WHAT PEOPLE AR
BARAGULA SERIE

Outback From Ba

Adventure, mystery, and romance wrapped together with a faith journey that tugs at one's heartstrings, Mary Hawkins' OUTBACK FROM BARAGULA is an entertaining and potentially life-impacting story of two souls learning to trust in the guidance provided by a heavenly Father's loving hand. Take a deep breath and enjoy the ride!

Kim Vogel Sawyer
www.KimVogelSawyer.com
Best-selling and award winning author

Like the movie Australia, Outback from Baragula is a suspenseful, wonderful slice of the country, especially living on a ranch in the Outback. The characters were engaging with real life problems and the suspense element kept you guessing exactly who did it.

Margaret Daley
www.margaretdaley.com
Award winning author

Return to Baragula (Book One)

I've loved all of Mary Hawkins' books but this is her best one yet. I was taken into the very hearts and souls of the characters and have to admit I stayed far too late last night because the story wouldn't let me go.

Lena Nelson Dooley
www.LenaNelsonDooley.com
Inspirational romance author

Whether Return to Baragula is your kind of story or not, whether it polarises you, challenges you, or affirms your core beliefs, the actions of the characters, their ups and downs, flaws, behaviours, struggles and growth will make you think, look at yourself, your life, your belief system and the way you want to examine, interact with and dwell in this world.

Jennie Adams
www.jennieadams.net
Best-selling, Australian romance author.

For more information and reviews visit www.mary-hawkins.com

MARY HAWKINS

*Greetings from Tasmania,
Australia*

Mary Hawkins

Outback from Baragula

Ark House
PO Box 163, North Sydney, NSW, 2059 Australia
Telephone: (02) 8437 3541
PO Box 47212, Ponsonby, Auckland New Zealand
Telephone: 0800 534 620
www.arkhousepress.com

All rights reserved. No part of this publication may be reproduced, stored in a retrieval system or transmitted in any form or by any means electronic, mechanical, photocopying, recording or otherwise without the prior written permission of the publisher. Short extracts maybe used for review purposes.

Unless otherwise noted, Scripture quotations are from the Holy Bible, New International Version, Copyright 1973, 1978, 1984, 1998 by International Bible Society.

© 2009 Mary Hawkins

ISBN: 9780980541472

Cataloguing in Publication Data:

Hawkins, Mary, 1940-
Outback from Baragula / Mary Hawkins.
9780980541472 (pbk.)
A823.2

Printed and bound in Australia
Cover design and layout by BBD Agency
bbdagency.com

Dedication

Dedicated to all the members and friends made a few years ago while my husband and I shared ministry with the Christian Celebration Church at Northampton, England.

However, for me this book will always bring extra loving thoughts and thanks to one of the members during those days, Mary Johnson, who edited the first draft of this book but has since gone to be with the Lord Jesus Christ.

"And this is the testimony: God has given us eternal life, and this life is in his Son. He who has the Son has life; he who does not have the Son of God does not have life."
1 John 5:11,12. (NIV)

Acknowledgments...

Besides a supportive husband and family, an author always has many folk to thank at the completion of a book. For Outback From Baragula there are several others who deserve special mention.

Thank you so much Ian and Helen Fraser for all your time and information as well as putting me in touch with your friend in western New South Wales, Kevin Blackburn. You all have given invaluable assistance in trying to help me get the setting right for the fictitious property and surrounding area of Davidson Downs. Any mistakes are entirely my own.

The members of Society Women Writers Tasmania have supplied at times much needed face to face "writer talk." Thank you so much for your fellowship, encouragement and support.

Thank you also Lyndle van Zetten and daughter, Rosita, for your encouragement when officially launching Book One, Return to Baragula, and even more for your invaluable, practical editing help and enthusiasm for this second book in the Baragula series.

Mary Hawkins

Chapter one

The quietness of the cattle station homestead was broken when one of the dogs in the yard near the sheds began to bark. The other one joined in for a moment before both fell silent. Then the barking started up again, this time more urgent. Angry.

The noise broke into Jillian Davidson's total concentration on the facts and figures of Davidson Downs' income and expenditure. As for the last couple of years, it was the expenditures exceeding the income that was particularly worrisome. Jillian raised her head and listened. Only then did she hear the increasing roar of the quad as it neared the homestead.

Jillian glanced at her watch and frowned. Surely John hadn't finished working on the prime mover already? It was only an hour since their early breakfast. And why was he on the quad? She hurried from the office and was on the back veranda by the time her twin brother had shut off the engine of the sturdy little four-wheeled, all terrain vehicle.

Her heart sank at John's set, tight-lipped face. 'What's up?'

John scowled at her as he sprang up the steps. 'Have to ring Coonamble and see if they can repair the starter motor. It's beyond me and I strongly suspect beyond any mechanics there also. If so, means a reconditioned one – or preferably a new one but of course we can't afford that! Should have known this would happen when Bob went on holidays the same time as Dad was still unavailable! I reckon that whole... whole *thing* is beyond repairing anymore.'

Jillian winced, knowing he was close to swearing a blue streak.

She bit her tongue as John growled, 'Anyway, reckon the starter will have to be added to the order for the brakes for the car. Would be a minor miracle if they don't have to order both the brakes and starter from Sydney.'

Jillian knew this was another expense they would somehow have to meet, but latched onto John's comment about the man who had been employed on the station as long as she remembered. 'Remember, Bob's nearly as old as Dad,' she said abruptly, 'and he's been trying to work too hard for a man his age, especially since we've had to stop employing full-time station hands without telling Dad we simply can't afford them right now. Bob needed a holiday even more than Mum and Dad and he'd set his heart on going to his family reunion in Tasmania!'

'I know that! It's just right at this time before harvest he...' John stopped.

His frown deepened and after a moment Jillian sighed and said soothingly, 'I know, mate. Anyway, you're nearly as good a mechanic now as Bob. I guess what we really need is what Bob suggested last year. The prime mover should have a complete re-conditioned motor. It would be awful if it broke down for the hundredth time right in the middle of hauling the wheat bin during harvest in a few weeks.'

'Yeah, right! What we really need is a whole *new* prime mover, but where are we going to get that kind of money, even for a reconditioned one? We need the prime mover right now, not only for that wheat bin but right after harvest to haul the cattle crates to get those animals to market. And we have to sell them just to stay viable this year. There's certainly no chance of coping with such a huge expense yet. I doubt we can even afford to pay someone else to transport the cattle!'

John stormed past Jillian and she refrained from reminding him they still didn't have the final bill yet for the helicopter service and repairs. She also refrained from voicing her own fears that perhaps they should have insisted on waiting a couple more years before they had agreed to their father's suggestions to diversify from just cattle into growing crops. As she'd been finding out all morning, the capital expenditure for that as well as their parent's new lifestyle had stretched their cash flow far too much.

She followed John to the laundry where he always scrubbed the grease off his hands before entering the house. 'Where are you off to on the quad?'

'I'm fed up with trying to put that motor back together again. Decided I need some fresh air and open spaces. Thought I might as well check on that fence along the boundary Bill Reed said he'd fixed while we were away. Would hate to have anymore of our cattle getting out into his newly-acquired Webster station while we're in the middle of harvesting. Aren't any fences over there and goodness knows where they'd end up – probably in the Reed's new wheat paddocks.'

'Oh, John, you said we could both go round that boundary fence as soon as I'd finished this rotten office work and you'd finished overhauling the truck.'

John glared at her. 'Well, we can't! I'm certainly not going to waste my time around the house waiting for you to finish when I can be getting on with something else. You said you had to get that paper work off to the accountant by tomorrow so he can finish our tax returns in time.'

And what about her own longing to get out of the house and away from the paper work John should be helping her with?

Jillian swallowed back her disappointment. It was no good making any further protests. She knew her twin brother as well as she knew herself and understood his stubborn expression. It was more than the need to escape the sheds and check fencing. John wanted time to himself in the wide open spaces.

His sombre mood and short temper lately had nothing to do with anything she had done or not done. She was also sure it was more than their cash flow troubles. 'Woman trouble,' her father would call it. John had been even more morose and withdrawn since they'd returned from Sydney a couple of days ago.

More than once over the last few months Jillian and John had regretted not telling their parents the true state of the lack of cash for everyday expenses. The family coffers had investments that could be sold, but not without their parent's signatures. But they had been so excited as they planned their round-the-world trip and the twins worried they would have refused to spend the money if they knew it was needed for the property. Besides, they had both wanted to prove they could handle things by themselves.

As well as a brief holiday the twins needed before the hectic harvest season commenced, the plan had been for John and Jillian to clean and air the Manly harbour-side house ready for their return. Jillian had not protested when John deserted her and spent every moment he could with his girlfriend. Amy Reed was in her last year of a science degree at a university in Sydney and they didn't see very much of each other.

Long before the twins were born, the two families had been friends – from the time Bill and Joan Reed had purchased the neighbouring cattle station, Jedburgh. Jillian and John had grown up with Amy Reed and her older brother, Scott, who was the same age as the twins. But it was not until Amy had gone away to university in Sydney that her friendship with John had started to develop into a much deeper relationship. Jillian loved Amy already as a sister and refused to feel lonely and left out when it had become obvious Amy wanted Jillian's twin brother to herself.

But now Jillian started to feel cross with John. 'Perhaps we should have stuck to our original plan on the way home from Sydney and stayed with Matthew at Baragula. At least I would have had some company for more then a few minutes every day.'

John glanced at her before continuing to scrub his hands and arms.

Their older brother was the local doctor in the small country town nestled in the mountains on the edge of the Hunter Valley north-west of Sydney. They had not seen Matthew since his marriage to Emily earlier in the year. Jillian had been especially looking forward to seeing their delightful little twins, Deborah and Daniel, who were now more mischievous than ever. The whole family was still recovering from the shock that Matthew had never known about the twins before Emily had returned to Baragula the previous year. However, at the last moment John had gruffly declared there was too much to do to finish getting ready for the harvest in a few weeks and rung Matthew to cancel.

John grabbed a towel. 'I was in no mood to put up with Emily and Matthew cooing at each other and saying prayers every meal and being expected to go to church.'

'Probably a few prayers would have done you a world of good!'

At the time, Jillian had held her peace and resigned herself to the long trip west over the Blue Mountains to the Western Plains of New South Wales and home to Davidson Downs. She knew their change of plans had more to do with John falling out with Amy. Anyway, she had tried to convince herself, it was just as well not to visit Baragula when there was every chance she would see Steve Honeysuckle. But her stupid heart was still very disappointed even that chance had been denied her.

John had been very quiet on that journey home, for once quite happy for Jillian to do the majority of the driving. She had not questioned him after he had tersely volunteered the news that Amy may not go back home to Jedburgh Station after graduation. She was considering doing a year's practical work with a veterinary clinic in Sydney.

Now, as John strode past Jillian into the kitchen and helped himself to a drink from the refrigerator, an increasing sense of loneliness made her protest. 'It's been several weeks since I've been out with you on the quads. I thought we said we'd take them on the ute and camp out over night at Windmill One out-station while we checked all the cattle in that area as well as those fences.'

John shrugged. 'And we'll still do that, but I thought the sooner I found where Bill said that fence was broken the better. I've been thinking about my conversation with him on the phone last night. Where he said that post had snapped I'm pretty sure was part of that new fence Dad helped me with last year. If it is that section, can't understand why. We used all new material. Do be an angel, Jillie and get me a few sandwiches while I ring Coonamble.'

As always, Jillian couldn't resist her beloved twin's coaxing tones. While she was making the sandwiches, the phone in the kitchen gave one brief ring. Jillian hesitated and then shrugged. Someone had either changed his mind or John had answered on the other extension.

Jillian finished wrapping the food and then hurried to the office to make sure John had picked up one of the portable Ultra High Frequency radio units they used on the quads. It was one of her father's strictest rules that no one ever went out on the vast property by themselves without one. John wasn't there but the radio was. Jillian scowled as she reached for it. She did wish John was more responsible about things like that.

Several minutes later, Jillian stood on the veranda and watched John negotiate the quad slowly past the sheds before speeding up along the rough track towards the north-west. He had taken the smaller of the two quads, leaving her the larger one. Seeing it, Jillian acknowledged a little bitterly, her brother had never intended taking her with him.

Unlike the larger one, his quad had only one seat for the driver and space on the back for a dog and tool box.

It was very dry and the air still. The brown dust cloud flung up by the quad lingered, marking John's progress even after he disappeared from sight past the station airstrip.

A strange sense of uneasiness filled Jillian. John had avoided looking directly at her – just muttered a brief 'Thanks' when she handed him the food box and the radio. And she'd forgotten to ask him who had been on the phone. Strange, he hadn't mentioned it either. She shrugged. It couldn't have been important.

Suddenly she wished their helicopter was not away for servicing and repairs. It would have taken a fraction of the time to fly it out to that back paddock.

Bluey again barked angrily at being left behind to nurse his injured leg, instead of hopping onto his favourite place on the back of the quad. As the sound of the motor faded, he gave up protesting. The stillness of the outback settled once more around Jillian. Not even the warbling of magpies disturbed the quietness and a deeper sense of loneliness descended on her. Well, perhaps not really loneliness. For some time now she'd become aware of an increasing emptiness deep within her.

What would happen to her when John eventually married, whether it be to Amy or some other unknown woman? Although it had never been discussed between them, she had always accepted that his wife would be mistress at the homestead.

Even though their parents had handed the management of the cattle station over to the twins, Jillian had always accepted that the homestead would one day become the domain of John's wife as it had become her mother's on her marriage. Unlike Jillian, her grandmother as well as her mother had been only too happy to move away from the heat, dust and flies.

Jillian doubted it had yet entered John's mind that his twin sister would ever think of leaving Davidson Downs unless she were to marry. No matter how well she got on with Amy, Jillian knew that living with a newly married couple simply would not work. Now the reality of that separation from her twin was growing ever nearer. With it grew fear of the future, of having no one who was hers alone to come home to. To love.

Jillian had always loved her home and the freedom of their lifestyle here at Davidson Downs. During three long years in Sydney getting her Business and Economics degree and, even with John there, she had hated every day away from Davidson Downs. It had not been until the upheaval of her sister Sonya's death and her parents moving away that Jillian had experienced moments of feeling unsettled, even lonely, despite her closeness to her twin.

And since meeting and being rejected by Steve Honeysuckle at Baragula, that feeling of loneliness and isolation had drastically increased.

That particular ache and gaping hole in Jillian's heart intensified. She turned away abruptly and tried to banish thoughts of the tall, handsome mountain man that had been nagging at her more and more these last twelve months or, more accurately, especially since Matthew and Emily's wedding earlier in the year.

A vivid picture of Steve in his special, three piece wedding suit rose before her. Jillian stilled. She had only ever seen him dressed casually before and even more often in his riding gear and one of the warm caps he wore through the forest instead of his usual Akubra around the rest of his family's property. That day, Steve's handsome face had been filled with happiness for his friend until he had turned and seen Jillian in the gold bridesmaid dress that she knew brought out the lights in her own brown eyes. His smile had been replaced for one moment with such an intense look of admiration she'd felt a blush sweep right through her.

Jillian drew in a sharp breath and strode back to the office. Thinking about that wedding inevitably brought more thoughts about Steve Honeysuckle. Unpleasant memories. She sat down in front of the computer and in the hours that followed, tried to force all thoughts of him from her mind. It took some doing, but at last she succeeded in immersing herself once more in the hated office work.

Hours later she had finished collecting the information for the accountant. She stretched her back and stood, knowing there was still work to do on trying to find the best strategy to minimise expenditure until cheques from the harvest and sale of the cattle had been banked.

The office UHF radio crackled to life. She always left it turned on when in the office and especially when John was away. Jillian reached for the hand held microphone, her mind still on her lists on the computer screen.

To her rather absent-minded, 'Hello' there was no answer. She straightened and checked the radio settings.

'Hello, it's Jillian Davidson speaking. Is anyone there?'

She flicked the switch to receive once more. There was some noise in the background like traffic, perhaps a motor. She heard the sound of a voice in the distance but couldn't make out the words.

'I'm sorry, I can't hear you. Perhaps you should try—'

'Jillie.' The deep, gruff voice startled her. 'Jillie Davidson. It's been a long time.'

The voice sounded vaguely familiar. She strained to think who it could be. The sneering tone made her wary and she said sharply, 'Who's speaking please?'

'Jillie, Jillie, I'm deeply wounded you don't remember your old friend.' There was a harsh laugh. 'Just wanted you to know you've now paid me back in full and I'm enjoying every moment.'

The voice was so full of malice Jillian felt the hairs on her neck begin to rise. Desperately she tried to remember whose voice it could be.

'If you don't tell me who you are immediately, I'm going to switch off and...'

The traffic noise increased to a roar. Another voice yelled. It sounded like a curse. There was a click and the radio went dead.

Jillian stared at the mike and slowly replaced it. She shivered. That man's last words had been full of hate and triumph. Who on earth could it have been? She racked her brains, tried to think of anyone she could have offended, tried to place the voice. She glanced at her watch. Should she try and raise John on the radio? But what would she tell him? Some lunatic on their frequency had scared her? She shook her head and dismissed the call as some crank.

And yet, the man knew her well enough to shorten her name as she only tolerated from family members and close friends. He'd also known which radio frequency to use.

Jillian shut down the computer and pushed a couple of paid bill envelopes into the correspondence bag. It would go to the post office at Coonamble the next time someone had to go there. Hopefully, if the dry spell continued and the prime mover was fixed, they would be able to start the wheat harvest in a couple of weeks, the end of November. There were still supplies to get in for the harvesting contractors and other workers who would be descending on the place.

Outback from Baragula

Jillian found herself staring into space thinking about that menacing voice, trying to remember.

She shook herself, muttered under her breath and forced herself to turn back to start on some more paper work. A dry wind stirred the curtains at the open windows of the office. A gust of wind flicked a couple of sheets of paper across the desk. Scowling impatiently, she stood up to close the window and pain lashed through her.

Jillian clutched her head with both hands. At the same time the muscles in her legs cramped. She groaned and fell back onto the chair. Then the pain was gone as fast as it had struck. She sat there, not game to move, waiting for it to return. Carefully Jillian stretched her leg muscles. Nothing. She slowly rotated her head. Still nothing.

And then she knew.

When they were kids John had complained about his arm hurting that time she'd been thrown by her pony. Her arm had been broken and John *felt* her pain. There had been other minor incidents discussed between them in awed whispers over the years, wondering if other twins experienced them, especially unidentical ones.

This time it was Jillian's turn. That pain had not been hers alone. Something bad had just happened to John.

Chapter two

The huge kangaroo bounded from the clump of bushes straight in front of the four wheel drive vehicle. There was a loud thump.

Steve Honeysuckle slammed down on the brake pedal before remembering the large horse trailer he was towing. He immediately lifted his foot and groaned.

'*Must* be tired. What a dumb thing to do when I've been driving so carefully for hours so as not to upset Punch and Judy more than necessary!'

That was all he needed after his horror of a journey – the two horses thrown down in their home on wheels because a wretched big grey decided to commit suicide.

'Thanks, Matthew, old pal, old mate,' he muttered between clenched teeth as he slowed gently to a stop in the middle of the one-lane, gravelled road that was little more than a track winding its way across the flat landscape. 'Why ever did your precious brother and sister cancel their trip to Baragula? Then I wouldn't have had to let you talk me into delivering their birthday presents. And now I probably have two even more nervous, if uninjured horses to calm down, as well as a wretched, injured 'roo to check on!'

Steve climbed wearily from the vehicle and strode to the trailer. Neither horse had been flung down as he had feared. The big black stallion tossed his majestic head at him and snorted. The more highly strung mare whinnied and stamped her hooves nervously. As they had each time he had stopped, they let him know very clearly that being cooped up for hours in a wretched little box on wheels was not at all to their liking.

'Sorry, old fellows,' he soothed as he patted the pretty grey mare. 'It's taken much longer than it should have to get here, but from what Matt said we've been on Davidson Downs since we left the main road. I reckon we must only have another few kilometres to go to the homestead.'

He looked around. Except for the patch of low scrub that had so successfully hidden the kangaroo, there were only a few small, straggly trees scattered among clumps of grass. The last light was fading fast from the wide expanse of cloudless sky. At least it was getting cooler now the sun had set. For a long time he had not driven over the slightest rise or seen even the hint of a hill. In the distance, outlined against the western horizon, was the silhouette of several taller trees. He fervently hoped they would be around the homestead site.

So, this was Jillian Davidson's precious outback home. For a mountain man used to the whispering of the wind through tall timber and unexpected valleys with tumbling, cold and refreshing waters, this looked lonely, desolate and nothing but light brown dirt with a few pathetic attempts at vegetation.

Steve shook his head. And yet all the Davidsons seemed fond of the place. Doctor Matthew Davidson had not lived here since the need for advanced education had forced him away to Sydney and then to his medical practice in the Hunter Valley. But he still spoke nostalgically of his old home, this huge outback property.

It was so still, so quiet.

There was a movement to his left. Several grey shadows bounded further away into the gathering darkness. Then the stillness descended once more.

Roos. And he had better check and make sure the one no longer with the mob was not lying injured and in pain.

After inspecting the front of the vehicle, he was relieved to see there was no damage. Because there were so many similar incidents caused by kangaroos, some insurance companies even refused to cover those repair bills. Just as well his father had insisted they get the big bull bars installed with the purchase of this latest addition to their vehicles.

With reluctance Steve hauled out his carefully stored rifle and went searching for the kangaroo.

It took him several minutes. Although he had been travelling slowly on this rougher road, a modern heap of metal had still collided with considerable force with soft flesh. The kangaroo had been flung a couple of metres. To his relief, it must have been killed outright. Then, to his dismay, there was a slight movement and a small head shyly popped up from the pouch in front of its mother. Pointy ears twitched and big eyes stared at him for a brief moment before popping back down out of sight.

A joey – and its mother was dead.

Steve hesitated. Even if it had not been injured the baby kangaroo would never survive alone. The sensible thing would be to give it a quick knock on the head.

After all, it would be one less kangaroo the cattle and sheep would have to compete with for feed and one less to invade any wheat crops.

After all, he'd brought his rifle after being warned by Matthew that Jillian and John would probably expect him to help in the constant war to keep down the numbers of wild pigs and kangaroos on Davidson Downs. He knew they were an even bigger pest out here than around Honeysuckle and Baragula.

The tiny head ventured up again.

After all, it wasn't the poor little blighter's fault his mother had been stupid enough to take on a large intruder to his habitat.

And after all, he was a soft touch.

Steve grinned wryly at himself. He hesitated for a moment, wondering if he should go back and get the blanket from his gear. Then he shrugged and took off his denim shirt. The little fellow might disappear before he got back.

He pulled the joey carefully and not without a struggle from its snug home. It was larger than he had expected and managed to get in a few scratches to his bare arms by the time he had wrapped it securely in the blanket on the back seat.

The air had cooled considerably in the last hour. Steve was glad to slip back into his shirt before setting off again up the narrow track. It was dark enough to need the headlights now. Keeping a careful lookout for more kangaroos feeding in the cooler part of the day on grass near the road, he drove slowly until a white house and the outline of several large, corrugated iron sheds loomed into view.

He almost stopped and then remembered that Matthew had warned him there was a smaller house some distance from the main homestead. It was usually vacant, used for seasonal workmen or even overflow guests. Sure enough, the house looked deserted, no cared for or fenced off yard, no lights on. The road curved around the house and at last the headlights lit up Davidson Downs' old homestead.

Steve whistled softly and brought the four wheel drive and trailer to a stop beside a gate in a neat wire and log fence that disappeared into the darkness. He sat still for a moment, staring a little grimly at what was lit up by the lights from his vehicle. A very wide expanse of green lawn contrasted sharply with the dried out vegetation he had been driving through for the last couple of hours. The homestead's dark shadow sprawled well beyond the reach of his headlights. But one thing was very evident. Davidson Downs' homestead was huge.

Suddenly Steve had a vivid picture of Jillian as she had looked around his home that first time she had visited Honeysuckle. There had been a curious expression on her face as she had surveyed the old stone and brick building. Then she had gone very quiet as she had sat herself in the rather shabby, old-fashioned lounge chair that his mother had often threatened to throw out but had never done so. And all these years since that sad time when Beth Honeysuckle had died, it still sat in that cluttered family room, declared to still be the most comfortable seat in the house.

He strongly suspected that this house would be at least twice the size of Honeysuckle. Undoubtedly his own comfortably untidy home, filled with old family photographs and treasures his father had accumulated, must have seemed cramped to Jillian. Just one more thing to emphasise the differences between them!

It had been obvious from their first meeting that Jillian Davidson was a well educated member of the old, wealthy squattocracy of Australia. His own grandfather had started out as a logger's labourer in the State Forest until he had managed to scrounge together enough money to buy his first few acres of the then cheap, mountainous terrain near Baragula in the Hunter Valley. Certainly his family had prospered since then but nothing to what Jillian Davidson was used to.

And yet, wealth and position in society wasn't even the biggest difference between them, Steve reminded himself sadly as he opened his door and looked up at the expanse of bright, sparkling stars. He tried

Outback from Baragula

to live daily by faith in Christ, while she had once scoffed at what she called his out-dated notions that God could possibly care what individuals like them did, as long as they lived decent lives. From his understanding of being a Christian, he was walking in Light while she was still in Darkness. And neither could exist side by side.

Wondering why no one had appeared to investigate the sound of his vehicle's arrival, Steve tooted his horn and after a long moment turned off his headlights. Pitch blackness descended. There wasn't a sign of a light anywhere.

He knew they did have electricity right out here. There had been electricity posts along the road from that first house to the homestead. He remembered too that Jillian had once tilted her chin at him and told him their station no longer needed their own power generator like a lot of outback properties still did. They had been connected to the state supplied electricity at considerable cost some years before.

The furiously barking dog somewhere behind the house had stopped its challenge. Only the restless movement of one of the horses broke the sudden silence.

Steve's heart sank. There was nobody home. If there had been, someone would have made an appearance by now, or hailed him from the sheds. And not to be at the house or out-buildings at this time of night meant Jillian and her twin brother must be off the property.

He should have insisted that Matthew not keep his arrival a surprise. But Matthew had merely grinned at his suggestion and reassured him he had made certain neither of his siblings was planning to be away again. As it was, after not even sparing the time to visit Baragula on their way back from Sydney when Matthew had intended to give them the horses, Jillian and John would be in a rush to get ready for the coming wheat harvest.

Steve scratched his head and ran a hand wearily over his now rough chin. Even if he had not hit the kangaroo it would have still been dark by the time he arrived – all because of those two flat tyres. The one on the horse trailer had been the biggest headache, causing him all kinds of problems getting help to unload the two horses and watch them while the tyre was replaced. As for that back tyre on the 4WD...

The dog started barking again. Another joined in. They paused for a brief moment and Steve heard what sounded like the distant roar of a motorbike. He peered around. It must be on a track approaching the other side of the house.

Steve relaxed and leaned back against the horse trailer. A slight smile twisted his lips. Was someone in for a surprise!

∽∅∾

The house was still in utter darkness. John wasn't home.

Jillian searched for the smallest glimmer of light, but the faint hope died that somehow the quad had simply broken down and John was now safely back home.

Once more she fought back the tears of fear and exhaustion that had been building for many hours. She was so sure a few moments ago there had been a light on the track leading to the homestead from the main road.

Jillian hesitated a moment before zooming the quad past the dogs' yard and heading towards the front entrance which only strangers to the place ever used. Bluey and Blackie were almost hysterical that she dared to ignore them, but she forgot all about the dogs at the sight of a large vehicle parked near the front gate. There seemed to be a caravan or something behind it.

Her heart leapt. She must have been imagining things after all. John had been playing games with her. Of course. It was their birthday this coming weekend and he loved to surprise her.

The quad headlights shone on a dark figure that straightened and moved away from what Jillian suddenly realised wasn't a caravan at all but a horse trailer still attached to what looked like a large four wheel drive vehicle. And John wasn't as tall as the figure now standing still, hands on his hips and wearing a cap instead of John's wide-brimmed Akubra.

And then her headlights lit up his face.

Jillian eased the quad to a stop and switched off the motor. For a moment, neither moved in the sudden silence.

'Steve?'

Her choked murmur of wonder brought that low, deep chuckle that never failed to vibrate along her nerve endings.

'Jillian?' he mocked back and moved out of the direct headlight's glare to stand staring down at her.

She fervently hoped her face was in the shadows so he could not see her expression as she hungrily studied him. Only then did she realise just how disappointed she had been not seeing him on the way back from Sydney.

Outback from Baragula

Jillian found her voice at last and fired at him, 'What on earth are you doing here?' She peered around him at the vehicles still lit by the quad's powerful headlights and asked urgently, 'Is John with you?'

Jillian saw his teeth gleam for a brief moment. 'No John, just Punch and Judy.'

'Punch and...' she began in a dazed voice.

There was a rattle and snicker from the horse trailer.

'Judy,' Steve said gently, 'Oh and Hoppy as well I suppose, although I'm not sure how welcome he is.'

Horses. Here. On Davidson Downs where there had been no horses since her beloved old pony had died over six years ago.

Jillian stared at the horse trailer and then back at Steve. She slowly reached up a finger and eased her wide brimmed hat back off her forehead. Mixed emotions seethed through her. Despite the dreadful few hours she'd just had, there was a sudden brief flash of exhilaration that the man who had been haunting her thoughts ever since she had last seen him at Matthew and Emily's wedding last Easter was actually here, on Davidson Downs, smiling down at her in that wickedly attractive way that never failed to distract her.

'Hoppy?' she squeaked still in that dazed voice that was nothing like her usual decisive tones.

'A now motherless joey whose mother committed suicide on my vehicle a few kilometres back.'

'Oh, that happens. We... we have a special enclosed place near the house where we...' she began automatically and then stopped, still disbelieving that Steve was here, talking some nonsense about horses and kangaroos and...

The wonder faded. A mixture of emotions swiftly followed, including bewilderment and then annoyance. 'Why didn't you let us know you were coming?' she barked out and then cringed. Hurriedly she added, 'Sorry, didn't mean that to sound so unwelcoming, it's just...'

Jillian's fear and worry nearly swamped her again. She swallowed hard on the rising lump in her throat and muttered bleakly, 'No John, you said?'

The tall figure straightened. 'Something wrong, Jillian?' Steve said in an altered voice.

'John hasn't returned or called in on the radio since leaving the homestead this morning on his quad.'

For a moment Steve was still, then took a swift couple of steps closer. 'You've been out looking for him?' Gone was any trace of humour in the sharp tones.

Jillian nodded wearily. 'For about the last six hours I think.' Steve gave a sharp exclamation and without thinking she added hurriedly, 'I just had this sudden weird feeling something had happened to him and when he never answered his radio I knew...' Jillian stopped dead.

She and John never mentioned to anyone except family, the strange incidents of sharing with a twin that had happened a few times over the years. They knew most people would consider them unbelievable, strange, too out of this world.

To her relief, Steve was still for a moment and then merely asked quietly, 'Have you notified anyone for help?'

She nodded. 'Only a couple of hours ago though. I managed to get onto our nearest neighbours, the Reeds. They'll do an aerial search at first light.' She drew a shuddering breath and said fiercely, 'I wish I hadn't waited so long to contact them now, but I was pretty sure I knew where John would be. He said he had to check out a fence along the back paddocks and when he hadn't returned I hoped he'd decided to check the bore on the Black Plain. He went by himself instead of waiting for me to go with him in a day or so. It's been so hot we have to make sure there's plenty of water for the cattle.'

Jillian swiped impatiently at a wayward tear that started to trickle down her cheek. At first she had tried to tell herself the quad must have simply broken down, run out of fuel or, at the worst, just tipped over and banged John's head in some way. His radio must have been damaged or even accidentally left turned off. But as the hours had marched on she had become more and more worried.

'When John wasn't at the Black Plain, I thought perhaps he must have been stranded in the Far Block. But there was no fuel left in the shack there where we always store it. Not even any empty containers.'

Jillian frowned again at the memory of that. If John had been there to fill up the quad, why had he not left the empty cans to be replaced later when they took the utility out there? Had John forgotten on his last trip to leave enough tins of fuel?

The words tumbled out of her. 'Fortunately I still had some left in the container I'd taken with me, but only enough fuel to come back here. I'm going to get out the ute, put this quad, some tins of fuel and stuff on board and go camp out at the Number One Windmill for an early start.' She stopped abruptly, knowing she was just putting her thoughts into words, not really expecting this mountain man to understand.

Outback from Baragula

Steve surveyed her for a long moment. 'You're exhausted, Jillian,' he said quietly at last. 'Can't you get a few hours sleep here first instead of camping out?'

Panic and fear suddenly overwhelmed her and Jillian voiced at last what had been tearing at her heart for hours. 'No! John's out there somewhere, injured, unconscious. Otherwise he'd have radioed in or at least heard my rifle and let off his gun in reply. It was a dreadfully hot day. What if he doesn't have his water bag? He just might be at Windmill One. Or... or near it. He... he might wake up, see my lights, a camp-fire, know I'm near. I've got to be there and...'

Her voice had risen. Jillian gasped, knowing she was verging on hysteria after her long, agonizing search. A sob tore through her. And then strong hands were lifting her up out of the quad and into strong, protective arms that soothed and comforted, even as Steve's deep voice murmured over and over, 'Fine, Jillie, that's fine. We'll do that.'

Then he was silent, just holding her trembling body for a long moment, before he whispered, 'And God is there looking after your brother even if you can't be.'

Jillian stiffened and Steve added swiftly, 'We'll both go, but you must have something to eat first. My guess is you haven't even thought of food, have you?' he soothed. 'And I must confess I'm starving. I know the horses must be too. It's been a much longer trip than I planned for and they've only had some water. Can you tell me where I can unload them?'

Jillian pulled away from him, battling for self-control, ashamed that this strong man had seen her give away even momentarily to her fear for John.

'What are they doing here, anyway?' she asked sharply. 'We haven't used horses on Davidson Downs for the stock for decades. Are you en route somewhere with them?' She immediately knew that was a foolish thing to say. Davidson Downs was hardly 'en route' to anywhere.

To her relief Steve ignored her question and referred to her comment about not having a horse. He unexpectedly grinned at her. 'You told me once before how sad you were when your old pony died.'

Jillian felt heat flood into her face as she remembered that first visit to Steve's home. He had proudly shown her over the stables on Honeysuckle and his special, obviously much loved horses. She had tried to explain how different her cattle station home of Davidson Downs was compared to mountainous Honeysuckle.

It had been such a strange day. She had met Steve Honeysuckle and felt she had so unexpectedly found a friend.

Matthew had not long started his general medical practice in Baragula and insisted he needed his sister's help to settle in. Then he had enthusiastically taken Jillian out to visit his new friends from church on their property some distance from Baragula. She had been enthralled by the picturesque mountain scenery, but nothing had prepared her for Steve Honeysuckle.

Jillian, who had grown up among tall men in her own family, had at first been awed by his height and the width of his shoulders. His steady, hazel eyes had stared back at her for a long moment. His large hand held hers a fraction too long. As his lips tilted in a welcoming smile, intense interest flooded his face. Then he had dropped her hand and looked away. When he had turned back his face had been strangely expressionless. Certainly he had been polite, even quite friendly, but some barrier had gone up.

At his father's request Steve had taken her down to see their beautiful stables and well kept horse yards. She had loved being near horses again and her enthusiasm had seemed to sweep away what she had thought of in regard to Steve's natural reserve. To her relief, he had relaxed and began to tell her about his hopes and dreams for the horse stud. She wistfully mentioned how sorry she often was that motor bikes and then the four wheeled quads had long replaced the horses on their station.

Before she knew it they had been chatting away like old friends, laughing and teasing each other as they strolled around the well-kept farm buildings. Jillian had found herself confiding in Steve about Davidson Downs' vastness, its isolation and her regret they no longer had horses there. She had felt as though in Steve Honeysuckle she had found someone who understood her, someone who could become a real friend. And then the atmosphere between them had for some unknown reason changed once more.

Suddenly Steve had gone quiet. After she had finished stroking the young foal that was obviously his latest pride and joy, he had told her abruptly that the others would be wondering where they were and led the way hurriedly back to the house.

Afterwards she had gone over their conversation word for word, trying to work out why he had changed, why from that time Steve had remained quite friendly but held her at a distance. When she had

Outback from Baragula

met him again in Baragula a few days later he had not said more than one or two terse words to her, leaving her at first bewildered and then deeply hurt.

Jillian had decided that for some reason Steve Honeysuckle found her lacking in ways she had only been able to guess at. There were other hurtful memories during several visits to Baragula, but now Jillian pushed them away. More important things concerned her now.

She turned her back on him and climbed back onto the quad. 'We can talk later,' she rapped out, 'it will be easier if you follow me. I'll lead you across to the old stables. They are in a pretty decrepit condition, but the yard there should still be fine for now.'

Still without looking at him, Jillian roared the quad into life, swung it around and headed back the way she had come. But the memories of nearly two years ago would not be so easily stifled, even with this dread in her heart about what might have happened to John.

Jillian cringed as she remembered she had tried to stifle her hurt feelings by deliberately provoking Steve on her very next visit to Baragula. Then there had been that Sunday a couple of weeks later. Embarrassment flooded her again as she remembered that morning and what had followed.

At first she had laughed off Matthew's eager invitation to go to the church service with him.

'That's a shame,' he'd said casually. 'Steve and his family also worship there each week and I'm sure they would be disappointed if you're not there.'

After narrowing her eyes at him for a long moment, her longing to see Steve again made her change her mind. She had deliberately ignored the sudden twinkle in Matthew's eyes.

The service itself had been wasted on her. Sitting directly behind the most handsome man she'd ever met had been far too distracting. Afterwards, she found out with some discomfort, that Matthew had previously invited Steve and his sister Madeline back to his house for lunch. She had glared at her brother for tricking her into going to church and then defiantly set out to deliberately tease and flirt with the tall, silent man.

Steve had been merely amused and practically ignored her. Jillian Davidson was not used to being ignored and had become more and more bewildered and upset. Then there was that visit to Honeysuckle a couple of days later.

To her surprise and bitter disappointment, out of the hearing of both their brothers, Steve's once friendly sister had been cold and downright unfriendly. Madeline had made sneering remarks about girls who tried to 'latch on' to any man like her brother Steve to relieve boredom.

'Besides,' Madeline had added with a dismissing wave of her hand, 'Steve would never be interested in anyone who didn't believe in God like he does.' Several other pointed remarks had followed about how different Jillian must find the mountains after the flat, dusty plains of the outback.

Her attitude so infuriated and upset Jillian that, after the men had rejoined them, her flirting with Steve had become more blatant and outrageous, even bringing a puzzled frown to Matthew's face. At last, after one highly provocative remark from Jillian, Steve had grabbed her arm. His face grim, he had dragged her down the garden until they were hidden from the house and swung her around.

Blazing eyes told her she had gone too far. She began to tremble and opened her mouth to apologise. Before she could speak he hauled her into his arms and kissed her furiously.

The fury in his kiss had lasted all of two seconds and then his lips and hands became gentle. Before she knew it she responded, swept away by feelings she had never experienced before. And then suddenly he let her go. For a moment they stared at each other. His eyes looked as dazed as she felt, but then contempt twisted his face into a scowl.

With a low cry she'd turned and fled, not heeding his strangled cry. 'Jillie, I'm so sorry!'

Shortly afterwards she gave some excuse and Matthew cut short their visit to Honeysuckle. Jillian was aware of her brother's disapproving frown at her behaviour. Still on the verge of tears, that evening she made up a forgotten appointment back home and returned there the next day. Aware that she had not fooled Matthew for a moment, she was grateful to him for not saying a word or asking questions.

That encounter had been unforgettable, as had been Steve's inexplicable attitude to her that never forgotten day when Honeysuckle homestead had been cut off by flood waters. At Matthew's request she'd flown the station's helicopter there to transport the sick little Debbie to hospital. Since then she had made sure she was never alone with Steve Honeysuckle, not even at Matthew's wedding. She had

Outback from Baragula

been too nervous; embarrassed by her behaviour that had provoked what she knew was such uncharacteristic behaviour for the rugged horseman Matthew thought so highly of.

And now, she acknowledged, too weary for any defences, she was even more scared of the impact Steve Honeysuckle had on her with his tenderness, his comforting arms.

Besides, she should only be thinking about her beloved twin right now. John. Who somehow had called out to her when something terrible had happened to him. Nothing mattered except finding John. And now she had help, even if it was Steve Honeysuckle, the man she simply could not forget, no matter how many times she tried to convince herself there was no future in thinking so wistfully about him.

Jillian drew in a deep, quivering breath and opened the gate into the old horse yard as Steve slowed his vehicle and trailer to a stop. She waved him on. 'There's plenty of room to turn around.'

And then, as Steve waved back and carefully drove forward over the uneven ground, Jillian wondered if, on all the tens of thousands of acres on Davidson Downs, there really was room to hide the impact this man from Baragula always had on her.

Chapter three

With his hands on his hips Steve surveyed the high fenced yard, partly lit by the headlights of both vehicles. Jillian had thoughtfully left the quad idling and trained its lights on the horse trailer.

'That water trough okay still?' he asked abruptly as Jillian ran towards him.

She answered in equally clipped tones. 'Yes, of course. This used to be the horse yard. Now we bring any of our small flock of ewes in here when they're ready to lamb.'

He looked doubtfully at the rickety looking gate. As Jillian swung it shut, one end dragged on the ground. He remembered what she had told him that first never to be forgotten day at Honeysuckle. Six years since this yard had been used for horses was a long time. Probably the logs on the top of the old fence would also be as dilapidated as the gate. However, it should hold for at least one night if Jillian said so.

'Come on,' Jillian added impatiently, 'the sooner we get your two horses settled the sooner we can get back out to...' she faltered a moment and then burst out, 'Why on earth did you have to bring your horses all this way anyway? And just what *are* you doing here at all?'

With his head tilted, Steve studied her for a long moment. She held his gaze then looked swiftly away and pushed her hat right back off her head. This time it dangled from its cord around her neck. He didn't think Jillian even realised what she had done.

'I'm... I'm sorry, Steve, that was very rude of me,' she whispered.

More than a little bemused, Steve watched Jillian run a hand over her forehead, pushing away strands of curly dark hair that had escaped her tight ponytail. He wondered why she had still been wearing the hat anyway. After all, it had been dark for some time now. Since the sun had set it was getting much cooler. Was it all part of the outback 'uniform'? In the mountains he usually wore caps rather than wide-brimmed hats. Even in the summer it could be too cold and windy for an Akubra.

Steve allowed himself a slight smile before he murmured, 'No offence taken Jillian and these are not my horses anymore.'

Jillian swung back and stared at him with a puzzled frown. One slender hand pushed back more strands of hair.

Suddenly Steve wanted her back in his arms. He wanted to hug her. He wanted to hold her close while he assured her that every moment of the drive that last half kilometre or so from the homestead he had been busy talking to his caring Lord Jesus about her and John.

Fighting for control, Steve turned abruptly away, glad she did not follow him as he strode back to the trailer. 'I'm just Matthew's birthday present delivery boy,' he flung over his shoulder. 'Stay there while I get them out. They're skittish enough already without a stranger getting too close.'

Steve saw to Judy first, soothing her with voice and hands as he backed her carefully out of the trailer. She started to prance a little, pulling on the short leading rein as he walked her over to where Jillian was standing very still in the light. She stared from him to the horse and back again.

'Judy,' he murmured, 'come and be introduced to your new mistress. Now, you be gentle with her just like I've been telling you.'

As he led her towards Jillian, Judy tossed her head up and down a couple of times. She gave a few snorts and snuffles, pranced forward a couple of small steps past him and poked her head in Jillian's direction. Steve tightened his grip on her halter, but to his relief Jillian very slowly reached out a hand to let the horse sniff at it before starting to stroke the long nose.

'She... she's mine?' Jillian asked in a dazed voice.

'Sure is, courtesy of your brother Matthew and Emily. Happy birthday for next weekend, Jillie,' he murmured gently, then slipped off the lead rope and took a step back.

Jillian patted the long nose. 'She's lovely.'

Her hand moved to touch the horse's neck, but this was too much for the weary and nervous Judy. She swung away and trotted off a few steps, tossing her head and whinnying loudly. There was an answering indignant snorting and much clattering of hooves from the horse still in the trailer.

Steve dealt with Punch swiftly. But as soon as the bigger horse was out of the trailer, this time he undid the halter and leading rein. Punch tossed his head and jumped away a few steps, his head swinging from side to side. He gave a piercing call to challenge any other horses that might be near and then began running around the perimeter of the yard, sniffing, thoroughly checking out this new territory.

'He'll take a while to settle down, perhaps even a day or so, but for a stallion he is a very placid horse,' Steve murmured quietly as Jillian stared after the horses, now only dark shadows against the furthest high fence.

For a brief moment Punch indulged himself at the trough with Judy before he was off again, round and round the yard rails.

Steve gave a low whistle. Judy raised her head and looked towards him. He gave another whistle. She tossed her head, snorted and slowly walked back to Steve. Swiftly he also removed her halter and then slapped Judy on the rump. She moved smartly back off into the shadows to investigate her surroundings.

'They... they are both so beautiful,' Jillian said as she stared after them. She looked back up at him and added in a wondering voice, 'Judy looks just like that young foal you showed me during my first visit to...'

She stopped as he grinned back at her. 'She is that horse, isn't she?' she whispered, 'but... but she was your pride and joy you said. You... you've sold her?'

'Sure have,' he answered cheerfully and refrained from telling her it had been for a much lesser amount to his friend than he could have asked for a horse of her pedigree and quality elsewhere. Besides, the simple fact was that Matthew had wanted the horse for Jillian.

At the sudden look of doubt on her face, Steve added swiftly, 'Jillian, I breed horses to sell and I couldn't think of anyone besides you I'd rather have Judy. And from what Matthew said, John is no mean horseman either and loves polo. He seems to think you might like to breed polo ponies with the pair of them. According to Matthew, the town of Quambone isn't too far away to take them in the horse-trailer and is well-known for its polo and horses.'

She stared back at him and suddenly he really wanted to see clearly the expression in those dark, chocolate brown eyes.

Steve turned away and cleared his throat. 'Right. Now, I'll just throw out some feed I've brought with me just in case, unhitch the trailer and—'

'No!'

He paused and raised an eyebrow at her.

'Throw out the feed, but it will take too long for the rest. Everything can stay as is until we get back. You can come with me on the quad back to the shed and the utility. We've got to get going.'

The strain and urgent note in her quivering voice made Steve's heart go out to her. Not even Jillian's delight in the horses had taken her focus off her brother's disappearance.

'Of course,' he murmured soothingly.

Steve hauled out a small bale of hay from the back of his four wheel drive. Jillian was already there with a pen-knife as he dropped it on the ground.

As she started to cut its ties, she ordered tersely, 'I'll fix this. You get your bag. I hope it's only small.'

'And the joey?'

Jillian muttered a curse that made Steve's brow crease for a moment. 'I was forgetting you said something about a kangaroo!'

He opened his mouth to explain but she added swiftly, 'We'll have to put it in the special enclosure to fend for itself until we get back.'

'I think that'll be okay. He's pretty big. I think he was probably almost ready to leave the pouch permanently anyway.'

A few minutes later they were both on the quad, Steve with a tight grip on the joey still secure in the blanket. They paused a little distance from the dogs' kennels. Steve was relieved to see that although the yard wasn't very big, it contained a shelter and was completely surrounded, including the top, with wire netting.

Jillian waited on the quad while Steve lost no time releasing the kangaroo. As soon as Steve climbed back on she revved the motor and they sped towards one of the open sheds nearer the house. The headlights lit up a small truck – no, on closer inspection it had high sides, a large utility. A small truck some may call it – with a ramp already in position. She pulled up near it and jumped off. While Steve was still climbing down from his seat she ran into the shed lit by the quad's lights and flipped a couple of switches. Powerful lights came on, including a large outdoor spotlight.

'I'll refill the quad's fuel from the main storage tank just outside. You start loading those extra cans of fuel onto the ute,' Jillian said briskly. She pointed towards a corner of the shed then nodded towards the house. 'The camping gear is kept in the other garage next to the car. We'll load up over there.'

Steve hesitated. In the bright light he could see the full extent of her exhaustion. Her face was pale and strained, her eyes bruised. Before he could protest, Jillian moved swiftly back onto the quad and disappeared. He shrugged and set about doing what she had asked. Several minutes later he could not help admiring her efficiency as Jillian returned on the quad and ran it up the obviously well used ramp and onto the tray of the utility.

He bit his tongue to stop the ready protest that sprang to his lips as Jillian helped him load a couple more heavy cans of fuel before she slammed the tailgate shut. Jillian left him to secure it while she reached up to a ledge and picked up a set of keys.

At Honeysuckle they would never dream of leaving keys around like that. They were always kept securely in the house. Steve smiled wryly to himself. Another difference between their properties. Obviously there were more people around their Honeysuckle farm than here on this outback station.

'I'm going to leave the lights on. They... they can be seen a long way off.' Her voice broke. Jillian swung away, but not before Steve saw her lips tremble.

As soon as he had climbed into the passenger's seat beside her, Jillian set the vehicle in motion. 'The camping gear is in a storage room at the back of the garage. I'll load it up while you—'

'No.'

She flung him a sharp glance.

'*I'll* load up while you make us a pot of tea and get some food ready,' he said firmly. "That will be easier than me trying to find my way around the kitchen."

She was silent, but after a moment his watchful eyes saw her nod. As she pulled the utility to a stop next to the garage, he added, 'And we're going to have something to eat before we head off.'

Jillian started to protest, but he leaned towards her and touched her on the cheek. 'Jillian dear, we are both tired. Exhausted might be closer to it for you. I haven't eaten since a bit of a snack at midday and I strongly suspect neither have you. We'll be no help to John unless we look after ourselves first and he won't thank me when we find him if you're a mess.'

She was still and silent. He heard her take several deep breaths and knew Jillian was fighting for self-control.

Immense admiration for her swept through Steve. He strongly suspected her break-down when he first arrived was very uncharacteristic.

According to Matthew, she and her twin brother had been capably managing the family station by themselves for the last four years or so since their mother and father had given up on the harsh conditions of the outback and gone to live in Sydney. Matthew had often told him yarns about his younger sister. At only twenty-six years of age, Jillian Davidson was undoubtedly a strong, capable, independent and responsible woman.

Perhaps too strong, too independent to ever admit she could need a Saviour, a Friend like Jesus Christ, to see her through anything that life could fling at her?

Steve devoutly hoped not.

༺༻

Jillian wanted to lean into that strong hand stroking her face so tenderly. She would have liked nothing better than to yield to the longing that swept through her to rest her weary head against Steve, feel those sheltering arms surround her once more.

She stiffened and moved her head sharply away from him. There was no time for this. Jillian bit down hard on her bottom lip to stop it trembling. She knew what Steve was saying made sense.

With a frustrated sigh, she gave in. 'There's a tent with attached ground sheet, sleeping bags, blow-up mattresses and...'

Steve was looking at her with one of his wry smiles.

Jillian stared back at him, then took a deep breath. 'Right,' she added quietly, 'you've been camping and know what to take. But there are some large logs between the house and the garage for the fire we'll need. Include as many as will fit. Unlike your mountains, there are very few trees and spare wood lying around where we're going.'

Steve had been wrong about one thing, Jillian thought as she raced towards the house. The last time she had eaten had been that early breakfast with John.

Then she had felt that sudden pain, that sharp sensation John needed her. She knew researchers had not been able to completely establish that twins, who are not identical, experienced things like she had that morning. Whatever it was, a twin 'thing' or some kind of supernatural experience, it had been so strong that Jillian had gone straight to the radio. When John had not responded at all to her increasingly anxious calls, she had phoned their nearest neighbours.

'Sorry to take so long, love,' a breathless Joan Reed panted just when Jillian had almost given up on anyone answering their phone. 'Just chasing some wretched sheep out of my garden. Rotten things have stomped all over my flower beds.'

When she had asked if by any chance anyone there had heard from John that morning, Mrs Reed had replied, 'Negative there, Jillian, unless Bill has on his two-way, but he's away over near our other boundary from yours. Scott left here a few days ago on some jaunt or other to Sydney. If you like, I could contact Bill and get back to you if he's heard anything. Nothing wrong I hope?'

Feeling a little foolish, Jillian had assured her that as far as she knew everything was fine. 'John's just probably away from his radio or has it turned off,' she said, knowing full well he never did so when she was alone at the homestead. 'But I would appreciate it if you ask Mr Reed when he comes in, if he noticed anything over our way.'

Without even thinking of food, after she had hung up the phone to her talkative neighbour as swiftly as she could, Jillian had grabbed her old hat, made sure the water bag on the front of the large quad was full and the tank filled with fuel. With the other two-way radio strapped to her waist she had headed off.

She knew John had been hoping Amy would marry him as soon as she had finished her degree. As Mrs Reed would then be his mother-in-law, there was no way his sister could mention that she 'felt' something had happened to her twin brother.

As they had grown up together, there had been a few times over the years when Jillian had known Amy resented the closeness between the twins. Until recently, John often put his sister first before Amy. As big-hearted as Joan Reed was, Jillian doubted if she had the imagination to understand that the strong link between John and his twin meant there had been times when one of them sensed 'things' about the other.

Like that time John had rung her at Baragula after that last visit to Honeysuckle and Madeline's nasty, spiteful words to her.

She put a brake on that memory. With Steve Honeysuckle right here on Davidson Downs, it was no time to remember past hurts, how upset she had been that evening.

And there was John to concentrate on now.

Besides food, Jillian would have given anything for a warm, soothing shower, but opted instead for a quick wash of her hands and face. One look in the mirror made her give a faint groan. She was definitely not looking her best for Steve to see her after so many months! She shrugged and made quick use of a brush, pulling her long, dark hair back again into a ponytail before rushing back to the kitchen.

By the time she heard Steve's heavy tread Jillian had swiftly prepared and packed food and drinks, including a large thermos of hot water. 'In here, Steve,' she called out.

He appeared in the large kitchen and looked around appreciatively at the modern setting and electrical appliances. 'Nice, very nice,' he murmured.

Despite her weariness and fears for John, Jillian smiled back at Steve. He could not have said anything that pleased her more. She had been responsible for the new, modernised kitchen, her mother leaving it entirely up to her.

'Its renovation was long overdue, about thirty years or so. I managed to talk Dad into it when the state electricity supply reached us at long last.'

Besides a large freezer in the huge pantry just off the kitchen, another one stood beside the refrigerator in the corner. Her father had told her a little wistfully the original, first kerosene refrigerator had stood there in pride of place when Jillian's grandmother had been a young bride. Of course it had been up-graded to an electric fridge before Jillian had been born, but the old thirty-two volt power plant had not been strong enough to support all the other modern appliances that now graced the house.

'It's much easier to cater for seasonal workers now, as well as for the occasional large parties like... like...' Jillian stopped.

Hoping her face was hidden from Steve, she busied herself packing the box on the bench. The party. After harvest a big party was planned for her and John's birthday.

Jillian braced her shoulders. 'I've made some sandwiches we can eat on the way,' she said abruptly in her best don't-you-dare-argue voice. 'If you'd like a cool drink, please help yourself to anything in the fridge. We'll have our hot one when we've set up camp.'

To her relief, Steve only hesitated a moment before making his way to the refrigerator and retrieving a can of drink.

'Want one?' he asked quietly.

Sudden tears blinded her eyes at his acceptance and understanding. Why did Steve Honeysuckle have to be so wonderful?

Jillian kept her face averted as she shook her head. 'I grabbed one and a mouthful to eat while I was working.' She lifted a box and headed for the door. 'There's a small bathroom just through there if you want to freshen up,' she added rapidly and escaped.

To her relief, Steve had packed the gear very well, leaving her room for their food supplies. When she returned to the kitchen, he met her in the doorway, carrying the other larger box and cooler. She looked at him searchingly. His hair was a little wet but he must have been very fast in the bathroom. Immense gratitude filled her that he understood her sense of urgency without another word spoken.

'This all there is?' Steve asked in his deep voice.

She nodded and held the outside screen door open for him.

Steve didn't move. 'Jillie, did you pack an adequate first aid kit? I couldn't see one in the store-room.'

His voice was gentle. For a moment the thought of why they might need the medical supplies closed her throat. 'It... it's...' Jillian fought to stop her voice trembling. 'In the other box,' she ended abruptly, 'and there's always a smaller one in the ute that we can take on the quad.'

'What about bringing one of the dogs?' Steve asked as they climbed into the utility.

'Bluey's still getting over an injury and Blackie's pups are due any day now,' she answered him briefly. 'John had to put them both in their yard otherwise we'd never have kept them off the quads today.'

They were both silent for several minutes into the trip, busily eating the sandwiches she placed between them. Jillian felt relieved Steve had automatically climbed into the passenger's seat. Too many times

Mary Hawkins

over the years she had met too many men out here who took it for granted they would drive.

Oh, why was there so much about this man she liked? Especially since that disastrous kiss when Steve had made it clear more than once that he was not interested in her.

'This is the way I drove in,' Steve commented at last. 'Are we going all the way to the entrance to Davidson Downs?'

She finished swallowing the mouthful of her thick beef and tomato sandwich and nodded. 'It's a bit further to go this way, but faster in the ute, especially at night. We'll travel along that road for about half an hour and turn off onto a track back into Davidson Downs to Windmill One. It's pretty central to where we need to. . . to search for John.'

The thought of her brother lying out in the dark somewhere, waiting for her to find him, needing her help, made Jillian grip the wheel tighter and her foot go down on the accelerator as much as she dared.

'We'll find him, Jillie.'

Steve's quiet voice was steady, confident. And suddenly Jillian was immensely thankful he was with her. But all she could manage was a slight smile in his direction. They didn't speak for a while after that and Jillian was so exhausted and worried that she was grateful for his silence.

At last she roused herself enough to say, 'I was so sorry we didn't see Matthew a few days ago. How do you think he has settled down with Emily and his instant family?'

Steve gave a faint chuckle. 'Very well for someone who suddenly has been thrust so swiftly into being the father of precocious six year olds like Debbie and Danny.'

Jillian found her own lips smiling at the memory of her brother's mixed emotions last year when he discovered that the woman he had met and loved so briefly all those years ago had become pregnant and had not one baby but twins.

Then she frowned, remembering how amazed the whole family had been when Matthew had been able so readily to forgive Emily when they had all been angry and upset for Matthew that she had deprived him of his children's first few years. There was absolutely no doubt about his deep love for Emily and their children. For Matthew's sake, Jillian had been very relieved to see Emily obviously adored him back.

She and John had discussed it. John had been furious with Emily and Jillian knew he was still stiff and unfriendly towards her. All they had been able to understand about Matthew's ability to forgive was the fact he had become so religious.

'Matthew's changed a lot these last few years,' Steve said quietly.

Jillian glanced at Steve and then away at once. He was watching her face. 'He's been a bit of a puzzle to us all. One moment he seemed to be a typical party going, pretty reckless medical student and the next he was very religious and all serious and dedicated to being a doctor.'

Steve was silent for a long moment. When he spoke Jillian had the feeling he was choosing his words very carefully.

'Matthew told me that the change in his life all started during that summer holiday at the Gold Coast with your sister Sonya, where he first met Emily.'

Steve paused again and Jillian said impatiently, 'He never told us anything about Emily, but Sonya did. She was furious with him for upsetting her best friend so that she left early on their last day without even saying goodbye. But Matthew didn't really change until after... after Sonya was killed.' Even if it was over six years since her older sister had died in a car accident, Jillian still found it hard to talk about that dark time.

'Although what transpired between Matthew and Emily made her faith weaken until last year, Matthew said that what Emily had told him about having a personal relationship with God had made him start to think.' Steve hesitated again and then continued quietly. 'And you're right. It wasn't until after he was devastated by your sister's death that he started a serious search to find out more about God.'

'Searching for God? For answers. Weren't we all wanting to know the "why"?' The memories of all her own bitter, angry questions at the time flooded through Jillian. Whatever answers Matthew had found, hers had still not been answered. 'Matthew told us that apparently when Emily had tried to contact him after she had discovered she was pregnant, it had been during the turmoil we were all in just after Sonya's death. I've never been able to understand why on earth Matthew would want to have anything to do at that time with a God who let something like that happen.'

'And yet you said yourself his personal relationship with God has changed Matthew,' came the quiet response. 'So don't you think he did find something life changing – or rather, Matthew is allowing

Someone to change him and give him answers?'

Jillian had no response to that. She definitely did prefer the kind and loving man Matthew had become to that younger one who had teased, but more often ignored, his younger brother and sister. But wouldn't Matthew have changed anyway as he matured? He had always been basically a good, decent man. Why give God all the credit?

What she had just told Steve was true. When Matthew had gone all religious, it was something that utterly confused her parents as well as herself. John had not been able to understand at all and for a long time even resented the changed Matthew who would not go to certain wild parties, drink alcohol as he used to, or even visit the casinos in Sydney anymore on a rare night out.

Jillian glanced across at Steve again. He too was different from any man she had ever met. She suddenly wondered if that had anything to do with his regular attendance at the same little church Matthew and now Emily went to in Baragula. Steve seemed as religious as Matthew, although so far he had never tried to preach to her as Matthew had several times immediately after he had become what he called 'born again.'

Thankfully, Matthew had quickly stopped trying so hard to bring them all to his way of thinking about God. Nowadays he still invited them to church, was always ready to try and answer any of their questions, but that was all. And yet, as she and John had discussed more than once, to their surprise Matthew believed, even more fervently as the years passed, than he had at the beginning of his 'conversion.'

Sometimes, Jillian found herself wishing she could believe in a loving God who cared personally for her. But she could never quite get around the fact that if God really cared He would not have let her beautiful sister die so young – or have Matthew miss out on knowing about his babies for so long. But still... Jillian had once discussed with John that becoming so religious had certainly seemed to help Matthew deal with Sonya's tragic death far better than the rest of them had.

A sharp pain shot through Jillian. *Oh, God... please. You've taken Sonya. Please... not John. You couldn't be so cruel!*

Jillian suddenly realised Steve was still talking about Matthew and his family. She tried to concentrate on what he was saying.

'Guess I've never seen a happier little family,' Steve was saying. There was a smile in his voice as he added, 'Although those two little terrors keep them both on their toes.'

Outback from Baragula

Jillian swallowed hard and managed to ask, 'Are they excited about having a new brother or sister?'

'You know Emily's pregnant?'

'Matthew still seemed in a state of shock when he contacted us shortly after Emily told him. Any chance it could be another set of twins do they know?'

Steve was relieved to hear Jillian's voice lighten. She had gone very quiet and he had carried on talking, careful not to mention faith in God again. As much as he longed to talk about Christ to her, it was not the right time. She was far too upset and exhausted.

He gave a deep rumble of laughter. 'Too early to know yet, or so Matthew said a few days ago. When I asked him that very same question, he looked even more excited and then not sure whether to be thrilled or a bit apprehensive at the thought of another set of twins like Deborah and Daniel.'

To his delight, Jillian responded with a faint smile. 'Those kids are simply gorgeous. And besides, what's wrong with having twins?' she asked in a mock indignant voice.

'Double the work, double the worry and double the wisdom needed,' he answered promptly.

'Double the gain, double the...' her voice faded a little, but she added in a forced, cheerful voice, 'double the pain, Mum always said.'

Steve was silent. At last he couldn't resist saying softly, 'And double the love. No matter what has happened, God loves you and is looking after John, Jillie. Do believe that, my dear.'

'I want to believe that, I really do, but...' she burst out, 'how can you be so sure God worries about these kinds of things? What about... what about Sonya? We're just specks in His universe.'

'Because His very nature is Love,' Steve began earnestly, 'and He showed His whole creation He cares when He became flesh in the form of Jesus and lived here amongst those specks. Jesus taught that every hair on our head is numbered. If He cares even to know that, if He cares enough to die so we can have a personal relationship with Him, if...'

He stopped abruptly and gave a low laugh. 'Oops, sorry Jillie. Guess I just kinda get a bit carried away, don't I?'

She was silent for so long he was suddenly afraid he had alienated her, made her angry with him for preaching at her.

Then, to his relief, she whispered in a choked voice, 'You sound like

Matthew does sometimes, especially when he first talked to me after he had become serious about his religion. I kind of laughed at him then, but now...'

Steve waited. Already he may have said too much at this time.

At last, to his relief Jillian said quietly, 'My big brother has just changed so much the last few years. This business of "a personal relationship with Jesus Christ" you and he talk about so much is really working for him – and apparently Emily now too for that matter. If... if you don't mind too much, Steve, I'd like us to talk more some time about what you and Matthew believe.'

His heart swelled with joy and hope. But instead of shouting out the thanks and praise filling him, all Steve allowed himself to say quietly and sincerely was, 'I'd enjoy that very, very much, Jillie. Anytime you're ready, we'll talk.'

Chapter four

A large, full moon had risen above the horizon by the time Jillian at last drove across a wide, cleared area and pulled to a stop a little distance from a couple of stunted trees. They both stared silently at the very tall windmill ahead of them. A breeze had sprung up, cooling down the countryside even more. The moon's silvery light gleamed on the windmill's slowly moving arms. Once the sound of the motor ceased there was only a faint creak and then the clang of the pump drifted towards them.

After a long silence, Jillian muttered, 'That windmill should be turned off.'

She had put into words what Steve was also thinking, but there was a hint of hope in Jillian's voice. The person who had set the windmill free to the whims of the wind had to have been her brother. But Steve knew there was one problem with that scenario. Before leaving, John Davidson would have relocked the windmill.

On Honeysuckle they never dared leave windmills free, especially ones that were a long way from the house. Strong winds could do a heap of damage to the windmill as well as wasting the precious, life-giving water the pumps still sucked up, even when the tanks were full.

Neither Jillian nor Steve moved or spoke again. They strained to hear a shout, the faintest sound that John was nearby.

For the last stretch they had been travelling very slowly over a rough, badly potholed, dirt track. It wound in and around a few patches of low scrub with only a few taller trees further back from the track. Not far from the windmill, Steve could see the dark outline of huge stock yards with what looked like a loading ramp next to the tanks. Beyond the yards Steve also caught a brief glimpse in the headlights of some kind of small shed.

Until they had reached this place, not a word had passed between Steve and Jillian for quite a while. Steve was feeling very weary. He could only imagine how exhausted Jillian must be. After her long day, he had known she needed to concentrate on avoiding the worst of the potholes since they had left the road, and remained silent. He had sensed her increasing tension as they neared the windmill silhouetted against the moonlit sky.

Well, at least that was what he tried to tell himself was the main reason that had kept him from speaking the last few miles. In reality, since they had left the homestead, Steve had become even more aware of the differences between Davidson Downs and Honeysuckle. The differences between his home and Jillian's. The differences between his belief in a loving God and Jillian's unbelief.

In the district of Baragula, Honeysuckle was recognised as one of the largest properties in the area, but the sheer size of this place amazed Steve. Certainly they had not been able to travel very fast most of the way, but it had taken at least an hour to get here to these back paddocks. Once Jillian had casually mentioned that the public road they had turned onto for a few kilometres followed the actual boundary of their station. Then, when they had at last driven over a cattle ramp off that gravelled road, they had driven for ages inside the property itself to this place. According to what Jillian had told him, Windmill One wasn't even in the centre, only near the boundary area!

Jillian stirred at last. 'We'll make camp well away from the water tanks and troughs.' Steve looked across at her and she added, 'Snakes. They're more likely to be nearer the water.'

Steve shuddered. 'If there's one thing I hate, it would have to be snakes,' he said grimly.

That earned him a faint laugh. 'Yeah, me too. Shame Australia has so many highly poisonous ones. And out here we have the Western Brown, one of the deadliest in the world, as well as the usual varieties

Outback from Baragula

like tiger snakes and red-bellied blacks.'

Jillian opened her door and then paused to add in a grim, carefully controlled voice, 'Guess the first thing we'd better do is get the pressure lamps set up and use those torches to scout around first. I need to lock that windmill down,' she finished abruptly.

She did not have to say out loud that her faint hope John might be here somewhere had faded. He may have unlocked the windmill sometime, but if John was nearby he would have heard the utility and, if able, called out by now.

Without another word, Steve turned on the big torch he took from the cabin and silently helped Jillian get a couple of strong pressure lamps gleaming brightly. He climbed up and placed one on the top of the utility, a beacon shining out to anyone lying helpless in the darkness on the plains.

Jillian hurried off with another lamp, a powerful torch clutched in her other hand which she used to swing in a wide arc to carefully check out the surroundings as she went. Steve would have liked to be the one to see to the windmill but she'd know its intricacies better than he.

Jillian gave a sharp exclamation. Before Steve had taken more than one hasty stride forward she called out, 'Be careful if you come this way. There's water everywhere.'

He stopped and drew in a sharp breath of relief before he waved his torch back at her. For a long, thoughtful moment he watched her taking a wide path away from the tanks until she disappeared behind one of them. Turning away he busied himself unloading the tent. He shone his torch around the clearing and then swiftly checked the ground the other side of the utility for the most suitable camp-site. Here the ground was darker than back near the homestead. It was also much drier, any vegetation either eaten, trampled on or dried to a crisp.

He kicked at the dirt thoughtfully. His lips tightened. Something was very wrong here. Jillian had been a long way from the tanks when she had called out. The ground here was so dry it would take a lot of water to extend so far. Either one of the tanks had a leak or someone must have unlocked that windmill long before John could have reached here this morning.

The wide expanse of bare dirt around him seemed to extend beyond the light of the torch. Only a few ghost-like trees were a mere moonlit smudge in the distance, and he guessed that most of them would be as bare and lifeless as most of the trees that had been visible beside the track they had just travelled over.

On the whole it had been a pretty dry year again out west. Steve wondered how the wheat crop had survived it. Then he remembered that Matthew had once said something about it being on the most southeasterly part of the property where they had put in water channels and irrigation pipes from the plentiful artesian water in that area.

Moving as quickly as he could, Steve carried the rolled up tent a little distance from the utility. He peered towards the windmill and tanks to see what Jillian was doing.

Steve froze. The tent tumbled to the ground.

Several metres up, a light was bobbing on the windmill. Jillian was climbing the narrow metal ladder in the dark.

As he watched anxiously, not daring to move, she paused just beneath the now still blades. Then the lamp flared brighter still. She would be pumping it up, making it fling its light as far as possible out into the darkness.

John's sister was leaving nothing to chance. If he was able to see the windmill, John would know she was there. Steve's own anxiety for John increased. Jillian was certain that John must be lying injured somewhere.

By the moving, faint light of the torch, Steve knew when she started back down. How he prayed she was using both hands, that the torch hung from her neck, that...

Unable for another moment not to be closer to her, his heart still in his mouth, Steve started towards her swiftly. Only when she was safely on the ground and striding to meet him, did his breathing start to even out again. And with his desperate relief came anger, more anger than he could remember in a long time.

He roared out, 'You stupid woman! Don't you ever try a stunt like that again. I could at least have held the torch so you could see more easily.'

Jillian paused in mid-stride.

Steve reached her, battling the temper that he had long thought controlled with the help of the Lord. Of their own volition his hands reached out to grip her shoulders. He didn't know whether to shake her or. . .

He hauled her against his body, hugging her tightly in the safe haven of his arms. Then he pushed her away slightly and peered into her face. Her lips were open, her eyes round and startled in the faint light. Steve pulled her close again to his own trembling body.

'I... I've climbed that windmill more times than I could... could count over the years.' Her voice sounded strangled and she tried to push him away. 'I'm not scared of heights.'

'Well I *am*. Especially in the dark! A rusty step could have been broken or...' He shuddered. 'Don't you dare do such a risky thing like that again!'

Then he did give her a little shake before reluctantly letting his arms drop. They felt even emptier than they had after she had wept all over him earlier. There was nothing he wanted more than to kiss her hungrily, desperately, keep her safe from all that could harm her.

The thought made him freeze.

Lord? Lord, help me. What's happening here? Help me!

His prayer was answered swiftly.

Jillian's response was sheer fury. It cooled his rush of blood.

'Don't you dare try and tell me what I should or shouldn't do! This is *my* place, my responsibility. I'll do what I please on my own property!'

Jillian actually swore at him, stamped her foot, then turned and strode angrily off towards the utility, stumbling over the rough ground in her haste to get away from him.

Well, you sure blew that one, Stevie old man.

For several moments Steve stood stock still. His heart pounded furiously. He had never felt quite like this before in his whole life. Despite all the thought and prayers he had given to his attraction towards Jillian Davidson and why it was all so impossible, Steve knew that his heart was in deep, deep trouble.

Another desperate prayer rose up to the Lord he had committed his ways to when still a teenager. This woman was not for him. Could not be for him.

Then why was it she drew him as no woman had in all of his thirty years?

⸻

Jillian trembled with anger as well as sheer exhaustion. How dare Steve Honeysuckle grab her like that, yell at her like that! Who did he think he was? Her hands were still shaking as she strode away.

One thing that had always attracted her to Steve was his quiet tones, his way of just doing what had to be done with no fuss or fury. Only twice before had she seen Steve less than his cool, reserved self. The time he had kissed her more in punishment than because he wanted to. The day she had flown their helicopter over the flooded areas of the Hunter River valley and onto that Honeysuckle property last year.

'You fly a helicopter!' he had yelled at her accusingly before she had even set foot on the ground after that dawn flight.

She had stared at him in absolute amazement and then yelled back derisively, 'Sure! Can't you?' She had then turned away with considerable relief as Matthew rushed towards her, his face at least alight with relief.

So, why had Steve been so furious, so uncontrolled again just now?

Suddenly Jillian stood still. Steve had been trembling a few moments ago, just the same as he had been that time beside the helicopter. Certainly that first kiss of punishment had been all anger. But that time beside the helicopter, and now... this was different. He'd been frightened for her. And flying the helicopter? She'd thought Steve was just being ridiculous about her, a woman, flying a helicopter. Had his fright for her been the reason also for his behaviour that day at Honeysuckle?

Jillian shook her head. It couldn't have been. He had been friendly enough, but even more reserved again when she had met him a few months later at Emily and Matthew's wedding in Baragula. In fact, his coolness towards her then, his ability to look right through her instead of *looking* at her in her beautiful bridesmaid frock had hurt something deep inside Jillian, even more than any of their previous encounters.

'Sorry,' Steve's gruff voice said from behind her.

Jillian jumped slightly. She bent and started straightening out the tent.

Steve audibly cleared his throat and added with ice in his voice, 'You were perfectly correct. I have no real reason to keep you safe just so I don't have you to care for as well as John.'

A ready retort on her lips, Jillian swung her head and looked at him. He had turned his back to her and was picking up the metal rods for the tent. She swallowed back angry words and concentrated on letting her anger out on setting up camp as fast as she could.

After a few moments, Steve rejoined her with a pile of tent rods he dropped nearby. She paused briefly and, not daring to look at Steve, muttered, 'I'm sorry I swore at you.'

To her surprise, after a long moment Steve gave a soft chuckle. 'Apology accepted, although they were very, very mild words compared to what some of our stockmen use at times.'

Jillian glanced at him. That was partly her problem. She had been around people who cursed so much over the years that it sprang too naturally to her own lips. But surely religious people hated swearing? She knew Matthew had certainly cleaned up his vocabulary the last few years and even chided her when she swore.

Not sure quite how to respond, Jillian remained silent, but was relieved that the remaining slight constraint between them disappeared as they set up camp. She found they worked well together, each naturally and easily doing what needed to be done with the minimum of talking and movements. And as they worked, Jillian relaxed even more. It was quickly apparent that Steve was very familiar with camping and soon their bedding and gear lay on each side of the four man tent.

Hands on his hips, Steve surveyed their camp mattresses and sleeping bags for a moment. 'Wonder what some of the old gossips in Baragula would think of—' He stopped abruptly.

There had been a touch of humour in his low voice and Jillian said dryly, 'From what Matthew has told me, probably the very worst. In fact, some of our neighbours out here would be as bad.'

Her thoughts flew to Scott Reed. She frowned slightly. He for one might subject her to another outburst. Unless he had taken to heart her strong words that last time he had dared to criticise her. Hopefully she had once and for all made it clear he had no right at all to object to anyone she was friendly with. Because she had known him nearly all her life, until that day she had several times deliberately ignored what she had perceived as his immature, proprietary attitude towards her in public.

Steve stared across at her for a long moment. He murmured, 'You know I would never want to compromise you or harm your reputation in any way, Jillie. I'd be quite happy to sleep in the utility if...'

'No way,' she snapped back at him. 'Don't be so stupid. Your Christian reputation's quite safe with me.' And then immediately wished she had not brought the 'Christian' bit into it.

He hesitated and then shrugged. 'Fine.' He turned away and she

Mary Hawkins

thought she heard him mutter, 'Thanks a heap, Lord.'

She gaped after him. What on earth had that meant? Was he thankful his reputation as a Christian upholding scriptural morals was quite safe? Somehow she did not think he had meant that at all!

Last of all they built the camp-fire in a carefully selected area so the smoke would not blow across their tent. They had scoured the few trees for bits of wood and bark, knowing there would probably not be enough to last until morning, even with the few big logs Steve had found at the homestead and heaved onto the back of the utility.

'It sure seems strange to me having to bring our firewood,' Steve muttered.

Jillian glanced at him briefly, thinking of all the beautiful tall trees on Honeysuckle. Without comment, she pulled out a cigarette lighter.

'You don't think we should wait until dawn so we can use the fire to heat some water then?'

She shook her head. 'Despite how hot it is during the day, here it's usually quite cold at night and, besides that, the... the smell of a fire travels a long way out here,' she finished rapidly.

To her relief, Steve helped without another word, as if he somehow knew the fire was as much for her sake as any chance of attracting John's attention.

However, they didn't wait to boil water on the fire, just used the hot water she had brought in the thermos for cups of coffee. Companionably they ate a couple more sandwiches as well as pieces of a fruit cake she had baked early to have to feed the harvest workers.

At last Steve sighed in satisfaction. 'That was great. Did you make the cake?'

Pleased, Jillie found herself grinning at his replete expression and, without thinking, said, 'You guessed it. Not just a pretty face after all.'

He turned his head and looked at her. Her heart took a high leap at the unsmiling, changed expression on the angular, handsome face lit by the flames from their fire.

'You are very beautiful, Jillian Davidson, but no one could ever think you were "just a pretty face" I'm afraid.'

Steve's tones were deep, throbbing with such unexpected feeling that she stared at him, unable to look away.

It was Steve who moved abruptly at last. He gathered up the remains of their supper and stored it away with the rest of their food

Outback from Baragula

supply safely in the utility. 'We'd better get some sleep, so we can be up at first light.' His voice sounded rather harsh. Then, without a glance or further word to her, Steve grabbed a torch and stalked off into the darkness.

Now, what had that all been about?

Warmth flooded through Jillian. Steve thought she was beautiful. The slight smile that tilted her lips faded. But he did not seem particularly pleased about that fact. Men! Who could ever understand them, she thought crossly, as she made her own preparations for bed.

Steve did not return for some time. When he did she had been lying stretched out in her light-weight sleeping bag for ages, starting to even get a little worried about him, feeling incredibly lonely. She relaxed at last with a sigh of relief when she heard the crunch of his footsteps.

She turned over, the tent wall only a few inches from her face. When she heard him enter the tent, she said quietly, 'Make sure you zip us in safely so we don't get any unexpected visitors.'

Jillian felt immensely relieved when Steve answered cheerfully in his normal, quiet tones, 'Sure thing. I'm glad we have a full floor cover zipped to the walls so none of those nasty slithery visitors can sneak in under them.'

'It actually wasn't those I was concerned about,' she said with a smile.

He must have heard her amusement for he asked suspiciously, "Oh, it isn't? What then?'

'Not saying. Might never happen and no sense mentioning them. Goodnight, Steve,' she added firmly.

After a pause he wished her a good night's sleep and there was silence.

Jillian was still and tense for a long while. Having Steve so close didn't help a scrap. She was so weary, but the moment she closed her eyes, events of the past day crowded her mind.

Why had she not been able to find John where he'd said he was going? Where could he possibly be? Something deep inside Jillian was telling her he was still alive. Surely she would know if he wasn't?

Wouldn't she?

This time she fervently hoped more than she ever had before that her 'twin instinct' was accurate this time. But one thing she was sure of now was that something had happened to John when that uncanny feeling and that brief, sharp pain had swept through her.

'Can't sleep, Jillie?'

The quiet voice reached out to her across the silent tent.

She had been lying flat on her back and rolled over. 'Over tired, I guess,' she said crossly.

There was a fumbling noise and a torch came on.

'Oh, I'm sorry, Steve.' She added, 'I'm disturbing you and you must be even more tired after your long trip with the horses.'

He didn't answer. His dark shape left the tent. A couple of moments later he was back and crouching down beside her. 'Try these,' he murmured and held out his hands.

'I don't want to take any filthy drugs!'

'Just a couple of paracetamol from your first aid box,' he coaxed in his irresistible, velvet tones. 'It'll get rid of any aches and pains and help you relax, Jillie dear.'

It made sense. Reluctantly she came up on her elbow and took the tablets with the water he had also brought.

'Thanks,' she muttered as he took the plastic mug back from her and she laid down again.

Instead of returning to his own side of the tent, Steve sat down on the nylon covered ground beside her. A large hand touched her, beginning to gently massage her head and neck.

She began to protest and his soothing voice murmured, 'Just relax, Jillie sweetheart. We *will* find John tomorrow, you know.'

'I'm just so scared!' Jillian felt Steve's hand tense and blurted out, 'When you were gone so long I felt lonely, so alone. I couldn't help thinking what it would be like if... if John goes from my life like Sonya did and... I'd have no one.' Her voiced choked to a whisper, hoping she had not sounded as frightened and confused as she was feeling. 'I'm sorry to dump all that on you, Steve,' she added in a determinedly brighter voice. 'Call it dark-time blues.'

Steve's hand slid down and clasped her trembling hand. She clung to it tightly. He was silent for a long moment and her embarrassment and misery increased.

'Jillie, I'm not quite sure how to put this without sounding... sounding pious and...' Steve paused and Jillian heard him draw in a deep breath. 'All I can do is say it straight out. After my mother died I got right away from everyone and took off up a mountain near our home. I felt as though my whole world was filled with anguish because she

Outback from Baragula

had gone, even though... even though Mum and I had never been particularly close – but that's another story,' he added hastily.

His words tumbled over each other as he rushed on. 'That day, high up on that mountain, I felt as though I was the only person on earth. I was angry, lonely and cried out to God. And then, I've never really told anyone else about this before, but I had an overwhelming sense of God's presence being there with me. And that sense of His nearness has never left me. His presence fills all the gaps and holes in my life. I know that even when I seem to be alone I never am. God is there. He's here with us right now.'

All the gaps and holes. She need never be really alone, empty... ever again?

Steve's voice dropped to a murmur. 'I... I've never told anyone else all that before.'

He had shared something with her he had never told anyone else. Jillian dared not move, trying to absorb what he had said, what it all meant.

After a few minutes, Steve whispered hesitantly, 'Jillie, I've already been doing this of course, but would... would you like me to pray with you for John?'

She stiffened. Then Jillian found herself nodding her head briefly. Steve must have felt it. He moved his hand and held hers gently as he began to pray.

It was as though he was just continuing a conversation in his quiet way with someone Steve knew very well. In simple, yet reverent words, he asked God to be with her brother and watch over him, keep him safe until they found him. He asked for wisdom as to where to search so that they might find John before the day became too hot.

There was a slight pause. Jillian opened her eyes. She lifted her head but stilled as Steve tightened his grip on her hand.

His voice filled with emotion. 'Oh, dear Lord, we do thank You for Your love, Your care of us and ask if You would keep us both safe tomorrow. Please grant Jillian Your peace and comfort. May she learn about You and Your presence with us by Your Holy Spirit. Would You bless us both now with the gift of Your healing, refreshing sleep.'

After his voice fell silent, they were both very still. Steve's grip on her slowly relaxed. A sense of peace flowed over Jillian.

'Thank you, Steve,' she whispered at last and squeezed his hand.

He squeezed hers back and then let it go. She felt his lips touch her cheek as lightly as a feather. A final squeeze on her shoulder and he was gone.

Jillian did not move for a long moment. Was it really possible to know God's presence like Steve had said? At last she sighed, turned over and was asleep within moments.

It was the snuffling and grunting that woke Jillian. She sat bolt upright. Very faint, pre-dawn light was beginning to fill the tent.

Steve's startled voice said loudly, 'What the...?'

There were a couple of squeals and then the sound of retreating little hoofs. A pungent odour reached them.

She laughed out loud. 'Well, at least they left us alone until daylight.'

Steve was already peering out through the tent entrance. He turned a stunned face towards her as she joined him.

'Pigs. Dozens of pigs!'

'Wild pigs,' she corrected a trifle grimly, 'the worst pest we have on Davidson Downs. Perhaps we can get a few before they all run off.'

She turned her back on him and hastily checked her clothing she had slept in before starting to pull on her sturdy work boots.

'Get a few?' Steve said in a puzzled voice.

She glanced at him. Memories of his soft touch and voice coaxing her into sleep returned with a vengeance. It made her voice more abrupt than she intended. 'Yeah, like in shoot as many as we can, although the ban on automatic rifles has made that more difficult than we'd like. Be careful though. As you would know, some could also attack us.'

Steve didn't reply. He stared at her for a moment and then grabbed his own footwear. The evening before she had been thankful to see they were also strong work boots.

However, their voices and then their appearance were too much for the dozens of feral pigs scattered around the camp site, the troughs and tanks. Before Jillian could retrieve the rifle from the utility, they disappeared among the few trees the other side of the cattle yards. Their squeals became fainter until the silence of the outback settled around the two people looking after them.

Steve stared in absolute amazement. 'We get quite a few wild pigs on our place but there must be about thirty or forty in that bunch!'

'More like fifty, I'd say,' Jillian replied grimly, 'I hope they haven't travelled south-east and managed to get through the fences surrounding the wheat. They will have flattened it right, left and centre. The

Outback from Baragula

'roos might eat some wheat, especially when it's just coming up, but the pigs cost us heaps. It's mainly because of the holes they make going after roots that it's so dangerous for horses these days. But even they aren't as bad as the wretched emus.'

'Emus!'

She smiled at his wide eyes and the way he immediately searched the landscape. 'Yeah, emus. Those large birds that I've wished many times *could* fly. They have those huge feet that can really flatten a lot of wheat each step. They don't just run anywhere and everywhere in a wheat paddock like the pigs do, they like to work very methodically in a straight line right across, flattening everything in their path. Fortunately we haven't seen any in big numbers for quite a while and... That's strange.'

Steve followed her gaze. Beyond the water tanks was the small shack he had spotted briefly the night before.

'The door of the shed is open,' Jillian said in a sharp voice. 'It was shut when I went past there last night.'

They strode quickly in that direction. 'That's where we keep spare drums of fuel, even a few containers of water locked away just in case,' she told Steve in a tight voice.

At a glance they saw that the large padlock and bolt on the old, weather-beaten door had been broken off. The bolt was still attached to a piece of timber hanging from the door. Certainly no pig or animal had broken that off.

Jillian pushed the door wide open and then stood still. Steve peered over her shoulder. There was only a smooth, hard dirt floor and all he could see in the dim shadows were a couple of empty plastic bottles in a corner.

'Why, they've gone!' Jillian moved right into the small building. 'Someone's been here and taken both the forty-four gallon drum of petrol and the diesel one!'

'You had drums that size here?' Steve asked sharply. 'They would take a vehicle bigger then a quad to...' He stopped abruptly and ran back outside.

Staring at the ground, he paced a few steps. 'I thought so,' he muttered and then called back to Jillian, 'you had any big semi-trailer trucks of any kind out here recently?'

She joined him and looked at the dual tyre marks still clear in the soft dust near the shed. 'None that I know anything about.' Lifting her head, she stared back towards the cattle yards. 'Of course, it could just have been someone who followed the track in off the main road needing water or something,' she muttered and then stopped.

'Last night, when I was going up the windmill ladder, I could smell...' After a moment, she added thoughtfully, 'And the breeze was blowing across from the yards. I don't suppose—' She stopped abruptly and shook her head. 'Surely not,' she said in a shocked voice, 'it must just be the cattle coming here to drink at the...'

To Steve's bemusement she started running towards the cattle yards. He caught up by the time she reached them.

'Cattle have been in here,' she said in a grim, tight voice.

'Well,' drawled Steve, 'it is cattle yards for cattle, isn't it?'

She shot him a withering glance and started climbing up and over the top rail of the nearest rough wood and wire fence. He followed her. It wasn't until Steve walked a few steps that the smell and its implications hit him. Around where they had camped several dried out pieces of cow dung had been scattered. Here the ground was covered in fresh piles.

'A large mob of cattle has been held in here very recently.'

Jillian nodded briefly. She strode through that pen and into the next, a much larger one. 'We haven't used these yards for about twelve months,' she said crisply as she looked around, 'but somebody has and only yesterday if my guess is right.'

They examined the loading ramp. Cattle had been driven up it recently. Strangely enough, no tyre marks were nearby. Pigs again or deliberate human intervention to hide the fact a truck had been there?

Steve was silent. He knew what it meant and his heart went out to Jillian. Cattle prices had been too depressed to sell any during the last twelve months if it could be at all avoided. On Honeysuckle they had managed by only selling one truck load. Davidson Downs had plenty of money behind it. They would not need to sell to keep their heads above water. However...

'Over the last few weeks, beef prices have been on the rise,' Steve muttered his thoughts out loud and then stopped abruptly.

Their eyes met.

Hers were dark with fear and fury. 'I just hope John never came across any idiots out here thinking they could get away with helping themselves to our cattle,' Jillian said furiously, putting her worst fears and his own thoughts into words.

Chapter five

As they hurried back to the camp, Steve said calmly, 'You mentioned you didn't want to worry too many people until you were sure John had not simply run out of petrol or broken down somewhere. Don't you think it's now time we checked in with those neighbours you mentioned? I hope that fancy looking radio in the utility will reach them from here.'

Jillian nodded briefly. Her voice was firm and steady, but her expressive, amber eyes revealed her inner turmoil. 'Think you know how to use it while I get the quad ready?'

Steve wanted to comfort her, wrap his arms tightly around her. Instead, he clenched his hands and shook his head. 'Sorry, up our way we use mobile cell or even satellite phones out in the bush.'

'Lucky you! We still have some black spots out here. Until the system's upgraded more we have to rely on UHF radios still.' Her voice was a little absent-minded as she surveyed the sky.

It was quite light now. The sun was just touching the eastern horizon with rays of pink before its brilliance would chase the softer colours completely away.

Jillian looked back at Steve. Her voice was husky with emotion. 'The Reeds should be able to get their plane up very soon to help search.'

Steve cleared his own throat and nodded as they reached the utility. 'Now, I can get the quad down while you get on that radio. And I suggest you contact other properties out here as well, but be careful what you say. If someone had or still does have cattle that don't belong to them on board a truck, they'll probably be listening to the airwaves too.'

She glanced at him and then nodded abruptly before tossing him the quad keys.

'Food, drink,' Steve insisted when she had finished her calls and he had the quad safe on the ground ready to go. 'And while you get some out for us to have now and pack more on the quad, there's something I want to check out.'

He saw her eyes widen. Her mouth opened but he turned and marched away before she could get a word out. After several paces he glanced back and was relieved to see she wasn't watching him, but had disappeared into the tent.

First of all Steve went towards the shed, but this time strode past it. He keenly examined the ground further on. On the harder ground the tyre marks were not as distinct, but he could see they started to sweep around in a huge circle before being wiped out by the hoofs of dozens of feral pigs. He wasn't quite sure, but thought there could be a trace of what he was looking for towards the north. He had hoped...

There. But it was very faint.

Steve gritted his teeth. He had to be sure. There was nothing for it but to climb the windmill. And that would take a tremendous effort of will-power and faith.

The year before he had started school, Steve had been foolish enough to climb one of the big old gum trees some distance from his home. It had been an exhilarating experience. He had felt king of all he surveyed; that was, until his foot had become stuck when he started back. He had looked down and suddenly frozen. The ground was a long, long way below. Dizziness almost made him lose his grip on the tree. He had been so petrified of falling he'd not even been able to yell out until his father, an eternity later, had come searching for his wayward son who should have been coming in for tea.

Since then he hated heights, avoided them at all costs. Years later at school, after he had been tormented and called a coward, shaking badly he had climbed up a ladder to retrieve a ball in a tree. He had still been so upset, unable to sleep that night, that at last the whole incident came tumbling out to his father.

Wise Ben Honeysuckle had told him he was proud of him for being so brave, but that he should just accept his phobia about heights and never let bullies ever drive him to do something he did not have to.

Big Ben had scratched his head and then patted Steve on the arm. 'Son, there are many different kinds of fear. Fear of heights is quite a common one.' He'd grinned sheepishly and continued, 'In fact, you may have got it from your old man.'

Wide-eyed, he stared at his father. He'd thought his big Dad was never afraid of anything. 'But I've seen you up ladders and you even climbed that tree the time when I was stuck.'

His father had given a chuckle. 'Yeah, but you didn't know how much I had to fight off feeling faint, or about my knees knocking all the way, or that they nearly gave out on me when we reached the ground. And you might have noticed I'm up and down any ladder mighty fast, never stay up there.'

Then the weathered farmer's face had become serious. 'There's even a big name for our abnormal fear of heights. It's called acrophobia. And while I want you to treat our difficulties with heights with respect, use your commonsense. There may be times when you are forced to overcome that fear. Then I want you to remember how many times God tells those who believe in Him to "Fear not" because He is with them.'

Ben had paused and smiled a little self-consciously. 'I prayed hard every inch up and down that tree. It sure was a high one!'

Steve had remembered those words many times over the years. Now, when he reached the base of the windmill, Steve put his head against the cold metal support and grasped a step on the steel ladder. He shut his eyes and prayed.

Taking a deep breath, Steve started up the ladder. He was breathless by the time he reached the now unlit lantern. Never daring to look right down, as he had been taught and learned to do over the years, he took several deep breaths and stared straight across to the horizon first of all. At last he slowly turned his head to survey the vast, flat landscape all around him.

There must have been a little rain during the winter before this dry, hot spring. There was a film of green in some places, but most of the clumps of grasses on the dark soil were already drying out. Cattle would need to travel widely to find food.

Very carefully Steve lowered his gaze a little. Beyond the cattle yards the few stumpy trees were scattered here and there but petered out to a totally flat, mostly dark plain. Gripping the ladder tightly, he turned and looked toward the area they had driven through. The main road they had turned off was not visible. A few thick patches of low scrub, with an occasional old gnarled gum tree towering above them, hid most of the track to the windmill. There was no sign of movement. Even the pigs had disappeared for the moment.

His gaze ventured lower to his immediate surroundings. The roof of the shed hid the place where he had swung his own powerful torch the night before. Reluctantly he climbed up a couple more rungs.

And there they were.

Past the shed, faint tracks about the width of a quad were visible for a few metres. They disappeared, undoubtedly obliterated by the many hoofs of the wild pigs, to reappear further away before they vanished altogether in the distance. He again searched the harsh looking countryside in a great semi-circle, but there was not another sign of human habitation, except—

'See anything?'

Startled, Steve automatically looked down. It was a long, long way down.

A wave of dizziness swept over him. His grip on the ladder loosened and he felt himself sway. Convulsively his hands tightened to a death grip on the metal rod.

'Steve? You all right up there?'

He had closed his eyes. Tight. At the sound of her anxious voice he opened them and stared out again across the vast expanse towards the far horizon where the early morning sun was rising.

After a couple of desperate swallows, Steve found his voice and croaked as loudly as he could, 'Yeah. I'm... I'm fine.'

'Well, come on then, stop admiring the view and get down here. We've got to be on our way.' Jillian's exasperated voice was tart.

He had never climbed this high before. Ever. That tree had been nowhere near this height.

He would fall. His body would plummet through the air for at least twenty metres to a helpless mess on the ground

There was no way he could move. No way he could dare loosen his grip with one hand to move it lower. No way he could lift a foot to grope for the next rung.

Outback from Baragula

When I am afraid, I will trust in You.

The verse his father had insisted he memorise years ago to help him overcome his fear flashed into his mind. Steve licked his dry lips and managed to whisper it out loud.

Then he repeated it a little louder. He moved his foot down. It found the metal rod.

'Psalm fifty-six, verses three and four,' he chanted.

His hand moved. He said the first verse out loud, then the next, over and over. Always he finished with the reference as he had learned to so long ago, when memorizing scripture.

'In God, whose word I praise, in God I trust; I will not be afraid. What can flesh do to me?'

He went down another rung. Another.

Breathlessly he continued to chant the verses and where they came from, concentrating on the words. Confidence and strength flowed into his tense body. Hand over hand he went down, the words fading to a hoarse whisper.

Ashamed. Hating himself.

Jillian knew her suspicions had been correct. Steve hated heights. She started up the ladder, her eyes fixed on the tall, frozen figure so high above her. Then she saw him move, start back down. She paused and called out his name again. He didn't answer.

She watched him for a moment. He kept coming. Slowly she retreated to stand on the ground at last with her hands on her hips, watching Steve descend rung by rung. She saw his lips move. He went down another rung, then another before he stopped once more. He muttered something but she could not quite make out the words. She opened her mouth to call out to him but paused when he started moving once more.

Then his feet were on the ground. Instead of letting go of the metal ladder he leaned against it for support and breathed rapidly as though he had just run a marathon.

Jillian took a step closer. 'Steve, you're white as a sheet. What happened up there?' She reached out a tentative hand and touched him. Tremors were shaking his strong frame and this time she couldn't keep the alarm from her voice.

Mary Hawkins

'Steve? What's wrong?'

He started and turned towards her. Colour returned to his sweat-soaked face in a sweeping tide of red. 'Sorry,' he gasped, 'be okay in a moment.'

She saw he was horribly embarrassed and turned away. Sympathy swept through her for this big, strong man who until now had been such a tower of strength to her. 'I'll go get the quad and we'll get under way.'

Steve didn't say a word as she strode off.

Jillian took her time double checking the first aid kit. The food and water were already tightly strapped onto the quad. As she at last started its motor, Steve joined her. She risked a swift look at his face. He was still a little pale, but she was relieved when he looked back at her with his normal, steady gaze.

'Sorry,' he said gruffly, 'I shouldn't have looked straight down when you called me.'

Her eyes widened. 'Oh, then perhaps I should be the one apologising. Did you see anything from up there to make your climb worthwhile?' she added swiftly.

His reply was terse. 'Yes. Quad tracks to the south-east.'

Excitement swept through her. 'Quad tracks? John *was* here then. Neither of us has been out here on the quads for months. It's too far from the homestead and as I told you, we bring them on the ute when we need to check things here.' She paused and frowned. 'But why on earth did he come over here yesterday? He never said anything about coming all this way. The boundary fence he went out to check is a long way from here.

'Perhaps he saw or heard that truck.'

Her lips tightened into a grim line. 'Let's go.' She nodded to the seat behind her and gunned the motor.

He hesitated. 'Got that first aid bag?' he yelled above the roar.

Her heart flipped in fear and all she could do was nod her head briefly. To her relief Steve climbed on, but before she could move the quad forward, he pointed toward the shed and said in her ear, 'That way, but take it easy, the pigs wiped out the tracks and we'll have to pick them up again further on.'

They had no real trouble finding the trail. Several times they had to double back and search. A good half an hour later, it at last petered out over a large stretch of pebbles and stones.

Jillian stopped the quad at last and turned off the motor. She didn't move for a long moment, listening intently.

Steve also was silent. He slid off the quad, stretched his legs and back before he stood still and examined the area.

At last, Jillian sighed and joined him. 'I suppose we had better...' She tilted her head up.

'Sounds like a plane,' Steve said quietly.

The distant drone of the engine came a little clearer and they searched the sky until Steve at last pointed. 'Over there.'

Together they watched the early morning sun glint off metal for a moment. The plane was not much more than a speck, flying low in a straight line. It banked and turned in a wide circle a little closer to them before heading back the way it had come.

Jillian tipped her hat back and shielded her eyes as she followed its path. 'Mr Reed's searching over the area I covered yesterday near that fence that had been repaired. From the direction the plane came I'd say he's had a quick trip over the roads out of here looking for that truck.'

'Why haven't you taken your helicopter up?'

Jillian looked at him, but he was still watching the plane disappear into the distance. She had wondered a couple of times why he hadn't asked that question before. There had been a terse note in his voice and she remembered his unexpected anger when she had flown it to Honeysuckle. She suddenly wondered if his surprising attitude that day had more to do with his fear of heights rather than what she'd thought at the time; that he was upset she could do something he could not. Already Steve had proven in several ways he was not the male chauvinist she had once thought!

'It went in for repairs and maintenance a couple of days ago,' Jillian said crossly.

'Bad timing.''

She had thought that same thing many times yesterday as she had bumped over the rough ground. 'Yeah, very bad timing,' she said wearily and swung around in a circle to survey the dreary landscape.

They were in a slight depression that stretched from east to west across the plain. There were no trees near them, only several of the low, scraggly eucalyptus trees a long way to the north-west.

'Dad told us the old aboriginals in the area always said this was once a big river. It's a long way from the Macquarie River but it sure does look like an old creek bed, especially where those trees are.' She paused and then added thoughtfully, 'I wonder if John kept in a straight line along this towards the west or followed it north a while. It might be easier following along this than dodging the holes among the clumps of grass. Somewhere, John must have headed north-west from over there.' She gestured towards where the plane once more droned closer.

Steve gave a sudden exclamation.

Jillian glanced at him curiously. He was looking back the way they had come and suddenly strode forward. They had been careful to travel over the other quad tracks wherever possible. When she joined him he had reached where the tyre marks had petered out on the edge of the stones and hard, sun-baked earth.

'How could we have been so stupid?' he said angrily.

Steve took off his peaked cap, slapped it against his jeans before flinging it back on his head again backwards and then pulling it around to the front. Jillian didn't think he even realised he'd done it.

Steve pointed at the two sets of tyre tracks. 'Notice anything there, Jillie?'

Puzzled, she examined where he pointed and shook her head. 'No, just the two sets of quad tracks, ours and...' She paused and then added with rising excitement, 'And only one set of John's.'

'And there should be two sets if he came and went this way. I was thinking he had travelled like us from north to south-east but he would have come from the south where the Reeds are searching. Tell me,' he added urgently, 'if he came from the homestead or the Black Plain's area, is this the only direction he could have come from and likely returned by?'

'He could have cut across to the west and come up from further south I suppose, keeping parallel with the road. But this is more direct and the way we normally come across to this section from the Plains. Except, we very rarely do of course because it's so far and the petrol supply could be dicey unless we planned for it. We usually bring the quads on the ute as we did last night.'

'There were no tracks at all in that direction,' Steve said abruptly. 'he's back somewhere closer to where we camped, or. . .'

Neither dared put into words that perhaps whoever was in that truck could have carted John off somewhere and he was still with them, or even worse – alone and hurt.

They headed back the way they had come, following mostly in their own tracks this time and taking far less time to cover the rough ground than before.

When their camp came into sight, Steve yelled in Jillian's ear, 'Stop where we found the tracks again this side, past where the pigs had scuffed them out.'

On foot, they searched along where the pigs had travelled from the north. Some distance from the windmill and tank area it was obvious the wild pigs had not stayed in one group.

'That mud hole made by the water leaking from the tank could have attracted them here,' Jillian told Steve. 'They can't go without water more than a couple of days at the most and, in big numbers especially, don't often go this far away from that creek area where there are usually a few small water-holes. They must be nearly dry.' She pointed to the distant line of trees a long way beyond the track they had driven along the night before.

Steve stilled. 'I saw something from the windmill in that direction. The weak sun glinted off something just before you called out to me. I thought it would have been just a patch of water near the trees, but if there's no water there...'

Jillian stopped dead and stared at him. 'It's very dry out here. Even river beds dry up most of the year. There's rarely any water near here on the ground at all. That's why Grandpop put in the windmill and tanks in the first place.'

They raced back to the quad. This time they sped past their campsite and then more slowly along the track to the road. Once again there was evidence of the pigs having at some time criss-crossed the track, but in a couple of places they again came across remaining signs that a large, dual-wheeled vehicle had travelled that same track.

At last they found them. Tyre marks of a quad ran some distance beside dual truck tyres but then suddenly disappeared. Jillian drove several metres further on but turned back at last, moving even slower this time while they searched the ground in a wider area. Then they saw them again. The narrow quad tyre marks were visible in a patch of softer ground, but this time they led towards a large patch of scrub.

Jillian's heart pounded as she steered carefully, slowly following the winding tracks through the bush.

Steve gave a shout and pointed. John's quad was half hidden in a thicker patch of bush.

She pulled up beside it. The quad was on its wheels but badly damaged. The front bull-bar and carrier above it had obviously hit something hard that had bent them all out of shape. All along one side had also been damaged as though it had been scraped or even flung over.

Jillian stared at it, starting to shake. Whatever the quad had hit to cause that amount of damage would have sent the rider flying.

Steve was already on his feet, examining the quad and then the surrounding ground. Suddenly he shouted something, pointed and started to run. She could not hear above the sound of the quad's motor and took off after him. Simultaneously she saw the trail where something had been dragged along the ground. Steve pushed through some bushes she had to swerve around.

And then she saw the crumpled body.

Jillian braked to a stop and plunged forward. Steve was before her, already crouched over the body that was lying far too still.

'John...' Her lips were dry, her heart racing. 'Is he...?'

'He's alive,' Steve snapped out and then stopped as John stirred. 'Get some water.'

When she returned, he told her briefly, 'There's a cut on his head and his leg's broken.'

John gave a deep moan. They eased his head up and Jillian splashed a little water on his face and lips.

She fought her tears and held the water bag to his mouth. 'John, wake up, dear. We've got you now. Have a drink.'

He groaned faintly again. To their immense relief his eyes flickered. He swallowed a couple of mouthfuls and at last his eyelids fluttered open and gradually he focused on their anxious faces. He stared at Steve. Then the faintest smile touched his eyes as he looked at his sister. 'I saw light. What... took... you... so... long... mate?'

One deep sob of relief burst out of Jillian. She reached for his nearest hand, but as she clasped it agony filled his face. He groaned a faint 'No' before his head fell back.

Jillian let John go as though she had touched a live wire. Agony swept through her that her touch had brought more pain to this brother who had been beside her even in her mother's womb.

'He's fainted again,' Steve said quickly, 'let's look at that hand of his.'

But it was the wrist, lying at an odd angle. It too was broken.

Steve and Jillian looked at each other. Tears had started trickling down her face.

Outback from Baragula

'I wish I had got you to show me how that radio in the ute works,' Steve muttered harshly. 'You'll have to go while I stay with him.'

She looked down at her twin brother and reached out to gently push back a dark lock of hair from his forehead.

Steve was silent and still. When she looked at him his eyes were closed and his lips moving silently.

Jillian closed her own eyes. A prayer of thanks that they had found John went up. And then another prayer, a cry for help, whelmed up silently from the depths of her heart.

They still had to get John to expert medical help. And that was still a very long, long way from this isolated patch of scrub in the outback.

Chapter six

After leaving the first aid kit and water with Steve, Jillian flung herself on the quad and roared back to their camp-site. She jumped into the utility and contacted the Royal Flying Doctor Base at Dubbo. Unfortunately none of their rescue helicopters were available. Satisfied that by the time they could get John to the station airstrip a plane would be there, Jillian tried the Reeds. There was no answer from their homestead phone or radio.

Perhaps Mrs Reed was in the plane with her husband? She tried the frequency for their plane and was relieved when Joan Reed answered.

'Jillian?' Her voice sounded anxious. Before Jillian could answer, she said hurriedly, 'We've been trying to raise you. Scott rang us just before we took off. When we told him John was missing, he said John told him on the phone yesterday he was intending to check your Number One Windmill as soon as possible. We're about to take off again and extend our search in that direction. Over.'

'No need. We've found him. Everything's under control.' Jillian's voice cracked, *Please, God. Let that be true!* She fought for that control. Remembering Steve's warning about the airways she added abruptly, 'I'll phone you later with details. Over and out.'

Jillian's hands were trembling as she replaced the receiver.

John had told Scott? Scott Reed was supposed to have gone to Sydney about the day they had returned from there. When had there been a chance for John to speak to Scott? She suddenly remembered the phone ringing yesterday morning and frowned. But why hadn't John then mentioned to her where he was going? Why hadn't he taken the quad on the utility as they normally did that far from the homestead?

There would be time to think of answers later. Now she had to concentrate on gathering what they would need to make John as comfortable as possible in the back of the utility until they reached the homestead airstrip. She grabbed their camp mattresses and sleeping bags. Jillian's mind raced at a frantic pace. She looked at the tent. It only took another few minutes to dismantle it enough to grab a few metal supports and throw them in the utility.

It took some effort, but Jillian didn't even think about the scratches and damage to the utility as she manoeuvred it slowly through the scrub and over the very rough ground. She backed as close as possible to where John was still sprawled on the ground.

Steve raced to meet her. His face lit up at the sight of the tent rods and sleeping bags. 'Good thinking. I've used the splint in your very well stocked first aid box on John's arm and was waiting for you to return before going for some branches. Did you get on to the RFD?'

Jillian nodded and hurried to peer down at John. 'They're sending a team and plane as soon as they can. How is he?' she asked anxiously.

Steve's face was grim. 'He came to long enough to swallow a few more sips of water. I even managed to get a couple of painkillers into him before he became unconscious again.'

Jillian swallowed but couldn't speak. Silently she set about helping Steve, thankful for his terse directions. Matthew had once told her, with considerable admiration in his voice, that Steve had done a pretty comprehensive first aid course. With Jillian's help, Steve splinted both John's legs together before covering him with a sleeping bag. They used other rods and one of the sleeping bags to make a stretcher.

'Both legs?' Jillian whispered at last when she thought her voice would not tremble too much. John had stirred and groaned deeply before becoming still once more as they moved his legs.

Steve's reply was terse, worried. 'Just in case. And we need to be very careful moving his back. There's considerable bruising on what I've been able to check of John's lower back and side. No sign of paralysis but the less we move him around when we lift him the better.

Could you hold this please?'

Jillian's hands were shaking. She was thankful Steve kept giving her quick instructions. 'I'm... I'm so glad he can't feel this.'

Steve's slight smile was comforting, but he didn't speak.

John was a big man. They were both panting by the time they'd carried him on the makeshift stretcher up the quad ramps and onto the inflated camping mattress. Jillian saw the worry in Steve's eyes and knew he too hoped John would remain unconscious until they at least had driven over the worst of the rough ground.

While Steve swiftly pulled the ramps up, Jillian crouched down beside her brother and gently stroked his forehead. 'Go straight to our airstrip, it's a little distance from the homestead and near the old shearing shed. Just turn down past the worker's cottages and you'll see it.'

Steve touched her hand lightly. She reached across and held his between both of hers and looked at him through eyes blurred with her tears. She opened her lips, but he touched them with a finger and smiled crookedly at her. He jumped down, fastened the sides on the utility securely before making for the driver's seat.

He opened the door and then paused. 'If you need me to stop, just thump on the cabin. In fact, if the jolting wakes him up we'd better try and get some more water into him.'

Steve's quiet strength, his ability to do what had to be done efficiently and without fuss somehow comforted Jillian. And then of course she knew he would be praying. Quite suddenly, Jillian wished with all her heart she could believe in prayer as much as Steve did. Nevertheless, she found herself praying many times during the journey that followed.

Getting back onto the track was the worst part. As the utility slowly rocked and jolted over the uneven ground, Jillian gritted her teeth and steadied John as best she could. A thought struck her. Why had John been so far from the track? Where they had found him there was no sign of damage to trees or scrub which he might have hit causing the quad to roll. Had he hit a kangaroo, a pig? No, a quad was slow enough to dodge them. An enraged bull? No. The only signs cattle had been anywhere near had been in those cattle yards.

There was but one answer. Human intervention.

Jillian forced her spinning thoughts away. Dealing with the hows and whys could wait. Right now she had to concentrate on keeping

John as still as she could on his improvised bed.

When at last they reached the track, Steve stopped and leaned out of the window to yell, 'Okay?'

'Okay,' she called back.

'It'll be easier going until we reach the road and better still then. I'll go as slowly and carefully as I can.'

Jillian nodded.

It was a slow, tortuous trip, but Steve travelled as fast as he dared. He did manage to speed up on a few good sections of the public gravel road, but once again was reduced to a crawl over most of the one-vehicle track into the homestead and airstrip. John groaned softly a couple of times, but never roused enough for Jillian to make Steve stop.

To their immense relief the Royal Flying Doctor plane was circling to land as they arrived. After a swift examination by the doctor, he commended their first aid and didn't touch the splints. An intravenous drip was swiftly commenced and pain killers administered before they moved John from the utility.

In answer to Jillian's anxious query, the doctor said briefly, 'He responds to pain stimulus, so his level of unconsciousness is not too deep, but he's dehydrated somewhat and in shock. Should do though unless there's internal injuries. We'll take him to Dubbo. The hospital there is the closest that has the surgical staff and facilities he needs.'

No time was wasted getting John into the well equipped plane. Before climbing in to accompany her brother, Jillian turned wordlessly to Steve.

He suddenly took off that ridiculous cap, put it on backwards and pulled it to the front again.

Somehow Jillian found her voice, even though it sounded nothing like her usual tones. 'The Reeds will fly in as soon as they can and—'

'I'll be fine,' he said abruptly.

She continued to stare at him. His face blurred as the tears threatened again. 'Steve...' she choked, 'how can I thank...?'

A couple of fingers on her mouth again stopped her. Then his big hands cupped her face. The gentlest of kisses touched her lips. 'Don't worry about a thing except your brother,' was all he murmured. 'I'll look after things here.'

Steve watched the plane lift into the air, level off and disappear into the blue sky towards the south-east. He felt as though it was taking his heart with him.

Slowly he climbed back into the utility. Weariness washed over him. For a moment Steve rested his head on his hands as they grasped the steering wheel. His prayer was more than words as he pleaded with all his being that God would watch over John and give Jillian the strength she needed to cope.

After a few moments he let out a slow breath and started the utility. As he drove the short distance back to the homestead, he thanked God for the Royal Flying Doctor service.

When medical help meant travelling on very rough roads over long distances and communication had been limited to the old pedal radios of the outback, it had been a Christian missionary, the Reverend John Flynn, who had initiated the Royal Flying Doctor mantle of care over the vast, remote areas of the Australian outback. At least at Baragula, even before the rural community had managed to snare Matthew to be their own doctor, they were only an hour or so by road away from medical care.

Steve decided to check on the animal population before returning to the windmill for the quads and the rest of their gear. The stallion was still restless, running around the enclosure's fence. Steve watched him with some concern. Obviously the trip had upset him more than he had realised. Anyway, now it would be a long time before John would be able to even see his birthday gift, let alone ride him.

Judy came at his soft whistle and let him pat her for a moment before snorting and walking away. In the light of day he could see the yard was bigger and the fences sturdier than he had thought. There was still plenty of feed. The trough was full, so he turned his attention to the dogs' welfare. But the cattle dog snarled ferociously at him and the very pregnant bitch waddled over to the fence with a few brief wags of her tail.

He hesitated and then said, 'Sorry, you two, haven't time to make friends now. I'll see what food there is for you when I get back.'

To his disappointment, the small kangaroo had pushed its way through a small hole and disappeared. There was no time to give him the care he needed, so it was probably all for the best anyway. Steve shrugged and made only a brief stop at the homestead to grab a couple of drinks before he headed back to the windmill.

When he reached the place where they had found John, he carefully examined the whole area, walking from the track through the bush to where John's quad still stood. The accident definitely had not happened where they had found him. Back at the track, he walked up and down a good distance until he found what he was looking for.

It was a grim-faced man who at last got back into the utility and slowly backed it up to the damaged quad. When he had at last managed to get it up onto the vehicle, he glanced around the clearing one final time.

With the injuries he had, it was impossible for John to have crawled so far from where his quad had been. Certainly, from his injuries he must have been flung off. The damage to the side of the quad made it obvious it must have been flung on its side as well as hit that tree head on. The only explanation was that someone had pulled it back on its wheels and then dragged it to this clearing. Was it John who had done this and did he do it before he had suffered his injuries? Very unlikely.

Nothing added up.

Steve prowled back to where John had been lying on the ground. From there his keen gaze searched the clearing.

His scowl deepened. Something was different since they had left the clearing. There were the tyre marks where they had backed the utility as close as they could to John, a few discarded bandage wrappers from the first aid box, but aside from that he could not put his finger on what his senses told him he should be seeing.

At last Steve shook his head and shrugged. Perhaps it was just that before he had been so totally focused on John he had not really taken in their surroundings. He walked back to the utility and started back to the windmill to pick up the rest of their camping gear. He would have to return later to get the other quad.

It was only when he drove past the cattle yards and saw the 4WD vehicle near the ashes of their camp-fire that Steve realised what it was that had been different in the clearing. Another vehicle beside Jillian's quad and their utility had made tracks there. Small branches of trees and bush on the edge of the clearing where they had not ventured with the utility had been crushed. The cleared area had been churned up by tyres where they had not driven.

Outback from Baragula

A figure strode swiftly toward Steve from the direction of the shack. The man was armed, the rifle in his hand similar to one Steve himself had once owned. He sat very still and watched the man come closer. With concern, Steve suddenly realised that Jillian's rifle must still be amidst their camping gear and not in the utility.

Now, this was going to be very interesting.

Chapter seven

'Look, Jillian, you know there's already too much work to get through for the two of us. I *can't* stay in here. At the very least I could man the phone and radio or even do the paperwork for you.'

Jillian stared back at the grey, pain-racked face so much like her own and tried to control her own frustration and mounting impatience. John had been in hospital just over twenty-four hours and he was already demanding in a loud voice to be discharged?

'Don't talk nonsense, John Davidson, you don't have any choice. The doctor says they want your leg to be in traction for days before they can do their carpentry on it.'

Jillian did not want to add that she had also been told they wanted him to recover more from his ordeal. They were also keeping an eye on his head injury for concussion and monitoring him for any bleeding from internal injuries. John's condition had to improve before it would be wise to give him a more extended anaesthetic than had been necessary for setting the relatively simple fracture of his wrist.

Hands on hips, Jillian glared at him. 'Look at you! You're lucky that thick skull of yours only needed stitches and did not crack when you flipped off the quad and broke your other bones. Although I'm beginning to think you must have lost some of your brains in the accident! You have concussion and that's not something to be taken lightly. And if you don't keep your voice down the nurses are going to kick me out very soon!'

Jillian closed her eyes, fighting her own exhaustion, fighting not to lose her temper with John. They had been arguing about this one way or another each time John had come out of a drug induced haze long enough to talk to her. She had insisted on staying with him all night. It was early afternoon now. Jillian had been back only awhile from a brief respite to grab something to eat while John dozed. Unfortunately, this time he had become very wide awake in her absence and was now arguing once more.

Memories of those dreadful hours just trying to get John into hospital flooded over Jillian.

She had rung Steve last night to let him know how John was doing. Steve had been very quiet and uncommunicative. They had not talked for long after he rather abruptly assured her he was managing well and not to worry. In fact, she thought again now, Steve had not sounded at all like the reassuring man who had been such a support to her. The call had been so unsatisfactory she had tried to ring him again earlier today when John had been sleeping, but Steve had not answered the phone.

'I just don't like you staying there by yourself! Er... Jillian?'

Her thoughts still on the handsome but enigmatic Steve Honeysuckle, Jillian stared at John.

'You didn't hear a word I said,' her twin accused. He stared at her consideringly.

She felt her cheeks warm and looked away. 'Yes of course I did, Johnny dear,' she defended herself swiftly, 'but no matter what you say, the fact remains you will not be well enough for ages, even after your leg comes out of traction and you have surgery.'

Feeling a little flustered at the way John was still studying her, Jillian added abruptly, 'Besides, I've stayed by myself at home plenty of times before.' She leaned forward in her chair and touched the back of her fingers against his cheek. 'You aren't indispensable, you know,' she murmured gently.

His free hand reached up and their fingers clung together. After a moment, John gave a big sigh and put his head back on the pillows, closing his eyes.

'Jillie, no matter what you say, you are not to be there on the property by yourself. It would be extremely foolish.' John's voice was fainter but no less adamant.

Jillian stiffened. John had not yet told her what had happened to him. She had tried to stop him talking too much at first. Then he had started on with all this nonsense about getting discharged as soon as possible. Through the dark hours of the night, dozing off and on in the comfortable lounge chair beside his bed, she had gone over and over what could have happened, coming up with the one thing. Someone had to have been there. Someone had to have dragged John under the shade of that tree. Someone who had no scruples about stealing cattle!

Deep, familiar tones growled from the doorway, 'I wholeheartedly agree.'

John's eyes opened and they both turned swiftly. Then Jillian was out of her chair and swept into a big hug by their doctor brother.

'Now, why did you bother Matt, Jillie,' John said crossly.

'Because I would have killed her personally if she hadn't told me.' There was a slight smile on their brother's face, but Jillian noted it didn't reach his eyes. 'Anyway, Steve Honeysuckle had already rung me before she was able to.'

Jillian pulled back and saw that Matthew was assessing the condition of the patient with medically trained eyes, keenly surveying the intravenous line and the traction on his leg. A feeling of immense relief swept through Jillian. She kissed Matthew on the cheek and hugged him again. The family always turned to the doctor in their family for all their medical advice. John would listen to Matthew.

'Don't you have enough of your own patients in Baragula, Doc?' John said cheekily as Matthew released Jillian and advanced on him. 'Have to travel a few hundred kilometres for another one?'

'Yeah,' Matthew drawled as he took John's offered hand. 'Problem is this thoughtless blighter who had to come off his quad and get himself smashed up a long way from Baragula.' He held onto John's hand and asked quietly, 'How are you, mate?'

John shrugged and then winced. 'Like you said, a bit smashed up.'

Jillian moved to his other side and raised an eyebrow at her twin.

'Yeah, well,' John burst out after staring defiantly back at her. He looked back at Matthew. 'As I was about to say, like a truck hit me and I've got a filthy headache.'

There was movement behind Jillian. She turned and met Steve's steady gaze. Her heart leaped. She could hardly believe how glad she was to see him.

'Hi, Jillian, you still look exhausted. This bloke keep you up most of the night again, did he?'

Suddenly she was tongue-tied. Emotion swept through her on a great wave of warmth and delight. He was here. Without giving it a thought she stepped eagerly towards him. She saw surprise touch Steve's eyes but his arms went out and then she was folded into them against his strong body. And it was so different from her brother's hug. For one awesome moment Jillian felt as if she had come home to a safe haven before she pulled back and looked up into his brilliant eyes staring at her with a strange expression.

'I tried to ring you,' she began. Her voice choked and she could not help but hug him again before taking a step back.

Steve wanted to drag Jillian back into his arms; to hold her tightly and never let her go. *Here we go again, Lord! I need your strength.*

He swallowed in an attempt to moisten his sudden dry throat. 'Must have already been on the way here.' Taking a step sideways he looked at John and then Matthew.

Steve ignored the rather startled expression on his friend's face as he stared from himself to his sister. 'Hello, Matthew, glad you could make it.'

He shook Matthew's hand and avoided looking at Jillian as he moved closer to the bed. He surveyed John keenly. He too was staring at Steve, but with a slight frown.

'G'day, mate. Reckon by the look of you, you survived our first aid after all,' Steve drawled softly.

A faint tinge of colour touched John's pale cheekbones. 'Yeah, reckon it takes more than your attempts to finish me off,' he joked. But Steve could see there was a wealth of gratitude in the eyes and masculine face so much like Jillian's.

It made him feel embarrassed and he blurted out, 'Just sorry you were so injured, John. And what was that about a truck hitting you?'

For a moment, no one moved. Steve looked at Jillian.

She shook her head slightly at him. 'Just a figure of speech. John's not feeling as bright as he likes to make out.'

John snorted. 'Well, this time you're wrong. A truck did hit me. Although, to be perfectly accurate, I suppose you'd have to say trying to stop a B Double cattle truck with a quad was probably the very height of foolishness.'

The other three exchanged glances. Jillian looked from Steve to Matthew and back again. Her eyes darkened and Steve knew she comprehended that he had already talked to Matthew about the truck wheel marks and their suspicions. But John had just described one of the large transports of a prime mover pulling two trailers, one trailer usually smaller than the other. There would have been nine axles at least and dual tyres on all except the front of the prime mover.

'I think perhaps we should talk about this later when you're feeling a bit better, John,' Jillian said hastily.

'No,' he said with a glare at her, 'I should have said something before but I didn't want to worry you anymore than you already are. But now that...' To her obvious annoyance he gestured towards the two men.

Steve winced. Ouch, that would not go down at all well with the independent Jillian. And he was right. Jillian thrust out her chin and put her hands on her hips.

But their older brother had considerable experience with these two. Despite their closeness, the twins were too much alike in their independent natures not to argue. As Jillian opened her mouth to blast that chauvinistic attitude, Matthew said swiftly, 'Jillian, we do need to know what happened before we contact the police. And I'm here to make sure the patient behaves, remember?'

It was John's turn to bristle, but after one glare of disgust at Matthew he looked back at Jillian.

She hesitated and studied John's pale face anxiously. They stared at each other. Some silent communication passed between them. Jillian gave a shrug and made for the chair beside the bed. 'What were you even doing over there at Windmill One, anyway?'

Without waiting for her to make herself comfortable, John replied slowly, 'That boundary fence was okay but I was worried there were so few cattle around the area. Thought more might have got through to Webster than Mr Reed said he'd turned back for us. The closer I got to the windmill, the more worried I was the fencing was down elsewhere because I didn't see more than one or two animals.'

John paused and added angrily, 'Only it wasn't the wretched fencing. My accident wasn't really an accident. The driver of that transport loaded with our cattle deliberately swerved enough to hit my quad.'

Jillian gave a little cry of distress but neither Matthew nor Steve moved.

John looked from one grim male face to the other and gave a mirthless laugh. 'Well, I did think you'd be a bit more surprised!'

Matthew looked at Steve and when he remained silent said mildly, 'Steve has already told me he thinks you must have come across some enterprising idiots stealing your cattle. It seems he's a pretty good sign-reader and detective.'

Steve straightened and looked at Jillian. She was even paler; her eyes wide and filled with horror.

For a moment he hesitated but then, with his eyes still on her, he said, 'When I returned to get the quads and the rest of our camping gear, I stopped on the way and had a very careful look around the area where we found John. There was a tree that looked as though something had slammed into it. It was near where we saw those quad tyre marks disappear beside the track. There were also more dual tyre marks on the edges further along.'

He paused and turned towards John. 'But I had hoped you'd just lost control of the quad while chasing the truck.' His voice was low and angry. 'Their leaving you without a drop of water was low enough, but this...'

'In all fairness to them, I'm not sure they really intended to hurt me as much as they did,' John replied swiftly. 'I came to a few minutes at one stage when they were moving me. One of the guys was very upset and wanted to radio for help. I think there must have been at least two of them.'

He stopped and frowned, as though trying to remember something. 'I thought the one wanting to get help sounded familiar.' He shook his head and muttered, 'There was something in my eyes and I couldn't see. Then I blacked out again.'

Steve glanced at Jillian. He saw her hand clench and knew that she too remembered. John's face had been coated with dried blood when they found him.

John reached for Jillian's hand. He didn't look at her, just stared from Matthew's grim face to Steve. 'The next time I came around there was an even more furious row going on. The driver of the truck was crouched down beside me. I'd seen him when he was yelling back at me to get away as I kept level with them; a huge, thick-necked brute of a man with tattoos all over his arm!'

Outback from Baragula

He paused and Steve asked sharply, 'You saw his face?'

John peered up at him and nodded. 'Then and when he was driving the truck. He shook his fist just before he pulled on the steering wheel. I saw the tattoos then and it was that same arm that grabbed me and started to drag me—' He stopped short and looked at Jillian. 'I don't remember anything after that, until you were there,' he muttered.

Steve saw that Jillian's knuckles were white where she was gripping her brother's hand. He knew she was thinking of what agony John must have been in when he had crashed. But then, to be dragged along by someone to lie under those bushes... !

Despite his own fury at the callousness of those men towards John, Steve's heart went out to John's twin. Jillian swallowed several times, obviously fighting to hold back the tears that were filling her eyes.

'That must have been...' Jillian looked down at their hands and John stared at her bent head. "I... I knew you'd been hurt, John,' she whispered.

The twins exchanged a look. John's eyes widened and Jillian gave a slight nod that puzzled Steve for a moment. Then he remembered the silent communication between another set of twins when Matthew's Debbie had been so ill and little Danny had felt her pain that dreadful night of the flood at Honeysuckle. Could it be...?

He looked at Matthew who was watching his brother and sister closely. He didn't look surprised or even puzzled, and Steve had his answer. Now he understood even more clearly the urgency that had driven Jillian to search so desperately, why she knew something had happened to her twin.

After a few moments, John said wearily, 'I've been thinking about it all. He deliberately swung that steering wheel so the truck veered towards me until it hit the quad.'

No one moved.

'Mind you, it didn't take much or with that load they were pulling he would have jack-knifed the trailer. He tried to side-swipe me a couple of times but I dodged. Then he swung the wheel again. I think in the end it must have been the side of his front bumper bar that hit me. The quad became airborne, spun straight into a tree. I came off and then it rolled on me.'

Steve glanced at Jillian. One hand covered her mouth and she had lost her battle with tears. They trickled down her face. He moved quietly and rested a gentle hand on her shoulder.

Jillian looked up at him. Agony had darkened her eyes.

And suddenly Steve knew. That was when Jillian had felt the pain and known something had happened to her twin.

Chapter eight

Jillian pushed her half-eaten bowl of breakfast cereal away and stared anxiously from Matthew to Steve. 'They are transferring John to Sydney by air-ambulance tomorrow. Will he be well enough by then?'

There was no mistaking the gleam of sympathy and caring on Steve's face. Their eyes clung and the sense of connection with him was instant. He smiled gently. Her heart pounded.

Confused, Jillian looked down at the table. No one had finished their breakfast. It was obvious the two men didn't feel like eating very much either. She'd been overtired last night, unable to sleep for a long time. There had been so much on her heart and mind to sort through.

Matthew said quietly, 'When I spoke to his doctor on the phone a few moments ago he seemed pleased with John's overall improvement and thought he should cope with the trip okay. After we left last night they gave him more pain relief. Apparently he had a reasonable night, but the sooner he can have that leg repaired the sooner he'll really start to recover.'

He paused a moment, his expression grave. 'Jillian dear,' he continued gently, 'his leg is a real mess. The doctors have decided John needs more expert surgery and after-care than they can offer in Dubbo. John knows, in fact he's quite happy to go off to the big smoke.'

Matthew's eyes lit up with a faint smile. 'He seems to think young Amy Reed might also be happy to have him closer. Even managed to speak to her on the phone last night. Besides Amy, I know when Mum and Dad get back in another couple of weeks they'll want to cosset him at Manly as soon as he's discharged. He's not going to be able to use crutches until his arm heals and he'll need some pretty extensive physio treatment to get him mobile again.'

'That means the running of Davidson Downs at the busiest time of the year is now solely in my hands.' Jillian bit her lip. 'Sorry, that's a horribly selfish thing to think of at a time like this. Matthew, John will get full use of his leg back, won't he?' she asked anxiously.

Matthew hesitated.

Horror filled her. 'Matthew! He...' Jillian's voice choked off. 'Steve?' she pleaded helplessly.

Steve reached out and tenderly stroked Jillian's pale cheek. 'Jillie dear, the doctors said last night they couldn't say for sure yet. There are multiple fractures in that leg and it's going to take a long time to heal.' He hesitated only a moment before adding steadily, 'We placed John in God's hands the other night, remember? He's still looking after your brother and will work all things out for good no matter what happens.'

'That's for sure,' Matthew agreed fervently.

Jillian looked from one to the other. Pain and despair filled her. Understanding, sympathy and something like longing swept across Steve's face. Was he longing to hold her as she wanted him to once more?

The thought made her angry, defiant. 'How *can* you be so sure? If God cares why did He let this happen in the first place?'

Before either man could respond, she added wearily, 'Oh, I know what you've told me before, Matthew. You believe God gives us free will, He doesn't make bad things happen, that He grieves too when we suffer.'

Matthew looked at Steve and shrugged helplessly. When Steve turned back to her there was a plea in his eyes.

His words were soft. 'Jillie, I know only too well that the hardest person to speak to about spiritual things could be your own sister. So, I... even at the risk of putting a rift in our friendship of these last few days, I...'

Steve straightened. Determination filled his face. 'There's so much

Outback from Baragula

we just don't know about the whys of suffering, but one thing I am positive about is that God is good, is *always* there with us right through our suffering, Jillie, as He has been with John.'

He took a deep breath. 'The doctor told Matthew that John's very fortunate we found him when we did. He was already in shock and becoming dehydrated. In another few hours his recovery prospects would have been very different. I believe God answered our prayers and helped us find him.' He finished simply with, 'So He does care and has everything else in control as well.'

Jillian stared at Steve. He smiled back at her, his eyes steadfast and filled with compassion. She looked swiftly away and felt the hot colour creeping into her face.

Dare she believe that God really cared about her personally? Could she dare believe He cared what happened to John, even though her brother was indifferent to Him and convinced Matthew had gone too far with religion by getting so involved with a church? And finally, what ever would John think about her own changing attitude to God?

Matthew said thoughtfully, 'Unfortunately there's evil let loose in this world we live in as well as good. Christians sure can't automatically expect it will never touch them. We can't pretend to know all the answers and I wonder sometimes if God doesn't permit things to happen to us for His greater purposes.'

Steve nodded and the two men exchanged a brief smile of faith and understanding. No one spoke for a long moment.

Jillian looked from Steve to Matthew and then back at Steve as he said softly, 'But there's one thing I'm absolutely positive about. Although He *is* Almighty, Creator God, I can never doubt He loves us and cares what happens to us as individuals.'

Jillian stared at his earnest face. His eyes shone with the same fervour and sincerity she had seen on Matthew's face at times over the last few years since he had become so religious – no, not religious, she corrected herself as Matthew once had when she accused him of that. If what Matthew had said then was right, being a Christian was more than 'being religious,' it was a whole way of living – Life itself.

Not for the first time, Jillian wished she could have faith like these two strong men. Sure, she believed there was a God. Who could doubt that when they lived so close to the earth and sky, to nature as she did? She certainly believed that Jesus Christ was an historical figure, that

He had even died for the sin of the world. Despite all the times she had spent thinking about God in recent days, she still wasn't at all sure where she stood. Stuff like going to church, the possibility of having a close relationship with the Creator of such vastness as the Australian outback, this world, the universe even, seemed so very improbable.

Jillian looked away, out of the restaurant window. After a moment she blurted out, 'Well, God had better have some good purpose in mind for this mess!'

'He will have,' Matthew said cheerfully, 'but now, we need to discuss something else with you, Jillian. How you are going to manage at home without John.'

She sighed. 'I've been thinking about that. Guess we'll just have to stretch the budget somehow to employ someone until at least Dad gets back. He'll be able to come and give a hand until John recovers.' She hesitated and looked quickly at Steve and then back to Matthew. 'On top of the harvest contractors I'm afraid we just can't afford anyone for more than a couple of weeks, or at least until we can sell some of our cattle or get a wheat payment through.'

Steve's eyes widened in surprise. 'You can't afford to pay wages?' he said in a puzzled voice.

Matthew straightened. 'Jillian! Are you serious? Are things really that bad?'

There was no amusement in Jillian's harsh laugh. 'Yes, Matthew, the last few years have taken a real toll on our cash flow.' She turned on Steve. 'Don't tell me you too believe the myth about us being filthy rich. Like a lot of property owners, we might be dirt rich, but there are times we are cash poor too, especially when we have to rely on produce sales money coming in on time.'

'Well, I... I...'

She cut across Steve's sudden stammer, saying wearily, 'It doesn't matter, Steve. Fortunately the Davidsons have had their prosperous times. Guess we have survived better than most on the land today because of past investments not all tied up in land. But we've also been hard hit these last few years like everybody else by the downturn in rural Australia. Then on top of everything else, this last drought has been a bad one. We didn't get much of that rain that flooded you out last year.'

Steve nodded slowly.

The drought had lasted much longer out west. Until this last year,

Outback from Baragula

most places hadn't had decent rainfall for a long, long time. Only the huge underground supply of artesian water had helped stations to survive at all. Honeysuckle had also felt the bad effects of drought, but being closer to the Great Dividing Range that stretched all the way down the eastern part of Australia meant they had received more rain.

'We've had drought after drought. Even our bores are starting to dry up. If this continues, it will inevitably mean increased costs of production. We'll have to cut back on stock, cart water and hand feed.' Jillian swallowed and sighed. 'When the seasons did come good for awhile, prices also went down. There are less and less markets for what we do produce. When the money went out of wool, why do you think we sold all except a couple of hundred head of sheep a few years back and now have increased our wheat cultivation to so many thousands of acres? And the smaller acreage we managed to put in last season barely paid the costs of irrigation this year.'

Jillian paused. Neither men spoke.

'Rich? Unfortunately we may have to go into debt until we get some money from the wheat harvest this year. We were planning to sell some cattle right after harvest if the prices stay up. That might tide us over without going into an overdraft.'

'And don't forget that after Sonya died there was the added expense of Mum and Dad buying that place in Sydney as well as all the travelling they've done since,' Matthew said swiftly. 'I said at the time you should have told Dad how bad things really were. He lost so much heart at that sad time and with looking out for Mum he let things slide downhill quite badly before you and John finished university and took over.'

Already bemused at learning of the true state of Davidson Downs finances, Steve looked at Jillian sharply. That was something else he hadn't known. Unlike Madeline, he had not continued on to tertiary education after Senior High School, content to help more and more with the farm work he loved. But now it seemed Jillian Davidson had a degree as well.

'Perhaps,' Jillian answered her brother wearily. 'Perhaps if Dad had sold at least some of the sheep before the drought killed so many of them. Perhaps if he had kept more cattle. Perhaps if he'd cleared that land earlier for crops. Perhaps if the 'roos, cockatoos, pigs and emus had not damaged so much of the crops. So many 'ifs'! But you know how distracted Dad was by his own grief as well as how much Mum needed to get away. She was a city girl when they married and, after all the years she put up with living out here, Mum had really set her heart on that house near the beach at Manly. Besides, with the cattle sold and this crop harvested safely, hopefully we wont have to go into debt after all.'

Steve looked from one to the other. So, the Davidsons might be so-called land rich and although certainly not really poor, at least nowhere near as wealthy as he had thought they were, even if they did move in the higher echelons of Sydney's society life. In fact, it seemed that his own family was much better off money wise at the moment.

One more hurdle knocked over. Money was no obstacle to...

Steve drew in a quick breath at his thoughts. Shame touched him. Suddenly he felt humbled and perhaps smacked by the Lord for his attitude to material possessions.

The barriers he had thought were there to stop him even dreaming of a relationship with Jillian Davidson were steadily, one by one, being destroyed. If John had a serious girlfriend, even the twin's close relationship may not be the problem he had thought it could be. Steve's pulse pounded in sudden elation.

Then his heart quietened.

There was still the biggest of all the barriers and something only Jillian could lower, the spiritual one.

He had noticed the deep sadness on Jillian's face when Matthew had mentioned their younger sister's death. Matthew had once told Steve about that accident. Sonya had been just eighteen and going home for the Easter weekend a few weeks after starting her university course. Her car had ploughed into a telegraph pole only an hour's drive from Davidson Downs. They thought she must have fallen asleep, one of the main reasons for single car accidents on the long, straight stretches of highways throughout Australia.

Steve's heart went out to Jillian. He longed again to fold her in his arms and comfort her with assurances of God's love and mercy, but he strongly doubted Jillian could fully understand or believe in those assurances. That thought made the ever dull ache in him for her flare into piercing pain.

At times Steve envied Matthew the happiness in his marriage God had brought into his life, but certainly not the pain of those years when he and Emily had been separated. Matthew had once told him that he and Emily had both made a bad, immoral mistake which had resulted in her losing her close relationship with the Lord for a long time, as well as him missing out on his children's early years.

But through the turmoil of losing Sonya as well as Emily all those years ago, Matthew had come to a deep faith and commitment to Christ. God was certainly blessing them now, exercising His wonderful grace to 'work things out for good' despite their sin and failure in the past. There was no doubting their utter devotion to each other now – and to Christ.

Sudden hope stirred in Steve's heart as he watched Jillian discussing with Matthew when they should let their parents know about John. God had brought Matthew to Himself. Emily's faith and love for Christ had been renewed.

Nothing was impossible with God. Surely a time could come when he and Jillian shared a deep, personal faith?

'John's condition certainly isn't life threatening now,' Matthew was saying, 'and besides, we're not even certain where Mum and Dad are at the moment. Didn't they have a coach tour of Europe booked about now?'

Jillian nodded. 'Yes, but then I thought they were flying from Heathrow to spend a few days again in the USA before eventually coming home.' She sighed. 'I think we'd better risk their wrath at not being kept informed and let them enjoy the last part of this trip they've had planned for so many years.'

'Besides,' Steve interrupted, 'I'll be helping you and all I need is my bed and food.'

He enjoyed the way Jillian turned and gaped at him.

She looked so beautiful with her dark hair curling attractively to below her shoulders. Her hazel eyes had picked up the green in the cool cotton dress he had carefully packed for her with some other basic things. When she had joined them for their late breakfast, he had been glad to see that the shadows beneath her eyes had almost gone.

A little to his dismay, those expressive eyes changed rapidly from astonishment to apprehension.

After all they had been through together that rather surprised Steve. It also hurt. But her expression changed again and this time included

Mary Hawkins

a good deal of scepticism and suspicion. That annoyed him considerably and he frowned.

'Steve! You don't think I can cope either!'

Steve opened his mouth to refute her claim but Matthew beat him to it.

'Of course we both know you could cope, Jillian.' There was impatience in Matthew's voice and she looked a little mollified. 'But you just said yourself you'll have to employ someone,' Matthew added swiftly. 'Besides John's transfer, that's what we wanted to discuss with you.' He held up his hand as Jillian started protesting. 'It's a pretty quiet period at Honeysuckle at the moment. That's why I could talk Steve into delivering your birthday presents.'

'Oh, Matthew! And I haven't even thanked you. Those horses are absolutely beautiful and John doesn't even know about them yet.'

'Plenty of time to tell him.' Matthew grinned at her. 'And of course they're beautiful. Steve breeds wonderful horses. But we'll talk about them later. Let's settle this first.'

As Jillian opened her mouth, Steve rushed in to say, 'Look, Jillie, we only have a couple of hundred acres of crop to harvest this year on Honeysuckle. If your wheat will be ready in the next week or so, your harvest will probably be finished before ours even starts. Besides, we have a good supply of employees at the moment.'

'Yeah and that father of yours still oversees everything anyway,' Matthew interrupted him. 'In fact,' he added with a smile, 'I think it'll probably do Ben Honeysuckle and your sister Madeline the world of good having to cope without you. Might make them appreciate you more.'

*

Jillian watched Steve glance impatiently at Matthew, before looking back at her. A smile slowly spread over his whole face. It transformed him and melted all her protests.

Steve raised an eyebrow. 'Well, Jillian Davidson, think we could keep working together as well as we did when looking for John?'

Work together? Have Steve Honeysuckle working with her every day? Have him sharing the responsibilities of looking after the harvest contractors? Dare she risk her heart anymore than she had already?

Jillian stared back at him helplessly. It was no doubt incredibly stupid for her heart's sake, but she knew she had little choice.

But... have Steve Honeysuckle there when she woke up, went to bed?

It would be sheer heaven.

So much so, that Jillian hesitated. Would Steve regret it? And most of all, what about her own pride? Would she be able to successfully hide how she felt about him, how she had been feeling about him for months?

'Come on now, Jillie,' Matthew coaxed, 'we both know that some of the men who come to work on Davidson Downs during the harvest are pretty rough and ready guys and there's usually one or two who could cause you problems.'

Jillian swallowed. She certainly would not like to have been by herself last year after a couple had wandered up to the homestead, especially after they'd relaxed with a few too many beers after work.

'What about...' She licked suddenly dry lips, frantically trying to think what to say. 'What about how it would look,' she blurted out.

Both men looked at her blankly.

'I... I mean... you're a man,' she said in a rush. She felt the hot colour flood into her face at the dawning looks of comprehension on both men's faces.

Jillian saw startled amusement fill Steve's eyes before he looked down to hide his expression. Feeling horribly embarrassed, she strove to hide it and tilted her chin. 'Remember we've got to think about what the contractors and their workmen, let alone the neighbours, would think. Everyone would know we were by ourselves in the homestead, unless of course you'd be happy to stay in the old house by yourself and then later with the harvester crews?'

"No," Matthew said decisively, "John would not be at all happy with you in the house by yourself at night. Sure, we've never really had to worry about security at Davidson Downs, but after what has happened to him...' He paused. Suddenly he smiled and snapped his fingers. 'I believe what you need is a chaperone.' Matthew's smile developed into a mischievous chuckle. 'And I know just the lady. She would be a great help in the house too while you were busy elsewhere, Jillian.'

Steve raised his head sharply. 'You're joking I hope, Matthew, if you're thinking of whom I think you are.'

Jillian looked from one to the other. A memory stirred and she said slowly, "Not long after Emily arrived at Baragula, you were sick and some epidemic was threatening the place. Emily had to stay and look after you as well as your surgery. You had to get another woman to live in. To still the gossips in the town and protect the purity of the local GP, you told me."

Steve looked disgusted. 'Mrs Henrietta Cobby. She taught me in Sunday School when I was a kid and sometimes still forgets I'm not one of her boys.'

'Then consider yourself very fortunate,' Matthew snapped at him angrily. 'Ettie Cobby is a fine Christian woman. I just wish the long memories in a small place like Baragula would give her credit for letting the Lord change her. If she was a nasty person there for a few years when she was going through a dreadful personal time, she's now very kind and caring. One of the best.'

Steve and Jillian stared at him.

Matthew looked a bit self-conscious and added in a milder tone, 'Sorry, but I'm rather a fan of Ettie. She's been very good to me.'

'No,' Steve said slowly, 'I'm the one who's sorry. We haven't had much to do with her in recent years, but I know she is a very hard worker at the church and in the community. She would be good to have at Davidson Downs during a hectic time.'

Jillian looked from one to the other curiously. Could God really be given the credit for such a change in a person, especially someone as middle-aged as this Mrs Cobby?

But then, Matthew had certainly changed a lot over the last few years. Before this she had thought it had been just because he had matured, had been as badly affected by Sonya's death as the rest of them. Now she was more convinced than ever it was much more than that.

'Think you'd feel safer with a chaperone?' There was a faint twinkle in Steve's eyes. 'Mrs Cobby is one woman who would protect you from me with her life and not only for your sake but so my personal relationship with Christ and my Christian witness wouldn't be tarnished in any way too.'

He smiled outright. His eyes filled with laughter and some deeper glow that sent complete confusion sweeping through Jillian. She felt her face go even hotter and looked away from Steve and straight into Matthew's eyes. His too were filled with amusement. They widened as he saw her distress. Comprehension suddenly filled them, which only added to Jillian's embarrassment.

Matthew looked troubled but just said gently, 'I'm sure Ettie would jump at the chance to visit the romantic outback, Jillie. Okay if I ring her for you?'

Jillian pulled herself together with an effort. 'Romantic outback?' she scoffed, 'why, we aren't even "back of Bourke." She'll find out soon enough we don't live in the outback. That's much further west.'

Both men chuckled.

'Matthew has already warned me that no matter where anyone out west lives they think the outback is further west from them again, or east I suppose if you live in Western Australia,' Steve said, still smiling. 'So, Jillie, what's it going to be? We risk the gossips – which would be fine by me, by the way,' he added hurriedly, 'or do we let Matthew work his charm on our Mrs Cobby?'

Jillian hesitated briefly before she nodded. "If you would please Matthew.'

She tried to gather her wits from where they had been scattered once more by the gleam that suddenly lit up Steve's eyes and managed to do so enough to ask, 'How will we get her here?'

Matthew drawled, 'Knowing my dear, independent Ettie, I'd say she'll want her own transport and drive herself.'

Things moved quickly after that. There was a profitable phone call to Mrs Cobby, who did insist she needed her own 'wheels,' before they went to spend some time with John. Eager to start his six hour journey back to Baragula, Matthew only stayed a few minutes at the hospital with them, bidding John farewell and promising to see him in Sydney as soon as he could.

The next morning John was air-lifted to Sydney.

Steve slipped his arm around Jillian and held her gently as they watched the plane take off. John had been heavily sedated and barely able to smile as his sister hugged him before he was wheeled from the ambulance into the plane.

Steve's sympathy and understanding were almost the last straw that nearly undermined Jillian's determination not to let him see her cry again. She moved quickly away from the comfort of his arm and body.

Steve stiffened.

Jillian glanced at his face but could not read his tight expression. She hesitated. Before she could speak he turned and strode towards the car park.

Knowing that Mrs Cobby would arrive that very evening, they had decided to set off for Davidson Downs straight away in Steve's big 4WD. To her relief, Steve smiled gently at her as she climbed into the passenger seat. They were both silent for some time as they headed towards Gilgandra.

Jillian suddenly felt exhausted. She put her head back on the headrest, fighting sleep. Vaguely she knew Steve had glanced at her a few times. Then she heard him say quietly, 'Why don't you have a sleep, Jillie dear?' and at last she relaxed completely and did just that.

As the car swept through the gently undulating countryside and then the flat plains once more, a feeling of contentment swept through Steve. He was going to spend the next few weeks with this woman whose beauty, courage, love and concern for those about her had crept into his heart.

Then the old warnings came back about giving his heart to an unbeliever and he sighed.

There was nothing I could do, Lord, except offer to help her out, was there? But I sure do hope Your Holy Spirit is working hard on her to give her a personal faith in Your Son. If she doesn't turn to You... Steve's hands tightened on the steering wheel. *Oh Lord, I've tried so hard but I'm afraid I'm falling deeper and deeper in love with her and heading for big, big trouble.*

At last he had really admitted to the Lord he loved Jillian Davidson! Steve glanced tenderly at Jillian's still pale, but relaxed face.

'Oh, God, keep me strong,' he prayed silently but none the less fervently. 'I yielded the other night and kissed her. And I know I shouldn't have. It wasn't fair to her – or to me for that matter. But she was so worried about John. Now I know kissing her that once wasn't enough. It just made me... just made me want to kiss her more, to hold her close, to...'

He gritted his teeth and stopped trying to justify his action to the One who knew his innermost thoughts anyway.

Keep every thought and intent of my heart pure towards her and before You.

A large transport vehicle roared past them.

Steve straightened and murmured out loud, 'And God, please help the police to find those rotten thieves and above all recover the cattle for her.'

'Amen to that,' Jillian said softly.

Outback from Baragula

He glanced at her swiftly. She was watching him and smiled a little bemusedly. 'And I wouldn't have minded hearing the words your mouth moved over before that either.'

Steve was heartily glad she had not!

'My, my,' she murmured mischievously, 'you're actually blushing. Must have been some words.'

Much to Steve's relief Jillian yawned and looked away at last. She sat up and peered back at the transport disappearing along the straight stretch of highway.

'Too much to hope that might have been our cattle rig we're looking for, I suppose,' she said regretfully.

'Afraid so,' he smiled at her. 'It was one of those big supermarket supply semis.'

She grimaced and then asked curiously, 'Do you often pray when you should be concentrating on your driving?'

He swallowed. Just as well he had not been murmuring all his recent prayers out loud!

Chapter nine

Jillian watched Steve's neck go a dark red as he glanced swiftly at her again. More than ever she wondered just what he had been praying to make him so embarrassed now.

His smile this time was a bit lop-sided. 'Yeah, afraid I do. In fact, it's a bit of a habit of mine.'

She gave a light laugh. 'So I shouldn't be worried if you suddenly start talking to someone I can't see?'

He looked a bit sheepish and then a note of slight alarm came into his voice. 'You sure I didn't say anything else out loud before?'

'No, or at least, not that I heard! That transport truck woke me up." Immediately she wondered why he had asked and added a little more seriously, "Why, were you praying something you didn't want me to hear?"

To her surprise, he looked even more embarrassed, and that made her more curious than ever because she suddenly knew she had been right. Steve had been saying, or praying, something he didn't want her to know!

Then Steve swallowed. 'I was praying for you, Jillie. Well, actually, I guess it was for us both.'

Praying for her? For both of them?

His voice was so tender, filled with such sincerity and honesty that her eyes widened and her heart warmed even while she said sceptically, 'You need prayer, too, do you?'

'Very much so, I'm afraid.'

There was such a wealth of weary acceptance in his voice Jillian frowned. Steve was a good man. Surely he didn't need prayer?

There undoubtedly were things going on in his life she was completely unaware of. After all, she had not seen him for several months. Sure, from time to time as casually as she could, she'd been able to ask Matthew or Emily how the best man from their wedding was getting on. And seeing she had been Emily's bridesmaid she thought that seemed perfectly normal.

Jillian caught her breath on an unpleasant thought. Perhaps there was a woman back at Baragula he would have to explain his extended absence to. Then she relaxed. Surely Matthew would have said something if there was someone who would want to know where Steve was.

'I haven't had a chance to ask after your father and sister,' she said politely after a slight pause. 'How have they been?'

He looked towards her with a raised eyebrow and she realised how abruptly she had changed the subject.

'Well, Dad's still courting Emily's Aunt Barbara.' That slight drawl that often crept into his usually quiet voice was there again. 'I'm not sure if he's ever going to pluck up the courage to pop the big question. And Madeline... well, she's just Madeline. Although,' he added in a more thoughtful voice, 'recently I've been wondering if she ever has come to grips with Mum's death, even though it's been seven years now. This last year particularly she doesn't seem very happy with life. She even tries to get out of going into Baragula now, especially to church on Sundays.'

Jillian thought of Madeline's less than friendly attitude towards herself the few times she had met her. For some reason Madeline Honeysuckle seemed to have taken an instant dislike to the local doctor's sister. Jillian had many times racked her brain trying to work out why that could be. Although initially she had liked Madeline, at last Jillian had decided it was just a clash of personalities and tried to forget Madeline's biting words when no one else was near.

They stopped at Gilgandra to stretch their legs, grab a drink and fill up the fuel tank. Jillian sipped on a drink and walked briskly around the Service Station driveway to get her circulation moving while

Steve paid for the petrol.

A car turned off the road way too fast, making Jillian jump out of the way. The car braked sharply. For a moment the scruffy looking, bearded driver stared across at her. His eyes widened in recognition. He turned to the passenger. The next moment the car took off again with a squeal of tyres.

'The idiot!' Steve's voice exclaimed behind Jillian. 'Are you all right?'

Jillian stared after the small, battered looking old car until it had disappeared down the road. She turned slowly to Steve. 'I'm fine, a bit startled, that's all. It came in so fast.' She paused, looked after the car once more and frowned.

'Jillian?'

She turned and smiled reassuringly at Steve's scowling face. 'For a moment I thought the driver looked familiar. Certainly when he saw me he changed his mind and took off as though he knew me, but I can't remember seeing that hairy face before. Now,' she added brightly, 'it must be my turn to drive. That is, as long as you don't mind a woman driving your big 4WD treasure?'

Steve relaxed and grinned at her. 'You must have been talking to my mate, Matthew. I don't mind in the least, but this time I'll keep driving. You're still recovering from only a little sleep the last couple of days.'

Jillian hesitated and then shrugged. She had to confess she was still feeling weary enough to be relieved that Steve had refused. But as she climbed back up to the passenger seat, she had a niggling feeling she should remember that driver who had seemed to recognise her.

Once back on the highway, a comfortable silence reigned with only an occasional remark until they reached the intersection where they turned off the main highway to head west.

'Sonya hit one of those telegraph poles a little further along here.'

Jillian knew Steve looked at her sharply but she stared blindly ahead. Even after all these years it still hurt to think of her baby sister lying alone in her crumpled car for who knows how long before another vehicle came along.

The verdict had been 'killed on impact with a telegraph pole,' but the thought that she may not have been, that Sonya may have slowly died alone, had haunted Jillian for years. Never once had she identified or mentioned this spot to anyone. And yet, for some reason, it had seemed natural to share this with Steve Honeysuckle.

'That must have been a terrible time for you all,' Steve murmured, 'Matthew told me they think she must have gone to sleep.'

Jillian sighed deeply. 'One of the big problems on country roads, especially on our long, straight stretches. We think when she reached here she must have relaxed because she knew there wasn't that much further to go.'

They were silent again for a few kilometres and then Jillian stirred and asked a question about the Barrington Mountains north-east of Honeysuckle. Steve responded, as though only too happy to turn her thoughts away from that tragic memory. It was obvious how much he loved the mountains near Baragula.

The atmosphere became relaxed, friendly, as though they had been good friends for many years.

Jillian sat up a little straighter. But they had not been good friends. Not until now at least. Feeling suddenly self-conscious once more, she leaned her head back against the seat and for the most part kept her eyes closed. She knew Steve glanced at her a few times and, after a couple of attempts to continue the conversation that she only responded to quietly in monosyllables, he at last also fell silent.

Jillian did not stir until she felt the vehicle slow down not far from the turn-off to Davidson Downs. With a feeling of relief that they would not have that far to go now, Jillian sat up.

Steve glanced at her. 'This gravel road further on is the one we drove along to what you call the Windmill One paddocks. It goes right along your property boundary and then further past your Windmill One. Where does it go to after that?'

Surprised, Jillian glanced at him.

He added swiftly, 'When I went back there to get our things, I noticed it looked as though the road petered out, not much more than a track past that entrance to Windmill One. It looked as though it wasn't used very much.'

'It isn't. Years back the Websters used to come this way to Sydney or Dubbo. Then the road the other side of their property and nearer their homestead was upgraded. The last few years we've been about the only ones on this road. The Reeds may now need to re-use it if they develop that end of the old Webster place.'

Steve lifted enquiring eyebrows and Jillian added, 'It leads to the back paddocks of Webster station. The main entrance is from the other direction – closer to the old Webster homestead, although I guess it's really not called that anymore. The station was on the market for the last few years and the Reeds managed to buy it several months ago. It's now part of Jedburgh Station.'

'Jedburgh Station?'

Jillian smiled. 'Apparently Bill Reed's ancestors were shepherds who came from near the town of that name in the Scottish Borders. As their back paddocks bordered ours as well, we'd have liked to buy old Webster out too but...' She gestured with her hands and pulled a face. 'Dad didn't want us to go into too much debt when Mr Webster first told him he was thinking of selling – which is just as well now, I'm afraid.

'For years Mr and Mrs Webster hoped their son, Billy, would return and help them on the property. Sad to say, that didn't happen and things deteriorated for them both in health and finance until it was either they be declared bankrupt or sell. Old man Webster dropped his price right down otherwise I don't think the Reeds would have been able to afford it either. As it is, I think they may have had to get a pretty hefty mortgage.'

Steve was silent for a long moment before he said thoughtfully, 'So, that road leads only to Davidson Downs and the back paddocks of what is now Jedburgh. I suppose the Reeds do use it though to ship their stock out sometimes?'

Jillian frowned. 'I don't think the Reeds have used it at all yet. As far as I know, Webster station was so run down the only usable stockyards left are the ones on the homestead paddocks closer to the main entrance. Mrs Reed mentioned once that all the tracks through Webster had been badly neglected, so I very much doubt they would be good enough for the big stock transport trucks – those B Double ones usually with the one short and the very long trailer are what we mainly use out here these days. Of course, if we ever needed to visit Webster we'd go that back way, but most people find it easier to go the longer way round on the better road.'

'Were the Websters good neighbours?'

Good neighbours? Jillian gave a little shiver. 'No.'

Her tone had been more abrupt than she intended. Steve glanced swiftly at her again.

'Bad neighbours, then?'

Jillian shrugged. 'Mrs Webster was all right. Dad and Mr Reed had some trouble over the years with Mr Webster, but they were reasonably friendly the last few years. Their son was a few years older than John and I. Billy had more to do with Scott Reed. We didn't get on with him.'

An understatement if ever there was one!

She continued swiftly. 'Billy went to the same boarding school John and I did for awhile but got in with the wrong crowd – alcohol, drugs. I... I couldn't stand him. He left home and we haven't seen or heard of him for years. Long before the sale finally went through his mother and father moved to be near family in Queensland.'

Jillian saw Steve glance at her.

'What is Scott Reed like? Is he a good friend?'

His voice had been so abrupt Jillian looked at him curiously.

Had he guessed she didn't want to have to think of Billy Webster ever again? Thankful for the change of subject, Jillian told him not only about Scott but the long term friendship between the two families.

Steve merely grunted a couple of comments until she fell silent. 'So, there's nothing personal between you and this Scott?'

'Personal between... Certainly not!'

Steve glanced at her sharply. He seemed relieved.

Silence descended. This time it was not a comfortable silence.

Jillian thought about Steve's question. When it had become more and more obvious John and Amy were falling in love with each other, she had wondered if Scott did want to deepen his friendship with her. Since she'd made it very clear to him she wasn't interested, things had not been easy between them. She pushed thoughts of Scott away. No matter what their old friend thought now, as far as she was concerned he had always been more like another brother.

As the miles slipped by, the slight tension eased. Jillian wondered if she had imagined Steve's interest in the Reeds, especially Scott, was more than casual. After a while, she closed her eyes again and dozed. She didn't stir again until she felt the car slow and start to turn. They were passing the large sign that notified travellers they were entering Davidson Downs.

'Afraid that needs some fresh paint,' she muttered. They jolted slowly over a couple of large potholes on the narrower road. 'And this road is one more job we haven't had a chance to work on since the rain last autumn. The grader also needs fixing.'

By Steve's sympathetic glance she knew he understood how difficult it had been for her and John to do all that had to be done.

'You have your own grader?'

Jillian sat up straighter and stretched. 'A very old one which has currently died. Dad has had it almost as long as I can remember. It's much too expensive to hire a grader to do up our private roads around the place as often as they need it.'

'I'm a fair mechanic, perhaps I can have a look at it,' Steve said quietly.

Jillian glanced at him. 'Afraid it needs more than a look. John said it was badly in need of some urgent transplants in its inner organs. But perhaps you could see what you can do with the prime mover. We'll need that for towing the grain bulk bin once harvest starts.'

'Sure thing.'

Once past the heavily corroded stretch of road, the vehicle picked up speed until Steve peered around and slowed down. 'I think it must have been near here.' At Jillian's enquiring look he added, 'Where I hit the kangaroo.'

She sat up straight. 'The joey! I forgot all about it. Was it okay when you left for Dubbo? And the horses, have they settled in all right? And the dogs, I didn't feed them!' Jillian cried out in distress. 'And the horses, I still haven't mentioned them to John.'

Steve chuckled and then said soothingly, 'I fed the dogs. They didn't let me forget them. Afraid my joey escaped and I'm quite sure your brother's had other things on his mind besides horses. Don't worry, Jillie, John will understand. Besides, you've not even seen them in daylight yourself yet.'

Jillian subsided. She glanced at him and blurted out, 'It was very good of you to bring them for Matthew, although quite honestly I have no idea when I'm going to get a chance to ride... what was her name... Judy?'

'Yep and Punch,' Steve said cheerfully. 'And I believe Matthew thinks you and John need to get off the property more. They are actually horses that have been trained for playing polo. I believe they do have a few tournaments around here?'

Get off the property more?

Jillian suddenly realised Matthew understood her more than she realised. She had certainly grasped every opportunity she could to visit him at Baragula until seeing Steve Honeysuckle had become more pain than pleasure. On her last couple of visits Matthew must have sensed her increasing restlessness with only John for company.

'Polo! Yes, the Reeds even have a playing field at Jedburgh. But you've got to be a really good rider for polo and I haven't ridden at all for years.'

Steve grinned at her. 'Then guess I'll have to give you a few lessons.'

The thought of spending time with Steve in any capacity was exciting, thrilling.

And downright scary.

Jillian swallowed and hoped he didn't notice the huskiness in her throat as she asked swiftly, 'You play polo?'

'Not for a long time, but I'll have you know I was once Baragula's star player.'

At Jillian's amazed look he burst out laughing. 'Why the surprise? Did you think I was just a lone cowboy roaming over hill and dale, combing the forest for cattle?'

Jillian laughed too. She stared at him, loving his deep, full-throated laugh. It was infectious laughter and she felt her spirits, that had taken such a battering the last few days, lift wonderfully.

'Ah, yes,' she replied in a pseudo-American drawl, 'an with ya six-shooters at ya side, Cowboy Steve – or should that be John Wayne?' she wondered in her ordinary voice before hurriedly continuing, 'Ya rifle ready in it's holster on ya saddle, y'all 'ed be ready to take on any of them thar cattle rustlers, anytime, anyplace.'

He roared with laughter and she joined in.

Still chuckling, Steve said, 'Well, Cowboy Steve sure has his work cut out for him chasing down rustlers these days. Especially when...'

He stopped abruptly. The smiles left their faces.

After a long moment, Jillian finished for him. 'Especially when they use road transports and don't hesitate to run down a man and leave him seriously injured in the bush?'

Steve looked grim. 'Yeah, they seem pretty ruthless crooks, especially that truck driver John described. But these days we also have better ways of catching criminals with the communication network and modern techniques the police have.'

He hesitated before adding in a quiet, yet firm voice, 'The police in Dubbo interviewed me this morning. They said you and John had given them clear, informative statements and seemed to think they have a pretty good chance of catching them. If it had just been a few animals, the thieves could have butchered what they took themselves and would be harder to trace. As it is, they're well branded and the sheer number they must have fitted in that cattle truck surely will not go unnoticed. The general belief is the thieves must be from the city with little real knowledge of cattle marketing.'

Jillian was silent for awhile and then spoke just as quietly as Steve. 'We need those cattle, Steve. And I'm thinking there must have been more than that one load. I was so caught up in looking for John at the time, but I've been thinking about what John said. Did you notice all that time on the quad looking for John we never saw one beast?'

'I didn't really think about it. I know you can't run many head per acre out here and just thought they must be too scattered elsewhere.'

Jillian shook her head. 'Not over that huge area we travelled across. Those crooks must have cleaned out around Windmill One pretty well, especially near the tanks. And then there was that damaged fence which John is sure now was deliberate. The cattle in that whole area were prime beef. After harvest we were going to have a muster ourselves. We intended to several weeks back when it was cooler, but the prices were too low for us to risk it.'

Steve frowned. 'Just how long were you away in Sydney, Jillian?'

'Ten days. We'd have been away the full two weeks if we'd stayed that planned weekend at Baragula.'

'Over that huge area and with so few head per acre, it would have taken some time to collect enough animals to fill even one truck the size John reckoned it was. If there were other loads, they could have been working the whole time you were away. It fact, it seems more and more likely they must have timed it to coincide with your absence.'

Jillian shrugged. 'Depends if enough cattle were grazing close to the main water supply near the windmill in that block. But if there is a large number that have gone, you're right. It would have taken days to round up so many cattle in that area. They somehow must have been following our movements closely to be so well organised. That we were going to Sydney was no secret over the airwaves. What puzzles me though is how they'd know when we left and how much time they'd have. I doubt very much we were ever that specific – except perhaps to a few close friends.'

'Someone had to tell them.'

Jillian stared at Steve for a long moment then nodded abruptly. 'Anything on this scale I'm beginning to think this must be would have to be very well planned. Mustering, transport and then disposing of them.'

'Disposing of them is the big question. Where could they possibly hope to rid themselves of so many branded cattle at once?'

She sighed and added tightly, 'It doesn't really matter now. They did it and, if we don't get those cattle back, we'll have to look at selling those on the poorer and drier areas further to the west. We can't sell too many of them or our herd will be depleted too much. Besides, we know they're not really ready for the sale yards yet and won't fetch anywhere near as good a price.'

Steve was silent. His hands tightened on the steering wheel. He was beginning to wonder if there were any cattle at all left on Davidson Downs.

They had slowed near the scattered old buildings and yards near the homestead when he said grimly, 'Then it seems we are just going to have to do what it takes to get your cattle back, aren't we?'

Steve had never felt quite so certain about anything in his life before. He looked at Jillian. She was studying him. Her eyes travelled from his eyes to the set of his jaw and back to examine his face.

A trace of awe entered her eyes. 'Although I was joking before, suddenly you do seem to have not only the very essence that made the hardy cowboys of the Old American West survive in their harsh, isolated lands, but the spirit of the men who first settled the harsh outback of Australia.'

Steve found himself smiling at her. Her awe was replaced with twinkling delight. They both chuckled.

'Well, I'm not too sure about any of that cowboy stuff,' Steve said in a lighter voice, 'but there's one thing I am sure of.'

Jillian stopped smiling. She put her head on one side and studied him. Before he could speak she said confidently, 'And I know what that is. Steve Honeysuckle won't rest until our precious cattle have been found.'

He nodded briefly. This wonderful woman was right. Grim determination took root in Steve's heart. With God's help he would find what had happened to the cattle and bring to justice the cruel men who had left Jillian's brother to die.

Outback from Baragula

Chapter ten

Neither spoke again as they approached the homestead. Knowing better now, Steve drove past the front entrance to the back gate.

In daylight, the landscaped gardens surrounding the sprawling house could be seen as mostly neglected and overgrown. Only the lawn immediately at that front entrance and around the swimming pool at the back had been mown recently. There were empty flower beds scattered among trees and shrubs in the large fenced area around the house. Once they must have been filled with annuals, but now only a few hardy bulbs had broken through the surface among the weed-infested soil.

It had made Steve sad to see the neglected grounds. In fact, it had all rather puzzled him until Jillian's revelation about not being able to afford wages. No doubt too, the garden would have been cared for by her mother. Despite the previous years of drought, somehow this oasis of greenery had survived – no doubt from sheer hard work and the plentiful underground water used to irrigate. But with no one but the twins and this Bob she had once mentioned now working the whole property, it would take all their time just to keep up to scratch the inside care needed for such a large house.

Before heading off to Dubbo, Steve had also discovered a tennis court further behind the house that looked as though it had not been used for months, perhaps even years. Matthew had once commented that he wished his brother and sister could still have some of the social life they'd enjoyed before they had taken on the full responsibility of the day to day operations of the property.

But the fenced off swimming pool was a different matter. It was spotless and obviously used regularly – no wonder, with the dry, spring heat that was already starting to soar during the day at this usually milder time of the year.

Jillian had told him that only complete strangers to Davidson Downs entered the house by its imposing front door. Everyone else came through the veranda and side entrance next to the large garages. There was plenty of space on the wide veranda to dump bits and pieces like food coolers and kick off old work boots.

Coats of all kinds hung from rows of hooks. There were only a couple of plastic rain-coats and they were covered in dust, testifying to how many months it had been since it had rained enough for anyone to venture out in them. The couple of good quality oilskin coats surprised him a little. They certainly had to wear them at Honeysuckle on the many freezing cold days in the mountain ranges, but somehow he had thought it would be too hot out here, even in the winter. Then again, he remembered he had heard of severe frosts out west. And those freezing westerly winds at Honeysuckle would also whistle across heavy frosts on these vast, sweeping plains.

'I hope you don't mind, but I found a bed in what looked like a guest room,' Steve said as he began to ease his vehicle to a stop at last. 'It had a French window nice and close to the swimm—'

He stopped abruptly as Jillian gave a frustrated groan and then muttered something under her breath. For one moment he thought she must be upset at him making himself at home the way he had, but then he followed her gaze and saw a small truck and caravan parked under the shade of a gum tree.

'Visitors?' he asked quietly.

'No,' Jillian answered briefly and swung open her door as he switched off the engine. 'Eddie Jones. I thought he wasn't coming until next week.'

She climbed down and stared at the grizzled, disreputable looking man ambling towards them. A limp, hand-rolled cigarette dangled from his bottom lip. Steve quickly joined Jillian, glanced at the less than pleased look on her face and then studied Eddie Jones.

The middle-aged man was thin and tall. His shoulders humped forward. Straggly, long hair was liberally sprinkled with grey. His clothes looked as though they had not experienced the touch of water and soap for many long days, if ever. And yet, Steve noted with some bemusement, his filthy jeans were tucked into slightly battered boots that he recognised were the very latest, best quality leather from a well known brand name. He himself had been the recipient of a pair for Christmas from Madeline, but they were so special, in fact such high quality, he had not liked to use them for everyday use and kept them for special outings.

Eddie Jones's sun-burnt, lined face was streaked with dirt and grime. He obviously had not bothered shaving for a few days.

He was also scowling.

'Where ya bin, Missy?' he drawled around the cigarette. 'I've bin waitin' here wastin' me time all bloo... bloomin' day.'

'Sorry, Eddie,' Jillian said tersely, 'a lot's been happening. You should have let us know you'd be here early.'

He looked up and down disapprovingly at her slim, neatly dressed figure in jeans and a good blouse. 'Ya bin' gaddin' again to town, I see. The boss around?' Curious eyes turned towards Steve. 'G'day, mate, you visitin' or workin'?'

Steve thrust out his hand and, before Jillian could speak, said crisply, 'Family friend, Steve Honeysuckle.'

A weathered, calloused hand gripped his firmly while sharp eyes studied him carefully. Steve had met many men of the bush and wide open spaces over the years and knew those keen eyes would miss very little. He suddenly grinned at the older man.

An answering spark lit the faded blue eyes for a brief moment, but his lips did not move around the dangling cigarette. Eddie Jones didn't say a word either, just nodded and turned back to Jillian.

'Steve's a friend, but he's also staying to give me a hand.' Jillian's voice was still abrupt. 'John's had an accident and will be out of action for some time. Now, Eddie, we wanted you to clear the paddocks around the wheat before harvest starts.' She looked pointedly at the cigarette he was now sucking on. 'And that means if I see another cigarette in your mouth we'll hire another professional. We can't risk you starting a fire near the crops.'

A slight smirk twisted the thin lips then as nicotine stained fingers tilted the cigarette. He defiantly sucked on it a couple of times before removing it and blowing out a cloud of smoke. Jillian's frown deepened, but to Steve's delight she refrained from comment.

Eddie waved what was left of the limp, home-made cigarette at Jillian. 'No one else around unless ya wanna git a bloke all the way from Broken Hill, like. But reckon I wouldn't wanna risk bein' burnt up meself. This'll be me last smoke.' The scowl returned to his face. 'Besides, before you was born reckon I knowed more'n you do 'bout what causes fire in the bush.'

He started to turn away but paused and asked a little too casually, 'John hurt hisself musterin' that mob in the Number One Windmill area, did he?'

Jillian stiffened.

Quickly, Steve spoke before she could say anything. 'Yeah,' he drawled, 'his quad hit a tree. You saw the cattle being yarded out there, did you, Mr Jones?'

Eddie Jones frowned. Keen, shrewd eyes examined Steve carefully once more. A glint of amusement and a touch of mischief briefly flared. 'Reckon only bank managers and them government blokes call me Mister, Stevie,' he muttered, with the cigarette once more dangling from one corner of his mouth. Still looking directly at Steve, he drawled, 'Hit a tree, hey? Wal, dumb thing to do and one thing these Davidson kids aren't, I reckon, like.'

He removed his wide-brimmed, tattered old hat and then tilted it more comfortably back off his forehead. 'Reckon I sure did see those cattle, mate.'

He nodded at Jillian and slowly straightened. Gone were the rounded shoulders. To Steve's bemusement, his drawl also suddenly disappeared.

In crisp, educated English, Eddie said, 'Good yarding it was, prime beef all right. You two young things have been doing a good job since your Dad let you take over. Called in to fill the van water tank and there was quite a mob already in the yards. No one about though. Couldn't even hear one of those quads of yours in the distance.'

He paused. His keen glance dropped from Jillian's tense face, from which the colour was slowly receding, to the cigarette once more between his fingers. He studied it for a moment before slowly raising his head and steadily surveying them each in turn.

'Surprised me a bit. Thought John said you were planning to get the wheat off first up.' The look he turned on Jillian became intent. 'You

Outback from Baragula

decided not to set up camp this year like you usually do when working out there?'

Jillian seemed not at all surprised by the abrupt change in him. Ignoring the curiosity in his face, she asked urgently, 'When were you out there, Eddie?'

'About four days ago, I reckon. Late one evening. Was moving camp and when I'm out there always fill up at your tanks.'

Jillian and Steve looked at each other.

'Did you by any chance see a B Double truck or road train there waiting to ship them out?' Steve asked quietly.

'None there that day.'

Steve saw the same disappointment that swept through him in Jillian's eyes as they exchanged glances again.

The cigarette butt landed on the ground and was squashed under the surprisingly well-shod foot. Although, now Eddie's speech had changed so much, Steve did not feel quite so surprised by those boots that were not in keeping with the rest of his appearance.

'Saw a big cattle truck day before yesterday though.' Expressionless eyes stared at them both before he suddenly turned away and started slowly towards his outfit again.

Jillian gave a strangled exclamation. They both started after him and Steve called out urgently, 'Mr Jones... Eddie, we need to know about that truck you saw.'

The erect, thin figure paused and then, as though making up his mind, swung around. 'Thought you might,' he said placidly to Jillian, ignoring Steve. 'Heard on the grapevine you were asking after it.' He paused and added a trifle smugly, 'Also heard the RFD was called out here the day after I spotted that there cattle truck, like.'

Jillian drew herself up. Her voice was rapid and shaky. 'Eddie, we've had cattle stolen from that Windmill out-station. The truck taking them out was more than a single-trailer cattle transport, John said. It deliberately swerved, only slightly, but still enough to send his quad crashing into a tree. The... the worst thing is they dragged the quad off the track to hide it and deliberately left a seriously injured man alone without even leaving him any of his water. John was flown to Sydney this morning for specialist treatment for a badly smashed up leg.'

Eddie Jones's expression had changed completely while she was talking. Suddenly he started to let fly with several vicious swear words.

'That's enough!' Steve snapped loudly above the tirade. 'There's no need for that in front of a lady.'

The middle-aged man broke off and glared at him. 'I'd say there's every need for it,' he barked, 'I've known these kids' old man long before he up and married.' He swallowed and asked anxiously, 'Johnnie's going to be all right, isn't he, girlie?'

'We... we don't know yet if he'll have any permanent injuries to his leg.'

He started to let fly with another expletive and then caught himself. 'The murdering swine!'

He marched forward and poked Steve in the chest with a heavily tobacco stained finger. 'A prime mover pulling two trailers roared past the paddock I was working in. It hurtled over that narrow, rough road far too fast and I thought it was funny, like. When I heard it again after dark it were funnier still, heading back and roaring even faster, like. As though it was empty, like.'

Steve and Jillian stared at him. Unfamiliar with the properties, Steve looked enquiringly at Jillian. Her eyes were wide and startled. To his dismay, her face had drained of colour. She swayed slightly and he instinctively moved closer.

Then, in a pain-filled, strained voice he hated to hear, Jillian asked slowly, 'Eddie, were you near the Websters' old place?'

He nodded once. 'Yep, been workin' just across from there. Got a good thousand tails,' he said, slipping back into his drawl. 'Reckon them pests been breedin' unchecked on Webster since the place got too much for the old couple. Course, ya don't have to worry, got lots of me quota still to go for your place.'

Jillian shuddered and closed her eyes.

Light dawned on Steve. 'A thousand! You... you must mean 'roos. You're a professional kangaroo shooter.'

'Yep and this year me government licence quota's been upped,' he said proudly, 'cause the 'roos especially round here, been breeding real fast these last coupla years. This is the first bad dry spell we've had again for a long time. Got ya permit of course?' he shot at Jillian.

She nodded briefly and said in a dazed voice, 'The 'roos thrive on the young wheat when it's just up and... Eddie, that semi. It must have been making for Webster up the back road. You didn't see the driver or get a license number did you?' she finished urgently.

Outback from Baragula

He shook his head. 'Naw, too far away, but a pale coloured prime mover, white or creamy I reckon with them cattle crate trailers'

Just as John had described it.

Eddie resettled the very old, sweat and grease stained hat firmly on his head. His shoulders slumped down. 'Well, when I heard tell about the Flying Doc and youse was lookin' for a truck, thought ya mighta bin interested, like, so thought I'd git over here early, like. Just sorry I didn't see it proper in broad daylight,' he drawled. 'Well, gotta get meself set up proper before sunset,' he finished abruptly, turned and started to trudge off again towards his truck and van.

'Thanks a heap, Eddie,' Jillian called after him. 'Make sure you call back for any supplies you might need and use the guest house anytime.'

He didn't pause this time, just waved a nonchalant hand over his head at her.

'He "heard tell"?' Steve murmured slowly, 'I'm beginning to think Baragula gossips have nothing on you outback people with your two-way radios.'

Jillian didn't answer. He glanced at her and then moved closer until their shoulders were touching. All his being longed to offer her comfort and support. Somehow he refrained from slipping his arm around her, but could still feel her tension as they watched the old kangaroo shooter start his vehicle and lurch slowly over the bumps until he disappeared behind a clump of trees.

'Mr Eddie Jones came early specifically to find out what was happening and tell us about something he "thought strange, like",' Steve said.

Jillian merely nodded without relaxing or moving away.

Steve remained staring thoughtfully after Eddie. 'What an interesting old bloke. He sure likes to play on that image of an outback character.' He drew a deep breath and turned to stare at Jillian. 'Seems we now may know where to start looking for a mob of Davidson Downs cattle.'

'Yes, it seems we do,' Jillian said in a clipped, absent voice. 'If Eddie's right, I... I...' Suddenly she shrugged and turned back to Steve's vehicle. 'Eddie Jones is quite a legend. He's a Vietnam Veteran and, as you said, a real character. Guess there are quite a few of them around if you look,' she added, with a sudden trace of anger tinged with bitterness.

Before Steve could comment, Jillian added wearily, 'Like Eddie said, we've known him all our lives, but only see him once or twice a year. I've never been able to understand the bloke, never understood how anyone could spend his life shooting kangaroos. If he's right this time...'

She opened the back door of the vehicle and dragged out the small case Steve had packed and taken to Dubbo for her. Steve took it from her and retrieved his own. She let him take it without a protest, just continued talking in a spat of nervous words that worried Steve.

'Every time we can get a permit to keep the kangaroo population down we use him,' she said a little breathlessly as they strode towards the house. 'I know they are just pests and I know we just have to do it for our cattle and sheep to have enough feed and for us to get a reasonable wheat crop return to survive. But I must confess anyone who can boast about killing thousands of kangaroos and do it year after year as a living...' She shuddered.

'I think it's more than that for him,' Steve said quietly, 'he just demonstrated there's not much goes on he doesn't know about and he revelled in being able to give us that information.'

They looked at each other. She was still very pale, with a strained, tense look about her that worried Steve even more. There was uncertainty and a strange fear in her eyes he could not quite fathom.

'So, we check out that road to Webster where that truck could have gone?' he ventured.

His own hope was not reflected in Jillian's face. She was very still for a long moment, just staring at him before she nodded at last.

Steve frowned. Jillian was scared about something... something triggered by the information from Eddie Jones about the Webster property being involved. She was not going to tell him what she suspected. He took a deep breath, fighting his sudden overwhelming need to hold her, to tell her she could trust him completely. But if she didn't know that already...?

Not daring to trust himself not to grab her and kiss her with all the longing that just kept getting worse, he swung away immediately, saying gruffly, 'We had better ring this through to the police.'

He headed towards the house, but to his surprise she did not follow him. When he reached the veranda he looked back. There was no sign of her. He hesitated and then shrugged before dropping the bags on the veranda and making for the phone in the kitchen. Jillian must need some private space right now.

Outback from Baragula

The detective in Dubbo was very interested, excited, but then said regretfully, 'Look, I'm real sorry, sir, but afraid we've had a homicide in the area here and all our resources have been ordered to concentrate on that. But we will get on to this as quickly as we possibly can.'

Very disappointed and disturbed, Steve hung up the phone. Hopefully the thieves may not risk the cattle being moved again if they had been left yarded. However, if the roads on Webster were still as bad as Jillian said and because of the incident with John, it was more likely they had been released not far from that unused gravel road. In the vastness of a property out here they could very quickly scatter far and wide.

He would have to investigate himself.

He? A brief smile twisted his lips. As though one independent woman would let him get away with doing anything without her.

Deep in thought, he went outside and after a moment's hesitation started towards the sheds. Then he heard a sharp yap. Despite his concern for her, he smiled a little as he heard Jillian's voice demanding, 'Blackie, get off me!'

The yard the dogs had been in was now empty. Steve stood quietly for a moment watching Jillian making a fuss of the very pregnant black and white collie a little distance from it. There was a sudden threatening snarl directly behind him.

Steve froze.

There was another, louder snarl and one deep throated bark. He ventured a glance over his shoulder. The red cattle dog was several feet away, ears flat, tail rigid, every muscle on alert. It took a limping step towards him and barked savagely again.

'Bluey!' Jillian called sharply.

It did not relax a muscle but stayed perfectly still, eyeing Steve balefully. Knowing what he did about intelligent, red cattle dogs, Steve decided to stay very still. One paw was raised slightly off the ground as though ready at any moment to rush him.

Before he could speak, Jillian strode between them.

'Bluey, heel!' she commanded, exasperation in her voice.

To Steve's immense relief, the dog relaxed, wagged its tail once and went over to Jillian and sat down beside her. Steve turned around and the dog was on its feet again with another ferocious snarl.

'For goodness sake, Bluey, I do wish you'd behave,' Jillian said in an exasperated voice. She bent down and patted the dog, then looked up at Steve with a wry grin. 'Just as well they were in their yard while you were here by yourself. He doesn't seem to like you. But please, don't take it personally, Bluey's like this with all strangers. Hence the high fence around their yard.'

'I assure you the feeling's mutual,' Steve said. Nevertheless he advanced very slowly and crouched down near Jillian.

'Now, look here Bluey, you dumb dog,' he began in his usual quiet voice.

The dog's ears pricked forward.

'Who ignored your very unfriendly demeanour and fed you the other night, made sure you had plenty to drink?' Steve continued with a smile in his voice. 'Hey, you ungrateful wretch, who risked your mistress's wrath by poking around her sheds and then her kitchen trying to find some dog food? Who ended up raiding the deep freeze and risked getting into even more trouble by micro-waving that huge and probably prime steak? And were you grateful? Oh, no, still showed those teeth at me so I left you both strictly alone.'

By the time he had finished, Bluey's tail was wagging furiously. He gave an apologetic little yelp and Steve could have sworn the dog grinned at him as though he understood every word. He held out his hand. The dog stiffened once more, but only for a brief moment before giving another friendly yelp. Tail whipping from side to side, the animal cautiously approached.

Steve heard Jillian give a startled gasp. He looked up. She was watching with a strange expression in eyes that were dark with emotion. A rough, wet swipe across his jaw drew his attention back to Bluey.

Jillian chuckled as Bluey started licking his face. Still cautious, Steve gingerly patted the dog and she said in a slightly breathless voice, 'Wow, that was quick work, Mr Honeysuckle. Seems you've already won his heart. It usually takes quite a few days after he tolerates a stranger touching him before he ever approaches of his own accord!'

Like his mistress, flashed through Steve's heart. Cautious at letting a man get too close to her.

That one time he had grabbed Jillian and kissed her on Honeysuckle, she had stiffened in what he realised long afterwards, when his flash of temper had gone as well as her, had been more than mere affront. He had badly frightened her, something he somehow still needed to

Outback from Baragula

apologise for. And yet... His heart leaped. There had been no fear the other night when he...

Suddenly Steve was very glad Ettie Cobby was on her way.

'Oh, of course,' Jillian was still chattering away, drawing his thoughts away from how tempting she had been that night in the tent, despite her pain and fear. 'You didn't speak before, just sneaked up on me and you no doubt kept your distance enough for Bluey not to recognise you or your smell.'

'Smell? I'll have you know I don't smell, Madam! Or at least, not like your friend Eddie, I should imagine,' he added hastily.

He felt rewarded when she giggled. It was so good to hear the laugh in her voice. 'You must have talked to the dogs a while the other evening for Bluey to recognise your voice the way he did just now.'

Steve cleared his throat. 'I didn't say more than a word or two to the dogs, but yeah, reckon I did talk out loud for a while near them.'

He hesitated, not really willing or sure if it was wise to open up himself even more to Jillian. 'After feeding the dogs, I stayed not far from them, enjoying the peace and wide expanse of God's starry, moonlit sky,' he began slowly. He avoided her gaze and fussed over the dog. 'I've always loved being out in the bush at night, but before now smiled when people spoke of the "silence of the bush." On Honeysuckle it's never completely silent. A lot of nocturnal animals wake up then. Night birds call out. In the mountains it's rare for there not to be even the slightest rustle of leaves in the towering eucalypts or the snuffles and rattles of animals in the bush. Here the other night, it was almost eerily quiet.'

Steve ventured a brief glance at her face. She was watching Bluey squirming on the ground with a thoughtful expression on her face.

'And I suppose you talked out loud to God like you did in the car,' she said unexpectedly.

He stilled. Without looking up at her Steve said as lightly as he could manage, 'Guess you're getting to know me a bit too well.'

Not even a breath of air had disturbed the silence that night he had poured out his heart to God. The horses had settled. The dogs were busy eating. Nothing moved. It had suddenly been as though he was the only person in the whole universe.

After several moments he had broken the silence and talked out loud to Jesus. To Him, his very best friend, Steve had poured out his fears for John – the need to find who could have left him so callously and stolen the cattle. He had poured out his rage at the cruelty of men who had left a seriously injured man alone to probably die. Then, not least of all, there had been all his increasing feelings for this beautiful, capable woman who he very much feared now may have stolen his heart for good.

'There was much to pray about,' Steve told Jillian softly.

She crouched down beside him. He could not see her face as Jillian patted the now quiet dog. He stood up, not sure what to say, waiting for a comment from her.

A thought struck him. 'Does Matthew know how Bluey acts around strangers?'

Jillian stood up, brushing her hands. The face she turned to him looked a little puzzled as well as relieved at his abrupt change of subject.

'Yes, of course. He's even had to be wary at first when he visits after a long time away.' When he remained silent, she added with a slight smile, 'And why would that make you frown, Steve Honeysuckle?'

He didn't answer.

She shrugged and added with a touch of impatience, 'Come on, let's check on the horses. I don't think I can resist any longer going to have a look at our birthday presents in the daylight.'

Steve bent to give Bluey a last rub behind his ears. Deep in thought, with the dogs running between them, he strolled behind Jillian to the horse paddock. His thoughts were racing. If Matthew, as well as John for that, knew that Jillian had such a fierce protector already, why had they both wanted him to stay and protect her?

'And now what are you grinning about? Having some silent conversation with God once more?'

He looked up. Jillian sounded a little peeved. She was waiting for him, leaning on a fence post and studying him with a curious expression on her face.

The sun shone down on her bare head, glinting off those dark curls. She was truly the most beautiful woman he had ever met. And somehow her two brothers knew he had recognised that fact. Especially Matthew. And yet, Matthew of all people, knew how different Steve was from his sister, knew how it was for a man who dared not love an unbeliever.

Sudden hope touched Steve. Perhaps Matthew knew that Jillian's attitude to faith was changing. His smile widened. 'Yeah, I guess so

Outback from Baragula

and I might even tell you – one day.'

Jillian stared back at him. Her eyes had gone very dark once again. Suddenly she turned her back on him and looked at the horses slowly walking towards them across their yard.

Steve's smile disappeared. *Please, God, take away this ever growing love I have for her or let her love me back.* Despite the desperate edge to his heart's cry, deep down he knew there was more than that involved.

Once again sadness swept through him when he thought about the big gap between them spiritually. If Jillian could not share his deepest passion of all, his love for Christ, any love between them would be marred, incomplete. And he would also be disobedient to the principles of scripture that warned strongly about being unequally yoked together with an unbeliever.

On that basis alone, any relationship between them could be a recipe for ultimate disaster.

Chapter eleven

'I wish we had time for you to saddle up and try Judy out,' Steve said quietly.

He had been silent while Jillian had been making a fuss of the two beautiful horses, especially Judy. Her own horse! She still could hardly believe there were horses once again on Davidson Downs.

Longing to go for a ride, Jillian reluctantly knew Steve was right. She gave the beautiful grey another rub on the nose and then moved back. 'You even brought saddles?'

Steve merely nodded. His face lit up with that heart-melting smile that played its usual havoc with her senses.

Jillian looked swiftly away. A deep sigh was wrenched from her. 'I wish so too,' she said rapidly, hoping she was managing to mask the real reason for that heartfelt sigh. 'I mean, I wish we could go for a ride, although I'm so out of practice. I'd like nothing better, but we haven't even eaten yet and I'm already days behind what I should have been doing this week. And now there's John's work to get through as well.' She stopped abruptly. Goodness, she had started to babble. Turning, she led the way back to the house.

'What would "John's work" be at the moment?'

Jillian glanced at Steve as he caught up to her. 'Before harvest started we planned to visit the bores and make sure the stock have water. We also check the fences, especially around the wheat and the boundary. The prime mover needs a reconditioned starter motor. John ordered one the morning before he left on the quad. He was trying to service the motor so there was less chance of it letting us down during the next few weeks. I think he said there were a couple of other things he was trying to sort out on it as well.'

She thought for a moment and then shrugged. 'He's already gone over the harvester and grain bulk bins, but otherwise I guess just checking everything, especially the machinery so we have less chance of interruptions while the harvest is on.'

Steve nodded briefly but was silent as she led the way into the laundry to wash their hands. He looked thoughtful, but once they were in the kitchen all he said cheerfully was, 'I don't know about you, but I'm starving.'

Jillian threw a smile at him and reached for the electric jug. 'So am I, especially as it's mid-afternoon and we only grabbed that drink when you filled up the petrol tank at the service station in Gilgandra.'

She was a little surprised, but very pleased when Steve offered to make some sandwiches. She was used to her father and John staying well out of the kitchen when food was being prepared. Opening the refrigerator, Steve pulled out the remains of a piece of cooked beef which she had only prepared and frozen a couple of days ago ready for the hectic days of harvest and mustering.

'Hope you don't mind,' he said a little apologetically, 'but I did go through your refrigerator and some of your cupboards to feed myself.'

'As long as you found plenty,' she murmured and reached for the cake tin holding the remains of the big fruit cake.

They spoke little, but it was a comfortable silence as they downed piping hot cups of tea with their hastily prepared meal.

At last Steve finished his second large piece of cake and gave a satisfied sigh. 'Thanks, Jillian that was great. Dare I ask if that cake is the one you made yourself?'

'Weell,' she drawled as she stood and started collecting their dishes. 'John's certainly not into cooking.'

'Amazing.'

She paused on her way to the sink and looked at him enquiringly. Steve was watching her with that tender look in his eyes which somehow always seemed to reach right into her, warming her – but also

Outback from Baragula

confusing and making her feel self-conscious.

Turning her back on him, she said as lightly as she could, 'Amazing that I can cook a fruit cake?'

She was starting to feel rather defensive, a little hurt that a simple fact like that highlighted how little he thought of her domestic skills. It reminded her only too vividly of one of his sister Madeline's snide remarks about her capabilities when she had tried to help get lunch on that visit to Honeysuckle.

'Yeah, amazing.' A teasing note entered the soft voice behind her. 'According to her big brother she is very proficient on the computer, doing nearly all the book-keeping for the property. She keeps house for her and her twin brother as well as helping with the cattle, driving tractors to plough paddocks, plant wheat. I know she even shoots wild pigs, so I reckon she must be something of a sharp-shooter.'

She swung around and stared at Steve. He was watching her with such a tender expression in his eyes that something deep inside Jillian melted in a puddle. She moistened her lips, but couldn't get a word out.

Steve looked at her lips before slowly letting his gaze wander back up to her face and into her eyes once more.

'I bet she'd even shoot kangaroos too rather than watch her sheep and cattle die because there wasn't enough feed for all, especially if those pests were threatening her family's livelihood.'

He grinned up at her. The hot blood rushed to her face at the blatant admiration on his.

'And now I know she cooks meat so that it melts in the mouth and a fruit cake like none I've ever tasted before. Besides all that I know first hand she drives a quad like a racing car driver and climbs windmills in the dark without turning a hair.' He stopped and looked away. His smile dimmed a little. 'And she also flies her own helicopter.'

Jillian studied him for a moment. 'Why does my flying a helicopter bother you so much, Steve?'

Her quiet question seemed to startle him. His eyes widened and he finally asked, 'Why do you think that?'

She shrugged. 'Mainly just the way you spoke to me at Honeysuckle when I flew in to take Debbie and her grumbling appendix to hospital during the flood there. And just now...' She hesitated, not quite sure how to express her disquiet.

He frowned. 'When we met up at the wedding I apologised for the way I spoke to you that day. I hoped you had accepted my explanation that I was in no mood to indulge in polite conversation that morning you flew in. We'd had little sleep for days while we moved our stock from the flood waters, not to mention that last night with poor little Debbie so sick and rescuing Matthew and Emily from a watery grave.'

She bit her lip, wishing she had not said anything. Even the way he was reacting now showed Jillian there was more behind his attitude towards the helicopter than he was prepared to admit to her.

'Oh, well,' she said at last, 'you won't have to worry about the helicopter for awhile yet. I rang the maintenance depot. They had to send away for a spare part and said it could be at least another day or so.'

'Pity, you could have flown over the area in the direction Eddie saw the cattle transport.'

Jillian was relieved that unusual element of strain was gone from Steve's voice and replied as lightly as she could, 'We'll just have to take the ute again instead.'

Steve opened his mouth and closed it again. His lips tightened. 'I'm very much afraid you're right.'

She had been gearing herself up to argue with him, expecting him to say they should leave it to the police, that the men involved had already proven how dangerous they were.

Steve was watching her face and gestured with his hands in defeat. He pushed his chair back and stood up. 'Oh, well, I knew you'd insist we both drove there anyway,' he muttered. The expression on his face was suddenly bleak. 'The police in Dubbo have a full scale homicide investigation on their hands and it has to take precedence over cattle stealing and the attack on John. So, if we want anything done at once it seems we'll have to start doing it ourselves.'

'I *was* going out there anyway, Steve.' By the resigned look in his eyes, she knew he had heard the implacable note in her voice and added calmly, 'Besides, I'm sure the Reeds won't mind helping—'

'No.'

The word was so sharp, so abrupt, it startled her. Then she guessed he was about to put into words the unwelcome thoughts of her own she'd tried to dismiss as Eddie Jones had driven off.

She doubted if anyone other than the Reeds had known their movements on a day to day basis, or even that the helicopter was not on the station, so there was virtually no risk of being disturbed while stealing cattle. If she and John had stayed away longer, stayed at Baragula as originally planned, no doubt that last load of cattle would have been long gone.

Steve was still scowling. 'Someone on Jedburgh could be involved, even if indirectly, with the whole sorry mess.'

Jillian nodded reluctantly. 'I do know they've employed a few different men since buying the Webster station.'

Of course, it was unthinkable that Bill and Joan could be involved. As for Scott... No, they'd grown up together. Sure, he had been showing far too many signs recently of wanting to be more than an old childhood friend and neighbour, especially since John and Amy had started getting serious about each other. Jillian had even begun trying to avoid him the last few months. Fortunately the last time she'd visited Jedburgh since their major confrontation, Scott had been away on one of his trips to Sydney.

'I don't think it's at all wise to let *anyone* know where we think the cattle may be,' Steve was saying. 'If those cattle are on the old Webster place and still yarded, they could be moved pretty fast before we have a hope of finding them. Now, I take it you know where they have stock yards on Webster, particularly any that are well away from the homestead?'

Jillian looked at him thoughtfully. 'We were never very friendly with the Websters. I haven't been there for years, but I'm pretty sure they had a couple of smaller stock yards as well as the main one near the old homestead. Unfortunately I can't really remember just where.'

'Of course, the cattle could have been unloaded and let loose in one of those massive paddocks you seem to favour out here. How long do you think it might take us to find them and what equipment do you suggest we take? I didn't bother to unload the camping gear. It took two trips to bring both quads back here; yours and also the camping gear are still on the ute.'

She stared at him. 'John's... the quad's motor still ran enough for you to get it up the ramp? I thought they must have pushed it to where...' Her throat closed up at the memory and horror of finding John.

Steve nodded briefly. 'Just going enough for me to get it up on the ute. Reckon that's how they got him so far away from the track where he hit that tree. But there's a lot of damage to the axle and steering. The tyres are also ruined.'

He stopped abruptly and turned his face away. Jillian saw Steve swallow rapidly and felt a sudden bond with him. He too felt John's injuries and what had happened almost as deeply as she did.

'Guess that means a trip to Coonamble one day to see if it can be fixed,' she said as steadily as she could. She cleared her throat and continued in a business-like fashion that brought his eyes back to her face. 'We might need the camping stuff again so it may as well stay and we'll certainly need my quad again.' She hesitated and added slowly, 'Steve, have you thought about taking the horses out in the trailer?'

'Yes,' he answered briefly, 'but from what I saw out there, I reckon it's wiser to use your modern means to chase the stock.' A slight smile twisted his mouth. 'Not as much fun as riding a horse, but at least no risk of getting a horse's leg down one of those holes scattered here and there.'

'Rabbits and pigs! Well, at least it was rabbits digging holes before the calicivirus virus started killing them. But we do still have some of their old warrens as well as the pigs trying to dig up roots. They were the main reason we stopped keeping horses for the stock. Men we employ at mustering times mostly still have them of course.'

She hesitated once more. 'There is a small motorbike we used a lot when we still had all the sheep. It will fit on our big ute with my quad. Afraid it hasn't been ridden for ages since we bought the second quad, but if we can get it going one of us could use that I guess.'

'Me,' Steve said cheerfully, 'we use a trail bike ourselves sometimes on our less hilly paddocks. I'd be better on it than the quad.'

'Right, but we shouldn't leave until your Mrs Cobby arrives. One of the unwritten rules out here is never to leave without letting someone know where you've gone.'

Steve nodded and looked impatient. 'Same at home. On any property it's only commonsense.'

She glanced at him and wondered why he sounded so irritable all at once, but he'd already turned away.

Steve muttered something about checking out the horses and disappeared.

Both of them kept busy the next couple of hours. Jillian prepared a guest room for their chaperone, smiling a little as she did so. A chaperone? How old-fashioned – and yet rather gallant perhaps. The fact remained if she and Steve had been going to get up to any of the kind of nonsense a chaperone might prevent, there had been plenty of opportunity in that tent in the middle of nowhere.

Outback from Baragula

Nonsense?

Would it be nonsense to get seriously involved with Steve Honeysuckle? The memory of that night they had spent together in the tent swept through Jillian.

Still clutching a pillow-slip, she sank down on the side of the bed and closed her eyes. So much had happened since then. All her attention had been focused on John and she had not allowed herself to dwell on it all. There, in that uncomfortable small tent, she had experienced something she never had quite the same before. Steve had cared for her in a way that had made her feel the most important person in his life.

But then... He had prayed for her, just her.

Were You really listening, God?

Her eyes flew open.

Steve had prayed she would sleep. Despite her turmoil of mind, the hard ground and her small blown-up mattress, she had slept like a log until those pigs had grunted and squealed.

Steve had prayed they would find John that morning before it became too hot. They had.

Steve had prayed God would watch over John during the night. John remembered nothing of that night except the light on the windmill. He remembered nothing of his pain, his thirst, until they were bending over him splashing water on his face.

God, can it be true what Steve said? Can You possibly care for us – me, Jillian Davidson? Have You been listening to my prayers lately too?

Jillian jumped up, not wanting to face any of her thoughts, and swiftly finished preparing the room. Then she retreated to the office and turned on the computer to have another go at checking the lists for harvest as well as paying more accounts. But Jillian couldn't shake off her restlessness. After a few minutes she realised she was just staring blankly at the screen.

Email. She'd better check to see...

There was one from her parents that had arrived the day before. They had cut their European trip short and had sent it from the hotel they were staying at in California. They were intending to spend another day at Disneyland before a visit to the Grand Canyon. They sounded happy and relaxed, even though they were looking forward to returning to Australia in another few weeks.

She hesitated, knowing she should send them an email to tell them what had happened. Then she shrugged. Matthew had promised to keep in close touch with the hospital in Sydney and contact their parents if he thought it necessary. Jillian returned to her paperwork, deciding to give it another day when they would have news of John's condition after his operation. But she still felt a little guilty as she tried to concentrate again on updating data on her files. Continually, Jillian's thoughts kept wandering to Steve. She wondered what he had found to do, and then she thought hard about what he had said about praying.

Steve had found plenty to do.

First of all, he had explored the various buildings closest to the homestead that he had not had time to check out the day before. It was his first visit to a property that in its heyday would have been almost a small village with the homestead and the buildings around it. He knew that on some of the largest stations further west in the 'real' outback this was still the case.

He had hoped Jillian would offer to show him around the place but hadn't liked to ask. She had so much more on her mind. But still, as he trudged towards the modern garage that would house at least three large vehicles, Steve wished she was there to tell him what the various, now mostly dilapidated buildings, had once been used for. There were even a couple of places where some dwelling had been pulled down, leaving only a chimney, a slab of concrete or a few foundation posts to show they had ever existed.

'And you can't quite talk, Bluey, can you?' he muttered to the dog that had appeared as soon as he had stepped outside and now limped after him wherever he went. At first Steve had kept a wary eye on him, but beyond a brief wave of his tail when he had first appeared, Bluey had just stayed near, occasionally taking time out from escorting him to follow up some interesting smell.

When he had grabbed the camping gear in the garage near the house, there had been little time to note the expensive, top of the range Commodore Holden. He had seen it in Baragula when John and Jillian had driven it there for Matthew and Emily's wedding. In fact, it had been used as the white bridal car. To him then, as well as the helicopter, it had appeared as another example of the wealth and different life-style that separated Jillian and himself.

Suddenly he again felt rebuked by the Lord. His attitude to what he had perceived was the Davidson's affluence and prestige was not becoming to one of Christ's followers.

Then, in a corner of the garage he spotted the small motorbike Jillian had mentioned. It spluttered at first, but to his relief it started up okay. He rode it slowly outside. There was a bark of delight and a red streak jumped up onto the platform behind him.

Steve laughed out loud. 'You like this method of transport better too, do you, Bluey? Okay, let's explore. Guess if it's going to be real busy around here I'd better know where things are.'

Matthew had told Steve once that Davidson Downs was now only part of a property that had once spread across hundreds of square miles. It had been originally settled well over a hundred years before by his ancestors, side by side with those of the Webster family on their property. For various reasons, in recent decades the Websters had sold off more and more of their original station. It was rather sad that now they'd completely sold out and left the district.

When Jillian's father had been a boy, although there had always been cattle, wool had reigned supreme and many stockmen and other staff employed to help run Davidson Downs. There would even have been a book-keeper or office manager who watched over the ordering in of supplies, paid any bills, made out the wages. According to Matthew there had also been a small store room where staff could purchase an amazing array of supplies. Now, with modern transport and established road systems, that was no longer feasible.

With the property so much smaller, wages so high, the wool industry collapsing, modern machinery and modern methods made it possible for John and Jillian to work the property with just employing seasonal workers when needed.

In many ways, it would be a much lonelier life now for the families on properties like Davidson Downs. Steve became even more sober and thoughtful as he wondered about this young woman and her brother who had taken on such heavy responsibilities.

A little distance from the homestead's enclosure he found a building containing a couple of rooms, one of which he realised must once have been used for butchering animals for the station's own meat. There was a rusty padlock still on the sturdy door – undoubtedly to lock when meat was hung there. The room had one small, screened and barred window but was spotless.

He grimaced. At least killing their own animals was one thing he'd never been forced to do at Honeysuckle, although according to his father it had been quite common even when his father had been a small boy to kill and dress their own meat.

About half a mile past the guest house and the airstrip was a massive old shearing shed. It reminded him again that sheep and their 'golden fleece' would once have been the main source of income here. Steve hesitated, tempted to ride over there, but decided to leave that inspection for another day.

He made his way to one of the large sheds not far from where the utility with the quad was garaged. He had seen the prime mover there. Its large trailer was parked beside the same shed. Hunting around a top rafter in a similar place to the one Jillian had found the ute's keys on, he soon found a set – and grinned. Even when a vehicle had its motor pulled down, the keys at Honeysuckle were kept in the house.

His smile faded and he scowled. Perhaps now, with thieves around, the Davidsons too in this isolated place would not feel as safe or free to do so any longer.

Steve had always serviced their vehicles – time permitting, of course. Over the years, to keep up to date with the latest technology, he'd done several courses so he could now do most of their own mechanical work. He frowned as he tried to start the engine. Certainly the starter motor needed replacing or reconditioning, but there were other problems too by the sound of it. Before long Steve was absorbed in trying to find out what needed to be done and then started to work on it.

The sun had dipped low in the western sky when at last there was the toot of a horn announcing Ettie Cobby's arrival. Bluey heaved himself to his feet and went on alert. He gave a couple of ferocious warning barks but looked apologetic when Steve sharply reprimanded him.

As he wiped the worst of the grease and dirt off his hands with an old rag before making for the house, Steve grinned at the dog. 'I'm beginning to think you are all bark and no bite, Bluey old boy.' Nevertheless, Steve was relieved when Bluey stopped trailing after him to head towards where Blackie was resting. At least Ettie would not be confronted by a snarling cattle dog the moment she set foot on Davidson Downs.

Outback from Baragula

A small sedan had pulled up at the front entrance. Steve arrived in time to see Jillian walking swiftly to meet it. Suddenly she paused. Then her face lit up and she rushed forward as the driver's door opened and a tall, tanned figure emerged.

'Bradley Hunter!' he heard her exclaim with delight. 'Oh, I am just so pleased to see you.'

As he saw his old school friend, Steve stood stock still. Jillian hugged the tall policeman from Baragula and his heart seemed to stop. For the first time he could remember, Steve felt deep pangs of envy.

Only in the hospital yesterday had Jillian Davidson greeted him with any sign of pleasure. But never with such unreserved delight. Never had she so spontaneously flung herself at him.

Until these last few days, she had always seemed more reserved around him than others she'd met at Baragula. If anything, except for that first visit to Honeysuckle when they had become so friendly so fast, Jillian had seemed wary and reserved with Steve. Then had come that disastrous day when, for some unknown reason, she'd started flirting and egging him on until his anger had exploded. And of course, after he had stupidly yielded to his anger and frustrated desire to kiss her that day, Jillian had avoided him. Several times here in the outback, especially that night in the tent, Steve had felt they were drawing closer but then in some indefinable way she retreated.

Was this another barrier, another hurdle he had not suspected? Was Brad Hunter the main reason for her reserve, her wariness around him?

Chapter twelve

Jillian stepped away from Brad and looked at the older woman climbing out of the passenger side of the car. She took a deep breath. So, this was the formidable Henrietta Cobby.

Footsteps crunched behind her. She turned to smile at Steve, but paused. Why did he look so ferocious?

'G'day, Steve.' Brad Hunter was grinning at Steve. They shook hands and then slapped each other on the back.

'G'day, mate, you just on holidays or here officially?'

Steve had responded with a broad grin that suddenly wiped Jillian's own smile from her face. Usually his eyes lit up warmly when he smiled. Now they remained cool and reserved. Only his lips had moved. That illusive dimple had not made even a brief appearance

Why was Steve not really pleased to see Brad who, according to Matthew, had practically grown up with the Honeysuckles? Surely Steve would be as pleased as she was that a man trained as a policeman, and a friend besides would arrive just when they could do with his expertise.

And then immediately Jillian wondered how she had come to know Steve Honeysuckle so well that she noticed when his smile did not quite reach his eyes.

'Holidays... well, kind of.' Brad gave a slight shrug. 'Matt rang me for advice. I was rather bored and at a bit of a loose end, so I rather jumped at the chance to get away.'

A car door slammed. Their attention focused on Mrs Cobby now looking rather uncertainly around her. Jillian remembered meeting the lady at the Baragula church and at the wedding. Ettie Cobby was the woman who liked wearing hats. There had been one incredible straw creation decorated with a wealth of artificial fruit. Matthew had seen Jillian's bemusement and told her he had never seen Mrs Cobby at church without a hat of some kind perched on her head.

'Mrs Cobby, it was so good of you to come, especially at such short notice.'

The sharp eyes surveying Jillian softened. 'You're Matthew's sister and he's family.'

Family? Jillian stared at the thought of Matthew having other family beside theirs. Undoubtedly the woman was a little strange, even if Matthew had once smiled and shaken his head when she had mentioned the lady in the unusual hat and asked if she was one of the town's eccentrics.

A beaming smile suddenly transformed the lined face. She gave a little chuckle. 'Sorry, my dear. No, I'm not really a long lost cousin or anything, but Matthew and I are part of God's family and I do hope you are too.'

Jillian stared. She was bereft of a response to the blunt statement. A part of God's family? She glanced a little helplessly at Steve as he joined them.

'Hello, Mrs Cobby.' This time his welcoming smile did reach his eyes.

The grey-haired woman pulled a face at him. 'Now, let's get one thing straight, the name's Ettie to you all.' She took the couple of steps towards him and gave him a brief hug before surveying his face intently. 'You're looking tired.' She turned her gaze towards Jillian and said gently, 'I'm so sorry about your twin brother. We've been praying for him and that you will recover your cattle from those rustlers.'

At any other time, Jillian would have smiled at the American West's term for the cattle thieves, but the compassion in the kind eyes made Jillian try to swallow a sudden lump in her throat. She managed to murmur a husky, 'Thank you' before looking a little helplessly towards Steve.

His return glance was full of understanding. 'Why don't you ladies

Outback from Baragula

get the kettle on while Brad and I bring in your things?'

Brad gave a light chuckle. 'Er, perhaps they should carry something too, Steve, or we'll be making several trips.' He swung open the back door of the car. 'Word gets around very quickly in Baragula.'

A few minutes later, Jillian surveyed the assortment of coolers and boxes of cakes and slices of all kind spread out on the benches in the kitchen with considerable astonishment. 'But where did they all come from at such short notice?'

Ettie beamed at her amazement. 'When word got out, folk just raided their freezers, even that Mrs McPhee. When Emily's Aunt Barbara told her about you all, she donated the fruit cake she'd made yesterday.'

Jillian remembered Matthew mentioning a Mrs McPhee, one of the banes of his life as Baragula's only doctor. She looked rather helplessly from the pile of goodies to the faces watching her. Jillian wasn't quite sure whether she should feel affronted at any suggestion she needed such help.

Before she could make any of the retorts hovering on her tongue, Ettie added cheerfully, 'Matthew said you were starting harvesting in another week or so and would have an influx of seasonal workers. We've all had some experience of what that means, even in our small village. With all the worry you're having, we guessed you may not have time for the extra cooking to feed everyone as well as all this to-do with John and the police and such.'

She paused for breath and beamed happily at Jillian, leaving her with absolutely nothing to say except to murmur a thank you. And after all, they were right. This week she had planned to do massive amounts of baking.

Still feeling rattled and trying to regain her control, Jillian turned rather abruptly to the two men. 'Steve, would you show Bradley to one of those bedrooms near yours? I... I'll bring some linen after I show Mrs Cobby...er, Ettie to her room.' She turned away from Steve's steady gaze and hurried away before he could comment.

Ettie followed her, looking around curiously. She stopped and Jillian had to wait while she oohed and aahed over the large, formal lounge room. 'Now, that's what I call a state of the art sound system.'

'You enjoy music?'

'Always have, but afraid I probably watch more tellie now than... oh!' Ettie stood in the doorway of the even larger family room and stared around.

Jillian smiled at the awe in her voice. 'This is the room we always seem to gravitate to and spend most of our relaxation time.'

A very large television with a video and DVD player stood in one corner before cosy lounges. A well used, old billiard table took up a large section and another corner held the old computer now used mainly for games and play stations.

'This old homestead is simply wonderful for a family. It's huge,' Ettie murmured and Jillian found her eyes misting over.

It was so many years now since they had been a real family enjoying each other here. Things had never been the same since Sonya...

Jillian strode across the room to the other door. 'We live so far from any town we have to provide our own fun and entertainment. Now, I've put you in this guest bedroom where you have your own ensuite.' She strode down a corridor.

Ettie's eyes were wide as she surveyed the generous sized bedroom. 'My, my, this house is beautiful! I can't get over how big the rooms are. Huge like the whole of this wide outback you live in, I guess.'

Jillian found herself looking at Ettie with some astonishment. 'It... it's just home,' she said a little awkwardly.

'And I would suspect there's not been too much fun here for you lately,' the older woman said shrewdly. She added swiftly, "Sorry, it's none of my business, but while Matthew was sick last year he told me he had been rather concerned for his young twin brother and sister taking on the whole responsibility of the family property the way you did when your parents moved to Sydney.'

Jillian stiffened in annoyance that Matthew would discuss family business with a stranger.

Ettie Cobby smiled so warmly at her that the sharp words Jillian had been tempted to speak dried up. "I told him straight that from what I had observed when you visited him you were a very modern, informed young woman who would not let herself be doing anything she hated doing and to mind his own business. That shut him up,' Ettie added with such satisfaction, Jillian found herself smiling at the thought of her inclined-to-be-bossy brother being put so firmly in his place.

When she was sure Ettie Cobby had everything she needed, she went in search of the two men. To her bemusement she found they had already raided the linen cupboard and were busy making the bed for her unexpected guest with clean sheets while they talked. They were so involved in their conversation they did not notice her in the doorway. Steve's voice was so angry, so grim, Jillian hesitated. Then what he was saying made her freeze to the spot.

'Matthew was very upset and adamant that we don't tell her or John yet about my suspicions. They've all grown up together and apparently she's very fond of him.' Steve straightened. He glared across the bed at his old policeman friend. 'Matthew said he had spent some time with the bloke only last week and doesn't agree he could have anything to do with what's happened. So, although I don't agree with Matthew, I did promise not to say anything to her until we've more to go on. He's afraid she'll just be upset unnecessarily.'

'And Matthew wouldn't be talking about his little sister being upset by any chance, would he?'

Both men looked swiftly towards Jillian. With her fists planted on her hips, Jillian stared balefully from one startled face to the other.

Steve and Bradley glanced at each other. Bradley Hunter's face was blank, perhaps something he had perfected over the years of being a policeman, but Steve looked dismayed and uneasy.

Jillian advanced into the room. 'Matthew's been trying to protect his "little sister" ever since she was born. Is there something you've discovered about John's accident that you haven't told me?'

Steve took a couple of steps towards her. 'Jillie, dear, it's all supposition and speculation at this point.'

He hesitated, searching her face. The depth of sadness and regret in his face suddenly scared Jillian. He opened his mouth, and closed it again as the dogs started barking furiously.

Jillian raised her head and listened. The sound of an approaching vehicle reached them.

'We didn't put Bluey back in his yard,' she said sharply, 'I better make sure he's okay with whoever it is.'

There were a few short toots on a horn, and she looked surprised. 'That sounds like Scott Reed announcing his arrival, but his mother said he'd gone to Sydney.'

As she turned away, Bradley said urgently, 'Whoever it is, please don't let them know I'm a policeman.'

Surprise shot through Jillian and then she nodded in comprehension. 'Of course, but this conversation is by no means finished. John is my brother as much as he's Matthew's brother. The cattle are my problem now and I insist you both tell me what those suspicions are I heard you mention – even if they prove to be without foundation.'

Bluey's barking was becoming even more ferocious. An impatient hand was now continuously on the horn. Jillian ran from the room.

The men stared at each other. Neither moved nor spoke for a moment until Jillian's running footsteps had disappeared into the distance.

Then Brad resumed tucking in the sheets on his side of the bed. 'This Reed bloke sounds pretty impatient,' he murmured blandly.

Steve's frown deepened. 'According to Matthew the fellow has been trying to latch on to Jillian for years.'

'But he told me once he's not sure how deep her feelings are for this Scott Reed. They've grown up more like brother and sister.' Brad looked up and briefly studied Steve's face. 'Come on, we'd better see how they do get on together. I'm also very keen to see his reaction when he spots you.'

As they strode towards the back entrance of the house, Steve wondered just how and why Scott Reed had come up in conversation in Baragula between his two friends. Had Bradley been checking out whether Jillian had a boyfriend already? Steve's lips tightened.

Jillian had a firm grip on the red cattle dog's collar, but Bluey was still snarling at the rather stockily built young man standing next to a large four wheel drive vehicle, even more ornate than his own. Steve changed his mind about the snarling dog once more. He could not help but feel a sense of gratification that Bluey quite obviously did not like Scott Reed one bit, whereas the dog had accepted himself quite fast.

'For goodness sake, Bluey!' Jillian yelled in exasperation. 'It's only Scott. Down, boy!'

She glanced across at the two men as they walked out onto the veranda and called, 'There's a dog chain near the steps. Could you bring it over here please?'

'You don't need just a chain, you need a gun for that mongrel,' Scott roared angrily. 'Why on earth you still insist on keeping that dangerous dog I'll never—' His voice stopped abruptly as Steve walked from the shadows of the veranda into the fading light.

Steve stared across at him for a long, considering moment before bending to pick up the chain near his feet. He strolled slowly towards Jillian and gave it to her. She snatched it impatiently and hooked it to Bluey's collar. Tugging the still snarling dog well away from Scott, Jillian tossed the other end of Bluey's chain over a metal stake in the ground, obviously there for the very purpose of restraining Bluey from eating any visitors he took exception to.

'G'day, Scott,' Steve said very politely, while wishing that Bluey had managed to take a bite out of the man he had met out at the Windmill paddock.

'What are you still doing here?' There was more than a trace of belligerence in Scott's voice.

'Helping control a dangerous dog?'

Bluey let fly with more ferocious snarling and barking. Steve studied Scott Reed's strained face with interest before turning his back on him and strolling over to the dog. Blackie also was waddling to join her mate.

'Now, Bluey, you've made your point. Stop all this noise at once. Sit!'

To Steve's satisfaction, Bluey obeyed his command and even tolerated a pat on his head without taking a bite out of his hand. When he looked up, Jillian was watching them with a twinkle in her eyes. He smiled gently at her and she swiftly frowned at him.

'Obviously it's far too long since I've been here. Perhaps it's time I had another go at making friends. I'd hate to have that animal on the loose when I visit and nobody's home.' Scott's resigned, yet amused voice set Bluey off again and he was shouting by the time he finished.

Jillian's eyes widened in surprise. 'Are you sure, Scott? You vowed last time you tried you wouldn't make the attempt again and that Bluey was never going to let you anywhere near him.'

Colour moved up into Scott's cheeks. 'I... things have changed. I really would like to try again.'

Steve's eyes narrowed. Now, what exactly did that mean?

'I suppose you could try,' Jillian said doubtfully, 'it has been awhile. Come on then, I'll hold him for you, but do be careful.'

Scott moved closer. Steve stood up but did not surrender his stance next to Bluey. Bluey bared his teeth and snarled at Scott but to the man's credit he just started talking to the dog in a quiet, soothing voice. It took quite a while, but Steve had to admit to a feeling of chagrin as well as admiration when Bluey's hackles gradually subsided and at last he sniffed Scott's extended hand of friendship and even tolerated a few pats from him.

To add to Steve's disquiet, it was obvious that Jillian felt nothing but admiration for Scott when he at last stood up and grinned triumphantly at her.

She looked really surprised. 'Well, I never thought you'd do it! Ever since you threw that gravel at her from your motorbike she's really hated you.'

A tide of red touched Scott's face once more. He looked pleased and yet a shade bashful at the same time. His voice was low. 'That was years ago. I guess dogs, or at least this particularly intelligent one, can sense when people have a true change of heart.'

Jillian raised a sceptical eyebrow at him, but turned as footsteps sounded on the path behind them. 'It seems, for some reason I haven't a clue about, seeing you didn't make it to Baragula for Matthew's wedding, that you already know Steve Honeysuckle.' She nodded towards the tall policeman. 'And this is Bradley Hunter, a friend of Matthew's from Baragula. Another friend, Ettie Cobby, has also just arrived to help me in the house.'

Bradley's smile was white and oozed friendliness as he strode forward with hand extended. 'I believe you're from next door.' He gave a light laugh and added, 'Well, not quite next door out here I guess, with your vast distances between each door.'

Scott studied Brad carefully before extending his hand. 'I've heard Matthew mention you.'

And undoubtedly mentioned Brad was a policeman. Steve saw by the resignation on Brad's face that he too realised it would have been natural for Matthew to mention Brad's occupation.

Steve sincerely hoped he was not expected to shake hands.

Jillian was frowning. 'You've met both Steve and Brad? I didn't know you'd been to Baragula, so where...? What did you mean about Steve still being here?' she finished crisply.

Surprise filled Scott Reed's face. 'He didn't tell you?' He stopped short and glared at Steve.

'Tell me what?' Jillian looked from one man to the other and waited with a raised eyebrow.

Steve opened his mouth, but Scott got in first.

'I drove out to Windmill One yesterday morning to see if I could help and he was there. Told me you had found John nearby and he was just picking up the rest of your things.' He gave a forced laugh. 'Afraid we nearly came to blows because I thought at first he was just some bloke trying to steal them.'

Outback from Baragula

Jillian's body tensed. She looked at Scott with an arrested expression on her face then turned swiftly to look hard at Steve and then Bradley. Without moving, Steve stared steadily back at Jillian. Her eyes widened. A rather strange expression crossed her face for a brief moment before she turned once more to Scott.

'Whatever were you doing way out there at Windmill One, Scott?'

He looked taken aback at the sharp note in her voice and frowned. 'Why, I heard you'd found John out that way. I went there first thing of course to have a look around to see what could have happened.'

Steve was watching her closely or he may have missed that, for a fraction of a second, Jillian did not move a muscle.

Then she said briskly, 'That was good of you, Scott, but I thought you were away in Sydney.'

He smiled at her. 'I only went there for a day and that was after spending a few nights with Matthew on the way. Meant to get back a couple of days ago but had some car trouble and stopped at that little motel near Gilgandra. Fortunately, I rang Mum and Dad on my mobile phone and heard about John being lost. I went straight out to Windmill One before heading home.'

Anger flashed into Jillian's eyes. To Steve's concern she tilted her chin and opened her mouth only to snap it shut when Bradley Hunter intervened.

'Well, you must be ready for a cuppa, mate,' he said heartily, 'I know I am after that long trip and, if I know our Ettie Cobby, I bet she already has the water boiling.'

Steve winced. A guest did not usually make his need for hospitality quite so plain. He waited for an explosion from Jillian and was proud of her when all she did was tilt that beautifully rounded chin a little higher at Brad and studied his unabashed face for a long moment. At last she nodded. 'Yes of course, let's all go inside.'

'No, no,' Scott protested, 'afraid this is a flying visit. Have already had to postpone a few more jobs Dad lined up for me since a couple of our men left unexpectedly while I was away and I need an early night for an early start.' He stared anxiously at Jillian. 'I just wanted to say how sorry I am about John's accident, see what the latest is on his condition and... and to tell you something I think you should know.'

He hesitated and glanced from Steve to Bradley. 'Of course, I also wanted to see if you needed any help but I can see you've got plenty for now. I'll be back as usual to help you with harvest though.'

'Oh, that won't be necessary thanks. You'll be too busy with your own on Jedburgh.' Jillian nodded briefly towards Steve and Bradley. 'Thanks to Matthew, it seems I've got plenty of help lined up already.'

Scott's smile disappeared. His frown deepened for a moment. 'Fine, but you'll need me to help them with our special far west conditions at harvest time. Afraid it's rather different from what I've seen of your Baragula hill country,' he finished with a grin at Steve.

'I wouldn't hear of you coming to help us so close to your own harvest, Scott. I know you've been very busy sorting out Webster since you took it over.' There was a distinct touch of frost in Jillian's voice.

Steve glanced at Brad. He was watching Jillian and Scott thoughtfully.

Scott's smile had completely disappeared. For a moment Steve could not help but feel a touch of sympathy for him. For some reason he actually rather liked the bloke despite... Steve cut the thought off abruptly, suddenly feeling ashamed at the jealousy that had seared him.

Scott shrugged. He glanced at his watch and said hurriedly, 'Look, I must be off. Perhaps we can talk about it later. Walk me back to my vehicle, Jillian?'

All Steve's sympathy for the bloke vanished as Jillian turned away obediently. 'Come on, I'll tell you the latest about John and you can tell me your news. You guys go ahead,' she tossed over her shoulder toward Steve and Bradley, 'won't be long.'

Steve clenched his fists and took a step forward as the two started off arm in arm.

'Leave them,' Bradley's clipped tones murmured very softly in his ear. Out loud he said, 'Bye for now, Scott. We'll catch up with you another time.'

Scott paused and turned. His hand went to his forehead in the mockery of a salute at the two men before he caught up with Jillian again. He started talking rapidly, their heads far too close together for Steve's liking. Then he saw Jillian stop dead and look up at Scott. She was very upset. Still talking, Scott reached up and touched Jillian's face.

Steve looked sharply away.

Bradley stood on the veranda staring across at Jillian and Scott. 'Get the impression we were firmly dismissed then, Stevie old mate?'

Steve growled, 'Yeah, right,' and stomped past him into the house.

Ettie Cobby was living up to her reputation. As the two men strode into the kitchen she turned from putting out cups and smiled at them. 'Ready for a cuppa, are you? Jillian and her new visitor on their way too?' Her smile disappeared as she saw their solemn faces. 'What's wrong?'

Bradley smiled slightly at her. 'Plenty, I'm afraid, but I think we'd better wait until Jillian is here. She's just saying goodbye to an old friend of hers.' He winked at Ettie and nodded towards Steve.

Her face cleared and she gave a low chuckle. Steve looked from one to the other enquiringly. 'What's so funny?'

They both grinned at him. He glared at them impatiently and pulled out a chair.

Brad joined him at the table. 'You are, mate. In fact,' he added reflectively, 'you usually are when you're around Jillian Davidson.'

That stopped Steve in his tracks. Heat started to rise up his neck and into his face as he stared at the two smiling faces. He sank slowly onto the chair.

Ettie's smile disappeared. 'Now now, Senior Constable,' Ettie chided, 'that'll be enough of that. From what you shared with me on the way here, *you* can't talk anyway,' she shot at him for added measure.

It was Bradley's turn to look discomfited and Steve's heart sank. So he was right. His old friend liked Jillian a lot. He was here more because of his attraction to her than the fact of his friendship with Matthew.

'Ettie...' Bradley began in a warning voice.

She smiled gently at him. 'I know. I promised, and not another word – as long as you leave poor Steve here alone.'

The screen door on the veranda slammed shut with unnecessary force. They were silent as brisk footsteps approached. All three watched Jillian storm into the room. She looked furious and upset.

'Okay you two, what's going on? Why did you treat Scott like that?'

Ettie put down the teapot in her hand. 'I'll just go and unpack and leave you to it.'

'No.'

They all looked at Bradley. His voice had been sharp, authoritative.

He stood up and pulled out a couple of chairs. 'Sit down the pair of you,' Brad added in that same brisk, no nonsense policeman's voice. 'There may be times when you'll be alone here Ettie and you should know all that's going on.'

Neither woman moved. Jillian glared at Bradley and then turned on Steve. 'Why didn't you tell me you saw Scott at the Windmill?'

Steve rose. 'Because you had enough with John and everything else on your mind.'

She didn't give an inch. 'Matthew was upset too, but you obviously told him.' Jillian paused and looked from Steve to Bradley and back again. 'You were talking in the bedroom before about Scott, weren't you? You think he's somehow involved in all this.'

Steve sighed and said simply, 'Yes. I was hoping we wouldn't have to tell you, not until we were sure.' He swept his hand through his hair. 'Look, it's only suspicions. Bradley's waiting for a couple of reports and...'

'Scott lied.'

No one moved. Three pairs of eyes stared at Jillian.

Jillian sank down onto a chair. She rested her face in her hands and murmured again, 'He lied.' There was a wealth of pain and disappointment in her voice.

Ettie said quietly, 'I think we do need that drink and something to eat before we talk anymore, Bradley.'

He shrugged and they were silent until at last they each had a cup of steaming tea in front of them. Ettie slid a plate of assorted goodies from the Baragula kitchens onto the table before taking her own place.

Jillian was pale and strained. Steve longed to have the right to reach across and simply hold her hand.

She looked across at him. 'What did Scott say to you when he met you at the Windmill?'

Steve avoided her eyes and took a sip of tea before answering. 'He said he heard that's where John had been found. At least,' he added reflectively, 'that's what he told me eventually, once I persuaded him I really was a friend of yours and he stopped waving his gun around.'

Startled brown eyes stared at him. 'Scott held a gun on you?'

He nodded. 'A nasty looking high-powered, automatic rifle.' Steve looked at Bradley and added dryly, 'I reckon your mob might be interested in it. Didn't look like it qualified as a legal one anymore since the new gun laws.'

Outback from Baragula

Jillian ignored Bradley's raised eyebrows and asked impatiently, 'What exactly did Scott say to explain his presence there?'

Steve hesitated and then shrugged. 'Scott said his father had told him, when he rang home on his mobile phone, that's where John had been found and he wanted to have a look around. When I told him the extent of John's injuries he was very upset.'

Jillian drew a deep breath. 'To start with, his father could not have told him any such thing, especially on a mobile phone. There's a black spot from about Gilgandra over a large area out this way, including both our properties. The phone company keeps telling us they are working on it but... Besides, I was so worried and his mother was in such a rush and panic when I asked them to use their plane to search for John, that it was only after I hung up that I realised I hadn't told her I thought John must be out near Windmill One.

'Remember, Steve, their plane was much further away. Then later, when I told her we had found John I'm sure I didn't say where. There was no time to go into details and you'd warned me about the thieves listening in on our radio frequency.'

She looked from one face to the other. Her sad gaze settled at last on Steve. 'So, it seems the only way Scott could have known to go there was if the skunks who had injured John told him.'

There was a pause.

'Or Scott Reed was one of the skunks,' Brad suggested quietly.

Chapter thirteen

'A council of war,' was what Ettie Cobby dramatically called it.

'More like men trying to lay down the law and keep me out of all the fun,' muttered Jillian.

Bradley gave a frustrated snort of laughter.

Jillian had drawn the line at believing Scott Reed could in any way be personally responsible for John's injuries. Because they could all see how upset Jillian was at their belief that someone she had known all her life might be involved to that extent, they had instead been discussing what they would do the next day to try and find the cattle.

Jillian had completely refused to stay at the homestead while the men went to investigate Webster.

Steve ran his hands through his hair. Defeat rang in his voice. 'And we may as well have saved our breath.'

Jillian glared at him. 'I'm only going to say this one more time. *I am going with you.*'

No one spoke. Steve looked at Brad and shrugged.

'I'm the only one who knows the way. It is my brother who has been injured by a bunch of crooks. It is our cattle that have been stolen. This is *my* livelihood at stake. And if you two men can't accept that, you are no longer welcome in *my* home!'

Brad was no longer smiling. 'But Jillian, this is a police matter too.

These blokes have already shown they're very dangerous and—'

'And because I'm a woman, would I be in any more danger than you two *men*? Will God only protect you two men?'

Jillian felt as though she was going to explode with anger, frustration and grief that Scott may be somehow involved with the whole sorry mess. She stared from one man's grim face to the other, knowing that she had to go with them to Webster station.

She made a tremendous effort to regain control over her anger and frustration. 'Look, I need to see for myself. Even if the cattle are there, it's no proof at all that Scott Reed could in any way be responsible for the theft or...or what happened to John.' She didn't give either man a chance to respond as she rushed on. 'Besides, you *don't* know for sure that Scott's involved in any way at all. What did Matthew think?'

'Matthew was very upset, but...' Steve paused and added slowly, 'he did seem very sure though that Scott's appearance out at the Windmill must have been simply an attempt to help.'

'I think I might know why Matthew thinks the best of your friend, Jillian,' Ettie murmured quietly, 'I briefly met a man called Scott Reed at his place a few months back.'

Jillian stared at Ettie in astonishment. 'Scott visited Matthew in Baragula? Neither of them has ever mentioned that.'

Ettie hesitated for a moment and then shrugged. 'By the look on this Scott bloke's face, he was under some considerable stress. I could see I'd interrupted a pretty intense discussion and left straight away. When he escorted me to the door Matthew murmured that he wanted me to pray for them both.'

Steve's eyes widened. 'Matthew did mention just a few weeks ago that a boyhood friend and neighbour of his family had contacted him. He'd been thrilled a short while before to be able to lead this old friend to Christ, but now he was in some deep trouble from past associates.' He paused before adding, 'Matthew said he couldn't go into details but really needed me to pray for both him and this friend. Apparently the guy could even be in some kind of danger.'

Jillian stared at Steve's thoughtful face. 'It must have been Scott. What kind of mess could Scott have got himself into? And why didn't he tell me or John? We're closer in age and have always been much closer to Scott than Matthew.'

She felt a tide of hurt which she quickly dismissed. Of course, it must have been Matthew's position of confidentiality as a doctor.

Outback from Baragula

And Matthew had asked Steve to pray.

Jillian suddenly felt regret that Matthew could feel so at ease contacting a fellow believer like Steve with such a personal request and not his family. But then, was this what Ettie had meant about being part of a church family? When he needed it, Matthew had support from fellow believers like Steve.

'Scott in trouble, danger?' she said slowly. 'He couldn't go to the wedding. I knew there must have been a very good reason for that, something that I've not been able to discover, but...'

The phone started to ring. Jillian rose to answer it. 'Anyway, I'm inclined to agree with Matthew. Why on earth would Scott steal cattle from us? Besides being our friends, the Reeds are well off otherwise they could never have bought that other property.'

'Unless they over extended themselves to buy it,' Steve murmured as she picked up the phone.

Jillian listened for a moment and then looked at Bradley. 'It's for you.'

She had only ever met Brad when he had been off duty and not in uniform. Listening to his brief words, his professional manner as he spoke crisply on the phone, brought home to Jillian the fact that Senior Constable Bradley Hunter was an experienced member of the police force. Then she heard his last instructions and glared at him as he hung up.

'You took Scott's registration number? And you actually asked the police to check him out?' She shook her head. 'I just can't believe he would have anything to do with hurting John.'

'Gambling'

Jillian stared at Brad.

'Gambling debts have made many a man desperate. At various times Scott has owed money at several well known gambling dens in Sydney. The casino my friend checked out also knew him as a regular customer until a few months ago. I've also had his bank accounts checked out.'

'Gambling?' Jillian whispered in horror, 'Scott's a gambler?'

Steve sighed and stood up. 'And in debt.'

Brad nodded briefly. 'Apparently he was very deep in debt to some undesirables at illegal gambling dens in Sydney's notorious Kings Cross. We know they can get very nasty when they're owed money for any length of time. It seems though that a few days ago Scott turned up with a pile of money and paid them out.'

No one spoke for a long moment. Then Jillian said in a dazed voice, 'But we've grown up together. John and Amy...' Her voice choked.

Steve took a step towards her. 'We don't know if Scott was actually in that cattle truck, Jillie, or that he would have condoned what happened.' He spoke urgently. 'There was no doubt yesterday – or today – that he's very upset. But it does seem somehow he not only knew John had been injured but where it had happened.'

Jillian raised her head and stared at him uncomprehendingly. Then it struck her what he was saying.

'Oh, Jillie, please, don't... don't cry.'

The compassion in Steve's voice showed once again his understanding of her pain and sense of betrayal. He shut his eyes tight. Was he saying a prayer again? She sure needed every one he could spare.

Then Steve crouched down beside Jillian and took her clenched fist between both his hands.

'Jillie...' He paused and she saw the reluctance on his face to speak. 'There's something else I haven't told you yet. It's why I really rang Matthew and why he immediately got onto Brad instead of us making it official. When I drove into that bush to get John's quad, another vehicle had been in there since you and I had left. Then I saw Scott poking around our camping gear at the windmill. Only those men in the truck could have known John was in that patch of scrub right off the track and gone straight to it.'

One solitary tear stole down Jillian's cheek. Steve reached up one hand and gently brushed it away. 'I'm sorry, Jillie.'

Jillian straightened and snatched her hand away from his comforting grasp. Anger and a desire for revenge consumed her. 'So am I sorry! And if he *is* involved at all, so will Scott Reed be by the time I've finished with him!'

The tender compassion on Steve's face was replaced with something that looked like disappointment. His expression hardened and he stood up and moved away.

Jillian tilted her chin defiantly and jumped to her feet. 'Right, Brad, how soon can we leave for Webster? If what our old 'roo shooter said is true and if Scott is involved, that seems even more likely to be where we should start searching.'

Bradley Hunter looked from her to Steve. After a long pause, he sighed. 'Okay, we *all* leave at first light in the morning.'

Outback from Baragula

Jillian saw Steve tense. As he frowned at her, she could see he was remembering her insistence last time they leave at once and camp out ready for a pre-dawn start. She knew she was right when he relaxed as she shrugged and then nodded. 'You're right. By the time we get there this evening we wouldn't have enough time to search before dark. But we'll leave here no later than four-thirty. By the time we get there it should be light enough.'

She turned towards Ettie. 'I'm sorry, Ettie, but it looks like we have to leave you alone on your first full day here. But I'll introduce you to Bluey and then leave him off the chain.'

Ettie smiled at her. 'No problem, my dear, I've lived on a property and been alone for a long time now. Despite what's happened, I'm sure out here is a lot safer than even Baragula.' She stood up and started efficiently clearing the table. 'But we'd better have our evening meal soon so you can all get to bed for that early start.'

No one argued about that, but Jillian felt sad. She wondered if Davidson Downs was actually far more dangerous now than Baragula.

Their food that night was also by courtesy of the Baragula residents. Jillian insisted she would heat a meat casserole and set the table while Ettie had a rest after her hectic day of packing and driving to Davidson Downs.

Jillian saw Steve had to hide a grin when she lost that battle.

'I doubt if anyone has ever won an argument with Ettie Cobby when she's all fired up for a good cause,' he murmured in her ear.

Just as they were ready to sit down, the phone rang again. When Jillian heard a hesitant woman's voice say, 'Jillian?' she stiffened.

'Madeline.'

Jillian saw Steve stare across the kitchen at her terse voice. He frowned and she turned her back on him.

There was silence at the other end of the phone for a moment and then Madeline said in a subdued voice, 'I'm so sorry about your brother.'

There was genuine regret in Madeline's voice and Jillian relaxed a little. 'Thank you, Madeline,' she said in a softer voice, 'would you like to speak to Steve?'

'Yes, of course,' Madeline said a little more briskly, but then hesitated once more before saying in a rush, 'Matthew said Bradley Hunter is also going there. Did he and Mrs Cobby arrive safely?'

'Yes, they arrived some time ago. In fact we were just having our tea.'

'Oh, I won't hold you up then,' Madeline said hurriedly, 'just tell them I rang and everything is going well here at Honeysuckle and Baragula.'

There was a click as the call was disconnected. Jillian looked at the hand piece a moment before slowly replacing it. Suddenly she regretted the abrupt way she had spoken to Steve's sister. Apparently Emily had grown up with Madeline Honeysuckle. Their friendship had been renewed after that time little Deborah had become so ill with appendicitis during the floods at Honeysuckle. But even though they had both been Emily's bridesmaids, Steve's sister had still avoided speaking to Jillian as much as possible.

'That was Madeline?'

Jillian forced a smile at Steve and nodded. 'She was just making sure Mrs Cobby and Bradley had arrived safely.'

As she spoke, she looked across at Bradley. A sudden smile lit up his face at her words but was quickly extinguished as Steve turned and looked at him.

Well, well. Was there something going on between the local policeman and the farmer's sister? Jillian looked at Brad thoughtfully for a moment and then hurried to finish helping Ettie dish up the food. Several times Brad had entertained Jillian while Matthew had been busy during her visits to Baragula. He was certainly a nice man, a good looking one too, but there had been no spark between them. Perhaps that may have been because they talked more about the Honeysuckles than themselves, she suddenly realised.

It wasn't until they were relaxing with cups of tea after a delicious meal that Steve said abruptly, 'Something's been niggling at me. Jillie, that private talk Scott had with you... Something else he said then upset you even more.'

Jillian hesitated and then shrugged. 'Oh, he just wanted me to know he saw an old neighbour in Sydney that we... we haven't seen for quite a few years, Billy Webster.'

There was a short silence.

It was Ettie who asked thoughtfully, 'And why would Scott Reed come all this way to tell you that?'

Jillian hesitated. She avoided their eyes and stared down into her steaming cup of tea. All the time Scott had been speaking to her she had only been thinking about one thing. He had just lied to her. Now she thought about what he had told her and went still.

Outback from Baragula

'If it's not something you think we should know, forget it, Jillie,' Steve said gently.

She looked up. Jillian studied Steve's face for a long moment before looking across at Bradley and Ettie.

'Actually, I've been wondering if I should tell you that Billy was always something of a gambler. He most likely introduced Scott to it. Billy Webster went to boarding school with John and Scott, but they didn't always get on.'

Jillian shrugged and gave a little laugh. 'Oh well, you might as well know. Billy was an only child and spoilt rotten by doting parents who for a long time couldn't see anything wrong with their wretch of a son. I never really liked him much, but then... afterwards I hated him.'

She paused, felt a touch of heat rise in her face. 'One night a few years ago, at a party at the Reed's, Billy tricked me into going outside away from the house and he... grabbed me, started kissing me and... and wouldn't stop.'

A lopsided, brief smile touched her lips. 'Oh, don't look so upset and angry, Steve. It was ages ago now. Scott heard me scream in time to stop him from...' She shuddered and looked away as she added quickly, 'Scott had noticed I was missing and was searching for me. John was close behind him. I'm afraid between them they gave Billy a rough time of it. Afterwards, Billy made all kinds of wild threats about what he would do to the three of us.'

'Was he ever charged with assault?'

Jillian looked at Bradley with surprise. He sounded furiously angry. Steve was looking pretty murderous also. Even Ettie was looking upset. These people truly cared about her.

A feeling of delight pushed old feelings towards Billy away. This time she didn't have to force a smile. Brad and Ettie's expression lightened but Steve still glowered at her. That made her feel a little confused, even embarrassed at the intense look on Steve's face.

She looked swiftly away and smiled again at Brad. 'Ever the policeman's mind, Brad? We always felt rather sorry for Mr and Mrs Webster for having a son like Billy so we didn't even tell our parents, especially when we found out the next day Billy had left home and gone to Sydney to try and get work. We thought he might be scared we would report him, but the three of us decided the hiding the boys gave him was punishment enough. He could even have had them up on a charge for his broken nose, jaw and a couple of cracked ribs! We never did find out how he explained his injuries to his parents.' Jillian's face became grave again. 'Besides, it would have upset Mum too much. She was still trying to cope with losing Sonya.'

She looked from one to the other. 'Don't all look so serious. It was years ago now. Billy had gone away before for lengthy periods, but sometime later his father told Dad he reckoned Billy had gone for good that time. It was the last straw and chance the Websters had of saving their station and why they put it on the market. This is the first time any of us have seen or heard of Billy since his parents left the area.'

Jillian's eyes suddenly widened. 'Billy! It was Billy – perhaps at Gilgandra too.'

Steve stiffened. 'The bloke in the car who took off when he saw you?'

She nodded and then looked uncertain. 'I'm not sure. It certainly could have been him. But I think it may have been his voice on the phone.'

'What voice?'

Jillian looked at Bradley's concerned face and put a hand to her mouth in dismay. 'How stupid of me, I'd forgotten,' she faltered. 'Everything that's happened drove it right out of my head.'

Swiftly she told them about the menacing, harsh voice on the phone, not long before she had gone searching for John.

No one spoke for a moment and at last Bradley said thoughtfully, 'And Scott thought you needed to be warned this old friend was back?'

'Friend?' Jillian shrugged and stood up. 'He was hardly that to me, just a neighbour. There was a rumour a while ago that Billy had got into serious trouble in Sydney with the police. John and I were included in those threats at the time and Scott's always been almost as over protective of me as John has.' Her face hardened. 'But now I'm beginning to wonder if I know Scott Reed at all.'

Jillian looked from one to the other. 'I'm probably wrong about Billy. He's been long gone from this area. For goodness sake, we've got enough things to worry about without adding more to them. Let's call it a night for that early start.'

No one moved. Brad was looking very thoughtful. Steve watched him for a moment, knowing the same idea had occurred to him.

In a soft voice, Ettie put his idea into words. 'I really think we need some prayer before we go to bed.'

Steve smiled at her. Ettie had remained very still and quiet but he was not really surprised at her suggestion.

Bradley looked at Ettie a little uncertainly and then they all turned toward Jillian.

She was staring at Ettie. A soft blush crept into her cheeks. Her gaze flew to Brad and then lingered on Steve. 'Now, why am I not really surprised at that suggestion?'

Ettie's eyes widened slightly.

Jillian gave a slight laugh and sat down again. 'Right, Ettie,' she said gently, 'I guess we need all the help we can get.'

She bowed her head. The other three looked at her and then at each other.

A smile twitched Steve's lips. He nodded at Ettie. 'Your turn,' he murmured.

Jillian opened one eye and then shut it again hastily as Ettie clasped her hands together and started to pray.

Steve grinned as he closed his own eyes.

It was a long, fervent prayer that included all that had happened and might happen in the coming days. In simple, direct words, each of them was individually committed into God's care and keeping. A fervent prayer for John's healing followed. Neither Scott Reed nor Billy Webster escaped as Ettie fervently talked to her Heavenly Father about them.

By the time Ettie at last said, 'Amen,' Steve was concerned Jillian might be annoyed at the length of the prayer.

Instead, he was touched when, with tears in her eyes, she merely whispered, 'Thank you, Ettie dear,' and gave her a quick hug before wishing them all goodnight and hurrying from the room.

Chapter fourteen

It was still dark the next morning when Jillian stumbled into the kitchen. Steve paused in setting the table and stared at her. Her soft, sleepy smile at him made him swallow several times. Even half asleep, Jillian Davidson was still beautiful.

'Good morning, love.'

Still in her dressing gown, Ettie beamed at her from where she was standing in front of the stove. She held a fork in one hand and the delicious smell of frying onions wafted towards Steve.

Jillian looked disconcerted. 'Why, Ettie, I didn't expect *you* to be up so early!'

Ettie turned and dealt with a saucepan on the stove, stirring it with a large wooden spoon. 'Thought you might have a long, difficult day in front of you all. And I can always go back to bed after you get away.'

'Mmm, is that onion I can smell?'

Ettie smiled at Jillian with a touch of shyness. 'And tomatoes, sausages, bacon and eggs. I do hope it was okay to raid your freezer, Jillian?' she asked and then looked relieved when Jillian nodded. 'They'll be cooked in another few minutes, but the porridge is ready.'

'Porridge,' Jillian said enthusiastically. She stepped forward and peered into the saucepan. 'Ettie, I haven't had porridge since Mum left. And I love the smell of frying bacon. You're a real Godsend!'

She gave Ettie an impulsive hug. Ettie kissed her on the cheek and laughed. 'Well, guess God has sent me here at that, but I've always believed God expects us to exercise our faith but also help ourselves and others as well as wait for His help. Eating sensibly I reckon is one way to do just that.'

Bradley strode in then and the three of them feasted as quickly as they could on the delicious breakfast. There was little conversation amongst them. All had been said the evening before. They had agreed this would be just an investigation, a 'look-see' as Ettie put it.

They had decided it would be best to take Steve's big four wheel drive for the rough terrain. The first thing would be to show Bradley and Jillian the place where Steve believed the quad had hit a tree, where they had found it and John. As the pre-dawn sky became lighter, Steve parked just short of the area. At Brad's terse order, they waited well back while he examined with a powerful torch where the quad must have slammed into the tree and the marks where it had then been pushed or driven towards the bush.

There were a few bird-calls, including a couple of white cockatoos, one of the pests of the area. Steve felt Jillian's hand slip into his. He glanced at her, saw her pale face and trembling lips. Steve squeezed her hand tightly before putting his arm around her and tugging her close against him. 'I knew this would upset you, sweetheart,' he muttered savagely, 'it's one reason I didn't want you to come this morning.'

She stiffened for a moment but it was a measure of her distress that she relaxed against him once more. Without a word, Jillian then let him hold her hand as they followed Brad along the track they had used to reach the small clearing where they had found John.

'Well, unfortunately your vehicles as well as animals have obliterated most traces,' Brad muttered at last. 'But Steve's right. There's been another vehicle driven in here besides yours and the quad.' He crouched down for a closer look. 'Steve, you said Scott was driving that big 4WD of his out here?'

Steve nodded. He could see Jillian was still battling her tears. 'Hard to tell, but this tyre tread seems smaller than those big ones he had on it yesterday.'

Jillian released a deep sigh of relief. Steve squeezed her hand and smiled crookedly at her. When they walked back at last to his vehicle none of them said a word. Her slim fingers clung to his until he had

Outback from Baragula

helped her up into the front passenger seat.

Steve avoided Bradley's assessing glance and asked quietly, 'So, Brad, do you need to have a look around the windmill and cattle yards or should we go straight to Webster?'

'Straight to Webster.'

As they travelled along the rough, rarely used gravel road, the grey sky gradually became tinged with pink in the east. The sun had not yet peeped over the horizon when at last Jillian said, 'There, that gate. That's the turnoff we always took.'

'Stop right here, Steve,' Bradley ordered sharply. 'You two wait while I see if there's any sign of dual tyres.'

It had been warm in the vehicle and Jillian shivered in the cool air as they stood beside it and watched Bradley move slowly towards the gate, examining the ground each step.

Steve moved closer and put his arm around her again. 'Cold for the end of November, isn't it?'

She stiffened slightly and then relaxed against his warm body.

'I don't think that fence would last long if a bullock decided the grass this side was greener,' Steve said thoughtfully at last.

'And that gate was pretty dilapidated the last time I saw it, but it looks even more rickety now.'

Steve smiled in agreement. The old, rusty, iron gate looked as though some effort had been made to mend it a long time ago, but now it hung on its hinges. All that kept it upright appeared to be where it had been fastened with a piece of rusty wire to a pretty rotten looking wooden post.

Jillian snuggled into Steve's warmth a little more, but remained silent. He glanced at her. She was watching Bradley trying to open the gate.

Steve grinned slightly. 'Looks like our fearless policeman needs a hand.'

'He's wasting his time. No truck has been through there.'

He looked at her sharply and then back at Bradley.

'No drag marks where the gate would have been opened, certainly no tyre tracks a turning B Double would make – even on that firm surface. Besides, I'd guess that gate would fall apart at the hinges if someone tried to move it," she muttered.

A few moments later, Bradley rejoined them and confirmed Jillian's thoughts. 'But I'm pretty sure dual axles of some kind have travelled along this road recently – as your old kangaroo shooter told you.'

Steve frowned. 'So, what now? Do we still follow this road, or go through that gate and search the property from here?'

'Search from here,' Jillian said decisively. 'I wouldn't be at all surprised if they have not simply cut the fence somewhere further on and got in that way. Besides, from here I have a pretty good idea where some old cattle yards used to be.'

Brad thought for a moment. 'I think you're right,' he said at last, 'and going through here might mean we can come up on them from a different direction before they know we've found them.'

'You think the men might still be here? Surely from what Eddie Jones said they must have unloaded the cattle and gone for their lives?'

Brad smiled grimly at Jillian's surprised face. 'Without leaving anyone behind to keep an eye on their loot? I think it's more likely they may have planned to cart off at least one load and return as soon as they think the coast is clear for the rest. John's appearance would force a change of plans. Might be why your old friend saw them head this way to unload the cattle and return with what sounded like an empty vehicle. Of course, it's more than likely they're long gone and trying to put as much distance between themselves and here after running John down. But there's still the risk they didn't and that we could meet up with Ettie's cattle rustlers. It's the main reason I didn't want you with us, Jillian,' he finished bluntly.

Steve saw Jillian's eyes start to flash and hastily intervened. 'Right then, we go in this way. I've got some tools that might help open that gate.'

Brad nodded. 'A pair of wire cutters would do. It's well and truly tied together with old bits of wire.'

The gate proved surprisingly difficult to open. The hinges were rusted and it took both men to lift and force it open once the wire had been dispensed with. The sun had risen by the time they had driven through the gate and refastened it as best they could.

'If there are cattle here, no sense in giving them an open invitation,' Steve insisted when he noticed Jillian's impatient scowl.

They drove slowly over what had once been a dirt track. Now it was barely discernible from the dried out, hard ground around covered by occasional clumps of dead or dying grass.

Steve surveyed their surroundings thoughtfully. 'It seems drier here than the ground we covered on the quad the other day.'

Jillian agreed. 'The further west we go out here, the less the rainfall. And lack of underground water was always one of the main problems on this property.'

Steve could feel the tension in her slim body as she searched the countryside for any sign of movement. There were only a couple of emus on the treeless plains and several minutes later, as they drew closer to a line of low scrub, several big red kangaroos straightened up. Their ears twitched at the sound of the intruder before they bounded away towards the distant trees.

'I simply can't get over the distances out here,' Brad said eventually. 'We've been travelling for a good half an hour since we went through that gate and seen one fence and been over one cattle grid. A bit different from Baragula, Steve.'

Steve smiled at him but it was a little forced. As if he needed any more reminders of the difference between here and his own home! 'Well,' he drawled, 'we've hardly been able to get out of bottom gear though and...'

Something moved under a clump of low scrub they were approaching. Steve reached for the brake pedal as Jillian exclaimed, 'Over there! Several head of cattle.'

'You're sure the Reeds haven't put any of their cattle in here yet?' Brad asked sharply.

Jillian didn't take her eyes off the cattle as they rolled closer. Her voice was terse. 'Too many fences need repairs, especially onto the main road near the old homestead. Mrs Reed said they have no time for repairs until after their harvest is in.'

Steve frowned. 'I really expected to only find cattle in stock yards, not any that would need to be rounded up once more. Any chance they could be a few strays the Websters left behind?'

Jillian looked swiftly at Steve and shook her head. 'Afraid not. Mr Webster sold every head.' She hesitated and then added reluctantly, 'In fact, John and I helped them with their final muster.'

Steve's tight lips relaxed a little. So, despite the bad blood between the families, the brother and sister had still acted neighbourly. He had heard it was taken for granted in the outback.

They drove forward until they all could see the distinctive tags that confirmed they were cattle that should still have been on Davidson Downs.

Steve glanced sympathetically at Jillian's white, angry face. 'Of course, they could have strayed here.'

'Possible perhaps, but I doubt it. Mr Reed mended a fence the day after we went to Sydney and told us he checked from the air and then drove a small herd back onto Davidson. That fence John reckoned was one he and Dad had renewed not that long ago, and the main reason he went to check it when he did on... on the quad.'

Jillian's soft voice became more and more choked. Her voice echoed her mixture of relief, grief and weary anger. 'He... he couldn't understand why it had broken. Dad and Mr Reed discovered years ago it didn't worry Mr Webster or Billy whether they branded calves belonging to cows with our brand as well as their own. So we've made very sure our fences bordering their paddocks were always in very good repair.'

Steve estimated at least thirty to fifty head of cattle were grazing in the immediate vicinity. 'So, whether they were trucked here or driven through your fence, looks like we know where some of your cattle are. Do we keep looking?'

Brad was leaning forward from the back seat. He nodded swiftly. 'Yes, I'd like to see where any cattle have been unloaded or even where they might be yarded again to put onto trucks.'

Steve hesitated. 'Which way do you think, Jillian?'

'The other side of those trees. And, as I remember it, you'll have to drive carefully over a wide and stony, dry creek bed.'

Steve reached out a hand to touch her clenched hands. 'I'm so sorry, Jillian.'

'You... you'd be better feeling sorry for Scott Reed if he did have anything to do with this!'

Fury and desire for revenge flashed into Jillian's eyes. Steve felt even sadder, but refrained from mentioning his own belief that if she continued to harbour such feelings the one to be more hurt spiritually would be Jillian.

And then he felt sudden shame. He was no better in God's sight. Hadn't jealousy and anger touched him also when he'd seen how friendly Jillian had been with that same man now causing her such heartache?

When they had first spotted the cattle, Steve had driven across country straight towards them. Now the 4WD slowly bounced over the increasingly uneven ground, dodging around stunted trees. They started to edge down a gentle slope.

Outback from Baragula

Jillian gave an exclamation. 'Stop! The creek's got water in it!'

'Good, that means your cattle at least have water to drink,' Brad observed as they rolled to a stop.

Jillian was already reaching for her two-way radio. 'Either of you hear the weather on the news last night or this morning?'

Steve glanced around at Brad. Both men shook their heads. A thought struck Steve. 'Before I left home there were some reports of heavy rain in the mountains a long way south of here.'

'I was awake for quite a while last night and didn't hear any rain here. Jillian,' Brad added urgently, 'don't give away where we are.'

She shot a derisive look at him. 'You're not likely to hear rain falling hundreds of kilometres away. Steve, we'd better not cross over until I check this out.'

Steve looked at the narrow strip of water trickling over the small pebbles. Had she forgotten they were in a four-wheel drive? And then he took in what was coming from the radio speaker.

It had been raining heavily many hundreds of kilometres away, mainly in the north but was also still raining around the head waters of the Macquarie in the south-east. The ground here might be very dry, the sun in a clear sky might be burning off any feed right here, but there were flood warnings out for all tributaries flowing into the Darling River to the west of them and especially for the large Macquarie and Bogan Rivers.

Jillian's face lost colour. 'This creek is part of the Macquarie network and we are right on a flood plain here.'

Unlike Brad, Steve knew what this meant. Both the Bogan and Macquarie were close enough that it could be very likely a major flood was on the way to this very area.

The Murray Darling river system was Australia's largest. The Darling was formed by several large rivers that rose on the western slopes of the mountains of the Great Dividing Range which twisted and turned thousands of miles down eastern Australia from the rainforests of Northern Queensland to the state of Victoria in the south. The river's many tributaries started hundreds of kilometres just inside Queensland, others flowed west in New South Wales to the Darling along its almost three thousand kilometres before it flowed into the mighty Murray River, which then emptied into the Southern Ocean. The Darling alone, with these many large and small tributaries, drained an area of almost six hundred and fifty thousand square miles.

During some years, parts of the Darling were little more than scattered chains of waterholes, but when it rained over the catchment area, with more water than the banks could stand massive floods took place.

In recent years small country towns with names like Walgett, Nyngan and Brewarrina had been inundated as the waters swept relentlessly down the river system. The water had burst banks to spread over vast areas of countryside, cutting roads, destroying crops, drowning or starving all livestock not herded or trucked out in time. It had isolated lonely homesteads for weeks. Some that had not been built wisely, too close to a river or not on high enough pylons, were flooded.

Brad put Steve's own thoughts into slow words. 'It's a phenomena of outback Australia that even if not a drop of rain falls locally on parched soil, extensive floods can arrive days, sometimes weeks even after it has been raining a lot in the catchment areas. So, that's what could happen here?'

Jillian did not answer Brad. She stared at that strip of water bubbling over the pebbles and flat creek bed that had virtually no bank.

'Jillian, this place floods even when it doesn't rain here?' Steve asked sharply.

She blinked as though brought back from memories of the past. Dark, expressive eyes looked at Steve. Jillian nodded abruptly. 'Yes, if it's a bad flood. This is a flood plain. I can remember a couple of times Dad helped the Websters move stock from this area.'

Brad scowled. 'Surely we'll have time to go a bit further and try and find those cattle yards before we have to get out of here? We need to see where they are and find any evidence before that truck comes back to take them off to whatever market they think they've found. I've heard it takes days for the water to spread out this far from the Macquarie River anyway.'

'Not necessarily." Jillian glared at him and turned to Steve. 'Get us out of here, Steve. We may not have enough time as it is to round up all the cattle and get them out of danger."

Steve hesitated. He looked at Brad's scowling, unconvinced face and back at Jillian.

She closed her eyes for a moment and then said in a tightly controlled voice, 'Look, when John and I were teenagers and allowed to drive over here by ourselves, Dad made us promise faithfully if ever we saw water in this dry old river bed we had to turn around immedi-

Outback from Baragula

ately and high tail it out of here, no matter how much we didn't want to miss a party at Webster. It would mean water was more than likely already over a wide area not that far from here. Not that we ever did come here again after...'

Jillian stopped. She swallowed and Steve saw her fight for control. 'Dad explained that any flood water in this area was unpredictable. If we went over the creek it might get so deep and wide we couldn't get back across and more than likely a few hundred yards or so further on, the ground could be covered in water or at least be too boggy for us to get out that way, even in a 4WD. We could become marooned in the centre of an ocean of water or at least have a battle royal to get the cattle out then.'

Her voice rose in desperation. 'Do you both *want* to risk having to be air lifted out?'

Without another word, Steve set the vehicle in motion. He heard Jillian's audible sigh of relief as he swung the steering wheel until they were heading back the way they had come.

'So,' Brad said slowly from behind them, 'now we not only have to find if there are more of your cattle here, but have to get them back to safety.'

'And fast – if it's not already too late,' Jillian said grimly. 'The transport truck is in pieces, so the best way to do that is for you guys to be on the ground with the quad and bike while I help muster them with our helicopter – if it's been repaired as promised.'

'Now, how did I know you were going to say that,' Steve muttered and then made a pathetic attempt to smile at Jillian's scowling, anxious face.

Chapter fifteen

Frustration twisted Senior Constable Bradley's face into a deep scowl. 'I guess you're right. Getting a few miserable cattle away to safety from a possible flood that makes this dry, cracked ground a quagmire and death trap for cattle has to take priority over trying to find rotten thieves who didn't hesitate to commit manslaughter, if not murder,' he ended sarcastically.

'Brad!' Steve glared at his friend. 'You don't realise just how important these cattle are to the financial well-being of Davidson Downs. But Jillian, are you sure...?'

Steve glanced at Jillian and stopped. Jillian had felt her own anger and frustration increase at Brad's sarcasm and knew it must be reflected on her face.

'From what John said, there could be hundreds of head of our cattle here. Hopefully we'll find most either in this area or at least not far from the old stockyards. Depending on how severe the flooding becomes and where the cattle have scattered to, we should be able to move them down the road towards the Windmill out-station and then further away from where the water is likely to reach. I'll check more with the surrounding properties when we get back home.'

Brad hesitated. He shrugged at last and looked apologetic. 'So be it then. I just hope we can get both the cattle and the men who put them here.'

He didn't add, 'and put John in hospital,' but Jillian knew that was what they were all thinking. She tried to control her own feelings to answer as calmly as she could. 'So do I! I want us to catch those low-life people who left John for dead. But I'm beginning to think neither of you really appreciates what an outback type flood is like! The sheer vastness can be... be unbelievable.'

'Hmm, I wonder if the cattle thieves realise the danger,' Steve said slowly.

Jillian snarled, 'If Billy Webster's with them, they should.'

'But city slickers are notorious for sneering at outback stories.'

Jillian glared at Brad's wry face, decided to ignore him and try to make them both understand the dire situation. 'Fortunately in the past, Davidson Downs has mostly escaped the devastation that Webster station has endured. Places do go under water, roads become impassable, especially when it rains here, but we are further away from the large rivers like the Macquarie, as well as its famous marshes. For the most part it only means cattle have to be moved closer to the homestead. Of course, that does mean we often miss out on the lush grasses that follow floods.

'Jedburgh Station is the same, even dryer in larger areas. It was one of the main reasons the Reeds had wanted Webster for the times when their own feed and water threatened to run out during the drought years that frequently follow the floods.'

Steve nodded. He looked grim and Jillian knew at least he understood her urgency. She stopped talking to let him concentrate on driving as fast as he could over the rough ground that jolted them around the cabin.

One time when a bad flood had come, she and John had still been students at home with the help of the Outback School of the Air. She remembered how Webster had become a lake of water, stretching over thousands of acres for weeks. Many cattle had drowned or starved to death.

Jillian thought again of that old promise made to her father. This was the first time she had seen that creek with running water and been called upon to honour that particular promise. It only flooded enough every decade or more to put any water in that creek. Perhaps even now, it might prove to be a mere inconvenience and not a widespread flood. For a moment she wondered if she should tell the men that, but dismissed it. She could not take the risk. Davidson Downs desperately needed those cattle even if rescuing them took priority over catching Ettie's cattle rustlers.

It wasn't until they had swung through that rusty gate and left the very bumpy ground of the Webster station paddocks that Jillian dared get on the UHF radio.

Steve murmured, 'Just as well we thought to show Ettie how to use the radio before we left this morning.'

Jillian glanced at him. That 'we' had been generous. It had been Steve himself who had suggested it might be wise to be able to contact the homestead, or Ettie to radio them if necessary. In fact, he had made sure he too knew how to use the two-way radio by the time she and Ettie had finished.

'Now I just pray she's not out feeding the dogs,' she muttered as she tried calling again. 'Oh, why don't those phone companies get their act together out here for us and clear up these huge black spots so we can use cell phones and save...'

The radio crackled to life. As Jillian had instructed her, Ettie's breathless voice said hesitantly, 'This is Davidson Downs. Over.'

'Ettie, thank God. We've got a problem here, I'll explain when we get home. There are a couple of phone calls I want you to make,' Jillian explained briefly and then gave swift, precise instructions. 'Do you think you can call me back when you've done all that, Ettie?'

'Of course I can.'

Ettie's voice sounded a little indignant and Jillian saw a slight smile ease Steve's tight lips. 'Right. I'll expect your call in say about ten minutes or so? Over and out.'

'Oh, well,' Steve muttered with resignation in his voice, 'guess it's only just over twelve months since I had plenty of practice with floods – and not the first time either. After all, Baragula even means 'flood-tide'.

Jillian glanced at Steve's grim face. She didn't like to remember how angry and disappointed she had been by Steve's angry reception towards her when, at Matthew's urgent request, she had flown into water-logged Honeysuckle during that flood last year. All their roads heading out had been cut by the raging waters and the emergency helicopters in the Hunter Valley had been busy elsewhere.

She raised her chin a fraction. 'It wasn't until I flew over the flooded areas in your Hunter Valley that I realised just how different floods are out here. Your flood waters rush down from the mountains sur-

Mary Hawkins

rounding the river valley, making usually pleasant, rippling creeks and waters raging torrents that eventually pour their mud and debris east into the Pacific Ocean.'

Jillian gestured to the flat plains that stretched as far as the eye could see. 'Most Valley folk had plenty of high ground but there are very few places out here that escape and become small islands – as long as the water gives up before it inundates them too. As well as water from down south, just here the water is being forced back up the creeks and tributaries from the larger rivers that have their catchment areas where it's been raining up north as well. Unfortunately any decent sized hill is many, many miles away. Often the animals just don't find even a small island in time.'

Steve glanced at her. The wheels hit a pothole, jolting them badly and he returned his attention to driving, slowing down just a little. 'Well, hopefully it also won't be as destructive as that last one that washed homes and bridges away. Far too many animals died and there were cars washed away and people even drowned.'

Jillian shuddered. 'Like Matthew's car off that flooded bridge. It was a miracle he and Emily got out in time.'

'They certainly kept God busy that night.'

There was dry humour in Steve's voice but Jillian shuddered. She remembered hearing about that dreadful foggy and wet night. Matthew and Emily had risked driving over flooded roads from Baragula to Honeysuckle because their little daughter, staying there with Emily's aunt and mother, had been so ill. 'I don't know how you can joke about something like that. As though the conditions weren't bad enough they had that crazy man following them.'

'After Matthew was swept away trying to free Emily, the man did drag Emily from the car though."

'Yes and then had to be rescued himself by Matthew.'

That had been a dreadful few days. Jillian had come close to losing her big brother that night, but instead of welcoming her when she had landed the helicopter that morning at Honeysuckle to get Debbie to hospital, Steve had been so angry and scornful. The couple of days that followed had hurt her deeply.

After that first angry confrontation, Steve – and Madeline as well – had practically ignored her while she was on Honeysuckle. Jillian had made a point of not seeing either of them again until the wedding had forced her to. No matter how many times Jillian had gone over and over in her mind why Steve could have been so angry with her, she had never found a reason except the laughable possibility that he had also thought she was 'chasing' him as Madeline had sneered. Now she wondered again if that episode on the windmill had been another clue.

Jillian bit her lip and glanced behind her to look at Brad. He was leaning back with his eyes closed. She hesitated and then decided to grasp the moment to ask softly, 'Steve, why were you so angry with me when I flew into Honeysuckle that morning?'

He did not answer her for a long moment but then replied, 'I couldn't believe a woman like you actually went up in a helicopter, let alone had one of her own and could fly it.'

Jillian gaped at him. There were plenty of women pilots these days. She never would have believed Steve Honeysuckle was a chauvinist. 'A woman like. . .like me? What on earth do you mean?'

Her voice had risen and Brad's amused voice answered for Steve. 'He means a woman who was the local doctor's sister from a huge, wealthy outback property family, who was not merely beautiful, well dressed, even glamorous but also someone not afraid of heights to the degree she flew a tiny helicopter of all things.'

Jillian turned and gaped at Brad. He grinned at her. She turned dazed eyes to look at Steve. Dark colour had risen up his sun-tanned neck. His hands gripped the steering wheel.

'Knock it off, Bradley Hunter!'

It was Steve's choked voice that brought the tide of heat to Jillian's own face.

She leaned back in her seat taking deep, calming breaths. Was that how the people at Baragula saw her, Jillian Davidson? From a wealthy family? Glamorous? Was that how Madeline had seen her and perhaps the reason for her antagonism?

And Steve?

Then Jillian remembered Steve's effort to descend the windmill. Was Brad right? Had it been Steve's own fear of heights that he had been reacting to more than the fact she was a helicopter pilot? She suddenly remembered Emily's terror stricken face in the helicopter on that second trip to the hospital with her and little Daniel to be with Matthew and Debbie. Her fear of heights had been very real and only her mother's heart had made her suffer that trip.

Jillian regretted mentioning the incident where Brad could hear. She badly wanted to continue the conversation, but bit her lip. This was not the time.

No one spoke for a long while after that. After a few moments, Jillian deliberately made the effort and forced herself to concentrate on what needed to be organised to get their cattle to safety.

Was there anything else she should or could do now? Ettie was ringing the airport to see if the helicopter was finished and someone could fly it over as a special favour. Ettie was also ringing the police in Dubbo to tell them where the cattle were. Would they be able to send anyone to investigate now some of the cattle had been found?

She gave an exclamation and reached for the radio again. 'The Reeds. I should let them know the waters have reached Webster.'

'No way.' Brad leaned forward. 'That will tip Scott off that we've been there. If he is involved, then the thieves will be warned we know where they've left the cattle.'

Jillian hesitated and then said urgently, 'But what if any of the Reeds are caught out in the back paddocks? What if they too should move their stock?'

The radio crackled to life with Ettie's anxious voice. 'Jillian, are you there? It's me, Ettie.' There was silence and then, 'Do answer me! Oh, I do hope I've done this the right way. Are you receiving me?'

'I'd answer if you would flick that switch back to receive, Ettie Cobby,' Jillian muttered.

The voice went on breathlessly. 'Anyway, praise the Lord the helicopter's fixed and after I explained how urgent it was someone is flying it out for you as soon as possible. But the phone rang just after I hung up and it was that young man that was here yesterday, that Scott Reed bloke. Said his Mum and Dad had gone to Tamworth for the weekend. Said he was ringing to make sure you'd heard the flood warnings that were being put out. Said to tell you he was about to take their plane up and see how far the waters have reached.'

Ettie paused. 'Oh, I do hope you're listening to this.' Her voice sounded as though tears weren't far away. 'That Scott Reed was most emphatic that I get a message to you to be extra careful. Apparently his parents couldn't have known about the flood warnings and reckoned you mightn't have either. Oh, are... are you receiving me? Oh dear, oh dear, I do hope I'm doing this right. And you've got a visitor who arrived here a little while ago and who...'

The radio went dead. Jillian waited a moment and then tried to con-

Outback from Baragula

tact Ettie herself. There was no answer. Brad and Steve remained silent until Jillian gave up in defeat.

Brad said calmly, 'Well, at least that eases your mind about your neighbours, Jillian.'

Jillian nodded. 'Partly, but now I'm wondering who the visitor with Ettie is.'

It was obvious by the way both men did not answer her and the way Steve increased their speed still further that they did also. Scott Reed's warning about Billy Webster was on all their minds. They spoke very little the rest of the journey until the trees around the homestead came into sight.

'I've been thinking,' Steve said abruptly, 'we need the horses out there. They'll go places on wet ground the quads can't.'

Jillian opened her mouth in startled protest at the same time as Brad said briskly, 'Exactly what I've been thinking, mate. But the quads are faster. We need both just in case. If you take your horse trailer I'll drive that utility with the quad and bike.'

'But the ground... you saw how many traps there are for horses,' Jillian cried out.

Steve smiled at her gently. 'We'll be extra careful, Jillie.' In the same breath he laughed as the guest house came into view. 'Well, I guess we know who your visitor is. No wonder Ettie sounded doubtful.'

The kangaroo shooter's caravan was parked beside the house, but a few moments later it was the sight of his old battered truck near the back entrance to the homestead that made Steve groan as he drew to a stop. 'Oh, no, he's probably scaring Ettie half to death.'

Brad had his door open before they had rolled to a stop. 'Who is?'

Steve grinned at his alarmed face. 'I doubt you'll need your police skills, Senior Constable Hunter. Brad, you're about to be educated on at least one eccentric outback character!'

Jillian led the way swiftly towards the house. She paused on the veranda and pointed. 'I somehow think your indomitable Mrs Cobby has held her own. Even Mum never achieved that.'

Steve's hand lightly touched her back as they mounted the steps. 'You haven't said a word for miles. I could hug even that smelly old 'roo shooter for bringing a smile back to your pale face.'

She turned her head and looked at him. For a brief moment she saw the tenderness on his face again that did strange things to her heart.

Then his face went blank and he looked back down at the pair of dirty, good leather boots placed neatly on the veranda near the back door.

Jillian was right. Ettie's beaming face greeted them at the door to the kitchen. 'Oh, good, there you are. I guessed you would be here soon. Just in time to help us eat this meat pie.'

'And I must say, an excellent pie it is too, Mrs Cobby,' said a transformed Eddie. He was freshly shaven and dressed in a white shirt and tie of all things. He rose politely and smiled at them until he saw Bradley Hunter. The veneer of politeness cracked. He stiffened and his eyes narrowed. 'Who are you?'

Ettie seemed to miss the snarl in his voice and the sudden tension in the air. 'Oh, Mr Jones, this is my friend I was just telling you about. Bradley Hunter was so kind as to accompany me all the way from Baragula. He was once in my Sunday School class you know – a real scamp too.'

Eddie Jones relaxed. He beamed brightly at Brad and advanced with an out-stretched hand. 'Well then, this gives me a chance to thank a gentleman who knows how to look after a lovely little lady like you. Nice to meet you, Mr Hunter.'

Brad didn't relax his stance or keen observation of the older man, but did shake his hand and murmur politely, 'Mr Jones.'

Ettie shook her head at them both. 'Now, now, none of that nonsense. And I've already asked you to call me Ettie, Mr Jones.'

'Only when you call me Eddie, my dear lady. Eddie and Ettie sound real good together.'

A muffled snort from Steve pulled Jillian's fascinated attention from the couple now beaming at each other. His eyes were full of laughter. Her own sense of humour came to the fore, but she frowned at Steve and hoped her own desire to laugh did not overcome her as she hastened to say, 'Well, we are always informal here in the outback. It's usually first names all round. How long have you been here for Mr... er, Eddie?'

Keen eyes observed her for a moment before Eddie relaxed. His eyes sparkled at her and Jillian realised he knew full well she had sounded a little too casual.

'Why, not more than a few minutes before yourselves – well, for lunch that is. When I first arrived I hurried over to tell you about the flood water starting to come up the creeks, but Mrs Cobby... er Ettie here told me you had already left. Then she kindly invited me back to share her lunch.'

Outback from Baragula

'And then you radioed me,' Ettie said and added anxiously, 'I did try to get you back but somehow I couldn't remember how you said to do it.'

'Oh, why didn't you say? I could have helped out there.'

Ettie's eyes opened wide at the old 'roo shooter, suddenly making Jillian wonder if she had not got the old reprobate's measure after all. 'Oh, by the time you got back all spoofed up there seemed little point cause I guessed they'd show up soon anyway. Now, while the veggies are finishing off perhaps I can give you the message now.'

Jillian opened her mouth but Brad got in first. 'No need, thanks Ettie. We heard you loud and clear although it seems you forgot to switch back to receive.'

'Oh my *dear*, I am so sorry!'

Jillian quelled Brad with a frown and smiled at Ettie's dismayed face. 'Not to worry, we got the message which is the most important thing. I tried to call you back but somehow you must have turned the radio right off. 'Now,' she added briskly, 'that meal smells delicious. We had better hurry to freshen up and get ready for it.'

Chapter sixteen

When they were all seated, to Jillian's astonishment it was Eddie Jones who said cheerfully, 'Right then, girlie, who do you want to say Grace?'

Jillian stared at him. He winked at her before closing his eyes.

She glanced across at Ettie. That lady was watching the kangaroo shooter with a slight smile. She caught Jillian watching her and grinned impishly. 'I think it must be my turn, Jillian dear.'

Ettie bowed her head without waiting for confirmation. Jillian saw Steve's slight look of alarm before he hastily closed his eyes as Ettie started to pray.

'Oh, Lord Jesus, we do thank You for all Your good and bountiful gifts, including having this man to eat with us even though he does shoot Your creatures and tries to hoodwink an old woman. Amen.'

No one moved.

Jillian continued to gape at Ettie. She hardly dared to look at the man whose temper she and John had often professed to be wary of over the many years of their childhood and youth. Eddie Jones eyes were open but his head was still bowed.

'Now, do help yourselves before it gets cold,' beamed Ettie Cobby as though there had been absolutely nothing untoward in her brief prayer.

A stifled sound came from Steve's direction.

Eddie raised his head and Jillian tensed, ready to order him from the room. He stared at the smiling woman who had picked up a plate of mashed potatoes and was offering them to him.

'Well, blow me down and strike me pink. Has this woman got guts or has she?' Eddie roared.

Steve started to chuckle out loud. Jillian looked at him with horror and dared at last to look back at Eddie Jones. To her amazement his grin stretched from ear to ear and he was looking at Ettie with considerable awe. He slapped the table with a gnarled old hand and gave a whoop of laughter. Perhaps it was a welcome relief from the tension of the whole day but in a moment all except Ettie were roaring with laughter.

She smiled blandly at them all. 'Now, do stop your nonsense and start to eat before it gets cold. I understand there is some urgency about these flood waters Eddie was telling me about.'

That sobered them fast. The food began to disappear rapidly.

'So, reckon you found those stolen cattle of yours, Jillie?'

Everyone paused and stared at Eddie Jones. He looked from one to the other and pointed his fork at Jillian. 'Well, like, stands to reason, like. You'd not be back so soon or be wantin' that there 'copter of yours so urgently, girl, less you'd found them beasts.'

'I didn't tell you about those cattle,' Ettie exclaimed, 'how...?'

Eddie grinned at her. 'You didn't need to. I had your frequency tuned in on me own UHF.' He stopped smiling. 'What did the police say when you rang them, Ettie?'

Ettie looked uncertainly from Eddie back to Jillian and then to Brad.

'It seems he knows everything else. He might as well share that info too,' Brad said calmly.

'They said they were extremely busy but would send someone out here as soon as they could.'

Eddie swore.

'Mr Jones, really!'

The man stared at Ettie's outraged face and after a moment had the grace to gruffly apologise before he said angrily, 'That means those dirty murderin' skunks will be long gone.'

Brad's face was grim. 'More than likely, although not if I have any say in the matter and we get back there as soon as possible. Perhaps

Outback from Baragula

Eddie here can help you round up as many of the cattle as you can and get them to safety while I do more investigating.'

Eddie eyed him thoughtfully. The telephone rang and Jillian jumped up to answer it. All conversation was suspended. Both Steve and Brad stiffened when Jillian turned and looked at them with a frown as she said briefly, 'Yes, it's me, Scott, and I'm glad I'm back too.' She listened carefully for a few moments. "Right, Scott, will do. See you then.'

She hung up slowly. 'Scott tried to get through on the radio from his plane but just landed back at Jedburgh to use the phone. He saw cattle out on Webster station where there shouldn't be any. He says to his knowledge they couldn't be theirs so reckons our fence must be down again. The floods are spreading out and already several kilometres from the homestead on Webster. He wants us to meet him at Webster's southern cattle yards as soon as possible.'

Brad and Steve looked at each other.

Jillian added steadily, 'That's not far from where we saw the cattle.'

Eddie shovelled the last mouthful of food on his plate into his mouth and jumped up. 'What're we waitin' for. My gear's still on me truck. Let's go.'

Steve stood up too. 'Hang on there, mate. What gear have you got? I'm going to take the horses out while Brad drives the ute with the wheels on board.'

Eddie stopped. He glanced at Brad, his face grim. 'Like I said, me gear – all I need whether it be chasin' 'roos, cattle or murderin' thieves.' He turned and disappeared. The screen door banged shut behind him.

Brad gave a slight grin. 'I don't think I really want to know everything he's got in that "gear". Best if we take all three vehicles anyway. It will take you a while to load the horses and by that time I could be well on the way with the utility behind the old bloke.'

While Steve started getting the horses ready, Brad and Jillian packed the small trail-bike and as many fuel drums they could fit on the utility around the quad and camping gear.

'Anything else we need I can bring out in the helicopter. Here, you'll need this too. I think you might know how to use it,' Jillian added dryly.

As he took the hand-held radio unit, Brad smiled at her. 'Reckon

I do at that.' His expression changed as he went on to say, 'Jillian, whatever you do, don't underestimate these crooks. We haven't any idea where they are but we do know what they are capable of. If you see anything at all suspicious when you get that whirly-bird of yours in the air, radio us at once. And you keep in touch. Let's always know where you are and what's happening.' His grim face eased a little. 'I'd hate to get on the wrong side of Baragula's only doctor if I let anything happen to his little sister.'

As soon as Brad drove off to follow the lingering dust left by Eddie Jones' hurried departure, Jillian raced off to assist Steve with the horses and make sure he knew how to use the other radio.

Pleasure swept through Steve as Jillian helped him. It was the first time they'd been alone together since Brad and Ettie had arrived. Suddenly there seemed so much Steve wanted to say to her. He could not explain the strange, uneasy feeling that gripped him deep within as he stared at this woman who was daily becoming more and more important in his life.

'Jillie, you and Ettie will take care, won't you? Are you sure you'll be okay using the helicopter with the mustering?'

She scowled at him. 'Probably safer than you will be on those horses I reckon.'

'I didn't mean...' Steve stopped. He wasn't quite sure what he meant. 'Just take care.'

They studied each other. Afterwards Steve wasn't quite sure whether he moved or she did. The next they were in each other's arms. He held her tightly against him and her strong arms held him just as tight. They were still for a long, long moment. Steve gave a deep sigh. He let go with one hand, but only to tip her chin up so he could find her lips.

Timeless moments passed before they slowly drew apart. Jillian's eyes were as dazed as Steve felt.

'Jillie, I'm sorry! I... I...'

'If you two have finished saying goodbye I'd better give you this hamper, Steve lad.'

They both jumped and turned to see Ettie standing next to the driver's door staring carefully down at the large picnic basket she had placed on the ground in front of her.

'Can I look yet?' she asked meekly. The eyes she raised were smiling, although Steve thought he could see concern on her face as well.

Outback from Baragula

Jillian's face was very pale. She stumbled back a couple of steps. Steve knew his own face must be red from the heat that had swept through him, making him lose control of his actions.

Steve stepped forward and hefted up the basket. 'Thanks, Ettie,' he managed hoarsely, 'I'll be off.'

As he slowly drove away, Steve's last glimpse of the two women was of Ettie stepping forward and placing an arm around the rigid figure of Jillian Davidson. Neither woman waved.

∽∕∾

Jillian was glad of the warm arm around her waist. She shivered and asked, 'Why does Steve keep doing that?'

Ettie's voice was very gentle. 'Doing what, Jillian?'

'When he... he kisses me he... he says he's sorry!' Anger made her voice start to rise. A solitary tear escaped and ran down Jillian's cheek. She brushed it impatiently away. 'Are all men like that?'

Ettie gave a low chuckle. 'Only perhaps those who steal a kiss they know they shouldn't have.'

'Why shouldn't he kiss me?'

Ettie was silent. When Jillian glanced at her, she avoided her eyes. The arm around Jillian tightened briefly before Ettie let her go. 'I reckon Steve has his own good reasons. Come on now, I know you must have stuff to do before that helicopter arrives and I've the kitchen to clear away.'

Jillian grabbed her arm as Ettie turned away. 'Please, Ettie, I really do need some answers. I need to know why Steve keeps giving me such mixed signals. One minute I could swear he loves... *likes* me and the next he seems so unhappy because he does. Is he committed to another woman somewhere?'

Ettie looked up at Jillian and studied her face carefully. 'Jillian dear, I can assure you that as far as I know there is no other woman.'

'Then... then *why?*'

Ettie looked undecided and then nodded her head as though making up her mind about something. 'I suppose it would be difficult for Steve to tell you at that,' she muttered. Louder she said, 'Let's go inside and I'll try and explain. Mind you, I've never mentioned this to Steve so I don't know for sure, but I do know that your own brother faced this same dilemma – well, almost the same,' she added in a troubled voice. 'And with Steve Honeysuckle's family history, as well as being the kind of Christian he is, I know it must be very much on his mind as well.'

Jillian had been striding beside Ettie, but at that she stopped dead. 'It wouldn't have anything to do with me not going to church like Steve does, would it?'

Ettie didn't stop and Jillian had to scurry after her.

'Look, my dear, it's not simply a matter of going or not going to church. It is much deeper than that. I know for a fact that Steve admires you greatly, but I also know he's a man fighting a man's attraction to a woman he can't help having feelings for but could never have a relationship with – or should not have one at the moment with the way things are,' Ettie corrected herself.

Jillian gave a bewildered laugh that was more a cry of pain. 'Do you mean because of the danger both he and Brad seem to think we still might be in or... or are you saying Steve Honeysuckle shouldn't ever love a woman like me?'

Ettie glanced up at her. 'Oh, my dear!' She looked really upset and uncertainty showed in her eyes before she turned away. 'Let's talk in the house.'

Once in the kitchen Ettie hesitated, looked at the untidy kitchen and then shrugged. 'I think we both need another cuppa while we chat.'

While Ettie fussed with the electric kettle and the tea preparation, Jillian started clearing the table. Ettie had not immediately denied that Steve shouldn't love her and she had the distinct impression Ettie was thinking about what she should or should not say. Well, that was fine with Jillian. While her own hands and feet automatically moved, her mind raced.

She was sure now that his religion must have something to do with Steve's attitude to her.

What else could be so terrible, so wrong about her, Jillian Davidson, that a fine man like Steve should not fall in love with her? She was a good person, had never done anything terrible, had always done her best to live honestly. Sure, she'd dated a few guys at university, but the closeness between her and John had always seemed to inhibit most men. Besides, after what had happened with Billy she had not been terribly interested in risking any other such incident.

She pushed that memory aside and thought about this religious thing. During various conversations with Matthew over the last few years she had challenged him about becoming too religious. In that first year after he had claimed to have handed his life over to Christ, as he had put it, she and John ended up avoiding him because every time they saw him he always wanted to force his new ideas about God down their throats. They had both been so relieved when Matthew had at last given up on them.

Or had he?

Jillian remembered how embarrassed she had been last year when Matthew had hugged her goodbye after his wedding and whispered in a matter of fact way, 'I hope you know, Jillie sweetheart, that I still pray very much for you and John.'

She had hugged him back, thinking he meant about them finding someone to marry like he had Emily. Now she suddenly wasn't so sure, remembering how years ago he had once fervently told her he was praying she would come to know Jesus Christ as her Lord and Saviour. Jillian had been embarrassed, even rather hurt that he should think she needed to be more religious. Over the years she had gone to church at least twice every year. Now she remembered how he let his religion affect every part of his life, especially his relationships with women.

Long before Emily had come back into her brother's life Jillian had teased him about finding a nice young woman and settling down. Of course, then she had known nothing of his history with Emily. Now she remembered him saying something about it being hard to find someone who could share his love for Jesus and that the Bible even warned about being 'yoked' together – or something – with an unbeliever.

Pain stabbed deep in Jillian's heart. She straightened. 'Is that it? Is it because Steve thinks I'm not good enough for him?'

The words had burst from Jillian and Ettie swung around. She stared at Jillian with dismay. 'Good enough? Of course not! Whatever do you mean, lass?'

Jillian sank down onto a chair. Ettie hesitated, then gave a resigned sigh, left her tea-making efforts and joined her at the kitchen table.

'That's it, isn't it? I'm just not good enough for Steve Honeysuckle.'

'Now my dear, please don't get angry. I...'

'Angry? That doesn't begin to express how I'm feeling! How dare that man think he's so superior!'

Ettie looked alarmed at her fury. 'Jillian, you're a very beautiful and talented young woman. I'm quite sure you are "good enough" for any man.'

'Well, perhaps I should have said not religious enough?'

Ettie was silent a long moment and Jillian knew she was right.

But then Ettie said, 'Jillian, there is a very, very big difference between being merely religious and being a Christian, or a "born again" believer as some call it. Have you ever personally asked Jesus to forgive your sins and come into your life to make you a new person who can enjoy an intimate relationship with Him?'

Although anger still churned with hurt and growing bewilderment in Jillian, she was taken aback by Ettie's bluntness. Except for Matthew in recent years, her family never talked about private things like this. And what she had been experiencing lately in the privacy of her own bedroom was no one else's business!

'Oh, you mean all that heavy nonsense Matthew professes to believe now that makes him so involved with church,' she scoffed, even as she knew she was being unfair to Matthew. He didn't just say he believed, he lived his whole life by his beliefs.

Like Steve did.

The truth of that hit Jillian hard. It had been so evident these past days.

There was a brief pause and then Ettie's quiet response. 'The mere fact you've just dismissed that which is the most important thing in the lives of people like Matthew and Steve – and myself for that matter – as merely "nonsense" should tell you something, Jillian dear.'

It was the sadness on her face and the tears in Ettie's eyes that silenced Jillian. She sat there, stunned.

It was obvious that Matthew and Steve's religion was very important to them, but this... this was completely beyond Jillian's understanding.

'The...the most important thing in their lives?' she whispered, 'even more than... than loving—' She stopped dead.

Ettie swallowed and then cleared her throat. 'You see, to start with you simply can't really understand what having a day by day personal relationship with Jesus Christ, having Him at the very centre of your life means to us until you too know Him as your Saviour and the Lord of your whole life. And a relationship that can lead to marriage simply does not work, or at least would only be a damaged one, especially in the long term, unless both understand and can share that vital part of life.

Outback from Baragula

'Even more than being simply commonsense, the Bible forbids it. Besides Jesus warning us not to be yoked together with an unbeliever, it says in Amos chapter three and verse three, "Can two walk together unless they be agreed?" The Old Testament contains many, many stories of the downfall of folk who married unbelievers. In fact I know people today too who...'

Ettie's voice broke. She bit her lip, obviously struggling for control. 'I'm afraid you will need to ask Steve as it is so private and personal, but I do know that Steve and Madeline Honeysuckle did not have an easy time growing up in that household with their mother and father before she died. Ben's a very different person nowadays.'

Jillian had been staring down at her clenched hands. At that statement she raised her head and stared at Ettie. For some reason she'd always thought Steve and Madeline had experienced a very happy family life. They were certainly very close to their father but very rarely spoke about their mother.

'Of course it makes sense that a married couple should be able to understand and accept the differences in the other person. But shouldn't that extend to differences in their religious beliefs too?' This was too much for Jillian. Anger filled her voice once more. 'Besides, how can you possibly have a...a "personal relationship" with someone you can't see? It's hard enough trying to have one with someone you *can* see!'

A smile touched Ettie's face and then she looked uncertain. 'That's true enough. I'm not sure I know quite how to answer that.' She thought for a long moment. 'Okay,' she started slowly, 'would you say you have a personal, or rather a deep and close relationship with Brad Hunter?'

'No way!'

A fleeting look crossed Ettie's face. Jillian thought it almost seemed like relief, but Ettie only nodded briefly. 'Right then, would you say you have one with your twin brother?'

Jillian frowned impatiently. 'Of course I do, I've known him all my life, Matthew too for that matter.'

'So, wouldn't you say your close relationship with them comes out of spending time with them, getting to know them, what they're really like, being able to trust them and to communicate with them on a deeper level than someone like say Brad, or me, who you've only just met, or someone you might just have passed a few times in the street

– er, outback?' Ettie ran out of breath at last.

Jillian didn't have to think about that. 'Naturally,' she snapped.

'God is a person and He made us in His image. So, that means we should be able to communicate with Him from the very depths of our being. Adam had that kind of fellowship with God until he blew it all. Just imagine,' Ettie said enthusiastically, 'Adam had an intimate relationship with his Creator who loved him more than we can begin to comprehend. When Adam disobeyed God he ruined it, not only for himself but he made it impossible for a Holy God to be intimate with us until sin was dealt with by the death of Jesus on the cross.'

Ettie's face had changed to a deep sadness. The rapid changes in Ettie's face touched Jillian more than her words.

She pushed the feeling away and scowled at the well-meaning woman. 'I know all that,' she said impatiently. 'I'm not a complete heathen. Mum and Dad dragged us all to church in Coonamble at least every Easter. But I don't remember hearing anything about what you call a personal relationship with Almighty God.'

The sadness on Ettie's face deepened. 'I'm afraid I went to church for years before I began to realise that a *personal* relationship is what God really wanted with me, not just my repeating words that I guess I did mean, but never really let Him into every area of my life.'

Every area of my life?

'But... but God can't possibly be interested in every little thing!'

'Of course He can. He loved us enough to send His only Son to die for us so we could have an intimate relationship with Him. Oh dear, I do wish I could put all this better. I'm afraid I'm not a very good Christian.' Ettie looked worried. 'I've never really talked to anyone like this about it all before. It's only been in the last few years I've known God like this myself and that happened at first because I was just so lonely after my son and then my husband died that I really let God into every part of my own life. Perhaps you should talk to our Pastor instead.'

Jillian felt more bewildered then ever. Hadn't Steve said that Ettie had taught him in Sunday School? And now she was claiming it was only a few years ago she too had come to know God in this way that she claimed was so all important.

She jumped to her feet and said through gritted teeth, 'It still all boils down to what I said before. Whatever it all means, one thing I do know is I was right. Steve doesn't think I'm good enough for him.'

Ettie looked even more upset. 'Oh dear, I've said it all wrong. Please, Jillian dear, you need to talk about all this with Steve sometime, perhaps even Matthew.'

Jillian simply didn't know how to respond. She heard the peel of the phone with a sense almost of relief. She smiled apologetically at Ettie as she went to answer it.

'Jillian? It's Scott.'

Jillian stiffened. 'Scott? Your voice sounds very faint. Where are you ringing from? I thought you'd be on your way out to help muster those cattle.'

'I'm ringing on my mobile not far from home. Look, I suddenly thought about your helicopter. I know you'd normally use it for something like this but I remember Dad telling me you said it's in getting serviced and why he took the plane up to search for John. Any idea if the helicopter's finished yet?'

Jillian was silent. His words about the helicopter hardly registered. 'You're ringing on a mobile phone?' she asked sharply.

'Yes, isn't it great? It seems the powers-that-be are fixing many of our black holes, although I had to drive away from the house to this bit of a rise to get reception.'

Jillian knew the place he must be ringing from. A very small hill a kilometre or so from Jedburgh homestead. And if *that* reception area had been fixed...

'But look, we'll talk about that later,' Scott was saying, 'is there any chance I could fly you to pick up the helicopter?'

Sheer relief swept through Jillian followed by a burst of elation. Scott hadn't lied after all!

'Yes, Scott, there certainly is every chance. I had a message they would try and get someone to fly it here but that would mean I have to fly the pilot back.'

'Much faster if I fly you there to bring it back yourself like I have before. I don't know why you didn't ask me yourself.'

She knew Scott well enough to hear a touch of hurt in his voice. 'Oh, Scott,' Jillian exclaimed fervently, 'you'll never know how glad I am you rang me.'

There was a small silence then Scott said slowly, with considerable surprise in his voice, 'No problem. We've done this before. I still don't know why you didn't ask me this time. See you as soon as I can. Afraid I have to check a couple of things here first. I'll radio when I'm in the air for you to meet me at your airstrip.'

The phone went dead. Jillian turned to Ettie with a wide smile. 'Ettie, Scott *has* got mobile phone coverage and that black hole may no longer be... I don't think he lied before at all!'

'Jillian?'

Jillian gave the puzzled woman an impulsive hug. 'I'll explain later. Now I've got to get busy on the phone to Williamtown and then make flight plans. Oh, the quad's gone and I don't have a car seeing the Commodore's still out of action. Ettie, could you drive me to our airstrip in yours?'

Ettie hesitated. A worried frown creased her forehead. 'Yes I will, but you do mean Williamtown near Newcastle don't you?' At Jillian's brief nod, she added rapidly, 'A long way from here even in a plane. Oh dear, do be very careful. I'm not at all happy about you going off with that man the boys were so concerned about!'

Chapter seventeen

When he arrived, Scott flew low over the house but they were already on the way to the airstrip in Ettie's car.

Ettie gave a brief, excited laugh. 'My, this sure is a different world out here. The next door neighbour comes to visit by plane, mustering with helicopters. How come you have a helicopter and not a plane?'

'I think my grandfather had a plane before they sold off some of Davidson Downs. Dad was never interested until John and I pestered him that a helicopter could land in many places a plane can't and we could use it for mustering as well as heaps of other things. I'm just thankful we already had it before the rural downturn.'

Ettie shook her head in wonder and was silent until they were slowing to a stop as Scott taxied his plane towards them. 'Jillian, dear, if you're falling in love with Steve as I think you are, I do want you to think seriously about talking with him sometime about what we were discussing before.' Her words were rushed and the eyes she turned towards Jillian were troubled. 'Perhaps you could even talk to Scott about what's been happening between him and the Lord.'

'Scott?' Jillian gave an incredulous laugh. 'Scott Reed's been less interested in spiritual things than I ever have.'

'Not any longer if he's the old friend Matthew mentioned.'

Jillian stared at Ettie and then looked towards Scott as he clambered down from the cabin of the small plane. 'Perhaps I will at that,' she muttered a little grimly, 'but first, there's a few other questions I want answers to.'

It took only a few minutes before the Cessna was once again rolling back down the runway. Jillian waved to Ettie and as the plane picked up speed, she glanced towards the old shearing sheds. For a moment she thought something moved near it and leaned forward for another look but the plane lifted into the air and swung away. As far as she knew there were no cattle anywhere near the homestead. It wasn't common for feral pigs to venture that close to the homestead. As she sat back in her seat she decided it might be wise to check it out when this current crisis was over.

'So, I take it Steve Honeysuckle and his friend from Baragula are out starting to move the cattle?'

Jillian glanced at Scott. 'Well, they're at least on their way. Have you heard the latest flood warnings and how far away the water is from Webster?'

Scott hesitated. 'I'm afraid not. What about taking a few minutes and checking it out before we head off east.'

'A good idea. Oh, I forgot to let Steve and Brad know I was going with you to Williamtown!'

Scott grinned impishly. 'I could always buzz them.'

Jillian laughed back at him. 'Not on your life, Scott Reed. I was with Dad the day you decided to do that. It took us another couple of hours to round up that mob of cattle you scattered. And Dad was not at all impressed and somehow I doubt if Steve would be either.'

'No, that man would probably decide it was a deliberate act of sabotage.'

Jillian drew in a sharp breath. There was no mistaking the grim note in Scott's voice above the engine noise. She hesitated. This young man had been her friend nearly as long as she could remember. And yet, she had to know.

'Steve thinks that somehow you're involved with what happened to John.'

'He made that perfectly clear,' Scott snapped.

Jillian waited for him to deny any knowledge or participation, but Scott remained silent. She at last opened her mouth to ask him outright why he was at the out-station when Scott spoke in such a quiet voice she wondered if she could have heard him correctly over the engine noise.

Outback from Baragula

'And it's been killing me wondering the same thing.'

'*What* did you say?'

Scott glanced towards Jillian. His face was grim, his eyes full of pain and worry. He opened his mouth but the plane suddenly hit a small air-pocket and he returned his attention to the controls. Then he banked the plane towards the north-west and Jillian saw the sun flash off what looked like a large mirror spread over a huge area of land.

She looked down and gave a sharp exclamation. 'Isn't the edge of that water not far from Webster homestead?'

The plane dipped and a couple of minutes later they both saw the large words 'Webster' painted on the roof of the house. Scott gave an exclamation. 'I didn't come over this far before. Looks like the water's coming more from the north-west rather than the south like it normally does here. Must have been more rain in the ranges north of us.'

'Well, that's good, isn't it? It means we have more time to get the cattle south back onto our place.'

'Yeah, I reckon. Depends how much water's flowing into the Macquarie and how quickly it backs up the creeks to this flood plain. And just as well we haven't had a chance to do anything to that dilapidated old homestead yet if it does go under water. Let's get out of here. The sooner we can get down and help your mates the better. At least the road has been elevated and hopefully will not be blocked off.'

Jillian glanced at Scott's set face and refrained from comment.

Scott suddenly exclaimed, 'What on earth...?' The plane banked sharply and began to swoop low. 'Look, down there. The homestead cattle yards are packed with cattle!'

Jillian yelled, 'Scott, get away from here! We don't want them to know we've spotted them.'

To her relief, Scott immediately swung away again and resumed his flight path towards the Hunter Valley and Williamtown.

'Did you happen to see if there was a cattle truck there?'

'A cattle truck?'

Jillian stared at the amazed face Scott turned briefly towards her. Relief swept through her. Scott knew nothing at all about the stolen cattle.

'Jillian, you don't seem at all surprised that our cattle yards down there are full of cattle that we know nothing about. Explain please.'

For a moment, Jillian closed her eyes. Then she drew a deep breath and did just that. She told him everything, including Steve and Brad's concern that Scott somehow was also involved in stealing the cattle. By the time she had finished, Webster station had been left well behind as they travelled steadily towards the south-east.

It was Scott's turn to be speechless. A flush of anger rose in his face. 'And what about you, Jillian Davidson? Did you also think that about your possible future brother-in-law as well as life-long friend?'

His quiet, pain-filled tones disturbed her more than if he had yelled at her.

'No way! At least...' She swallowed and said pleadingly, 'Not until I was convinced you had lied about ringing John on your mobile from Gilgandra when I still thought that was a black hole there and impossible to make calls.'

'So that's why you were so cold and withdrawn yesterday.'

'I'm so very sorry, Scott.'

Jillian waited for the explosion, the hot, furious words and bad language that in the past had always come when Scott was really angry.

It didn't come. Scott remained silent for a long moment. The colour slowly left his face. When he at last looked at her he was pale and drawn. 'And then I rang you again and you knew I really could use the mobile now. No, you don't need to be sorry, Jillian,' he added so quietly she could barely hear him above the noise of the plane. 'I deserve your suspicion and much more, but I swear it was unintentional.'

To her relief, Scott's radio crackled and he became busy with ground control.

Jillian tried to make sense of his last statement and when he had finished on the radio said crisply, 'You need to explain that last statement, but I don't think this is the time or place, Scott. Besides it may be best to tell me when Brad and Steve are there also.'

They were flying towards the distant smudge of mountains, part of the Great Dividing Range. Before long they would sweep above the beautiful Hunter Valley, perhaps even over Baragula on the way east.

They travelled in a tense silence for a long while. At last Jillian knew she was wrong. This couldn't be put off any longer. This couldn't be left until later.

As casually as she could above the sound of the plane engine, she said, 'Ettie Cobby mentioned she saw you once at Matthew's home in Baragula. You never said you'd been there to see him.'

Scott flashed a glance at her. She was relieved to see he had regained his natural colour.

'I've been to see him a few times now.'

Jillian remained silent. It was none of her business what Scott Reed did.

The silence stretched so long, Jillian thought Scott undoubtedly agreed with her until he spoke so quietly she had to strain once more to hear him above the noise of the plane.

'I stupidly got myself into some trouble in Sydney and the first time went to see Matt in sheer desperation. I knew he was someone used to keeping secrets as a doctor.'

Jillian hesitated, not willing to admit she knew anything about Scott's problems. She remained silent, but her curiosity got the better of her at last.

'Ettie also said Matthew was real thrilled because an old friend of his had... had "committed his life to Christ," was the way she put it. She thought it might be you.'

Scott looked startled. He opened his mouth but the radio crackled to life and for a few moments Scott was busy once more. He changed course and headed directly east. When the plane was steady again, he glanced at Jillian.

'Yes, I am that bloke.'

The colour deepened in Scott's cheeks and he spoke quickly before Jillian had a chance to respond. 'I'm still coming to grips with it all. Old baggage and that trouble I was in are still dogging my footsteps, but I've discovered that God is very real. I'm even finding He answers my prayers and despite everything there's a... a sense of peace that's truly amazing!'

There was a reverent, awed note in Scott's voice. He gave a self-conscious laugh. 'Why, God even made it so I ran into this bloke in Sydney when I went to pay off some debts to... Well, no need to bother about who,' Scott said hurriedly, glancing at Jillian. 'I'm still discovering the hard way that even though my sins are forgiven there are consequences that still have to be dealt with. But Matthew has even helped me to sort a couple of pretty bad ones out.'

'My sins' – Scott Reed was actually talking about sin? Jillian stared at him with disbelief. This sounded very much like Matthew all those years ago.

Then Jillian noticed the look of shame in Scott's eyes. It saddened her. So Brad's information about Scott's association with known criminal gamblers must be right. But where had Scott suddenly got that money to pay off his gambling debts?

She remembered something else he had just said. She stiffened. 'Scott has Matthew's help by any chance included lending you money?'

Scott looked startled. He swallowed a couple of times and then nodded briefly.

Jillian relaxed. One more puzzle answered. 'You have no idea how pleased I am about that, Scott dear.'

Surprise coupled with questions filled his face. He opened his mouth and then closed it. There was a brief silence until Scott said fervently, 'I owe Matthew so much. Your brother's a great mate. What's killing me is how I've repaid him by contributing to his brother getting hurt!'

Alarm again filled Jillian. 'Whatever do you mean?'

'I am so very, very sorry, Jillian. I've been going over what you've just told me. I think it could be partly my fault that your cattle have been stolen and even why John was there at all and left for dead.'

'Scott!'

'Oh, Jillie, don't look at me like that.'

The words tumbled from Scott in a tormented voice and washed over Jillian in a torrent.

'A couple of days ago when I went to pay some debts that Matthew had given me the money for, this bloke told me about Billy Webster and his boastings about getting even with us all. I headed straight home instead of staying in Sydney like I'd intended. Then... then when I was at Gilgandra at the motor repair place, Billy Webster actually walked in. He was taken aback at first when he spotted me. Then he became full of threats and saying stuff like at last he was making us all pay for what we'd done to his family.

Scott stopped and swallowed hard before continuing. 'I wish I'd never rung John that morning after Billy left. I told him what Billy had said and suggested John ought to check on your fences and the cattle right across to Windmill One. We both thought Billy must be damaging the fences, perhaps even the water supply. I never dreamed it could be worse than that. Then, when I heard John was missing I drove out to Windmill One out-station as soon as I could.'

'So it *was* Billy Webster I saw in Gilgandra.'

'You saw him?'

'Yes, Steve and I called in for petrol on the way home from the hospital in Dubbo. I didn't recognise him then. He looked awful and was driving a car and took off fast when he saw me. It's a wonder Billy didn't come over and gloat to me as well,' she ended bitterly.

Scott shook his head. 'Billy was always pretty keen on you, Jillian.'

Jillian gave a snort of derision. 'He had a pretty funny way of showing it!'

To her surprise, Scott nodded this time. 'You're right, although not quite in the way you mean if you're thinking of that night he'd had too much to drink at our place. Billy has always had a real problem relating to girls. I think that was initially his father's fault and the example he set Billy with his mother.' He glanced at Jillian. 'John and I have discussed that night several times over the years. Afterwards, when our tempers cooled, we actually felt rather bad about giving Billy such a thrashing.'

Jillian was speechless. John had not once talked about that night to her. Was it because he felt rather ashamed of it?

When she found her voice she muttered, 'Do you think that's why Billy must be involved in this mess we're in now?'

'From what he said, I think it's a lot more than that one night. He accused you all of cheating him and his parents out of their property. Sounded as though he thought you had bought it and not us. Before I could put him right he stormed off.'

Scott's voice became indignant. 'As though either of our fathers would ever cheat anybody. In fact, we all told Dad he should have tried to beat down old Webster on the price he wanted for that run down cattle station. Billy's words didn't really make much sense but I was worried. There was something almost triumphant about him so I rang John at once. Unfortunately I had to kick my heels there in Gilgandra for another full day waiting for the car to be fixed. Then when I did get home and Mum told me about John missing I tried to ring you and the next day went straight over to Windmill One as soon as I could.

"I just knew Billy had been up to something. He said things, vicious things, that made me think he'd been messing with your cattle. Despite what he tried to do to you that night when we were kids, I never dreamed he'd hurt John like that. For goodness sake, we certainly were never buddy-buddies but we grew up together!'

Jillian felt sick. She had tried to blot out of her mind the sight of

Billy Webster's passion-filled face that horrible night he had attacked her. And yet, as Scott had just said, Billy had been the worse for drink that night. Was he really capable of leaving John to die in the bush? And yet... if he hated them still so much after all this time?

'Oh, Jillie, I've been praying so hard these last few days. I didn't want to tell you about my part in all this but I guess God's been telling me I had to. If I hadn't let Billy introduce me to some unsavoury places years ago I should never have gone to, this may never have happened. And now God's put us together like this I knew I had to tell you.'

Scott Reed was talking about God like this when he too had once scoffed at Matthew's new found faith? Jillian found herself shaking her head in wonder. Scott saw her and his words showed he misunderstood her disbelief that he could change so much.

'I've been kicking myself I didn't ring Dad as well as John that morning. I thought I'd be home later that day and that it would be best to discuss it all with him then. I tell you again, Jillian, I never dreamt John could get hurt. You've just got to believe me!'

'Of course I believe you, Scott.' She reached out and patted his arm. He still looked very distressed. 'At least, I believe you about John. But it just sounds very strange hearing *you* talk about God as though you actually know Him.'

Scott went red. She watched him curiously as he swallowed and then tilted his chin. 'That's because I do know Him now that I've asked him to forgive me because of what Jesus did for me on the cross. There is still so much for me to learn about it all, but I've become a Christian and it's the best thing I've ever done.'

To Jillian's relief, Scott had to attend to the radio once more. To speed up the whole thing, he had made special arrangements for the helicopter to be flown to meet them at a small airstrip just west of Newcastle and the main airport at Williamtown which was used by commercial jets as well as the Australian Air Force. While he verified their time of arrival she was thankful not to have to respond to his quiet, amazing words. If she had been surprised and taken aback before, those frank words about 'becoming a Christian' dumbfounded her.

They remained mostly silent for the rest of the flight. It was obvious from the glances that Scott gave her from time to time he was concerned about what she was thinking. And there was no way she felt she could reassure him. She wondered how Brad and Steve would

Outback from Baragula

react to discovering what Ettie had suspected was true. Somehow, she knew Steve would be thrilled but she wasn't so sure about Brad. Would he be as sceptical as she was?

Scott didn't mention it again until he stood near the helicopter saying good-bye to her before flying back to Jedburgh.

'Jillian, it's obvious those cattle at Webster must be yours,' he said crisply. 'As soon as I land back home, I'll take our new B Double truck over to help shift them back to Davidson Downs.' He looked her straight in the eye. 'But above everything else, I do want you to know I've discovered that what Matthew has been trying to tell us all these years, about it being possible to really know God, is all true, Jillie. It's all new for me but I would like to talk to you about it sometime. It... faith in Jesus Christ as my Saviour and Lord is giving me something I've never known before.'

There was no mistaking Scott's sincerity. Then anguish filled his eyes. 'I know God has forgiven me but I do need yours and John's forgiveness also for the mess I've made of things. If I hadn't got into so much debt and become known by those associates of Billy's, all this may never have happened.'

There was such pain and regret in his eyes that impulsively Jillian took a step forward and hugged him. 'You've been like another brother to all of us, Scott. Of course I forgive you. I know you wouldn't have wanted this to happen for anything.' She paused, and then said rather shyly, 'And I would like you to tell me more about this having sins forgiven stuff. I'm afraid I have a few too many of my own,' she added, trying to make a joke of it.

But deep down, Jillian knew her words were true. She had watched and listened to Scott dealing with the airport officials and there was no mistaking that the once cocky, even slightly arrogant Scott Reed had changed. Her thoughts flew to the way he had controlled his temper on the plane when he had been so angry, the way he had dealt with Bluey and made friends with him.

Then memories of that other tall, handsome man who had also watched Scott and the angry dog make friends intruded. A sudden desire to have Steve tell her more of what *he* believed about God began to fill her.

And this time she knew she would listen. And listen hard.

Chapter eighteen

Steve stopped the quad and turned the motor off. He wiped off some of the dust on his face that had been kicked up by the small mob of cattle in front of him and lifted his head. He studied the blue skies intently for the hundredth time. The sun was no longer directly overhead now. They had been at work for hours rounding up the cattle. He wasn't sure how long the flight to and from Williamtown would be but Jillian had hoped to have been here before too long.

He listened intently. Even Bluey was silent now. He had managed to sneak a ride with Eddie Jones and was proving invaluable despite his sore leg. There was no sound except a few protesting bellows from the cattle moving steadily across the shallow, but ever-widening strip of water in the creek.

The roar of a motorbike intruded. Steve looked to where Eddie Jones appeared driving several animals to join his own mob. In a few moments Eddie drew to a stop beside him and pushed back his battered old hat.

'Heard anything from Brad, Stevie?'

Steve scowled. 'Not since he deserted us. I'm sorry I let him talk me into his riding Punch over towards where you said the homestead cattle yards are, instead of waiting until I could go with him.'

'Reckon he was right though about it making sense those rotten crooks would make off if they spotted us or heard a vehicle coming.'

Eddie had not taken his eyes off the cattle and suddenly gave a piercing whistle. A red streak went after another bullock that wanted to wander off by itself. The animal realised Bluey meant business and trotted obediently after the other cattle ambling towards the gate onto the road.

As Steve surveyed the sky once more he growled, 'By the way Bluey responds you could have handled getting them started down the road by yourself. I wish Brad had waited until we had all the cattle we could find in this vicinity rounded up and on their way out of here. Unless they've already trucked the rest out, there must be a heap more somewhere. And I can't contact him because Brad said he was turning off his radio in case it started up when he wanted to be quiet.'

Eddie nodded. 'Made sense to me. He's a copper isn't he?'

Steve stared at Eddie.

The older man glanced briefly at him and then back to watching the cattle. He gave a harsh laugh. 'Suspected it when I first met him. And when he started giving orders I was sure of it.'

'Had a bit to do with policemen in the past, Eddie?' Steve drawled.

Eddie gave another whistle and Bluey went into action again. 'You might say that,' he answered shortly at last, 'when I was young and stupid like that Billy Webster. Boozing is easy to get into when you're lonely in the outback. And too many police out here in my young days knew nothing of the pressures on stupid young shearers let loose with their pay packets in a country pub after weeks on the road working in those sheds in the blistering heat. Whacked us into the clink as quick as look at us. Reckon I was lucky I was called up to do a stint in Vietnam. Reckon what I saw there drilled a bit more sense into me. But it's still a lonely life out here.'

It was the longest speech Steve had heard Eddie make. He knew that Eddie was only one of many men who now regretted their early wild days and their run-ins with the law, whatever their reasons. He shouldn't be surprised, it was true the man had been a soldier. Who knew what Eddie had been guilty of when drunk? And who knew what could get into men like Billy Webster and even a Scott Reed?

They were both silent until Eddie gave another piercing whistle. Obviously it was not the first time Eddie had worked with the Davidson Downs' cattle dog.

'Reckon Bluey and I can take over this mob now. You go and see

Outback from Baragula

how your mate's getting on. Anyway, I reckon that flood water's pretty well stopped spreading here. Dry ground's just soakin' it up,' Eddie finished abruptly, 'so it's not so urgent, like, now.'

Before he could comment, Eddie revved up the bike and took off. Steve gave a wry grin. Brad Hunter wasn't the only one used to giving instructions!

Steve watched Eddie weaving towards the cattle. Once again he wondered just what Eddie carried in that heavy knapsack on his back he had insisted he needed. An antennae protruded from it, so at least there was a radio unit in there.

A check on the fuel gauge on the quad made Steve sigh. Time to head back for more before he did anything else. He hadn't gone far when his radio beeped.

'You there, Steve?'

Steve's sudden hope died at Brad's quiet voice. Where *was* Jillian Davidson?

'Yeah. Found anything?' he asked cautiously.

'I reckon. Heard anything from Jillian yet?'

'No. Want me to send her over your way if I do?'

There was a pause. 'Didn't she say she thought she'd be here soon after midday? And I haven't been able to get Ettie to answer at the homestead either. I thought Jillian made sure she knew how to use the radio properly this time. Think she could have stuffed it up again?'

Alarm swept through Steve. "No way, not Ettie. She was so upset that other time. I'll try her from here and get back to you.'

'No! I've got company here and they might hear the radio when I get closer – or even be listening. I'll get back to you. If you get on to Ettie, get her to tell my... er, my *friends* in Dubbo to get themselves here as swiftly as they can.' The radio went dead.

So, Brad had come across 'company.' Steve's anxiety increased. He immediately tried Ettie. No answer. He started the quad again and raced towards where they had hidden the utility and horse trailer as best they could in a patch of low scrub. As he reached it the radio came to life once more. It was Jillian's brisk voice. Steve closed his eyes in thankfulness.

'Jillian, where are you?'

'Just approaching Webster. Scott flew me to collect the helicopter and on the way we spotted what we've been looking for yarded nicely for us near the homestead. Scott's gone back to Jedburgh to get his big new truck for us and should be there soon. I'm going to land there and meet Scott. Where are you?'

Steve froze in horror. 'Meet Scott...! Jillian, don't fly to the homestead whatever you do! Scott might be there now, but Brad just radioed me. Something's very wrong. Said he has company you don't want to meet up with. I'm on my way to help Brad. At the moment I'm a bit further on from where we saw that first mob near the creek. Eddie's herding some cattle towards that gate. But at the moment we're worried about Ettie. Can't reach her. Will you try and raise her.'

'Will do.'

As fast as he could, Steve raced to the utility and grabbed a fuel can. Jillian came on the radio once more.

'Ettie's not answering. I'm going to check her out.'

'Brad wanted her to phone his friends in Dubbo to get out to where he is as quickly as they can. I think he's still worried our radio calls could be monitored.'

Jillian's puzzled voice said, 'His friends in... Oh!'

Steve suddenly heard the drone of the helicopter. He searched the sky and yelled into the radio, 'You're just to the south of me, Jillie. Take care!'

She didn't answer. Steve watched the speck in the sky rapidly disappear towards Davidson Downs. He hesitated and then looked towards where Judy was tethered near his trailer. He couldn't risk the quad getting stuck in mud.

In a few minutes, he had Judy saddled. He set his jaw and collected his rifle before swinging into the saddle. Steve prayed he would have no need to use it.

To his relief, Brad came on the radio once more. 'I'm on my way with Judy, mate,' Steve told him crisply.

'Good. I heard what Jillian said. Think Scott Reed could already be here?'

'I don't know. Depends how long after him Jillian left Williamtown. Doubt if he's had time though.'

'Right, mate. Let's just hope that bloke's still on the way – *and* bringing his transport for the right reasons. There's already one here a couple of guys are loading right now. We need to stop them leaving. Head north-east and you should find an old track. You'll be able to follow it until you come to a bunch of scrub. Turn north. When you hear the bawling cattle I won't be too far away. I'm making for the concrete tanks to get as close as I can without them spotting me. I think they're too busy to bother listening to our radio frequency.'

It took awhile to find the track. A sense of urgency made Steve grit his teeth and kick the horse into a run. 'I'm sorry to risk doing this to you, Judy, girl, but something tells me we've got to get to Brad as quickly as we can.'

The horse willingly broke into a gentle gallop. Steve watched the ground for the notorious holes that Judy could stumble in. The scattered trees became a little denser until at last he pulled the mare to a walk. It was then he heard the drone of a motor. He stopped and eagerly surveyed the sky. But the engine was different, certainly not the helicopter.

Steve frowned. It was a plane and by the sound of it far too low. It suddenly roared right over his head, almost touching the tree-tops. Judy reared in fright and it took a moment to calm her. When he looked once more, the plane was flying erratically. It soared into the air and then dipped sideways before turning sharply once more. He could hear the motor straining as it climbed steeply. The next moment it levelled out and headed west into the sun so he could no longer see it.

Somewhere ahead of Steve, several rifle shots rang out. He loosened Judy's reins, ready to start her running once more, but his radio came to life.

It was Jillian's voice. 'Steve, I've just landed. Ettie's here.' Her voice rose in alarm. 'There's something wrong. She's running and waving and... Oh, there's a man running from the hangar behind her. He... he's grabbed Ettie! He's hit her and... oh, dear, oh dear! She's on the ground. I don't believe this! He's coming... Why, he's got a gun! I think it's—'

Every hair on Steve's head stood on end. 'Jillian, get out of there!' Steve roared.

He heard someone shout. A man's voice. There was a loud bang and the radio went dead.

'Jillian!'

Steve tried to raise her on the radio again and again but she didn't respond. Frantically he started to radio Brad, but the policeman got him first.

'Where are you Steve? They saw me. Slammed shut the truck gates and made for the cabin. I need back up. Now!' Rapid gun-fire rang out again, drowning his voice. Then he yelled, 'Hope you've got your rifle with you, mate. They've gone berserk. Using a rifle. My handgun's too short a range.'

'Something's happening to Jillian and Ettie!'

Brad cursed. 'And something's happening here! I need your help. Right now!'

Steve kicked Judy into action. The sporadic bursts of gun-fire came closer. Several minutes later they rounded a clump of bushes at a run. Steve saw the clearing, cattle yards and water tanks. As he spotted a B Double cattle truck, the engine roared to life.

The sound of a fast motorbike reached Steve. Without so much as looking at him, Eddie came up behind and roared past. Steve saw the headphones he wore and knew immediately he'd been monitoring their radio calls again. The bike rounded a clump of trees and made for the truck. Steve heard men yelling frantically above the bellowing of frightened cattle.

Brad waved to him from behind a tank some distance on the other side of the slowly rolling truck. 'Steve!'

A rifle roared. The policeman staggered slightly and jumped back. The rifle cracked again. Dust shot up beside Judy. She put on a burst of speed. Steve crouched low in the saddle. In a moment the large tank hid them from the front of the truck that was now starting to move.

He pulled Judy to a stop just as Brad gave a shout. 'What does that idiot think he's doing!'

Eddie Jones had driven up behind the trailer. He steered one-handed and held something else in the other. Rapid fire spat out. Firing as he went, he swept along the driver's side of the long trailer. He skidded around in a burst of flying dirt and wheeled to the other side and out of sight of Brad and Steve. More shots rang out. The slowly moving vehicle slumped sideways.

'He's shooting out the tyres!' Steve yelled. 'He'd better not get the fuel tanks!'

'Get out of there. Get out of there!' Brad was chanting to Eddie as the truck lurched to a stop. 'They'll get you with that gun of theirs.'

'Not if we distract them,' Steve said through gritted teeth. He kicked Judy forward as the truck door flew open on the passenger side. A man pointed a nasty looking weapon towards Eddie. Rapid shots spat out.

Steve roared, 'Drop that gun!'

He swung his own rifle up and let off a wild shot. Somewhat to his

Outback from Baragula

surprise the man threw his weapon to the ground. But he wasn't even looking at the crazy man on the horse heading his way. He was staring towards the front of the truck.

And then Steve saw Eddie. He was calmly sitting on the motorbike, his legs on the ground balancing him. He let off another burst of fire over the roof of the cabin from the snub-nosed, deadly looking black weapon in his hands.

Eddie bellowed, 'If you don't want me to blast out what few brains you've still got, get outa that truck!' More bullets zinged into the ground directly in front of the prime mover.

'Now!'

The truck driver and his passenger wisely decided to do just that.

Eddie didn't even look towards Steve as he yelled, 'Get right away from the truck both you pieces of dog's meat! Stevie, get their gun and watch out they don't find another one.'

Steve dismounted. He kept his own rifle ready as he swooped up the gun on the ground.

'Both of you come here to the front bumper bar!'

'Are you crazy, man?' one of them yelled in a shaking voice.

Eddie graciously ignored that. 'Arms out. Face down on the ground. Move!' Eddie roared.

Steve thought for one moment he heard a soft chuckle burst from Eddie as he swiftly joined him. Then he was sure he must be mistaken as the man bellowed at the passenger who stubbornly stood beside his open door. 'You too. Around here and join your mate. Arms out. Face down on the ground. Now!'

Steve reached Eddie and there was no mistaking the 'roo shooter's delighted grin from ear to ear as the man hurriedly threw himself on the ground beside his partner in crime.

'Always did wanna say that,' Eddie muttered, 'but I reckon I'll let that copper do the official friskin' bit. Hope he's got his handcuffs on him too.' Eddie peered past Steve and added in a suddenly worried voice, 'And I think you'd better see why he isn't already on his way to claim his bit of the action, Stevie boy.'

Steve gave an exclamation and rushed back to Brad.

Brad's face was pale. He was holding very tightly to the calf of his leg. Blood seeped out between his fingers.

'Sorry, mate,' he gasped, 'don't think it's too bad. Get those men trussed up before you worry about me. Sorry, no handcuffs. See if there's rope in the truck.'

Steve hesitated and Brad added rapidly, 'A bullet ricocheted. Think it's still in there. It's sore but not too bad. I've had worse.'

Brad was right. After Steve had carefully and thoroughly tied up both men, it was Eddie once more who was prepared. A small first aid kit materialised from his knapsack. A dressing and bandage stopped the bleeding, but when Brad insisted on standing it was obvious he was in considerable pain. Despite their protests, he hopped across with Steve's support to check on their captives.

"Righto, youse guys, reckon youse can handle things now. Oh, you might like to know, like, none of these nice gents is Billy Webster. Gotta get back to me job with Bluey and the cattle.'

Brad's head swung around but his protest was lost in the roar of the motorbike. Eddie grinned at them. With a nonchalant wave he took off. All both the men could do was stare after this odd, outback character as he disappeared swiftly back the way he had come.

Angry frustration in his voice, Brad called out, 'Did you see what kind of gun that... that maniac was using, Steve?'

Steve couldn't help it. Admiration for Eddie swept through him. He stifled a grin at the expression on Brad's face.

'Can't say I really know what kind of gun he used. And I think it best we don't ask. It disappeared into that bag on his back very fast. Surely it doesn't matter much? Did the trick, didn't it?'

Brad swung to face him and staggered. Steve grabbed him and eased him to the ground. Through all the turmoil of the last few minutes, one worry was still pounding in his head, his heart.

Steve stopped feeling the slightest amusement. 'Afraid we have another more important problem to deal with, Brad' His voice faltered. 'Jillian... she'd just landed at Davidson's airstrip. There was some bloke there pushing Ettie around. Her radio went dead and then I heard your trouble here.'

Brad stared up at Steve from a pain-filled face. 'Matthew told me John talked about some heavily tattooed guy being the driver who ran him down. See any on these two? Does this Billy Webster have tattoos?'

A sense of urgency gripped Steve. 'I don't know. Are you saying we still may have one and possibly two more out there somewhere?' he asked as he grabbed his radio transmitter. 'Neither of these two beauties has a tattoo between them.'

'I'd like to know just where that Scott bloke is this minute,' Brad said through gritted teeth.

Outback from Baragula

'I guess you were too busy trying to stop those guys to see that plane just before I got here.'

Brad shook his head. 'No, I saw it all right. At first thought it was going to try and land somewhere right here, then wondered if it was going to crash before it soared up and away.'

'It looked about the same as the Reed plane – although I only saw it before from a distance. I'm wondering if that Scott has pitched some yarn to Jillian and...'

Steve stopped. He stared towards the miserable, now trussed up duo on the ground leaning against the truck. He stiffened. 'Brad, did you see what's printed on that truck?'

'Yeah, mate, afraid I did when I first got here,' drawled Brad grimly, 'Jedburgh Station. I sure reckon that Scott Reed has a few more questions to answer.'

Fear filled Steve once more. 'I just hope and pray Jillian and Ettie are all right with some stranger chasing Ettie with a gun,' he said.

'Steve! You said nothing about a gun before!'

Steve nodded grimly. 'A gun she said. And we're so far away from that airstrip at Davidson Downs!'

Chapter nineteen

'Give me that! Get out of that 'copter!'

It had to be a dream. Jillian stared at the furious man who cursed her as he wrenched the radio microphone from her hand and flung it behind him.

'Get out I say!'

Two hands gripped her painfully and hauled her out of the helicopter. She landed in a dazed heap on the ground.

Ettie's angry voice cried out, 'You cowardly bully! Your mother must be *so* ashamed of you.'

Jillian shook her head to clear it and sat up.

'Shut your mouth old hag. My mother?' The man's voice rose hysterically. 'Don't talk about my mother. She never did anything for me. Just let my old man hit me whenever he wanted to!'

And this time Jillian recognised the frantic voice. 'Billy? Billy Webster?' she whispered.

Slowly she got to her feet. Not for a moment did she take her eyes off the man glaring at Ettie. Billy's face was working. His bearded, dirty and dishevelled features looked distraught, and suddenly she was terrified the gun he was waving from Ettie to herself would go off.

Several feet away, Ettie limped a couple of steps towards Jillian. 'You all right, love?' she called in a strong voice.

Billy screeched and pointed the gun arms length at Ettie. 'Get back or I'll use this!'

Defiantly Ettie took another step. The shaking of Billy's body scared Jillian more than anything.

'Do as he says, Ettie!'

To Jillian's relief, Ettie stopped dead. She put her hands on her hips and glared. Ettie opened her mouth again but Jillian spoke rapidly before she could infuriate the obviously unstable man anymore. 'Billy, what's the meaning of all this?'

His eyes and gun swung back to Jillian. To her dismay, out of the corner of her eye she saw Ettie take another couple of swift steps towards them. Ettie's eyes were fastened on something on the ground behind Billy. To Jillian's relief she paused. The man's eyes flashed back to Ettie for a brief moment before settling again on Jillian. Some emotion flashed through the dark eyes as they searched her face.

Jillian fought to control her own fear. She attempted a slight smile. 'Hello, Billy,' she managed and was proud that her voice only trembled a little. Surprise flashed across his face and she added quickly, 'I'm sorry I didn't recognise you. It's been a long time since we said hello.'

His expression changed again and Jillian knew she had said the wrong thing. The last time she and Billy had been face to face was that terrible night he had attacked her at Jedburgh.

'Yeah, like not knowing me makes you sorry. You didn't even remember my voice on the phone,' Billy sneered, 'and you didn't even wave to me in Gilgandra.'

'So that *was* you!' Jillian straightened. 'I couldn't be sure. You've changed so much of course I couldn't recognise you. And you probably won't believe me but it does make me very sorry.' Genuine regret flowed through her. Tears stung her eyes. 'Really sorry. We go back a long way, Billy. When we were kids we played together, did a lot of things together over the years.'

Until you went off the rails, Billy, and changed so much.

Impulsively she asked, 'What happened to us all, Billy? The Reeds and Davidson kids should have all grown up good friends with you.'

Billy studied her face. Surprise flashed in his eyes. His gun arm relaxed a little. A harsh laugh broke from him.

'Who are you trying to kid? You lot want to be friends with that no-good Webster kid? Even that Scott Reed proved that a few weeks back, saying he wasn't going to meet me in Sydney any more.'

Jillian frowned. However Scott was mixed up in this had to wait. 'We had some great times together,' she insisted, 'and you *were* a good kid until you went away to that boarding school with John and Scott.'

'But I could never compete with them, could I? "Why aren't you more like that Scott Reed? Why aren't you as good looking and smart as that John Davidson?" That's what my father used to growl and say to me every holidays until I couldn't stand them anymore – or him!'

Jillian stared at Billy in astonishment and pity. 'And then you got in with that rotten crowd,' she muttered, remembering things John had hinted back then about Billy Webster and drugs and gambling. 'Was that why you went away from Webster so much when we were at University?'

'University!' The word sounded like a curse, a cry of pain. 'You were all gone. Dad never forgave me for not getting good enough results to go too. I never even wanted to go on to do tertiary stuff, but he nagged and nagged. I would have been happy simply working on Webster, but he was never satisfied. I could never do anything right for him. The more he drank the more he belted me.'

His voice rose to a screech once more. A dirt-coated hand brushed across his eyes. 'I had to work from dawn to dark. Day after day. While you all lived the high life in Sydney.'

Jillian stood frozen. How could they never have known what was happening on Webster? A small voice inside her whispered, 'Because he's right. You never really did think of him as a friend. You had your sister. You had John. You even laughed about Billy Webster with John.'

Billy's voice dropped to a low murmur of pain. 'I was so lonely after you all deserted me. If it wasn't for Mum... He started hitting her too after awhile. I wanted to leave so many times but there was Mum. I had to be there for Mum, but in the end I failed at that too.' His voice started to rise. 'She wouldn't go with me! And then...'

Pity filled Jillian. 'Oh, Billy, why didn't you ever tell us? Dad would have helped and—' She stopped abruptly as Billy glared at her and raised his head.

'Help?' he sneered bitterly, 'yeah he helped by trying to buy Webster! And then when I ended up in... in jail, they forced Dad to sell out. You've stolen my land, my heritage!'

Horror swept through Jillian. 'In jail? Oh, Billy! But it's not true about Webster, Billy,' Jillian cried indignantly, 'your father stopped working the property and the bank was going to foreclose. Dad couldn't afford to buy it. Mr Reed paid your mother and father more than a fair price for the run-down station it had become. Didn't you notice how bad things are there? Even the homestead?'

Billy's eyes widened. 'The Reed's bought Webster? But that rotten Harding told me—'

There was a movement behind Billy. Jillian cried out, 'No!'

She was too late. As Billy started to swing around, the lump of wood in Ettie's hands clouted him over the head. Without a sound he fell to the ground.

Ettie swept the gun from his limp hand. 'That'll teach you to call me an old hag!' she screamed, plonked down on the ground and burst into tears. 'Oh, Lord! Please don't let me have killed him,' she sobbed hysterically.

For a horrible moment Jillian thought Ettie could have done just that. She shook with fear as she crouched down beside Billy's slumped body and felt for his pulse. It beat steadily. She stood up on shaking legs and stared down at the pitiful heap on the ground.

He was filthy, as though he'd been sleeping rough for days. His cheeks were hollow and he was very thin. Jillian's heart filled with shame and guilt that someone so close to her and John had suffered so much and they had never once suspected what he was going through.

A sob rose in her throat. 'Oh, Ettie,' she wailed, 'I do wish you hadn't done that. He's been hit and hurt enough. He was telling me... So much makes sense now.'

To her utter relief, Billy groaned and stirred.

Ettie was on her feet at once, the gun clutched in a trembling hand. 'Whatever he's told you he's still the same bloke who left your brother in the bush to die!'

Billy groaned again. They both heard him mutter, 'No... tried to stop Harding... went back to help John. Not there. And Harding dumped me after we saw you in Gilgandra. Had to walk... so far... not there. Came to warn you but *he* was there. You... you've always been kind to me. Had to tell you he's dangerous,' Billy groaned and held his head between his hands. 'Couldn't let you tell anyone I was here. Got to get away. Had to tell you... warn you 'bout *him*.'

At first the disjointed words didn't sink in or make any sense at all.

Guilt and pain for a life that had been damaged so badly right under their noses continued to sweep through Jillian. Tears stormed down her face.

She heard Ettie gasp, 'You came to tell us *what*?'

Jillian sucked in her breath. 'Billy? Billy, tell us. Who's dangerous? Where is he?'

Billy didn't respond to her frantic questions. He was unconscious once more.

Jillian raised her head. The two women stared at each other.

Ettie's face was full of horror. 'He was coming to warn you!' She rubbed a hand over her face and put her fingers on her lips for a moment. 'He crept up on me just after you flew off with Scott. Scared the life out of me. He... he was hysterical, looked so rough. He yelled at me. Wanted to know why you'd gone with Scott, where you were going. I was sure he must be one of those rustlers. I yelled and hit out at him. He went berserk, knocked me flying and pulled his gun on me. He took forever to calm down but still wouldn't talk to me. It was simply awful. He made me sit in the hangar until we heard you coming back. I... I ran, tried to warn you, but he...' Ettie choked.

Jillian swallowed hard. 'I think your attack on him might have brought back some bad memories, Ettie dear.'

She tried to bring her whirling thoughts under control. Never would she have thought she could feel sorry for Billy Webster as she did at that moment.

'Stay with him,' Jillian ordered, then sprang up from crouching beside Billy and climbed into the helicopter.

The radio was wrecked. Billy had ripped at it in his frenzy to stop her. Steve had said Brad had company at Webster homestead and Billy had risked everything to try and warn her. Was it about the 'company' at Webster? And now...

Jillian grabbed the bottle of water she always carried and swiftly rejoined Ettie. 'Your car still here?'

Ettie nodded.

'He's busted the radio in the 'copter. Brad and Steve are in trouble at Webster homestead and have been trying to reach you to get help.'

Ettie had pulled herself together. 'Where's that Scott Reed?' she asked sharply.

Jillian stared at her. 'You think it's Scott Billy was trying to warn us about?'

Ettie just stared back, her lips tight.

'I don't believe it,' muttered Jillian, 'and he did mention that other man in the car with him. What was the name... Harding? But Scott went back to Jedburgh to get their new... new B Double cattle transport. B Double!' She stopped dead and felt her suspicion of Scott start to rise once more. 'I've got to get out there!'

'And what about this bloke? And what's a B... whatever truck?'

'A very big one with two trailers, usually a small and a large and...'

Billy stirred and groaned. Jillian stared down at him. "We can't leave him here. We'll have to get him back to the house.'

'Back to the house?' Ettie's eyes were wide with fear. 'He needs a doctor too.'

'That will have to wait. I'm sure you couldn't have hit him that hard. He's so thin he's probably more exhausted and hungry than anything.' Jillian thought for a moment. 'We'll lock him in an old storage room in the old meat building. I don't think he'll be able to get out and you can check on him through a small window without opening the door.'

Ettie bit her lip and stared apprehensively down at the pathetic figure curled on his side in the dust.

Jillian touched Ettie on the shoulder and forced a smile. 'I'll stay with him while you bring the car as close as you can.'

Billy became conscious enough to be able to stand with their support and get into the small car. Several minutes later, Ettie insisted on carting some bedding from the house for a very subdued and pathetic Billy in his small prison, while Jillian raced to the office. The answering machine on the phone was flashing. It was the police in Dubbo.

The brisk voice said briefly, 'We will be on our way as soon as possible to pick up your injured friend and the men they've apprehended. Air Ambulance will be on way ASAP. They're worried about you there at the homestead. Please ring us as soon as you get this.'

All Jillian heard were the words 'injured friend.'

Steve was hurt! Bad enough to send the emergency services into immediate action!

She started for the door.

The radio started to hum. Scott Reed's controlled voice called, 'Mayday, mayday. Emergency landing attempt west of...' A voice in the background starting cursing, almost drowning out Scott's voice. It rose to a shout. 'Mayday. We're going down. Position west of...'

The radio went dead.

Shock upon shock kept Jillian frozen for a full minute. Steve hurt. Scott... What was he doing in the plane? By now he should be on the way to Webster in Jedburgh's truck.

Jillian turned and fled. She was nearly to Ettie's car when Jillian heard her voice frantically calling her. She looked blindly at the woman running towards her.

'Jillian! Whatever is it?'

'Steve's hurt and... and Scott... Got to get there.'

Ettie beat her to the driver's seat. Jillian somehow managed to tell her what she had just heard. Ettie put her foot down and they made it to the airstrip in record time.

As Jillian swung her door open, Ettie grasped her arm. 'Now, love,' she said soothingly, 'calm down so you can get yourself safely in the air. Just remember whatever has happened to either Steve or Scott they both are God's children and their Father has them under His control. And I'll be praying for you all.'

Jillian stared at her numbly for a brief moment and then stumbled to the helicopter. Fuel. She turned back to Ettie. 'I'll need your help to refuel.'

With two of them it still took time she hated. Her hands trembled as she at last started the engine. She looked out at Ettie standing beside her car. Her head was bowed.

Jillian closed her own eyes as she waited for the motor to warm up, the rotor blades to pick up speed ready to lift off. Disjointed words burst from deep within her heart.

'Oh, God, keep him safe. All of us. Please. Help me,' she gasped finally and opened her eyes.

She automatically studied gauges and controls in the cabin as she had done so many times before.

'I'm choosing to trust You, God!'

Slowly Jillian's hands stopped shaking. Taking a deep breath she looked out once more at Ettie and returned her wave. To return Ettie's smile was still beyond Jillian. She took another deep breath and forced herself to concentrate on her take off.

When at last the whirling blades had lifted her into the air, Jillian was tense but her shaking had completely disappeared. She set her course towards Webster once more. Something touched her knee and she looked down. Only when she saw the wires swinging did she remember that in her initial panic she had not phoned the police back or tried to get Steve on his radio.

Jillian gritted her teeth. No matter she didn't have the radio to support her. She had to get to Webster. To Steve.

'Oh, God, please let him be all right!'

―――

Steve only realised how hard he had been listening for Jillian when he heard the first faint thump of the helicopter. The thump increased rapidly to a roar. A deep sigh of heartfelt relief escaped him when the small helicopter soared overhead. Jillian came down so fast his heart was in his mouth. The helicopter landed in the clearing. It wasn't far from where Steve had managed, despite the flat tyres, to manoeuvre the truck several metres back against the loading ramp to unload the cattle.

The huge rotor blades whipped up the dirt into a heavy cloud.

Brad had been lying down in the truck cabin. Steve started towards the helicopter just as Brad yelled something that was lost in the roar of the engine. Steve turned his back and tried to shield his face from the stinging cloud of dirt that whipped at his hair, his clothes. When it eased a little, he could still hardly see the helicopter. And then Jillian appeared out of the thick dust cloud and raced towards him.

'Steve, Oh Steve, I thought they said you were hurt. You're okay. God's kept you safe!'

And then his arms were full of a trembling woman who clung to him. Her hands moved rapidly over his back, his face, as she leaned back and searched his eyes, making sure he was uninjured.

'Me! You were the one who had a man with a gun coming for you,' Steve tried to say, but his voice choked up.

Warm, alive lips touched his cheek, his forehead and then settled on his lips and he drank deeply.

They clung together until a voice roared, 'Break it up you two. Time for that later.'

They lifted their heads and turned towards Brad yelling at them from the open door of the truck. Steve wondered if his face looked as dazed as Jillian's.

'Brad? It's Brad who's hurt?'

'A bullet in his calf muscle. We don't think it's too deep.'

Outback from Baragula

Steve filled his lungs with air. *What had that kiss been all about?* He tried to think rationally. 'A spent bullet off the tank. He's pretty sore but will be okay once they've dug it out.'

Jillian's hands left him. Her shoulders slumped. Embarrassment filled her eyes before she looked down. 'They said "my friend". I'm sorry. I didn't even think it might be Brad who was hurt.'

'Forget Brad!' Steve burst out. His hands gripped her arms as she took a step back. 'What happened to you?'

To his horror, tears filled her eyes.

'Not Ettie,' he groaned.

'No, no! Everything's fine now. It was Billy. He... and now Scott's sent out a mayday. I think he's crashed somewhere!'

Horror whelmed up in Steve. 'Billy and Scott... they—'

Brad yelled at them again.

Steve found his voice with difficulty. 'We'd better join him and you can tell us everything just the once.'

As they hurried over to Brad, Jillian saw the men, tied up in the shade of the truck.

'Steve!'

He followed her appalled gaze. 'And that they are there so nicely trussed up waiting for the police to arrive is thanks to your Eddie. But let's hear what's happened to you first,' he added swiftly as they joined Brad.

When Jillian finished her account of the events with Billy Webster, both men stared at her and then at each other. Both men spoke at once in awed voices.

'*Ettie* hit him so hard she knocked Billy Webster out?'

'My old Sunday School teacher attacked someone?'

Brief amusement flickered in Jillian's eyes. She nodded and added haughtily, 'We women coped very well capturing one of our cattle rustlers, thank you.'

'Ettie didn't by any chance call Billy Webster a rustler in front of him, did she?' Brad asked in a faint voice.

Jillian nodded. 'From what I can gather a lot more while they were waiting for me. She... she thinks it's why he was so angry when I arrived. She was dreadfully upset at the thought.'

Her composure cracked. She clasped her hands together. Steve saw them starting to shake and immediately covered them with his own hands. Every hint of laughter had fled from her face.

"She called him that again as we were getting him to the storage shed and also that she thanked God He'd not let her kill Billy.' Jillian shuddered. 'It was all pretty dreadful. For one awful moment I thought she might have done just that. Fortunately the old piece of wood she'd found near the helicopter was so rotten *it* broke instead of Billy's head. He... he made me so sad. Billy's changed so much. He's really very pathetic, looks so much older than any of us and he's nearly the same age.'

They were all silent for a moment.

Brad's pale face was stern. 'Well, I'm afraid his looks won't improve where he's going when the police and the judge have finished with him after this last stint of his.'

Jillian bit her lip and studied Brad.

Steve tensed. Knowing her, he suddenly had an idea what she was going to say. Something about letting her childhood friend get away with what he had done. Steve straightened. Brad was in no mood or fit state to listen to any pleas for Billy Webster.

'A plane flew over just before the excitement here started,' he said swiftly, 'we thought it was going to crash for a moment but then it climbed sharply and headed west. Jillian, you said you had a "mayday" from Scott. Could that plane have been his?'

Brad sat up.

Jillian stared at Steve. 'I don't know. Probably. It's most unlikely any other planes would be around here today. But what was he doing still flying?'

Brad echoed Steve's own thoughts. 'And do you think now, despite all Billy told you, that Scott may still be involved in all this somehow?'

Jillian shook her head. There was no hesitation in her voice. 'No he's not. He can't be. Scott told me he would bring his truck to load the cattle from the yards here and get them out in case the place flooded. But I can't understand why he was still in the air at all and who that other man could have been. Unless... unless it was someone who cursed and yelled a lot.'

Her eyes widened. 'Surely it couldn't have been that Harding man Billy was raving on about could it? If Billy had to warn us, surely it means he thinks Harding is still in the area somewhere? But why would he be with Scott?'

Despite her words, Steve saw the doubt about Scott start to dawn in her eyes. He caught Brad's eye. 'The guy with the tattoos that John told us about?'

Brad shrugged. 'Could be.' He tried to ease his position on the truck seat and gasped with pain.

Steve hoped medical assistance was not far away. Brad had lost a fair bit of blood.

Brad brushed aside their concerned offers of help. 'Well, why is he in his plane with that bloke if Reed is so innocent?" he said tersely. 'According to what he told Jillian he's supposed to be arriving here any minute with his truck – which seems to already be here!' He paused and then looked thoughtful. 'Unless... Jillian, do you know if Jedburgh has more than one truck?'

'Mr Reed did mention when they bought Webster they would need another one, but I haven't heard they've actually got one yet. Why?'

'You didn't notice the name on the side of this one?'

Jillian stared at Brad and then stepped back to look at the outside of the open door. Her face went white. She looked at Steve. 'I've... I've never seen this one before. I didn't even know they intended to have their name...' She bit down on her lip.

'So Scott could have been going back for this one or, knowing that this was already in use here, going back for the other one to clear out the rest of the cattle.' Brad nodded towards the animals milling around the huge yards several metres behind them. 'Or Reed could have been simply lying to you.'

'No!' Jillian raised her chin. 'He knew I was intending to come here straight away. And except for Billy, I would have been here by the time he should have arrived. What I can't understand is why he was still flying his plane! How long ago did he fly over?'

When they told her, she looked bewildered. 'But he couldn't have had time to refuel! Normally he'd have topped the plane up before he flew back but he wanted to get to Jedburgh to try and get their truck here as quickly as possible because of the flood waters creeping closer.'

'Eddie reckons it's slowed right down, even stopped.'

Brad scowled at Steve and looked sceptical, but Jillian smiled shakily and looked very relieved. 'Great! Eddie would know. Clear skies all around the mountains did make me hope. So that's one worry less.'

The smile disappeared. Jillian's lips trembled. 'I still don't believe

Scott had anything to do with the cattle,' she insisted stubbornly. 'He told me heaps of stuff when he flew me to get the helicopter.'

Several things she'd said suddenly made sense. Steve's heart nearly failed him. '*He* flew you to Williamtown?' he roared. 'How could you get into a plane with him after all that's happened?'

Jillian's eyes flashed. Angry colour flooded her face. 'Don't you yell at me, Steve Honeysuckle! I got in that plane the same way you're going to get into that helicopter with me right now and be my spotter.'

Speechless, Steve stared at her.

Brad snorted.

Jillian glared at them both. She put her hands on her hips and turned belligerently to Steve. 'Well? I can't do it properly or fast enough by myself! We've got a pilot, a *friend* that gave a call he was crashing somewhere west of here and we've got to try and find him. There's no guarantee anyone else heard his call. Can't you trust God like I've had to, Steve Honeysuckle, praying I was doing the right thing and to keep me and you safe?' By the time she'd finished she was yelling at them both.

Steve swallowed. The thought of even watching this woman he loved flying that infernal machine so far above the earth filled him with horror. And she wanted *him* to fly with her as well? Look over the side and search for a plane that may not have crashed, for a possible criminal who had conned her into believing him?

'Steve, I know your phobia. I saw evidence only too well when you came down that windmill and I'll never forget your face – or your quoting of the Bible.' Jillian took a couple of steps closer to him. Her eyes pleaded with him for understanding.

'We've got to try and find Scott. There was someone else in that plane with him, someone who turned the air-waves blue with his swearing. Billy became conscious enough to tell me that he reckoned that man he called Harding would try and steal a vehicle and try to get out of the district. What if he was waiting at Jedburgh and forced Scott to fly him here the same as Billy was going to force me to get him away. He told me he met this Harding bloke in prison. I'm betting he was the one who worked out the whole scheme. I'm sure Billy's not really a criminal type. I'm guessing he simply got caught up in it all and was used by this horrible man simply because Billy desperately needed three things enough to go along with it all.'

When Steve still didn't speak, she opened her mouth but it was Brad

Outback from Baragula

who said quietly, 'Revenge, money and self-esteem?'

Jillian nodded. Slow tears started to trickle down her cheeks. She scrubbed at them impatiently. 'He was so pathetic,' she cried desperately, 'he's all screwed up but he's suffered so much and we – none of us – cared about him enough, weren't there when he needed help. And John and I haven't even been there for Scott either! What kind of friends, people, are we? And now, don't you understand? I've just *got* to help them!'

Jillian paused and scowled at Steve accusingly. 'And now, despite all your words, it doesn't seem you have enough faith in the God you've talked so much about after all. Don't you believe He'll get you through a flight with me in a helicopter I've been flying for years without an incident?'

Steve realised she had not told him everything Billy Webster and Scott Reed must have told her. And whatever had been said had changed the angry, revengeful Jillian of that morning to this distraught one who was challenging him to exercise faith in the God he professed to believe in.

He had no choice.

Swiftly Steve took the couple of paces that separated him from this woman he loved more each moment for her courage, her caring and her undoubted stirrings of belief in God. He grabbed her gesticulating, pleading hands.

'Let's go, Jillie dear,' he said firmly, hoping she could not feel the tremors he could not control in his hands. He just hoped his legs would not shake too much to stop him climbing into her helicopter. 'We're wasting precious daylight time.'

Chapter twenty

Only when Steve actually had climbed into the seat beside her, did Jillian really believe he would go through with it.

Admiration flooded her. She had seen him on that windmill, knew how heights affected him. Despite his efforts at appearing cool and in control, his face had lost colour as he strode to the helicopter beside her. She saw his hands shake as he fumbled for the seat belt. And she had also seen her sister-in-law's panic that time she had flown her to the hospital last year over the raging flood waters in the Hunter Valley. Memory of that trip gave her an idea.

Jillian handed Steve his radio headset and said cheerfully, 'Just be thankful it's not summer yet and hot enough to take off the doors on this bird.'

Steve stared at her in horror and she bit her lip at adding to his fear of flying in a helicopter. Jillian busied herself starting her checks, very conscious of the rigid figure beside her and knew she had to do something. She started to fling a string of instructions out to keep Steve busy. Hopefully it would help take his mind off the fact that he would soon be soaring hundreds of feet over the solid earth he liked his two feet firmly planted on.

'There's a bag on the floor under your seat. I'll need the navigational maps in it. Hold it on your knees for me. First, are your ears on so we can talk? And don't forget that seat belt.'

Jillian started the motor as he fumbled to put on his set of headphones and then bent down to find her briefcase. Above the increasing roar, she yelled, 'Can you hear me?'

Steve turned his strained face towards her. He didn't speak and she repeated her question. Relief swept through her as he nodded jerkily. For one awful moment she had thought Billy's panic and fear had also damaged the headphones and they would have to do without internal communication as well as make do with one of the portable UHF radios she had grabbed from Steve. She just hoped the radio's range would be strong enough for whatever they would need it for.

'Okay, get those couple of maps out and spread them across your knees.' She didn't add *and they will also hide the ground a bit more as it gets further away*. The cockpit was surrounded by a bubble of glass to their feet that made it easier to muster cattle – and to search for downed planes – but it wouldn't help anyone with acrophobia.

'Now Steve, you'd better promise you won't tell Brad whatever you do. I neglected to mention to him we are quite illegal taking off without a flight plan to central control. He also doesn't know the helicopter radio is out of order and no long distance radio to air traffic control means we shouldn't be doing this. We'll fly low and hopefully there won't be too many aircraft crowding our space right out here.'

That did earn her a faint smile to replace his stunned look at the damaged radio near her knee.

'Now, spread those maps right out. That's better. Now, see if you can find Quambone and Bourke on it. As you know we're somewhere between the two towns. Quambone's west of Coonamble. The Mitchell Highway running north-west between Bourke and Nyngan would also be handy. We may fly over it.'

Jillian thought it wasn't necessary to mention she had flown west from here several times over the years and already knew what landmarks to watch out for. In fact, if Steve was allowed to by his companion she'd heard in the plane, he'd try to follow the highway and well known landmarks. As soon as the maps hid more of the bottom of the cabin and Steve was focused on his search, she set the helicopter straight up as smoothly as she could. Her old flight instructor would have been very proud of her.

While still concentrating on her flying skills, Jillian kept plying Steve with urgent instructions to pin-point just where they were at

Webster on the map, where they had to go, what landmarks like waterways and homesteads they might fly over. She got him to call out the already familiar ones she knew to look for, to guide her. In between she kept up a barrage of comments and instructions. She needed a pair of gloves that had conveniently fallen between their seats. There was a bottle of water behind him she needed to quench her thirst. She needed the chewing gum in her bag.

At last she ran out of things for him to do and Steve folded the maps into smaller units and sat up. Out of the corner of her eye Jillian saw him stiffen as he realised they were already far above the ground and heading out.

'Look straight out to the horizon, Steve,' she yelled.

But he was already doing that. At her comment he nodded but then closed his eyes tightly. Jillian's heart sank. What help would he be if he couldn't even keep his eyes open. Then Steve's lips moved silently.

Jillian knew what he was doing and said her own brief prayer under her breath and then muttered out loud, 'Okay, Brad, I know you were rather embarrassed even while you said it, but I sure hope you're praying with Steve and me right now like you promised you would, mate!'

Steve must have heard. He turned his head towards her. His face was a sickly white. Panic still flared in his eyes but his lips shaped in the semblance of a smile. 'I feel such a fool. So stupid.'

She hardly heard the choked words but beamed back at him. 'Never! I see a very brave man facing a phobia head on.'

Surprise flashed across his face. He swallowed and looked away.

'Keep looking at me, Steve. Keep trusting me – and God to answer our prayers.'

While I try not to reveal how your looking at me makes me self-conscious, aware of you in ways I probably shouldn't be while I'm trying to fly this bird!

To Jillian's relief, Steve kept his head turned towards her. What else could she say to take his mind off just where he was at that moment? She went with the question that had been eating at her.

'So, Steve Honeysuckle, what's all this stuff Ettie Cobby has been trying to tell me about why you keep saying you're sorry after you kiss me? Although,' she added reflectively, 'I must confess I haven't heard one yet for that last humdinger!'

Jillian glanced at him again and immediately looked away. To her utter relief his attention was caught. As he stared at her, a touch of colour brightened his cheeks. Jillian didn't wait for him to answer but ploughed ahead.

'Ettie tried to tell me she's convinced you're scared of any kind of in-depth relationship with me because I'm not a Christian like you are. I hope she's wrong because it sure made me feel as though you don't think I'm good enough for Steve Honeysuckle.'

'Not good enough? What utter rubbish! You're the most wonderful woman I've ever met.'

Good. She had really caught his attention now. And his anger, if she was any judge.

Then she realised what he'd just said and gulped. *The most wonderful...*

She forced her mind — and heart — back to his phobia problem, even managed a smile. 'I'm real glad you think that, but it hasn't stopped you pulling away from me like you're scared stiff we might get involved. Ettie said you've good reason to be like you are but I'd like to hear any excuse you might have, Mr Honeysuckle, Sir.'

'It wasn't only—' The word was cut off by a gasp as the helicopter hit a mild air pocket.

'I'm afraid these contraptions are not only noisy but more at the mercy of air currents,' she apologised matter of factly. In the same breath Jillian let herself sound cross with him when all she wanted to do was wrap her arms around him and assure him he was quite safe. 'And if I'm so wonderful, why don't you relax just a bit more? I've been flying this bird for years!'

Jillian was beginning to wonder if Steve would be able to control his fear of heights soon enough so she could dare ask him to look around at the landscape and help her search for a plane on the ground; hopefully an intact one that had only made a forced landing somewhere on the vast plains below them.

She rushed on with the topic that had taken his attention before. 'And if it wasn't only my spiritual state not reaching your standards, Steve Honeysuckle, what other obstacles are there to. . . to kissing me, might I ask?' Memories of sleepless nights, of tears shed over this man made her anger start to rise and put a real bite in her voice.

His answer was not at all what she expected.

'*Are* you a Christian, Jillian Davidson?'

Steve knew only too well what Jillian was trying to do. Matthew had told him once how Jillian had used her sharp-shooting comments to distract Emily from her fears in the helicopter. And as with Emily, Jillian was succeeding with him. But there was still a long way to travel and what better time to ask the vital question he had long wanted to ask her?

Angry colour flooded Jillian's face. 'That's a very personal question!' she snapped.

'But if your being a Christian or not has any bearing on any future relationship between us, don't I have the right to ask it?'

'And you didn't answer my question,' she came back at him. 'What other obstacles besides my spiritual state do you perceive?'

Steve swallowed, remembering how systematically those obstacles were being wiped out and commented, 'You mean besides my fear of heights and you mustering cattle with a helicopter?'

She grinned. 'I think we're sorting that one out right now.'

He managed a rather shaky smile. 'Well, I'm a mountain farmer and you're used to these flat, outback plains.'

The glance she flung at him was derisive, as was the tilt of her well shaped nose. "I love the mountains more than you can know and I especially loved yours on and around Honeysuckle and Baragula. Sure, I'd miss my own home and would always want to visit, but that's perfectly normal, isn't it?'

His heart leapt. Jillian wouldn't mind living at Honeysuckle?

Then she added sharply, 'Who says it would be essential to live at Honeysuckle? Your father may even have his own ideas about that. From what Matthew's said about him courting Emily's Aunt Barbara, it's more than likely. Anyway, that's a very minor point to my mind!'

She turned and glared at him. 'Any couple from different backgrounds have to make compromises. The important thing is we both like farming, the outdoor life. Would *you* mind starting out fresh somewhere else – perhaps half-way between both properties?'

Steve thought about that. It made sense. 'Certainly worth thinking about.'

Jillian flung him another mocking glance. 'Okay, one problem solved. Is that all? Or are there more excuses? Perhaps you simply don't love... like me enough.'

Steve stared. Colour flooded Jillian's face at her boldness. He sure wanted her to be truthful and not just trying to take his mind off his phobia with shock tactics. Hope took a great leap and his heart lightened. It took him a moment before he could answer.

'Well, there *was* the one where you were rich and I was poor.'

'You thought...! You snob! I think we've sorted that one out, or we had better by now.'

The glare Jillian shot Steve's way was not in the least friendly and he saw deep hurt in her eyes that, to his horror, were too bright. Surely she wasn't about to cry! While flying this machine so far above...

He gulped. 'I'm really sorry, Jillian.'

'And so you should be,' she snarled.

Jillian's face was bright red now and the look she directed his way should have scalded him. He must have been mistaken about any glistening moisture in her eyes.

'I've never heard so much rubbish!' she said in a shaky voice.

Steve knew that indeed he had hurt this brave woman he'd acknowledged before God he had fallen in love with – even though he had no idea where it all could go.

Jillian wasn't finished with him. Her voice no longer shook as she snarled, 'Now, if you can exercise just a little bit more of that faith you want *me* to have, how about you help me start searching the ground for Scott's plane. And this conversation is by no means over. For your information, at this moment I'm probably exercising more faith than you are!'

Despite the angry words, there was still something, a touch of vulnerability, of shyness, of deep hurt on the angry face she swung briefly towards him again. Steve's heart ached. Her eyes were definitely moist this time and suddenly he believed her. Something had been happening to his Jillian these last few days.

His Jillian?

Oh, Lord, Lord, is this really happening? Are you giving us to each other?

Steve realised Jillian was speaking again. He forced himself to concentrate on her words and not that beautifully shaped mouth that he so many times had wanted to drink deeply from and feel the yielding warmth.

Full of exasperation, her voice yelled in his ears, 'Are you listening to me, Steve Honeysuckle?'

Outback from Baragula

'Sorry... I... what were you saying?'

She glared at him and he was thankful when she looked away, her gaze searching the ground.

'My calculations indicate that from the time you think it was when the plane flew over and headed in this direction to when I heard Scott's mayday call, we should be almost in the area he could have gone down.'

'That is,' she added grimly, 'if he kept flying directly west. He could even have been trying to make Bourke airport. I'm going to maintain this height while we have a general look around and then I'll go lower. Are you going to be okay?' She shot a look at him and Steve saw the worry for him on her face.

Steve took a breath, a very deep breath. *God, give me the strength.*

He looked out towards the horizon. Very slowly he lowered his eyes to scan the ground and braced himself to control that sickening sensation of falling. It didn't come. He looked further down, right through the bubble glass that disappeared just before the floor plate they had their feet on.

'The sun could reflect off any metal on the ground, but it's also coming off large patches of water as well,' Jillian called crisply after a brief glance at him.

He smiled at her and gave her a thumbs up sign. Relief chased her worried frown away and she beamed back at him. Trouble was, she looked at him a fraction too long and the helicopter tilted.

'You just fly this thing safely and I'll do the looking,' Steve roared in fright.

She pulled a face and muttered something that sounded suspiciously like, 'Not completely okay' and then said loudly, 'I tried to see on the map if there were any homesteads in this area that may have an airstrip or paddock Scott would make for, but the only thing I could see were a couple of tracks. It's very flat out here and more isolated than back home. We're also closer to the main rivers and if they're in flood a lot of the ground will be treacherous for any attempted landing.'

They continued to search for what seemed like hours to Steve. He was amazed how little time had really passed when Jillian banked the helicopter higher and exclaimed, 'Although I've only been out this far west a few times, we flew over the highway before so I'm pretty sure that wide river must be the Darling. This is really "back of Bourke" country now.'

Steve thought he heard her mutter, 'And now is the time with the radio working I'd have been able to contact Bourke air-traffic control.'

Jillian sounded worried. Hopefully she *did* know where they were or they too could get lost in this vast, sparsely populated land. Not a good prospect without a longer distance radio set-up!

She didn't speak for several moments. 'I think we'd better circle back towards Bourke. Perhaps Scott's gone down near there.'

The outback. Steve stared down in wonder at the vast, red plains that stretched out below them. It made the area around Davidson Downs look quite heavily timbered and grassed.

Something flashed back a streak of light.

'Down there! Is it water or metal the sun's shining off?' Steve yelled.

Jillian made a tight turn and swooped lower. They both saw it at the same time. It was the plane. Steve caught his breath. It was tilted on one badly crumpled wing and the nose crushed into the ground.

Steve's heart sank. Could anyone have survived? Even as the thought flashed into his mind, Jillian gave a shout as they quickly descended. Someone was lying a few feet from the plane.

'Can you see if it's Scott?' Jillian called frantically.

Steve was concentrating so hard on that lonely, sprawled figure he gave no thought to the ground coming up swiftly beneath them. 'Yes, it is,' he exclaimed with relief, 'and he's waving. But he must be hurt or he'd be coming to meet us.'

'Be careful, Jillian,' Steve called after they landed and she jumped from the helicopter and started to run. 'Remember you thought he wasn't alone. That Harding bloke could be here too.'

But no one else made an appearance as they reached Scott. He slowly forced himself to sit up a little and smiled faintly from a dazed and heavily blood-streaked face. 'Am I glad to see you guys,' he said in a faint voice and promptly fell back again with a low moan.

While Jillian raised his head and gave him a drink of water, Steve examined him. Scott's face and arms were covered in cuts and bruises. One ankle and knee were badly swollen but Steve doubted they were broken. Blood still trickled from a nasty wound on his head, but everything taken into consideration, Scott Reed had been very fortunate. They gave him what first aid they could from the small box Jillian had grabbed from the helicopter.

Despite Jillian's confidence in her old friend, Steve still was not con-

Outback from Baragula

vinced he had played no part in this whole sorry mess. As he worked to stop the bleeding, his voice was terse. 'Were you unconscious at all?'

Scott nodded. 'The last thing I remember is the machine being flung around just as I touched down. The wheels hit something I didn't see in time.'

Jillian straightened and looked at the skid marks that scarred the very uneven, red ground for some metres.

'Are you trying to tell me you tried to land the plane on this?' She looked puzzled. 'And I'm sure I heard someone else in the plane when you sent your mayday. Why didn't you radio sooner and give your position? Where's your passenger? Is he badly hurt?'

'That idiot!' Scott's voice rose and he raised his head. 'He just wouldn't believe we were out of fuel. Until the motor cut out, thought I was trying to make him let me land and then it was too late. When I came to, he'd gone.'

'Gone!' Steve and Jillian had exclaimed together and Scott added grimly, 'I was still tangled up in the wreckage. Had a ghastly time freeing myself. Just as well there was no fuel left to catch alight. He'd disappeared and didn't even pull me from the wreck.' Obviously exhausted, Scott let his head fall back.

Jillian looked swiftly at Steve and put into words his own thoughts. 'Perhaps he thought you'd been killed.'

Steve nodded grimly. 'And if he is who we think he is, perhaps you should be thankful he thought that.'

Anger once again swept over the pale, blood-stained face. 'If you mean the man responsible for stealing the Davidson's cattle, running John into a tree and then leaving him to die, you're right. Joe Harding *is* responsible. He even boasted about it!'

Scott gestured to the water bottle again. His voice was husky with pain when he continued after a couple of swallows. 'And Billy Webster was in on it too. Harding used Billy's hatred and knowledge of the area to help him. Even got Billy to introduce him to me! And then dumped Billy completely when he apparently turned chicken over John being hurt. Was furious he'd stolen Harding's old car one night and defied him to drive back the next day to apparently get John medical help. Boasted how he caught him and kicked Billy out of the car in the middle of nowhere. We've got to find Billy.'

Jillian and Steve looked at each other. That explained the other tyre marks in the clearing.

Steve shook his head at her. They could tell Scott their story another time and how Billy must have walked a long way to Davidson Downs to warn her. They had more to worry about now.

'You knew Joe Harding?'

Steve's question was sharp and Scott stared defensively back at him.

'I met him in Sydney. A couple of months ago Dad gave him a job when I wasn't home. He claimed I'd told him there was a job for him at Jedburgh. I didn't say anything because I didn't want Dad to know...' Scott closed his eyes again for a long moment and then looked pleadingly towards Jillian. 'Harding only worked for us a few days on Jedburgh before it became obvious he had lied through his teeth about having worked with cattle before, or on any property for that. To my utter relief Dad fired him before I had to say anything to get rid of him.'

The disgust and regret on Scott's face was unmistakable. 'He'd also pitched Dad some yarn about being a friend of Billy Webster. Knowing a little of what Billy's been mixed up with in recent years, I know now I should have warned Dad at once but I... I let it go. Besides, I couldn't tell them it was Billy who...' He broke off and stared helplessly from Jillian to Steve.

'It was Billy who introduced you to gambling?'

Surprise and dismay filled Scott's face at Jillian's grim question. 'How did...?' He stopped and closed his eyes once more as if to shut out her face. 'Yeah, it was Billy who took me with him once to the Casino, but after... Matthew's been helping me,' he muttered at last in a dazed voice.

'Matthew? What's he got to do with...' Steve stopped, remembering what Ettie had said about an old friend of Matthew's becoming a Christian.

Scott was silent. At last he opened his eyes and looked at Jillian pleadingly. 'Matthew *did* lend me money to repay all my gambling debts.'

Steve saw the swift glance Jillian sent his way. She didn't look surprised. Scott must have told her before. For her this was more proof her old friend had been foolish but innocent of anything else. Not enough for Steve, though! There were still unanswered questions.

Scott paused and frowned. 'But Jillian, how did you know about Billy?'

Outback from Baragula

'How do I know? Billy told me himself a few hours ago.'

Alarm flooded Scott's face. 'Billy told you? Where—'

Steve interrupted. 'A long story. We'd better sort you out for now and get out word about this Harding bloke.'

Scott stared at him. Once again he struggled to sit up. Steve reached out and supported him when he swayed and gave a stifled groan. 'Take it easy, mate. You must have a ferocious headache. Close your eyes again and lean against me for a few minutes and then we'll try getting you to the helicopter.'

Jillian stood up. She surveyed the plane, the surrounding ground and frowned. 'You sure picked a pretty bad place to put her down, Scott. What happened?'

'I told you. No fuel left, no choice.'

'You took off without refuelling!'

Scott gave a harsh laugh and then grimaced in pain. 'Didn't have much of a choice with a gun stuck in my back.'

'He forced you?'

Scott stared at Steve. 'Of course he... You think I was helping him get away!' His voice rose in anger.

Steve thought back to when the plane had flown over them. He and Brad had both agreed Scott must have seen them and changed his mind about joining his comrades in crime. Neither had realised there were two men in the plane.

'According to Harding he was some distance away from Jedburgh when he watched me fly off to pick you up, Jillian. From what he said, he'd been keeping an ear on our radio and an eye on our movements ever since he and Billy got their heads together when Billy found out...' Scott paused. He shut his eyes and once more swallowed several times.

Jillian looked at him with a worried frown. 'Perhaps you'd better tell us the rest later after we get you to—'

'No! I might go unconscious again and it's been killing me knowing...' Scott stared up at her, his face working with regret. He looked away before saying, 'I met Billy in Sydney but Harding was with him. Had to pay off those debts with all the money I had. But it wasn't enough. They got really ugly. That's why Matthew...'

Scott stopped and glanced defiantly at Steve. 'Anyway that's when I mentioned to Billy you and John would be off to the big smoke to get that place ready for your parents' return. According to Harding that was just the information he was waiting for. We were even obliging enough to buy our B Double transport truck in Coonamble a couple of weeks back and leave it there for repairs and some paint work. He boasted at how trusting the old geezer there was to believe Harding's story about us sending him in to pick up the truck. A couple of his mates drove it to Webster. I was furious when I saw it there.'

Steve grimly remembered the erratic behaviour of the plane as it flew past. At last he too was convinced Scott was telling them the truth. Relief filled him for Jillian's sake.

Scott gestured towards the water bottle again. He gulped a few mouthfuls and, despite their protests, continued rapidly with his story.

'After what happened to John, Harding knew they had to move faster and get as many cattle out as they could. He went to Jedburgh to get our other truck. Seemed surprised I was still around at all. Had been listening to our radio and knew I was off checking the flood waters and Mum and Dad away. After I flew off to pick Jillian up he drove to our house to grab the keys to our other transport. Apparently decided while he was there to try and listen into the radio to see if there were any reports. Heard you and Brad and knew his friends had been spotted.

'Then he heard me coming back and decided I was his passage out. He was almost hysterical with fury at the thwarting of his careful schemes. After John saw them, his original plan had been for one of them to get on his way with the big load while the other guy stayed to help him load the second smaller truck. Instead, he radioed his mates at Webster to tell them we were onto them, make do with what they'd loaded and to get out of there. He was going to drive his car and join up with them further north.'

Steve's eyes narrowed. 'So that's the reason they spotted Brad so quickly. They were watching for him!'

Scott never paused. The words poured out. 'When I returned, Harding decided flying would be better than driving, give him a better chance to get right away. Wanted me to drop him off up north somewhere his mates could pick him up. He insisted we fly over Webster to check they'd got away. When he saw the truck still there and you and Brad, he went berserk!' Scott groaned and grabbed his head.

'That's enough!' Jillian glared from Steve to Scott. 'Anymore can wait until I've got Scott to a doctor. He's probably got concussion as well as a couple of busted ribs. I've already told you Scott's our friend. Surely you don't need anymore convincing.'

Steve nodded curtly. 'No, I don't.' He looked at the distance back to the helicopter and studied Scott doubtfully. 'Think you can hobble that far with our help, or do we have to carry you?'

Scott gritted his teeth. 'Let's give walking a go.'

It took a long time. Scott was almost a dead weight, only able to swing on one leg with all his weight on Jillian and Steve. By the time they reached the helicopter, Steve and Jillian were breathless. Scott was barely conscious.

When he caught his breath, Steve gasped, 'At least I don't have to gear myself up for take-off.'

Jillian stared at him with concern. Without speaking, both had known she could only take one passenger and she nodded. 'Steve, I can't even be sure I'll make it back here before dark. It could be morning before...'

'Jillie dear, I'll be fine.' He smiled gently at her. 'Just make sure you know exactly where we are here so you can find me again.'

She stared at him. Her face softened. 'That's one thing you can be sure of. I'll never lose you again, Steve Honeysuckle. And we both have the Creator of the universe watching out for us.'

Steve thought about those words as he waved the helicopter off and watched until it disappeared. He thought about them as the sun sank low in the west and at last dropped behind the horizon.

What had she really meant? Was Jillian still hung up on God being too Almighty to be really concerned about what happened to individuals? Steve sighed and poured out his heart to the One who had been there from the very beginning of creation: the Word made flesh, Jesus.

Oh God, thank You that Jillian does seem to be reaching out to You. But help her, help me, to understand more and more about our personal relationship with You through Your Son.

For the first time Steve let his heart have free rein as he dwelt on the beautiful, courageous woman who had sparked his interest from their very first meeting. The burden was lifted. They were both in God's hands.

And it had been Jillian who had reminded him.

Chapter twenty-one

As soon as Steve had run well back from the helicopter, Jillian took no time lifting off. She headed directly south-east to Davidson Downs.

She had heard a groan from Scott in her ears as she took off. As soon as she could, she glanced at him and yelled, 'How are you holding up, Scott?'

There was no answer. Scott didn't move. His headset was still in place but his head was slumped onto his shoulder.

'Right,' Jillian muttered through clenched teeth, 'perhaps it's just as well you stay unconscious until we get there, Scott, my dear. But next time we get a bigger helicopter, Dad! Once again I need another passenger seat.'

Her thoughts immediately flew to another trip with an unconscious man, her beloved twin, in the back of that large utility. Anger swept through her. If Scott had not been so stupid, if Billy Webster had not allowed himself to be so influenced by his upbringing, John would not have been so badly hurt, so nearly killed.

Suddenly, some part of her was glad that Scott was suffering too, glad that Billy Webster had been knocked out by Ettie Cobby. They both deserved to be punished.

God is so ready to forgive us when we are truly sorry and expects us to be the same towards those who have sinned against us and hurt us.

Matthew's words when she had challenged him about being so ready to forgive Emily.

His eyes had been filled with pain at the thought of the wasted years when the woman he still loved had not tried harder to find him and tell him he was the father of Debbie and Daniel. And now Jillian knew that even being the believer Matthew had become did not mean it had been easy for him to forgive. Forgiveness wasn't the natural way of things, but one other thing Matthew had said had stuck in her mind.

Forgiving is God's way.

Jillian squirmed in her seat. She knew those other words must also be true that Matthew had quietly said after she challenged him. So, even if that night in the motel in Dubbo, in sheer gratitude for John, she had dared to breathe that hesitant, scary prayer to God, how did she get to be as good a Christian as Matthew? How did she get to the point of being able to forgive others herself? Why, she hadn't even been brave enough to admit to Ettie or Steve what she'd done that night! Or was it that she didn't fully understand it herself?

She puzzled over it all as she soared high over the red, bleak plains, the flood waters and then the familiar, browner paddocks of Davidson Downs.

Scott didn't stir until she descended and flew low over the house. She hoped Ettie would hear and come and pick them up. To her surprise, Ettie's old car was already at the airstrip and Ettie waving to her enthusiastically as she landed. With a sense of relief Jillian switched off. Now she only had to contact the Royal Flying Doctor, refuel and head back to Steve.

Only it proved not to be quite as simple as that.

As the motor of the helicopter died away, Jillian swiftly unbuckled her seat belt and leaned over to help Scott. He sat up and gazed around him with a dazed expression.

'We're back at Davidson, Scott,' she started to tell him and then paused. Only then did she hear a swiftly approaching aircraft.

It was a much bigger helicopter than her small mustering one. A police helicopter! As soon as it settled, someone in uniform jumped down and helped Brad Hunter out. Then before Jillian could do more than shout a useless protest, the policeman was back in the helicopter and it roared off once more.

Jillian deserted Scott and raced towards Brad. Ettie was before her, slipping an arm under Brad's shoulder.

'Why didn't they wait?' Jillian shouted above the roar of the already steeply ascending aircraft. 'I've got a badly injured man here who could have gone with them.'

'Oh, Jillian, my dear, I'm so glad to see you're back safely. Did you find the plane?' Ettie looked very upset.

Brad was breathless. He gasped, 'We were worried about Ettie being here by herself with that Billy Webster. The RFD plane is on the way to pick us both up and take us to hospital.' He looked towards her helicopter. 'Where's Steve?' he asked sharply.

Relief that the Royal Flying Doctors would be there soon swept through Jillian. 'I've got another patient for them. Scott Reed's with me. He was injured when his plane took a nose dive. Steve had to stay behind.'

'And Joe Harding?'

'Gone!'

Brad stared at her. 'What do you mean, gone?'

'While Scott was unconscious he took off,' Jillian said grimly. 'From the tracks leading away from the plane he's headed into a very inhospitable part of the outback. I had to leave Steve out there by himself. I just hope that creep was well away and doesn't decide to circle back. As soon as I get Scott out and refuel I'm going back to pick Steve up.'

Brad swayed. Jillian grabbed him. He was very pale.

'I don't know how much *you* can do to help here. Ettie, drive the car right up to us,' she ordered crisply. 'Was there any word when the RFD team thought they'd get here?'

It was Ettie who shook her head.

There was nothing Jillian wanted to do more than go back to Steve but knew she had no choice.

'Right, guess I'd better help you get these two guys into the house before I leave. They can't wait here. Goodness knows how long before the RFD can get here if they didn't specify a time.'

Both women were exhausted by the time they at last had both men in one of the twin bedrooms. 'So I can keep an eye on them both at the same time,' Ettie had insisted. Now she said a little hesitantly, 'And I guess I'd better radio the Flying Doctor base and tell them they have three patients here instead of two.'

Jillian smiled faintly at her. 'So you're an old hand now at the radio.'

Ettie grinned at her weakly and turned away.

Jillian glanced at her watch and then at both pale men lying with their eyes shut. She hesitated a moment and then moved swiftly after Ettie.

"Ettie, are you sure you can manage here. It's now so late if I don't leave as soon as I've refuelled I'm not going to get back with Steve before it's really dark. But I just can't leave him out there all night by himself.'

Ettie paused. She studied Jillian's face carefully. 'I was going to ask you to go with me to check on that Billy fellow. He's been fed and was sleeping soundly as I told that Eddie Jones when he was here a while back, but I'd be happier if I knew he was okay.'

'Eddie was here?'

'Yes,' Ettie said briefly and turned away. 'He said to tell you your cattle were safe and he was sorry but he had to move on at once. On my way to the airstrip to wait for Brad, I saw him drive off towing that old van of his. Oh and he brought Bluey back and put him in the dogs' yard.'

Jillian was puzzled and then shrugged as she followed Ettie. Come to think of it there had been no sign of Eddie's caravan near the guest house. But nothing that old eccentric did should surprise her. Although, it wasn't like him to disappear before he found out if Scott was okay. Then she remembered what Steve had told her about Eddie's high powered, automatic gun that had dealt so efficiently with the cattle thieves.

She relaxed with a grimace. In case awkward questions were asked, Eddie would be putting as much distance as he could between himself and the police to undoubtedly hide his high-powered, automatic weapon.

Ettie paused and turned around. 'Oh, the old rascal gave me a message for you, Jillian. It doesn't make any sense to me but he was very serious and made me repeat it to make sure I had it right. He said to remind you that he's always thought of you seven as his own kids. He's looked out for all of you over the years but still didn't help Sonya or Billy and he's sorry.' She shook her head and added indignantly, 'He was most emphatic that I had to remember the seven and the apology. As though I'd forget. Now, let's go. That Flying Doctor call can wait while I run you back so you can be on your way.'

Jillian frowned. Seven? Her father had laughed with exasperation a few times over the years that the old kangaroo shooter was forever contacting him to check on them all when they were kids. So had he also kept his eye on the Reeds and Billy like that as well?

And Eddie was a law unto himself. A thought struck her.

'Ettie, after all, I think I'd better check on Billy for you before I leave.'

A strange expression flashed across Ettie's face. 'Yes, I think that's a very good idea, my dear. We can do that on the way.'

Ettie helped Jillian to grab the few things she and Steve might need overnight and together they made their way to the old shed.

'As well as feeding the poor starving creature, I hauled that mattress and bedding over to keep him comfortable,' Ettie said as she pulled the padlock key out of her pocket. She stopped. 'That's strange. I'm sure I locked this last time.'

The door swung open. Jillian wasn't surprised to find the room empty. She glanced at Ettie who was eyeing her uneasily and not looking surprised either.

Jillian swung away before Ettie saw the smile she tried hard to stifle as she exclaimed, 'Well, looks like our prisoner has done a runner, Ettie. The police are going to be rather disappointed.'

Ettie was silent for a moment and then said quietly, 'Yes, it does seem like that, my dear.'

'And I'm afraid there's simply no way I can spare the time to search for him now. As it is, I have to put enough fuel in the helicopter to get back to Steve and try to get home again before dark.'

The two women stepped outside the dimly lit room and stared at each other. Ettie looked anxious. Jillian turned and surveyed the open padlock swinging on its catch. Deliberately and slowly she closed the door, reached out and replaced the padlock the way it had been when they reached the shed. From a distance it would look as though it was still locked.

'I'm so sorry you forgot to relock this, Ettie, as I'm sure the police will be too.'

Ettie stared from her to the lock and back again. Relief spread across her face. She swallowed and said rapidly, 'When I got into my car to go to the airstrip, the key was sitting on the dashboard but I haven't had time until now to check on Billy.'

But you knew Eddie Jones had.

The unspoken knowledge flowed between them.

Ettie opened her mouth, swallowed and remained silent.

'Very wise,' Jillian said steadily, 'sometimes I do think it best not to say very much at all, especially when age makes us so forgetful.'

Indignation filled Ettie's wide eyes for a brief moment. Then her expression changed again as she grasped the excuse Jillian was giving her.

Jillian permitted herself a small grin when she wanted to laugh out loud at the expression on the good woman's face.

'Just so.' Jillian cleared her throat. 'In fact, I don't think it really is necessary to contact the RFD again today. We've plenty of pain killers in stock and bandages. I'm sure you will be able to cope. Best to stay right off the radio altogether for... er... some time, I think.'

Time to give Eddie a chance to disappear into one of his outback hideaways.

She thought of his love of monitoring their radio calls. It wouldn't hurt in the slightest to keep the old scoundrel guessing for days. In fact, she would use the phone to contact the RFD tomorrow.

Immense relief filled Ettie's face. Her eyes started to dance.

Jillian made a production of looking at her watch. 'Oh dear, dear, I've got to go!'

Both women climbed into the car. Ettie reached for the key in the ignition, but then paused and put her head to one side. At the same time, Jillian heard the unmistakable sound of a vehicle approaching the homestead. She groaned out loud. Ettie gave a stifled chuckle and then both women were laughing rather hysterically.

Ettie wiped tears from her eyes. 'We really are terrible, Jillian Davidson.' She gave a small gasp of surprise. 'Why, that looks like Ben Honeysuckle's big old sedan!'

She was right. By the time they had driven around to the front of the homestead, the car had stopped. Emily's Aunt Barbara was beside the driver, Steve's father.

Ettie gave a low laugh. 'Well, well, so those two are still spending more and more time together, even coming all this way. Like a real pair of love birds.'

But it was the woman in the back passenger seat who wiped the smile from Jillian's face. Madeline Honeysuckle jumped out and advanced towards them. Jillian groaned and saw Ettie look at her curiously as they got out of the car to greet the new arrivals.

Jillian planted a welcoming smile on her face but whispered urgently, 'Ettie, I simply can't leave Steve out there by himself and I don't want to worry his family. You'll have to act the hostess for me.'

'No worries,' Ettie murmured back. She greeted the new arrivals in a hearty voice. 'Well, if the Lord hasn't sent us help just when we need it.' She grinned and hugged Madeline. 'I know a young man feeling pretty sore and sorry for himself who will be very glad to see you, Mattie, my dear.'

Alarm filled Madeline's face. 'What's happened to Brad this time?'

Jillian paused in her greeting of Barbara Page and big Ben Honeysuckle. Strange. Surely Madeline should think of her brother first of all. She eyed her curiously. Perhaps Madeline's attitude towards herself had more to do with a certain policeman liking Jillian Davidson than her interest in Madeline's brother?

'Matthew told us you were having some excitement out here with cattle thieves so we thought you might appreciate some help,' Ben was saying in his gruff voice.

Barbara was beaming at her. 'And I knew Ettie might need help in cooking for you all for the harvest,'

Ettie gave her old friend a hug. 'I certainly do and you don't know the half of it. There's two injured men now to look after and one with a bullet still in him!' she ended dramatically.

Madeline's face went dead white. She swayed.

'Brad's fine,' Jillian hastened to assure her.

Relief filled Madeline's eyes and colour crept back into her pinched features.

'He does have a bullet still in his leg though, and we're...'

A multitude of expressions swept across Madeline's face. 'A bullet! Oh, no, not again!' She swung on her heel.

Jillian watched her storm towards the house and felt a touch of sympathy for Brad.

'And Steve? Where's my son?'

There was alarm in Ben's voice and Jillian hastened to reassure him. "Steve's fine. Or was when I saw him last. I was just on my way back to pick him up, but now...' She glanced at her watch and looked towards Ettie. The sun was already very low on the horizon.

Ettie went into action. 'Right you two. You might as well hop into the back of my car. I was just taking Jillian to the airstrip so she could get away.'

'The airstrip!'

'Yes, Barbara, isn't it exciting?' Ettie bustled both the startled new arrivals towards her car. 'I'll explain on the way. That helicopter has to leave immediately.'

'Helicopter!' The older couple chorused.

Jillian was busy with her own thoughts as Ettie started filling in their bemused passengers on the last – or some of the last – twenty-four hour's events. Second thoughts were stirring. Was she doing the right thing about Billy?

There was no chance to speak privately to Ettie until after the helicopter was refuelled. She pulled Ettie aside and murmured urgently, 'Ettie, I...' She stopped.

Ettie leaned over and gave her a swift hug. 'I know what you've been thinking, my dear. It's okay. Billy isn't really a bad man, he's a very tormented one. Certainly he's responsible for his actions, but we talked a lot before he went to sleep.'

'The police will look for him?'

'And they will find him if that is what the *Lord* wants to happen, despite anything that old Eddie might get up to. Now, you go and care for that other fine young man of yours. And we'll be praying for you. What goes for Billy goes for that other crook still out there somewhere. God is just and will deal with him too.'

Jillian barely heard Ettie's last couple of comments.

Yours.

The word haunted Jillian as she once again took to the air and waved one last time to the three watching her. Was Steve Honeysuckle really hers?

Oh, God, do make him love me like I love him.

Chapter twenty-two

After the sun went down, Steve gave up on Jillian returning before morning. He started to drag the seats from the plane to try and make himself as comfortable as he could on the ground.

At first he thought he was imagining it when he heard the distant thump in the sky. Then against the last light in the cloudless eastern sky he saw the small dot approaching fast. The sound increased to a steady roar and the distinctive sound of helicopter rotor blades as they swept through the evening sky. For a moment he wondered if Jillian had sent someone else to pick him up. But then the small helicopter that was now so familiar dived steeply towards him.

Only then did he realise how careful Jillian had been with him on board! He still hated the thought that soon he would have to fly in it once more and yet he was relieved to note he didn't dread it as much as he had. Probably his fear of heights and his vertigo would never completely leave him. He would always respect that weakness of his, but with God's strength it would never control him.

Steve waited a respectful distance until the motor died away and the dust and dirt began to settle. Then he started to run. Jillian met him half way.

Steve wanted to roar at her for taking such a risk. In another few minutes it would have been too dark to find him. When he saw her glowing, laughing face, he caught his breath.

All he could gasp as she flew into his arms was, 'You crazy, wonderful woman, Jillie Davidson.'

'Didn't think I'd leave you out here all by yourself in this savage outback country, did you, Stevie Honeysuckle?' she mocked him gently. 'You were going to be pretty hungry and cold by morning without my blankets and Ettie's food parcel.'

'You've been right back home?'

'Sure thing! I thought about dropping our patient off at Bourke but knew they wouldn't let me take off again to come back here without the radio, so home it was. As it happened the police arrived just as I did. Fortunately they were in too big a hurry to ask awkward questions. They dropped Brad off to wait for the RFD plane. Brad was not in a very happy mood to find our man out here has disappeared. There's been no sign of him has there?'

Steve gaped at her. Her tumble of words had his head spinning. He pulled himself together and shook his head. 'If he's got any brains, Joe Harding will be putting as much distance between himself and us as he can.'

Jillian shivered. 'I wouldn't like to be on foot out here. I wonder if the man realises he can walk for hundreds of miles west without seeing a single soul. In fact, if he isn't found, his chances of surviving at all are pretty slim. At least Billy...' she stopped dead.

Steve had already been remembering stories of people who had disappeared without a trace in the relentless outback of Australia. It took a moment for Jillian's comment about Billy Webster to register.

She had turned swiftly away and was staring at the plane seats on the ground. 'I think I can make us more comfortable with the things I've brought. We'd better get them before it's completely dark.'

'What were you going to say about Billy?'

Jillian didn't pause. Her long strides carried her to the helicopter. He followed but she didn't speak, merely thrust a small box at him and turned back to reappear with a couple of sleeping bags.

'Jillian?'

'It seems Billy escaped from Davidson Downs.'

He stared at her in consternation. 'Billy Webster escaped?'

Jillian took a deep breath. 'I don't know about you but I'm starving. Let's make ourselves comfortable and then I'll tell you why I'm so late getting here.'

Outback from Baragula

She avoided looking at him. Grimly Steve remembered when he had thought she had been about to plead for Billy to Brad. He still felt pretty murderous himself towards that man who had helped bring such pain and suffering to the Davidsons.

Once Steve held a mug of tea in his hand from the thermos, he looked at Jillian with a raised eyebrow and waited. She'd hardly said a word while she poured him his tea. Now she stared back at him and gave a big sigh. In a few words she told him about Brad, finding Billy had disappeared and the arrival of the folk from Baragula.

Steve put his cup down very carefully. Jillian had stared out at the shadows around them as she told him about Billy's disappearance. She hadn't looked at him once. Something wasn't quite right.

'I guess I should have expected Dad would want to be in on any action. But Billy Webster disappearing has me worried. Are you sure he's not hiding somewhere in those old out-buildings around the homestead?'

'Our old storage room door had been unlocked from the outside and he was gone.'

Jillian avoided his gaze a moment longer and then shrugged. She looked up at him with a perfectly straight face but he could see the smile trying to break out on her beautiful features.

'Well, you see, according to what Ettie *didn't* say, I'm pretty sure Billy had some help.'

'Not Henrietta Cobby! She would never...'

'No, no, not our Ettie.' A chuckle broke from Jillian. 'Although I'm sure her conscience is still worrying her because I've a strong inkling she suspected what her partner in crime was up to but did not do a thing to stop him.'

Once again, Steve gaped at her. Jillian threw back her head. Her hearty laugh rang out across the plains surrounding them.

He thought rapidly. 'You would have to be referring to our Eddie Jones,' he drawled at last.

Jillian nodded. 'In all fairness to Ettie, I don't think she knew what he intended to do. She was truly horrified when we found that shed empty. But she didn't seem really surprised. I think she must have been suspicious after Eddie gave her a message for me. He even made her repeat it.'

Steve raised an eyebrow and Jillian told him the message.

'*Seven* of you?'

A dimple peeped again on Jillian's beautifully curved cheek. 'Seems Eddie Jones has quite a family. He thinks of the Davidson, Reed and Webster families as his very own.'

Steve knew what was coming. He'd seen old Eddie in action himself, knew that this part of the world Eddie Jones considered to be his own little kingdom to deal out justice how and when he saw fit.

Jillian went on to confirm his suspicions. 'When I flew over the homestead, there wasn't a sign of Eddie's caravan. I didn't give it much thought until Ettie gave me his message. After he sorted out yours and Brad's problem he must have deserted the cattle and raced back to Davidson to sort out Billy. There was no time to try and spot them from the air if I was to get back here before dark.'

A chuckle escaped her. 'I'm sure we won't see that old scoundrel for a long time and wouldn't be a bit surprised if the next time we hear of him he has an offsider helping him to keep the kangaroo population down to acceptable levels.'

Not quite sure how he should feel about it all, Steve stared at Jillian in fascination. One part of him was glad for Billy Webster, although he strongly suspected he should feel sorry for him. He was not in for an easy time with that strong ex-shearer, ex-soldier, surrogate father and straight out old outback reprobate!

When he didn't speak, Jillian scowled at him and tossed her head defiantly.

'John didn't actually see Billy in that truck. What good would be the evidence of a badly injured man who "thought" a voice was familiar? We've only Billy's confession to go on. He could have been long gone from the whole area but he felt worried enough to walk a long, long way to warn us. And I'm sure, as much as dear Ettie can talk, she'll be very tight-lipped about someone she thought she might have killed!'

'And this is the woman who expressed such anger and vengeance before towards the men responsible for John's injuries and the theft of the cattle!'

Jillian dropped her head at his quiet words.

'Is she really okay about this old friend she had grown up with getting away with all he's been responsible for?'

Long, slender fingers rubbed around the rim of Jillian's cup for a long moment. At last she glanced up at Steve and searched his eyes. A trace of vulnerability in her own once more touched that deep part of his heart as no one ever had before. It took a real effort for Steve to remain silent. He waited.

'Steve, in the helicopter, you asked me a question which I haven't answered yet.'

He hoped he didn't show his surprise at her seeming change of topic. And then he remembered what his question had been. His heart accelerated but he simply nodded.

'I didn't say anything because I simply don't know the answer – not for certain.' Her voice was low, urgent. 'How *do* you know when you're a Christian? Know for sure? All my life I've taken for granted I am one. I've always known about Jesus dying on the cross, about doing good deeds. I've gone to church at least a couple of times a year all my life, but Matthew insisted that alone didn't make him or anyone a Christian. He talked a lot of stuff about personally asking Jesus to forgive your sins, about establishing a personal relationship with God through Jesus. Ettie spoke about that too.'

Steve heard her draw in a deep, long breath. His own pulse thundered in his ears. He reached out and grasped Jillian's hand. It trembled and then gripped his firmly.

Was she...? Had she...?

'That night in the motel in Dubbo I couldn't sleep and I... I'm just not sure if I've done it right. If God really heard me. If I...' The faltering words became a torrent. 'I've seen the huge change in Matthew. I've seen how your faith affects you, how Scott is changing. How do I get like that?'

Wonder and thanks nearly choked Steve. He closed his eyes.

Jillian tugged on his hand. 'Steve?'

'Oh, Jillie dear... What did you actually say to God?'

The words he longed to hear came low, shy – and rushed. 'That I was sorry I'm a sinner, that I believe He dealt with that on the cross, that I'm sorry I had so little faith in Him loving me and could Jesus please help me to have what Matthew and you do.'

Never had Steve's heart rejoiced as it did at that moment. He couldn't speak.

'Steve dear, your cheeks are wet.' There was alarm in her raised voice. 'Why...why, you're crying! What is it? Did I say something very wrong? Are you sick? What...'

Steve made an effort and pulled himself together. 'No, no, my darling, I'm just so happy.' Half a sob, half a laugh ripped from him in exultation. He knelt in front of her and gently, reverently put his arms around her trembling body. 'For you. For me. But oh, for you above everything, my darling, darling Jillie.'

Her reaction was not what he expected.

She pulled herself away and scrambled to her feet. 'You...you... I've been trying to get up courage to tell you and ask your help and you...you're laughing at me?'

'No, no! Never! How could I when I've been praying so very long for you to tell me you want to know Jesus in a personal way.'

'Well, I do. I need to know how to be a dinkum Christian. Right now,' she flashed back at him, 'so start talking.'

Steve kissed her first. Her angry, tense body resisted for only a moment and then melted against him.

It was timeless moments later before Steve surfaced enough to gasp and hold the now pliant body close, burying his face in the dark hair that curled around her face and shoulders to tickle his own rough, unshaven face.

She sighed deeply and lifted her head to stare at him with – of all things – a scowl that demanded once more he 'start talking.'

Curled up in each other's arms, Steve pulled himself together and did just that.

He shared with Jillian many of the things he had known for so many years, things he had longed to share with her and hardly dared to trust or hope he ever could. He realised that above all she simply needed God's assurance of her salvation and new relationship with Him.

That he was right she proved when at last she slowly sat up and moved a little away from him to stare out across the red plains now faintly lit by the rising full moon.

'That thing you've just told me. Does the Bible really say if I've accepted God's gift of salvation through his Son, Jesus, then I'm now His, a child in His family?'

'The Gospel of John, chapter one and verse twelve says exactly that,' Steve said promptly.

He waited as she remained silent, reluctant to interrupt her thinking about that wonderful fact – and the working of the Holy Spirit in her life. Steve knew no matter how much he told her it was the work of God to convince her.

At last he added very softly, 'There are many, many more verses I can show you as soon as we get hold of a Bible.'

'So you don't think what I prayed that night was just from emotion because of all that had happened?'

'Only you can answer that, Jillie,' he said tenderly, 'but I don't believe you are the kind of person who would do something like that without really meaning it. Are you?'

She slowly shook her head.

'What happened to John undoubtedly left you emotional and exhausted. But the human heart is so independent, that if it thinks it can do without God and solve all a person's problems without Him, that God is unnecessary, sometimes God has to allow circumstances to develop that make us cry out to Him. Then we discover that God's been waiting simply for us to acknowledge our need of Him!'

Steve waited, but Jillian still didn't speak for a long time. Then at last she whispered in a voice of wonder, 'So then, from what you say, I'm definitely in God's family.'

Steve sat up. He reached out and turned Jillian's face towards him so he could stare right into her eyes. 'When we get that Bible I'll show you many other verses. This isn't just what I say, it's what God says in His Word and we just have to believe God, that He keeps all His promises. We'll read what the apostle John wrote in his first letter to believers who also apparently needed God's assurance. Part of chapter five says, "Everyone who believes that Jesus is the Christ is born of God and everyone who loves the Father loves His child as well." And also, "Anyone who does not believe God, has made Him a liar because he has not believed the testimony God has given about His Son".'

Steve paused and then spoke softly, reverently. 'Dad made me memorise those passages many years ago, also "And this is the testimony: God has given us eternal life and this life is in His Son. He who has the Son has life; he who does not have the Son does not have life." No ifs or buts, Jillie dear. Certainty!'

It was a magical night under the stars that neither Steve nor Jillian would ever forget. They snuggled together in their sleeping bags to keep warm. Neither slept very much, despite their traumatic day. The ground was hard; the night air they breathed in became quite cold. They dozed intermittently in between nibbling on the goodies in Ettie's basket, sipping hot drinks and talking about God, about the events of the months since they had first met.

They laughed together when Jillian reminded Steve it was hers and John's birthday in a few days. She sighed. 'And I still haven't ridden my birthday present yet.'

'Well, Judy gave me a lovely ride,' Steve teased her, 'and after his ride to Webster on Punch, Brad was mourning that he was John's horse instead of his.'

Steve then confessed how jealous he had been of Brad.

Jillian responded by teasing him about having a possessive sister.

'Hmm,' he muttered, 'poor Madeline. I wasn't the only one scared stiff you and Bradley Hunter were just getting a mite too friendly!'

Jillian ran her hand gently down his cheek.

'Ettie said something about you and Madeline not having an easy time of it over the years. She inferred it contributed to your pulling away and refusing to ever consider a relationship with someone like me who didn't share your faith in God and a desire to obey Him, to walk the way He would want a married couple to.'

Steve didn't answer.

Jillian added hurriedly, 'I'm sorry, Steve. I didn't mean to pry. I know how very close you are to your sister and father.'

Steve stirred. 'You aren't prying and you have a right to know why I... I know I've hurt you and I'm so very, very sorry for that. I just couldn't seem to keep away from you – or not to kiss you it seemed. I guess I've always been so scared of making a mistake like Dad and Mum did. Apparently when they first met, Dad was a devout Christian. Well, at least from what I can tell he was. He was very involved with the church at Baragula from when he was a boy.'

'Ettie mentioned although she'd been to church all her life, she still didn't have a personal relationship with God until recently.'

'So I believe.' Steve shrugged. 'Perhaps that was the case with Dad too when he first met my mother. I don't know, but Mum certainly wasn't a Christian for many years.'

He stared up at the wide expanse of dark sky filled with brilliant, twinkling stars. Steve was thankful Jillian was silent and didn't ask him to expand that statement. Some of his memories were too painful to share with her yet, especially on this magical night.

'In fact, I've always been especially wary about the scripture's warnings of marrying an unbeliever because I saw for myself the impact not being able to share faith together in a marriage had on my own parents and family. Although we tried hard to hide it from people at Baragula, our house was more often like a battlefield than a home. I've been thinking recently that Madeline has been even more affected by our secret home life than I have. It was only just before she died that Mum committed her life to Christ.'

'Oh, Steve dear, I'm so sorry.'

Steve received her gentle, comforting kiss willingly. They both fell silent and eventually dozed off to sleep again in each others arms.

As the early morning light started to pour across the stark outback landscape, Jillian stirred first. Her movement startled a flock of white cockatoos resting on the plane fuselage. They rose in a cloud of screeching indignation.

Steve woke and smiled up at her from his sleeping bag. 'Brrr, it's cold. I'm sure glad you brought these sleeping bags with you.'

She smiled back but turned to continue her search of their surroundings.

'I wonder where Joe Harding is and how he survived. We can't be very far from a waterhole if the birds have come out here. Do you think the police will find him?'

Steve crawled out of his bag and stood up. 'I certainly hope so. In fact, someone like him will inevitably get caught – if not for this offence for something else. But we are done with him. It's up to the police now.'

He reached down. Jillian placed her hands in his and let him haul her to her feet from her snug, make-shift bedding. With his head on one side, Steve studied her face.

'Good morning, Jillian Davidson. Will you marry me?'

Jillian stilled. Then she pulled her hands away, ran a hand through her tousled hair and then rested both fists on her hips in mock indignation. She carefully inspected Steve's filthy clothes he had worked in all the day before. She reached out a hand and rubbed it over the rough bristles on his chin to snatch it away as he reached for it. The hand returned to her hip once more.

Concern flashed into his eyes and she couldn't stop the smile that insisted on springing to her face.

Steve relaxed. His eyes started to gleam.

'Well, really, Steve Honeysuckle! You're not even going to make sure I won't be swearing anymore? And couldn't you at least wait to propose until a girl's had a chance to wash her face, comb her hair and see if we've any tea left in the... Steve!'

Mary Hawkins

He had grabbed her by both shoulders. 'Jillie, I was violently attracted to you that first time we met,' he said rapidly, urgently. 'It's been a terrible struggle for me to obey God all these months and not spend more time alone with you. And now He's plonked us down together in the middle of the outback of all places. And I'm quite sure He's going to continue to change us both to be more like Jesus. And...'

Steve stopped. In his intensity he gave Jillian a little shake. 'Marry me. Please.'

He didn't give her a chance to answer before his lips plundered hers. Strong arms whisked her close to him until Jillian felt as though she could hardly breathe.

When he at last let her up for air she was breathless, her cheeks fiery hot.

Her arms reluctantly slipped away from him as he took a step back and looked at her. The satisfaction and triumph that gleamed in his passion filled eyes could not go unpunished.

'Well, really, Mr Honeysuckle, Sir!' she began with a toss of her head. 'I'm not sure I'm at all keen on your surname. Not sure it's a good name for a hero. Jillian Suckle might even sound better.' She sighed heavily. 'However, seeing everyone in the outback and probably Baragula by now also, undoubtedly knows we have now been guilty of spending two – mind you, *two* – nights alone together in the bush, Mr Honeysuckle, Sir, I suppose we have no choice,' she finished mournfully.

To Jillian's delight, Steve took a step back and bowed deeply, his arm sweeping out like a gallant of old. "I do declare you're right, Miss Davidson, ma'am. Sorry I can't do anything about the name, but we have absolutely *no* choice left – even as nothing happened we're at all ashamed of!'

He straightened. They laughed at each other, but his eyes were full of the love Jillian had always longed to see in those expressive hazel eyes.

Tears wet her eyelids. She savoured her unspeakable joy at being at the start of getting to really know God personally, that He was giving her this wonderful man to share the incredible journey into the future.

Steve came closer. 'I love you with a love that God has given me for you that can't be denied any longer!'

His words echoed her thoughts and her heart sang with thankfulness. Her laugh rang out joyfully, across the wide expanse of God's creation they would shortly soar over on the way back to the new life together He had been preparing for them all along.

'Come here and kiss me, my wonderful Steve. I love you so very, very much. Of course I'll marry you.'

Jillian stiffened and remembered. 'There's just one condition I have. You'll never say sorry ever again for kissing me!'

Steve tried to speak. Failed. Shook his head as though to clear it. Nodded fervently.

And then he kissed her.

Questions for Discussion

1. Steve Honeysuckle saw the damage to his parent's marriage by the differences in their faith and personal relationship with God. How has this affected him when he realises his growing attraction to a non-believer like Jillian Davidson? How have you dealt with things in your past that affect your relationship with God and others?

2. Jillian is deeply hurt by Steve's attitude to her. Is there anything Steve could have done – or not done – to prevent this? Do you know any non-Christian who may have been made to feel 'not good' enough to be a girlfriend or boyfriend of a Christian?

3. What do you think about marriage between believers and non-believers? List some problems they may have to face.

4. Matthew, Jillian's brother was aware of her attraction to Steve. Should he have asked Steve to take the horses out to Davidson Downs?

5. Do you think Steve is a coward because of his phobia? Is there any problem like this that makes you go regularly to God for strength? How does He help you?

6. Eddie Jones, is a Vietnam Veteran and an eccentric 'outback character.' Did you agree that while it may be considered a repugnant occupation, Davidson Downs needs to employ such a person?

7. What did you think of Eddie's reaction to what happens to John, meeting Ettie Cobby, his actions on Webster Station and his final disappearance? What about Ettie's reaction to Eddie?

8. As Christians, were Jillian and Ettie right not to immediately report what happened to Billy Webster?

9. Ettie tries to point out to Jillian the difference between just going to church and having a 'day by day personal relationship' with Almighty God, the Creator. She tries to explain why she believes God desires an 'intimate relationship' with us. Ettie mentions 'spending time' with God as essential for this. How can we do that more than weekly church attendance?

10. Some are hinted at and mentioned throughout this story, but can you list ways to help us to know God intimately on a day by day, moment by moment basis as Steve, Matthew and Ettie try to? If you can, mention scripture verses.

11. Did you think Jillian should have told someone sooner about her reaching out to God while in that motel? What do you think actually happened then in her relationship with Him? Was there anything else she could have – or should – have done right then?

12. Besides those mentioned in that last chapter, can you think of other passages of scripture Steve could have shared – or should *not* share – with Jillian at that point of her Christian walk?

Return to Baragula

Did you miss meeting the folk in Return to Baragula?

Emily Parker's actions as a teenager not only impacted her own life but the lives of many others.

Now, six years later, she returns reluctantly to her home town of Baragula only to discover the man at the heart of those actions, Matthew Davidson, is the community's respected doctor.

Disease attacks the community while danger from another source threatens Emily and her family. Through it all, will Matthew and Emily's faith be strong enough to forgive each other and put the past behind them?

coming soon....

Justice at Baragula

In various ways, life-long friends Madeline Honeysuckle and Senior Constable Bradley Hunter have wrestled with life's injustices. They are both still suffering from their own physical and emotional scars when the man responsible in the past for so much hurt to both of them reappears and threatens the peace of small town Baragula.

Why doesn't God always intervene in their lives to bring about His truth and justice? Two wounded people have to discover in deeper ways that God alone is just and righteous.

Alive & Christian Woman

Australia and New Zealand's leading Christian magazines.

Alive is a valuble resource for daily living and a tool to propel you into living your life as God intended you to - fulfilled, blessed and leading others to Him.

Health, Parenting, Real stories, Leadership, Hospitality + much more...

For over 50 years Christian Woman has been inspiring, challenging and encouraging women of all ages in their daily lives.

alivemagazine.com.au
christianwoman.com.au

More great fiction from Ark House...

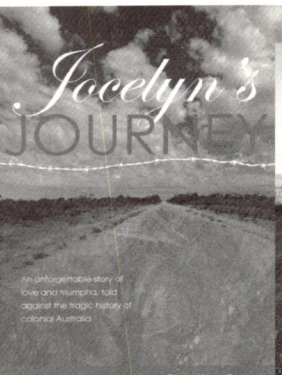

All the days of my life — Jo-Anne Berthelsen

Nemesis Train — Nathan Brown

no eye has seen — Graham Carter

Fire in the Rock — Rita Stella Galieh

Jocelyn's Journey — Caroline Fraser

Return to Baragula — Mary Hawkins

www.arkhousepress.com